EXPLORING THE RULES

THE DATING PLAYBOOK, BOOK: 4

MARIAH DIETZ

EXPLORING THE RULES

1

CHLOE

- ~~Sunscreen~~
- ~~Phone charger~~
- ~~Portable charger~~
- ~~Headphones~~

I check the last few items off of my list and nervously bite the end of my pen. I know I'm forgetting something—can feel it nagging in the back of my mind.

"You have everything," Vanessa assures me.

"I feel like I'm forgetting something," I admit.

She shakes her head. "You've been making that list for a month. Trust me. You have everything." She turns her attention to her phone, likely checking in with Cooper for the hundredth time this morning. She's jittery with excitement and nerves, and it's starting to become contagious.

My conviction to be calmer and less 'high strung' as my ex, Ricky Benson, so eloquently put it before we broke up last month, has me shoving my list into my purse to keep from checking it a fourth time.

Those weren't my only traits that annoyed Ricky. He hated my list-making and planning, as well as my habit of focusing on laws and rules and regulations—both defined and unwritten, like telling your best friend she has something stuck in her teeth or not stopping in the middle of a busy sidewalk. Rules are important in this world where so many things are blurred, and few things give me as much comfort. Maybe it's because I'm the oldest—albeit only by seven minutes—or because I'm majoring in astrophysics to be an astronomer, where every law of physics is fundamental—but rules bring me purpose, structure, focus, and a sense of security.

I look down at our bags and panic begins to swell in my chest like a balloon being blown up as I consider how many rules will be stretched and broken this summer as we travel across the country with my best friend and Vanessa's latest crush, Cooper Sutton.

"This has to be the worst idea ever." I grip my purse even tighter, trying to ignore the fact my palms are sweating from nerves.

"Chloe." My sister makes my name four syllables. "We've definitely had worse ideas than making a cross country trip with our best friend. Plus, the meteor shower. California. There's no way we'd have been able to go without Cooper driving us," Vanessa reminds me again as she toes one of the suitcases, lining it up with the others.

"I know, I know," I try not to grumble my admission because as much as I'd like to pretend otherwise, she's right.

At the beginning of summer, we ended our sophomore year at Brighton University in Seattle, Washington by putting most of our things into storage and flew home to Jacksonville, Florida. We've spent the past two months lying by the pool, picking up shifts at The Grille that our Uncle Pete owns and where he's offered us employment since we were sixteen, and finding every excuse to take naps and visit the beach.

It feels like summer just began, and already it's ending.

That sour note, combined with the fact we're going to be in a car for long periods with Cooper, who I know Nessie will be flirting with, has tainted the appeal of this trip—even seeing the Perseids meteor shower. We're watching it from the Aether Observatory in San Francisco, where I was personally invited by their astrology team to come and celebrate and witness the annual event that has become something I look forward to each year like a holiday. The shower leaves trails of bright lights in the sky like fireworks—beautiful and mesmerizing.

My short nails bite into my palms as my thoughts veer back to Nessie and Cooper. Cooper is my best friend aside from Vanessa. Sometimes it feels like Nessie and I are two halves to a whole, but Cooper is like my carbon copy, making him equally easy—sometimes easier—for me to understand. He's also a nice guy, which is a big change from the guys Nessie generally goes for and the only reason I'm trying to find hope that her feelings are genuine. Well, that and because although he hasn't outright told me, I know Cooper has been in love with Nessie for the past decade ... maybe longer.

Coop and I became instant friends when we were in the third grade. Back then he preferred chess to football and chips to cookies, and unlike most of the guys in our class who were starting to become cruder and grosser as they neared puberty, Cooper was grounded and kind and quiet, and we found solace together in the library and the treehouse Dad built with us over spring break.

Jealousy plays a small factor in my hesitation for them starting a relationship. I'm terrified to consider what might happen when they break up; a harsh thought, but considering Nessie's longest relationship has been three months, it seems nearly inevitable.

Mom and Dad head toward us, ending my thoughts and making my breath catch in my throat. Mom's face is red, tears building on her lower lashes. I hug her first. She rubs soothing circles on my back as I make a vow to myself not to cry yet again.

"You guys are going to have the best time," she says. Her long hair, which is mostly gray, is curled in relaxed waves that tickle my face, but I don't attempt to pull away or brush them aside. She smells of lavender and honey from the homemade soap we make in large batches each year. I attempt to memorize it all, knowing how much I'll miss them this fall.

Guilt and regret are like tectonic plates in my chest, hitting and creating a mountain of doubt. I don't know why I agreed to leave with Nessie nearly three weeks early to travel back to Seattle. I could spend these last weeks with our parents, soaking up more of the Florida sun, taking another trip to Disney World, and enjoying time with my family and friends, but instead, I chose a meteor shower.

Mom pulls back, the gold chain she wears around her neck catching the light of the sun before she hugs Vanessa. Dad engulfs me in a bear hug. I appreciate these moments with him. I've watched some dads get weird around their daughters—hugs become side-hugs, and they act like hearing the word tampon or period will scar their manhood. Our dad has immersed himself into the world of being a girl dad and embraces the fact, loving us to the point he learned how to French braid, the names of each Disney Princess, and the value of good chocolate when one of us was having a bad day.

"You guys will remember to text us periodically? And *stick together*. No drinking or texting while driving. And no picking up any hitchhikers," Dad says as he pulls back, his eyes red and heavy from lack of sleep. He hasn't been subtle about his concerns for our trip, which is likely why I've kept my concerns mostly to myself until this afternoon. It's not that his concerns aren't valid—some of them even match my own—it's just that hearing his concerns about something that started as my idea makes me wish even more that I could be easygoing.

Stubborn and strong-willed are my middle names, hyphenated only by my love for adventure. However, this trip was supposed to be a girls' trip. We were supposed to drive across the country with our good friend Meredith, sightseeing along the way and soaking up the feeling of independence and freedom before going back for our junior year and apartment hunting, job hunting, and full-time classes.

Then everything changed.

Meredith broke her femur and is now flying back to Seattle in four weeks. Vanessa got tired of discussing the pros and cons of different apartments in and around Seattle, and unbeknownst to me, chose the smallest on our shortlist that had only been on it because of her insistence. It's the most expensive, tiny, and has no patio. Then, to turn things into full upheaval, she made plans with Cooper to take this trip that has us leaving two weeks earlier than originally planned because he has to be back in time for football season.

I'm grateful, it just feels like the one time Mom made mashed potatoes and burnt the bottom layer—the top looked okay, but it still tasted burnt.

I take a deep breath of the humid air and remind myself why this will be okay. Arriving earlier than planned will allow us more time to job hunt and get settled, and though I'm concerned about what might happen between Nessie and Cooper, there are far worse ways to spend the last few weeks of summer than on a road trip across the country.

Nessie pats my shoulder like she can hear my silent resolve. "This is going to be amazing. Epic."

"Is that them?" Mom asks as a large black SUV slows and turns into the driveway.

I shake my head. "N—" I start, knowing Cooper was planning to drive his grandma's old Honda.

"Yes," Nessie says, cutting me off, her lips pulled wide at the corners as she winces.

Panic sets in.

Mom and Dad move down the driveway to welcome Cooper as Nessie leans closer. "This was the only way. It's going to be a short trip, we're going to see several cities, and it's going to be amazing." Her words come out rushed.

And then Tyler Banks appears from the driver's side, and every reason for not wanting to go multiplies tenfold.

"What is he doing here?" I hiss, my attention cutting to my sister as accusation drips from my words.

The biggest, cheesiest, and fakest smile she can muster slowly appears on Nessie's face. "He's going with us?" It sounds like a question. One I'm hoping to debate.

I grip Nessie's arm as she starts to turn away. "What are you talking about?"

"He has a work thing, and this worked out perfectly. His car is bigger, and we'll save a ton on hotels."

"No." I shake my head, still believing I have some say in the matter.

Nessie drops her chin. "Come on. It won't be that bad. Tomorrow, we'll be in New Orleans, dancing to jazz music and eating all the amazing food. Focus on the positives."

"I can't believe you didn't tell me."

"I couldn't. I knew if I did, you'd say no."

I glance toward the car to ensure they're out of earshot. "Because I hate him," I hiss.

Nessie frowns. "Don't even start. You barely know Tyler. You spend all your time avoiding him."

I try not to glower. "I know enough about him to know he's an asshole—hence why I avoid him."

Vanessa stamps her fists onto her hips that, despite our similar genes, are narrower than mine. Likely because she's a cheerleader at Brighton University and works out like it's her job. Meanwhile, I spent the summer indulging in Mom's homemade food and the cookies Dad hides in the bread box, knowing Mom won't find them there because she doesn't like bread, which is almost as strange as it is appalling. "He's not that bad."

"He's so cocky. And last year when you made me go to that Halloween party, I saw him make out with three different girls. *Three*. At one party."

Nessie shrugs. "I've heard worse."

"That doesn't make it any better."

Before she can reply, Dad's beside us again. "Do you know how much that car's worth?" His voice is lowered into a whisper.

Cooper turns from where he's talking with our mom and smiles in our direction. Though much about Coop has changed in the past four years, his smile has not. It still exposes one dimple, and his cheeks are still slightly rounded, too soft for being twenty-one. His eyes are a dark brown that matches his finger-length hair, which is swept away from his face in a tidy mess. Once, Cooper was gangly and short, but now, he still has a few inches on me even when I wear heels. And while he's still on the thinner side, defined muscles cord their way over his body—which we saw firsthand all summer in our pool.

"Hey," Cooper says, waving.

"Hey, Cooper." Dad moves closer, greeting him with a handshake and starts confirming our travel plans, but I don't hear the conversation because Tyler Banks steps forward. His disheveled dark blond hair, piercing blue eyes, and rounded lips that hide his emotions nearly as well as his silence. It's like he read a manual on how to be broody and decided to master the skill set.

"Mom, this is Tyler Banks," Vanessa says, extending a manicured hand toward Tyler, who surprises me by flexing a small smile and shaking her hand.

"Pleasure to meet you." His British accent—which is notorious at Brighton and likely all of Miami where he's from—makes our mom practically swoon. I'm pretty sure Dad's even developing a man-crush as he stares at Tyler's car and biceps and starts recounting Brighton's undefeated football season last year and his own glory days from Brighton.

"That's a nice car you drive," Dad says when Tyler moves to help with our bags.

Tyler glimpses over his shoulder, his gaze stopping at me for only a second before meeting the target of his Tesla. I'd argue that it's elaborate and screams ostentatious, but Vanessa is starting to tell Cooper which bags she's going to need access to and which can be buried, and Mom's asking me about our hotel room confirmation for tonight.

"I didn't make them, remember?" I ask, awkwardness edging its way into my voice and making my discomfort grow rapidly. I should have been concerned when Nessie assured me she and Cooper had it all taken care of—should have been more suspicious when I asked for details, and she gave me blanket answers about Cooper having gotten great deals through a friend. I hadn't considered that friend was Tyler Banks, heir to one of the largest hotel chains in America. A British playboy who grew up bouncing between continents and leaving a trail of tabloid stories and broken hearts in his wake.

Nessie's right, I don't know Tyler Banks, but I also have no desire to know him. Guys like him promise nothing but bad judgment and questionable motives that all lead to disarray and chaos.

"That's right. You made the reservation?" Mom turns her attention to Tyler.

I spin to Nessie again, accusation most likely written across my face. *How did Mom know?* I silently ask her, realizing this was in the cards all along.

"I can send you the information if you'd like. We'll be at the Banks Resort in the Garden District of New Orleans."

Mom sighs, lifting a hand to her chest. "The Garden District. You guys are going to have the best time."

Dad cringes. "You guys stick together. Don't drink anything that someone hands you on the street, and if someone offers you beads—"

"Dad!" Vanessa cuts him off with an alarmed look.

"They know about the beads, honey," Mom says, patting his arm. "They're smart, and everything's going to be fine."

Nessie steals a look at me. *Can you believe him? How embarrassing!*

I shrug. *At least he hasn't asked for copies of Tyler's driver's license or taken any pictures of his license plate like he did our prom dates.*

Nessie's gaze darts to our bags. "We should probably get going so we don't get stuck in traffic."

Tyler reaches for a bag, and I cringe when I realize it's mine, knowing it weighs a ton. Dad asked me to help him carry the same bag down the stairs, afraid it would throw out his back. But Tyler lifts it easily, his biceps and forearms flexing to accommodate the weight.

"Do you guys want a cooler for the ride? I've got some extra ice packs. We could throw in some water and snacks in case you guys get hungry." Dad eyes the garage, likely already picking which of the dozen coolers we own that he's going to send with us.

"I think we'll be okay," I tell him.

"You guys don't have to stop at gas stations with an electric car," Dad objects. "I've heard these things can go upward of six hours."

"We'll be okay," Nessie says, and though her voice is verging on condescending, Dad barely blinks. He's still debating what to fill the cooler with. Stubbornness is a Robinson trait, written into our DNA.

Mom hugs me again. "Have fun *before* getting to California, okay?" Mom is our free spirit, a trait she shares with Vanessa and one I envy furiously because I don't possess a single ounce of it. She holds my hands, giving me a reassuring smile that serves like a balm on my growing nerves.

I assumed freshman year would be the hardest—pulling off the Band-Aid and moving across the country to attend Brighton, where our parents are both alma maters. However, this year feels harder, like I'm nearing the end of summers to have the excuse to return home.

Nessie wraps her arm around Mom and me, holding us—binding us. "Don't worry. I'll make sure she has fun."

Mom sniggers, the planes of her cheeks creasing with laugh lines that she always points out with dismay in each photo that's ever taken of her. I love those laugh lines. They feel like a map of our childhood— blanket forts and makeovers and drinking too much pink lemonade that we always have in our fridge. "Look out for each other." She kisses Vanessa's forehead and then mine. "Be safe and be smart, my beautiful girls."

My throat is tight with emotions that I don't know how to articulate. Vanessa weaves her fingers with mine, extending a sense of comfort and strength, and reminding me how as hard as it is to leave—I'm beyond grateful that I always have her.

Dad sidles up beside Mom, his arms extending along her shoulders and mine, security to her like Nessie is to me. "You guys are going to have your own rooms at each hotel, right?" he asks, his voice lowered as his brows knit with unease and doubt.

"Definitely," Nessie assures him, but her voice is all bravado and lacks the sincerity I wanted to hear.

"And I'm serious about the beads," he adds.

The rest of my emotions ease as laughter bubbles out of my throat.

"I'm serious," he says.

Vanessa's objections wash away as she looks at me, and then she too starts to laugh, our hands still linked as we slowly back toward the car. Dad's grip on Mom's shoulders tightens as they remain by where our luggage had been.

"You sure you don't want the cooler?" he asks.

"Positive. But we love you for offering. I promise, no one will get dehydrated." I smile.

He sighs, resigning over the decision though I can see he wants to argue his point, likely thinking of how we might need it in case we get lost, the car breaks down, or a dozen other possibilities that my mind races through like I'm on the same telepathic loop.

"We'll let you know when we hit New Orleans," Nessie says, taking another step back so the barrier between us and home grows.

Cooper grins as we near the hood of the Tesla then moves to open the rear passenger door, which slides up instead of outward.

Vanessa's jaw drops. "This car is insane."

I climb into the SUV that smells like it was driven off the lot this morning and wave goodbye to our parents.

"This is going to be so much fun," Vanessa says, running her hands over the tops of her thighs.

I suck in a breath as our house falls out of sight, hoping beyond hope that my sister's right.

2

TYLER

I don't know how Cooper talked me into this nightmare.

Driving across the country with him will be a stretch of my patience—adding Chloe and Vanessa Robinson is guaranteed to be a train wreck. For starters, Chloe looks at me like she'd rather claw my eyes out than acknowledge my presence.

Apparently, her regret for kissing me freshman year is a level red alert.

I've tried to recall the details of that night numerous times to understand what happened that has her always making excuses to leave whenever I show up; to see if I'd done something that warrants her reaction. But our kiss was two minutes and hardly anything to get worked up over. Likely, it's because she was expecting a call or promises to spend every waking hour with her like some freshman couples do as they explore their new freedoms and get their first taste of an adult relationship.

I'd been at a party with Cooper, and he'd gotten hammered with only three shots, a perpetual lightweight. Chloe had been outside, nursing a beer and staring up at the sky. I'd formally met her an hour before that when Coop had introduced her and Vanessa.

I'd made a joke about the beer being flat. She'd smiled, and when I'd asked what she was doing, she pointed at the inky sky and told me she'd found Camelopardalis, and thanks to years of learning Latin, I laughed, positive she was trying to blow me off or sound like a genius because I knew Camelopardalis translated to giraffe. When I laughed, so did she. And I no longer cared if she was trying to sound smart or telling me to get lost, I closed the distance between us and stared blankly up at the sky.

"It's one of the hardest constellations for me to see, but I think the beer helped," she told me. "The giraffe was fairly unknown and exotic in the seventeenth century, so its species name refers to it having a body similar to a camel but the colors of a leopard, so they called them camel-leopard. That cluster of faint stars is supposed to be the spots on the giraffe."

She'd had too many details for it to be a lie, and still, it seemed implausible and strangely fascinating as my buzz waned with another drink of water, my attention focused on her rather than the sky. And when she glanced back at me, her light brown hair blew in the breeze and seemed to charge something inside of her that made her green eyes brighter and fuller, and then she leaned forward and kissed me. It had been a gentle kiss—a question that I answered ardently with a swipe of my tongue across the seal of her lips. But before I could taste her, a group of guys stumbled outside, laughing as they lit a joint, and Chloe straightened, her smile and that spark both gone. She disappeared inside like Cinderella, only when I saw her again, she wasn't eager or relieved that I'd found her. No, instead she ignored me like she had no idea who I was.

That was fine with me.

I didn't want drama or a relationship. I was finally out from under my father's thumb, and I wanted to relax and have fun and not have to worry about who was watching me or what anyone thought.

So, how did I get here? Driving across the country like a fucking chauffeur for a girl I kissed once who avidly avoids me, her sister who I am only kind of friends with, and my teammate?

That, my friends, is the ugly side of giving a shit.

Not about the twins, or my insignificant kiss with Chloe, or caring about the daggers she shoots my way—no, this is about friendship. My friendship with Cooper—lightweight, in bed by ten, all-around nice guy —Sutton, who is the closest thing I've ever known to a sibling. We met freshman year through football. He was serious, focused, and determined while I was pissing away my time and dodging calls from my parents about my missed classes, and when Coach Harris told me I had to either focus or ride the pine, it took everything in me not to tell him to shove it up his arsehole. I was tired of expectations and was about to quit when Cooper made some bullshit excuse for me and started picking me up every day to ensure I'd be at practice on time. That escalated to going to the gym and tutoring me when I fell dangerously close to failing a mathematics class I should have been acing.

Cooper dug me out of the crater I'd made with not giving a shit. I was trying to skate by on my looks and name, and he helped me rebuild a semblance of balance with football, school, and my sanity that the fans and hype that comes with being a football player at Brighton hacks at nearly as often and hard as the paparazzi when I'm in London. And because Cooper has had a crush on Vanessa Robinson since before his balls dropped, I couldn't tell him no when he proposed the plan to go across the country with them to allow him to get closer to her.

Call me motherfucking Cupid.

"Which stop are you most excited for, Chloe?" Cooper asks, twisting around in his seat so he can see her. "Vegas?"

She scoffs.

I glance up into my rearview mirror to catch her reaction, surprised to find a contradicting smile. "You know me so well."

Cooper chuckles, but the joke is lost on me. While Cooper is like a brother to me, Chloe is still his best friend. The two of them are close, which makes her actively avoiding me that much more apparent.

"She's been looking at all the best places to eat in each city," Vanessa says. "She has a list of dessert shops she wants to stop at."

Cooper's laughter grows. In the rearview mirror, I catch the gentle lift of Chloe's shoulders. "And coffee. Don't forget coffee."

"Cooper already knows you're an addict. I'm sure he assumed." Vanessa moves her feet, the shine of her sandal catching in my peripheral vision. I consider how much they're going to talk and request to stop. How Cooper and I will be responsible for them in the cities we stay over in, and how my car's going to smell like a girl's perfume by the time we reach Seattle. The mounting warnings have me considering driving through the night and trying to shorten this trip and tell my dad that the hotels were all fine. I'd take his wrath and disappointment, accept his look of condemnation at the dinner table over Christmas break if it meant I wouldn't be stuck in a car for two and a half weeks with shrill giggles and social media updates and selfies.

Then I consider how the dominoes might fall if I were to do that, how my dad is grooming Scott Lewis at this very moment to know every-thing about the Banks Resort and Luxury Hotel chain from the ground up. They're currently in London, visiting our original hotel that was opened over a hundred years ago by my great-grandpa. They're going to be traveling across England and up into Scotland, then over to Ireland before going through much of Western Europe. Our American hotels represent nearly seventy percent of our company's revenue, but Dad insisted on taking Lewis abroad to teach him the history of the company as well as understand where the mission statement for Banks Resorts and Luxury Hotels was born and how it became the world-renowned chain it is today. Lewis wasn't a bad choice. He's worked for our family for ten years and has an impressive resume packed with awards and accomplishments that will take me, at minimum, a decade to achieve. In addition to being smart, he's savvy, well-liked, and he delivers one hell of an interview—something I can't do even with a written and rehearsed speech in my grasp.

Dad claims Lewis is the backup plan. However, I've seen the writing on the wall since I was a kid, when I preferred tossing the football around with my uncle Kip to sampling which flavor of coffee or what thread count of sheets should be used. It wasn't that I didn't care, it's just I had two loves—the hotel chain that's been in our family for three generations and football—and my father never understood how I could love anything more than money.

During these next two and a half weeks, I will be stopping at several of our hotel sites, checking in with a few of our poorest performers, and some of our best. My goal is to reconcile the differ-ences between them, learn what our top performers are doing right, and leverage that with ones that are struggling. I'll report my findings and ideas for improvement to my dad on August twenty-eighth when he and Lewis fly to Seattle to discuss how their European tour went.

And I plan to be prepared because while Lewis has me beat in practically everything except for his last name not being the one on the buildings and letterhead, ingenuity and innovation are where I strive. This was why when I was twelve, I made a thousand bucks one summer while staying with my parents in Miami by recognizing the need for our neighborhood to have a drink stand outside of the fitness and pool center. To me, it seemed like a no-brainer—Miami is hot as hell. People were working out and sweating. Boom. Not only did I make a thousand bucks, I only worked for the first week, and then neighborhood kids worked for me, and I paid them while I lounged by the pool. My mum found this opportunistic and made me give the kids I'd employed more money when she'd found out. Dad, however, tripled my profits and invested the money for me, telling me I had a keen eye for business.

"What about you, Tyler? How was your summer?" I have to look in my rearview mirror to see which of the sisters spoke. Vanessa smiles at me. She's pretty, beautiful even, with long brown hair highlighted around her face, wide green eyes, and a mouth that could make any man have wet dreams.

I glance at Chloe, expecting to find the mirrored version of Vanessa like I had when Cooper first introduced us. At the time, I'd seen every guy's teenage dream flash before me as the two laughed at something, my lack of familiarity drawing an identical image of the two. Now, it's easy for me to tell them apart. Chloe has the same hair color, the same eyes, the same erotic mouth, even the same jawline—but their voices are different, Chloe's a bit grittier, and she's a little taller, her lips slightly rounder.

It's their similarities that had the football team making so many threesome jokes when a rumor circulated about our kiss after one of the potheads shared the news.

"Life in Miami is basically living the dream," I tell her as I sit back in my seat, one hand gripping the wheel as I fall into the role I created—the role my family created. "Sun, beaches, parties. I can't complain."

"Ty spent half his summer on a yacht and the other half at poker tables." Cooper glances at me, envy shining in his eyes.

I smirk in response, knowing my tanned skin and the different photos of me people shared over the summer fit this narrative perfectly, regardless of the truth.

In the rearview mirror, I catch Chloe watching me, her brows pinched before she notices my gaze and quickly looks away.

"You guys didn't pack as much as I expected," Cooper says.

"We left most of our stuff in storage over the summer, remember?" Vanessa asks him.

"Oh, I remember. We talked about how if you do it again, you won't pack all your books together in the same boxes." Cooper shakes his head at the memory.

Vanessa laughs. "I'm bummed summer's over, but at the same time, I'm really glad to be returning to Seattle. I have a feeling this is going to be the best year yet."

"Did you guys decide on an apartment?" Cooper asks.

"We did." Vanessa's tone isn't nearly as confident as Chloe glances at her.

Cooper laughs. "I take it you won the coin toss?" he asks, looking at Vanessa.

"I just made the executive decision. It's a little smaller, but we'll be downtown. We can walk to get coffee, and to the library, and to pick up dinner..."

I could kick myself for watching their expressions and trying to read between the lines because I don't care—yet, I recognize the annoyance that flashes across Chloe's face and the nervous energy from Vanessa.

"It's going to be an epic year," Vanessa continues. "And this is the perfect way to kick it off." She sits back in her seat as I return my focus to the road to keep myself from comparing the sisters.

My thoughts move to Cooper and how he'd reacted when he'd heard about my micro kiss with Chloe. He'd been ready to go fisticuffs with me, and that was when I learned not only was my friend a posses-sive wanker, but he liked one of the sisters. I'm pretty sure *like* is an understatement considering he chose Brighton over a handful of more prestigious schools because this is where Vanessa is going. He works his arse off and loves football, but he doesn't live for it, and he doesn't feel like a piece of him dies when we have a bad game. No, Cooper's smart and ambitious and wants to start his own programming company and stay in Seattle, far from the hot and humid summers of Florida.

Cooper avoided me for a full week after confronting me about the kiss and then was defensive and cagey when he finally demanded to know what had happened. Relief practically poured out of him when I told him I'd kissed Chloe—not Vanessa.

WE DRIVE MOSTLY in silence until Chloe and Vanessa both fall asleep.

"What do you think we should do tonight?" Cooper asks.

I shake my head, my thoughts converging on what information I need to focus on once we arrive and how the meeting I've ordered will go. Are they going to stare at me like some uppity little shit who had everything served on a silver platter? Will they try to work with me? My thoughts have been so consumed with the hotel that I haven't given a second of thought to what we'll do in The Big Easy.

"It sounds like your tour guides already have everything planned out. Desserts and coffee, didn't you hear?"

Coop sniggers. "Come on, man. We're going to be in New Orleans— we have to do something fun."

"Does that translate to getting Vanessa drunk enough that she might end up in your room tonight?"

Cooper's gaze flashes to the backseat, and then to me, a warning clear in his eyes, worried she overheard.

I chuckle. Guy's got it bad. "What do you want to do?"

"I don't know. What do people do in New Orleans?"

"Now *I'm* the tour guide?"

His lips thin with annoyance, but his gaze turns desperate.

"We're staying in the Garden District, so we'll be a short ride to the French District where there'll be all kinds of tourist shit. We can go down Bourbon Street tonight, and if the girls like to dress up and go clubbing, there's a masquerade club that's big with the tourists." Because a simple mask that barely covers one's forehead and nose somehow manages to conceal all inhibitions. "Drinks, beads, dancing."

"You can get us in?"

I glance at him, surprised he's asking until I remember how few and far between Cooper's requests go. It's one of the reasons I trust him and why our friendship has become a brotherhood—he doesn't ask for things and expects even less. I reach for my phone and hit a couple of buttons to reach Anika, our family's primary contact for social events, travel, and nearly anything that's requested of her.

"Mr. Banks," she answers on the second ring. "What can I do for you, sir?"

"Anika, I need four VIP passes to Façade for tomorrow night."

I hear her typing in the background. "No problem. I'll contact them and send directions and contact info to your phone. As a reminder, your meeting tomorrow is at nine A.M. sharp." Anika has been with my family my entire life, yet our interactions are always borderline sterile. She doesn't know me any better than I know her.

"Great. Thank you. Also, did you hear back from San Diego?"

"Not yet, but, I'll be calling them again this afternoon."

I swallow my reply. My father's not the only one who has doubts regarding my ability to lead and be the next CEO of Banks Resorts. Many appear to be working against my efforts, ignoring my calls and emails, and failing to accept meeting requests. I can't tell my father this, and they know it, and therefore I've been stuck playing a game of cat and mouse where half the time I'm left feeling like the fucking mouse chasing the bastard cat.

"Thanks, Anika," I say and hang up.

"It was that easy?" Cooper asks.

I nod, though the question feels loaded—or maybe it's the answer because few things are that easy, specifically when it comes to my role with the family business or even Anika.

Cooper leans back in his seat, taking an audible breath.

"You okay?" I ask.

He nods, his gaze flicking to the back seat again, making his thoughts apparent. I don't delve into them or try to understand—I already know I won't. The very last thing I have time for is a relationship and even less time for the idea of chasing a girl whose feelings are unknown. "Just tired."

"Take a nap. We've got four hours until we get there."

"You sure?"

I nod. "Positive. We'll have to stop before we get there to charge the car, but we're basically following the coastline, so you'll see more of this." I point out the window as signs invite us to exit for Panama City Beach. "Recline your seat, and take a nap."

Cooper plays with the controls and settles into his seat. I'm relieved. I don't want to analyze his relationship with Vanessa or make more plans for the trip. I have enough to focus on with New Orleans.

3
_____

CHLOE

I open my eyes and realize we've come to a stop.

I don't remember falling asleep. The car is nearly silent, creating the perfect setting for an afternoon nap.

I sit up, looking over at Nessie to see she's still lost to dreamland, and ahead of her, Cooper is asleep as well. Tyler's outside, leaning against the hood of the car, hovering over his phone.

My legs feel cramped, itching with the desire to move, and I wish we'd taken Dad up on his suggestion to bring a cooler because I'm thirsty and hungry.

I look around, hoping I can ascertain where we're at and how much farther we have until we hit New Orleans. Outside my window is a wall of Annabelle hydrangeas, the kind our grandma grows that have the giant white, cone-shaped blooms. Behind them is the main road where a billboard towers, touting "Mobile, Home of the Best Flea Market in Alabama."

I've never been to Mobile, but when it was Nessie, Meredith, and I planning this trip across the country, we'd discussed stopping here after seeing pictures of their white sandy beaches and abundance of seafood restaurants. The memory has me bending down to look out the other windows, hoping I'll catch sight of the coast. But the more I move, the stiffer my muscles feel, and the more I regret having my fourth cup of coffee this morning.

I debate waking Vanessa up so she can go with me but decide against it as she hums in her sleep. I know she's exhausted. Mom and I had lain across her bed, talking about our road trip and this next year while Nessie finally started to pack. I woke up in her bed this morning, and she was already awake, trying to finish getting her things together.

I pull in a breath, realizing my bladder won't make it to New Orleans. The car door opens without a sound—rising again instead of outward. It's so weird and so cool, and yet I try to act unfazed by this because Tyler's turned and is looking at me. I press for the door to close, and it does, silently again like the engine. Dad would love this. We're parked at a bank of chargers, in the same parking lot as a Target and strip mall. The skies are a dark shade of gray, filled with rain clouds that make the air feel heavy and sticky.

"Is there time for me to walk over to Target?"

He glances at the red and white contraption that leads to his car to charge the battery and then at the store, as though gauging the distance and how long it might take me. The action makes me bristle. I know it's not his fault—not entirely. There's just something about Tyler Banks that grinds my gears. Maybe it's the way Cooper talks about him and views him like he's a god among men or because every other girl at Brighton falls at his feet. Or maybe it's because his arrogance is obvious in the casual manner with which he carries himself and brief words that have me feeling like an inconvenience despite us having barely spoken. Or perhaps it's the fact that five guys saw me make the giant mistake of kissing Tyler Banks and—

"We still have twenty minutes left," he says, cutting me off mid-thought.

I won't lie, the bullseye of a Target usually leaves me in a hypnotic state that makes hours feel like mere minutes, but I'm determined to go inside and find the restroom and coffee and be back in twenty minutes.

"Do you want anything to eat or drink?" I ask because although Tyler makes my teeth grind, he's single-handedly the only reason we're able to afford this cross-country adventure in a way that doesn't require pitching a tent each night.

He shakes his head, his attention back on his phone. I stare at him for another moment, trying to understand the appeal that has so many girls lusting after him. His angular jaw and straight nose and blue eyes make him look like a cross between a young Charlie Hunnam and Matt Damon. But not *Good Will Hunting*, smiling Matt Damon. No, more like Matt Damon *à la* Jason Bourne: silent, intense, and angry at the world.

I tighten my grip on my purse and walk past him, the heat radiating from the blacktop, telling me the temperature is well over a hundred degrees, making me yearn for the beach and an umbrella.

I avoid the dollar bins and the cute swimsuits on sale just feet away and remain focused on my purpose and short timeline. I make a quick detour to the restroom before heading to the Starbucks, where I order a coffee and a passion tea for Nessie and get a couple of bottled drinks for Cooper and Tyler because although he said he didn't want anything, it feels almost rude to get things for the others and not him. I stare at the cookies and muffins that make my stomach grumble, but the idea of bringing any of them into Tyler's pristine car prevents me from ordering them, and that thought makes me wonder if he'll mind me bringing drinks into the car.

I grab a handful of napkins and take my icy-cold coffee and the other drinks and head back out into the blazing heat. Vanessa and Cooper are awake, standing outside of the car with Tyler, laughing about something.

"You read my mind," Nessie says, reaching for her tea. "Thank you."

I hand Cooper the bag of bottled juices and coffees. "Since you always change your order, I didn't know what to get you or Tyler, so I just picked up some stuff."

He accepts it, a quick smile flashing across his features.

"I can't believe I slept so long," Nessie says, rolling her neck muscles while Tyler disconnects the car from the charger.

"I can. You barely slept last night," I say.

She combs her fingers through her hair, her brow creased with concern as she silently asks me if it looks all right. We both inherited our mom's cowlicks that make the right side of our hair go straight up and out unless it's tamed and coated in product, but humidity and sleep can steal any semblance of calm we wrestle it into. I give her a quick nod of approval that has her sighing before taking a long pull from her drink.

"Where are we?" Cooper asks.

"Mobile, Alabama," Tyler says. "We're about two hours from the hotel."

At the sound of his voice, I swear, a woman passing us sighs.

"Do you mind us bringing drinks into the car, or should we finish them out here?" I ask.

Tyler stares at my drink and then my face, folding his arms across his chest, his tight black tee straining against the muscles in his biceps. He grins. "You're asking permission to bring a drink in the car?"

My cheeks heat with embarrassment. It hadn't seemed like a stupid question considering his car is worth more than what most people make in a year. Especially considering my mom still grumbles if we take drinks into her car after Nessie spilled a McFlurry—eleven years ago.

"Next time, I'll be sure to order a cookie," I grumble.

His brow furrows with confusion, but I ignore it and Nessie's complaints about the heat and get back into the car.

Once we've all piled in, Vanessa grins at me as she says, "I have an idea. Why don't we play a game?" Warning bells echo in my thoughts as her eyes light up.

"What kind of game?" Cooper asks.

"Truth or dare," Nessie tells him, leaning forward.

I shake my head. Nessie turns her attention to me and smiles, taunting me about my new motto to go with the flow and be spontaneous. I stop my silent objection and busy myself with my coffee, fishing for some of the whipped cream with my straw and licking it off of the end.

"Cooper," Nessie begins. "Truth or dare?"

He chuckles, leaning his head against the seat. "Truth, I guess?"

Nessie grins. "What's the most embarrassing thing in your room?"

"In Florida or Washington?"

"Both."

Cooper runs a hand through his dark hair. "In Florida, I still have a box of Pokémon cards, and in Washington... Shit, I don't know?"

"Definitely that awful pink stuffed bear on your desk," Tyler says.

"Stuffed bear?" Nessie asks.

"Your truth didn't require subtext," Cooper says, shaking his head.

"That was before I knew a pink bear was involved."

I giggle, sitting back in my seat and feeling surprisingly happy for Nessie's suggestion to play as I slurp down my coffee, feeling the jolt of caffeine.

"It's garbage," Cooper says.

"The more elusive you are, the more I'm going to press you on this, you know that, right?" Nessie leans forward.

Cooper releases a heavy sigh. "Claire gave it to me."

"*Claire* Claire?" Nessie asks, her eyes on me, wide with shock and a glint of pain. Cooper dated Claire Mayfair freshman year at Brighton. At first, I assumed it was his way of moving past his crush on Nessie— seeing her on dates every other night couldn't have been easy. But then one date turned into three, which turned into five months. I knew he was hurt when she dumped him and moved on to a new guy a week later.

"Were there multiple Claires?" Tyler asks.

Cooper shakes his head dismissively. "Just the one. She won it while we were at the county fair, and the thing was so hideous that it creeped her out, so she put it on my desk."

Nessie stares at me with stretched eyes, but doesn't pursue any more information.

"Okay, my turn." Cooper reaches into the bag of bottled drinks and picks out one of the fruit juices. "Chloe, truth or dare?"

My stomach lurches, but remains intact, knowing Cooper won't be too harsh. "Truth."

Nessie laughs at my obvious discomfort.

"What's something you've never told anyone else?"

I mull over the question, my face likely puckered as I try to think of something that isn't going to be humiliating or reveal just how crazy my thoughts sometimes wander. "Um...I once cheated on a test for AP History."

Nessie pulls her chin back with surprise. "Really?"

I nod, feeling both relieved and embarrassed over the simple truth. School has always been something I've worked tirelessly at and have taken seriously. I've known since middle school that I want a career in astronomy. "I'd missed three days after having my wisdom teeth pulled, and the painkillers made it impossible for me to stay awake or focus, so when I got back, and Mr. Bradenburg gave us a pop quiz, I cheated and looked at someone else's paper."

"Is that really cheating?" Cooper asks, twisting around in his seat. "I mean, if you were out, why didn't he just give you a pass?"

"In Chloe's rulebook, it was definitely cheating. We took Spanish together our freshman year of high school, and she'd even get mad at *me* for cheating off her work."

I scoff. "I still let you, and look how that ended for us."

"Busted!" Cooper yells.

"We both served detention for a week," I say.

"That wasn't the worst part. Afterward, I had to sit on the other side of the class next to that Ben kid, and he was even worse at Spanish than I was." Nessie shakes her head.

"Your turn, Chloe," Cooper says with a smile.

Rules of inclusion tell me I should be asking Tyler next, but I know how competitive games turn back on you, and the last thing I want is for him to ask me the question in return. "Nessie, truth or dare?"

She grins. "Dare."

"Kiss the person on your left!" Cooper yells.

"Why would I dare her to kiss me?" I ask him, rolling my eyes as I glance around the car. "Okay. Call one of your friends, and sing the chorus of the next song to them."

Nessie leans forward, giggling as she reaches for her phone. My sister is confident and brazen with nearly everything in life, making her easy to admire and even easier to like and want to be around. Her laugh is quick and contagious, and she's always looking for ways to have fun, so I shouldn't be surprised that the dare doesn't even make her blink as she scrolls through her phone and calls someone. She puts the phone on speaker and then belts out the chorus, her voice cracked and uneven because singing might be the only thing Nessie doesn't excel at. She giggles wildly as the girl on the other side laughs in response.

"What are you doing?" the person she called asks.

Nessie wipes a tear from her eye. "Just wanted to serenade you. I have to go. Bye, Britt!" She hangs up and beams.

"We might have to stop at a karaoke bar," Cooper says.

"All right, Tyler, truth or dare?" Nessie asks, ignoring Cooper's suggestion.

I catch his blue gaze in the rearview mirror, finding humor and intrigue enrobed with what I think is a reluctance to participate as he remains silent for long seconds. "Dare," he finally answers.

"I dare you to get the phone number of the next car that drives by us."

Tyler glances out the window, and I follow suit, catching sight of a minivan with an older couple starting to pass.

"Going to get me bloody arrested," Tyler says, accelerating to match their speed.

I'm already struggling to keep my laughter in, and he's only rolled his window down.

"Better than the guy behind them," Nessie says, turning to look at the motorcycle following the van.

"Bloody hell." Tyler rolls his shoulders. "Coop, you watch the road."

I slap a hand across my face with my fingers spread so I can still see. "This is a terrible idea."

Nessie places her hand on my knee. It's meant to be calming, but right now, my eyes are glued to the road. Tyler is waving at the couple to catch their attention.

The woman in the passenger seat starts to lower her window, and then the husband looks across, shakes his head, and uses the control on the driver's side to close it again. The woman turns to her husband, clearly objecting as she waves an arm, and then turns and starts to lower the window again. My guilt ratchets higher as humor works to join the party. She probably thinks he's trying to warn them their fuel door is open or something legitimately important.

"Have you ever wanted to become a cougar?" Tyler yells over the road noise.

"Oh my God," Nessie giggles into her cupped hands.

Cooper raises a hand to shield his face.

"What?" the woman yells back, her face pinched as the wind blows against her.

"Can I call you sometime?" Tyler asks, his full attention on her, requiring Cooper to lean over and grab the wheel.

"Call me?" the woman asks.

The wind displaces Tyler's dark blond hair as he sticks his head farther out the window. "That's right."

The woman ducks back into the car to say something to her husband, who is the easiest to see from my vantage point. He pulls his shoulders back and starts to say something, but the woman is laughing as she faces the window again and starts reciting a string of numbers and then cheers before her husband changes lanes and speeds up.

"That was easier than I expected," Tyler says, rolling his window up.

Nessie is in stitches. "She really seemed like she wanted you to call."

"Nah, she was trying to get her husband worked up. Did you see him carrying on?" Tyler shakes his head and runs a hand through his hair, unbothered by the fact Cooper is still steering the car.

After what feels like a millennium, he takes the wheel, his smile cocky. "All right, Chloe, truth or dare?"

4

TYLER

Chloe cringes, reminding me of how low her expectations of me are. The realization has half of me wanting to be a total dick and ask her something scandalous and embarrassing, and the other half of me feels guilty for having asked her.

"Truth," she says reluctantly.

I hadn't thought about what I'd ask, so it takes me a moment to come up with a question that isn't going to up the ante of her dislike of me. "What's something that most people think is true about you but isn't?"

She blinks, but I can't read her expression as I'm pulling back onto the freeway. When I finally glance up, she's looking at Vanessa. "That I'm Vanessa?"

"That doesn't count," Cooper says, shaking his head.

I was going to give it to her because while it's an obvious answer, I hadn't set any parameters.

"It's true," she objects.

"It's still a cop-out," Vanessa says, earning a wide-eyed stare of accusation from Chloe.

"Okay, how about that I can tell them their horoscope because I'm majoring in astronomy?"

Vanessa laughs. "I knew you were going to say that."

"Because it happens every time anyone asks what I'm studying!"

Vanessa laughs even harder. "Last week, she was explaining the difference between astronomy and astrology to Kira from high school, and after like a five-minute explanation, Kira told Chloe she was a Capricorn and asked if she could tell her astrological predictions for the year."

"This doesn't surprise me," Cooper says. "I had to be lab partners with her."

"Chloe gave her a fake horoscope filled with warnings about this fall and told her that listening was going to be imperative and..." She looks at Chloe. "What else did you tell her?"

Chloe laughs, shaking her head. "I don't remember. But I know I've explained to her what astronomy is at least three times, and I think all she hears is stars. It was mean. I blame it on the tequila."

Vanessa laughs again as she nods. "That was a fun night."

Chloe flashes another smile as she fishes more whipped cream from her cup and licks it off the tip of her straw, distracting me from the road and how normal she seems in these stories compared to the shy, standoffosh girl I generally encounter. "Okay, my turn. Cooper, truth or dare?"

Cooper blows out a breath. "Dare."

She smiles too fast, reaching forward with a balled fist. She smells like oranges and coffee and something floral that makes me think of that night freshman year, recalling the way her gaze had blazed seconds before she leaned forward and kissed me.

"Oh, God. What is it?" Cooper asks, reaching to take what she's offering.

In the back seat, Vanessa's already giggling.

"Ketchup?" Cooper says, smoothing the small packet.

"I dare you to drink it all," Chloe tells him.

Cooper cringes, and the laughter between us grows.

"I have to record this," Chloe says, reaching for her phone.

He flips her off as she starts recording him, giving a brief summary. "How did you have ketchup on you?" he asks, tearing the top open.

"Someone dropped it in the parking lot. I picked it up."

"Oh, great. So, it was probably injected with heroin."

Chloe's smile spreads as she reaches up, brushing her hair over her shoulder. "Likely. Now do it."

Cooper tips his head back, squirting the contents into his mouth. He gags and chokes, making us laugh again.

"Don't spew in here," I warn him.

He coughs, pounding his fist against his chest a couple of times as he breathes through his nose. "God. Where are those drinks you bought?" he asks, reaching for the bag Chloe had given him, digging out a purple juice that he downs half of in one drink.

"That was the best," Vanessa says.

"That was terrible," he replies, taking another drink.

THE GAME CONTINUES, and with each new truth or dare, the mood in the car lightens. I'm cautiously optimistic that this trip won't be as bad as I thought. When we reach the I-10 Twin Span Bridge, Chloe skips her turn, staring out at the ocean with a peaceful look in her eyes.

"Is this the bridge you were talking about?" Vanessa asks.

Chloe nods. "This is the longest bridge in the world."

"Doesn't it seem like the guardrails should be a little higher?' Cooper asks.

"You sound like Chloe," Vanessa tells him.

"Are we close?" Cooper asks.

"Another thirty minutes or so," I tell him, pointing at the GPS.

Cooper groans with his protest. "I'm so glad we have a couple of days off before we drive again."

The rest of the drive is mostly silent, save for Vanessa's occasional grumblings about the scenery's lack of diversity.

"New Orleans," Chloe announces, pointing at a sign as we near the outskirts of the city.

Traffic is congested; the weekend draws large crowds to the city. Cars are honking and changing lanes erratically, working to beat the traffic. I slam on my brakes when a car cuts in front of us, the driver one of the many arseholes trying to leap forward a mere foot.

I punch my horn and throw both hands into the air. Few things get under my skin as much as bad drivers and busy roads. "Make that an hour," I tell Cooper as we creep forward, and then come to a full stop as the GPS announces an accident ahead.

. . .

Chloe

TYLER WASN'T FAR OFF. It takes us fifty-five minutes before he pulls up to the hotel. It's massive, sprawling across a full city block and towering several stories into the air. Tyler comes to a stop under an extensive covered area that's made of stone and six car lengths wide. Broad wooden pillars are adorned with lanterns that warmly flicker, creating a warm ambiance. Two men from the valet dek and are dressed in black suits approach the car.

"Greetings, Mr. Banks," a man with raven-colored hair combed to one side greets him personally. "How was your trip, sir?"

I glance at Vanessa, who's already looking at me, her eyes wide with excitement and amazement.

My door opens, and the other valet smiles and offers his hand to me. "Welcome to New Orleans, Ms. Robinson."

This is so far outside of the economy hotels we generally stay at that I have to blink back my surprise at him knowing my name.

"Would you like all the bags brought up to your rooms and unpacked?" another valet asks, joining us.

Tyler nods in response, and though I want to ask how in the world they'll be able to tell our bags apart, I keep this question to myself as they begin unloading the bags out in record time.

A woman with white-blonde hair and an elegant suit approaches us with a smile, greeting Tyler again by name.

I stare at Cooper until he feels it and turns to look at me. "Is this a prank?"

Cooper shakes his head. "I think this is how the other half lives."

It's difficult to wrap my head around the possibility that enough people can afford to stay at this hotel to allow it to not only remain open but be in nearly every major city across the world.

We step through large glass doors and are greeted by the air-conditioning, which is welcome compared to the humid night. The air smells like vanilla and citrus—rich. I never knew rich had an aroma, but now

I'm sure of it as we enter the expansive and elegant lobby, my shoes too loud against the white marble floor. Vaulted ceilings make me tip my head back to see the coffered ceiling several stories above. A round table that could entertain fifty is covered by a bouquet of exotic flowers—*real* flowers. I don't think I've ever stayed at a hotel with real flowers or with perfumed air.

I lower my gaze to keep myself from openly gawking and follow the others to the front desk to check in.

"You're staring," Cooper whispers.

There's too much to see to look at him. "Why aren't you? This place is crazy."

He chuckles, wrapping an arm around my shoulders. "Way better than the trip you were planning with Meredith, am I right?"

"Too soon," I tell him, shrugging off his touch.

"Greetings. Welcome to New Orleans! I hope you all had a nice trip here. My name's Natasha Benting, and I'm the general manager. It's a pleasure to meet you, Mr. Banks." A woman wearing a pristine navy suit and coral blouse greets us, her dark hair flawlessly curled. She's probably forty but looks twenty as she smiles at us with a practiced grace that makes her look like she walked off a Hollywood film set. Paired with her Southern accent, it makes her the definition of a Southern belle. I'm not even remotely shocked to find Cooper and Tyler both staring at her for a full second while the woman recites a list of things about the accommodations and the hotel before confirming Tyler's meetings tomorrow.

Meetings?

I want to ask Cooper what the meetings are for but don't. The car ride here and all of our laughing created a false sense of friendship that just proves why I don't trust Tyler. I don't doubt where our alliances and the lines of our relationship have been drawn and have no interest in approaching them.

Fool me once, shame on you. Fool me twice, and I'm the only one to blame.

I know the rules.

What's more, I know the score.

"Please follow me to your room," Natasha says, moving out from the desk with a stack of key cards in her perfectly manicured nails. It's not her fault I'm measuring myself against her, comparing all of her perfections to my imperfections and feeling slightly more defensive and inadequate with each one noted.

A man moves to take her place behind the desk. He has dark brown hair and blue eyes that are a shade so dark they're nearly violet. He's striking and so distracting I nearly collide with Cooper as he starts to move forward.

Nessie chuckles, grabbing my hand and spinning me around to follow them into the massive lobby. "Do they hire models here?" I ask as I steal another look back at the guy who grins at me before he winks and makes me feel like I've just won front-row tickets to a concert.

"Is this a freaking atrium?" Nessie asks. "Oh my gosh, there are crocodiles! Chloe, are you seeing this?" she whisper-yells, clinging to my arm as she points at a sign.

Tyler glances at us, and Nessie tries to smile and play it cool although she's visibly still bouncing and freaking out as we stare with wide eyes at the lobby and the glass ceiling.

Natasha leads us to the bank of elevators and goes to the one on the far right. "You'll need to remember that this is the only elevator that goes up to the presidential suite," she explains.

Presidential suite?

Nessie's fingers dig into my arm with the same thought.

The doors open immediately, revealing white marble tiles patterned with smaller black and gray ones. The walls are dark wood with carved accents. There's a large ornate mirror on the opposite side of the doors, and below it is a leather bench seat.

"Oh my gosh," I whisper as quietly as I can manage. "There's a couch in the elevator."

"They don't get out much," Cooper says, ushering us forward when the others remain still, waiting for us to step inside the elevator's cab.

"Sorry," I say, quickly moving forward.

Natasha swipes one of the key cards and hits the top floor: eighteen.

"Do you guys have plans for tonight? Do you need any dinner reservations? Chef Babineaux is here tonight, and she's prepared numerous specialties and would be honored for you all to dine in the restaurant," she says.

Tyler nods. "That will be great. We'll be down in an hour."

Natasha nods. "Most certainly. Your table will be ready."

The doors open with a chime, leading straight into a massive and elaborate space with no additional door or hallway. We step right into a foyer with bright white tiles that gleam from the warm lights that fill and warm the space. More fresh flowers are set on a round table; all perfect blooms. Ahead of us is the fanciest living room I've ever stepped into, which is saying something because I've been to parties that Ian Forrest, another member of the football team whose family is ungodly wealthy, has thrown in his mansion in Seattle. This suite makes that place look like a shack. Floor-to-ceiling windows stretch the span of the room, revealing the bright lights of the city. Sleek couches sit in a U-shape, and beyond them is another group of couches with a massive fireplace and a grand piano. Along the wall is a bar with lights glittering across a sleek black counter.

"I'll have them take care of the luggage while you're dining. Would you like all of the garments hung? And does anyone have any requests for temperature or any oils?"

Nessie and I exchange another glance before looking at Tyler. "I think we're fine, thanks," he tells her.

Natasha nods again, her smile tight. "If you need anything, please let me know." She hands Tyler the stack of key cards with a smile.

"Thank you," he says with a casual nod, making me realize this is his norm. He didn't bat an eye at the full atrium in the middle of the hotel or the fact there was a freaking couch in the elevator or that this room is more opulent than I could have even tried to imagine.

Natasha heads back toward the single elevator and disappears behind the elegant wooden doors with intricate paneling that barely resembles an elevator.

"There are only three bedrooms. You two are welcome to the master," Tyler says.

Nessie stares at me, and I quickly shake my head. "No. You should definitely take it," she replies.

"I'll take it," Cooper says, his head dropped back to take in the high ceilings and expansive windows.

I press my lips together to keep from scoffing or laughing because either reaction seems plausible during this completely implausible situation.

"Come on. I'll show you the rest of the suite." Tyler steps forward, passing the couches and then the other set of furniture. When we reach the piano, I notice a staircase and elevator. "The elevator goes up or down. The stairs only go up."

"I thought she said there was only one elevator to go back to the lobby?" I ask, chancing a look at him and regretting it and the question instantly. His clear blue eyes are narrowed, watching us like he's expecting us to steal or harm something.

Tyler nods. "This one goes down to the private pool or up to the bedrooms."

Nessie turns to look at me, but I ignore her, realizing it's likely our continued shock and surprise that has him so defensive and annoyed. We need to chill. I pull in a deep breath that I hold for five seconds in an attempt to calm my features into passive. Tyler continues up the stairs with Nessie close behind. I steal another look around and then at the elevator that leads to the pool—the *private* pool—and realize there's no chance I'm going to be able to remain cool and calm. We've just won the travel lottery.

Cooper chuckles, placing a hand on my shoulder. "Wild, right?"

"This doesn't even seem real. I had no idea places like this existed, much less ever expected to stay in one."

"I bet the food is going to be so good," he says.

I pause. "We can't afford to eat at a place like this. I'm sure it's over a hundred bucks a plate."

Coop shakes his head. "Ty said it's part of the experience, and we'll be helping him by offering our feedback. He's doing this to report back on some of the hotels that are struggling."

"Struggling? This hotel is struggling?"

Coop shrugs.

"I feel like a fish out of water," I admit.

"You've gotta fake it till you make it. Once my company's big, we're going to be flying around the world, staying in places like this." He weaves his fingers together and stretches them out in front of himself.

"Don't get too big for your britches," I warn him, recycling the saying his grandma frequently uses when he talks about his plans for anything from school to football to his dream career.

He laughs, dropping the pose and slinging his arm around me. He propels us forward to catch up to where Nessie and Tyler stand at the top of the stairs. It's another living room filled with more couches, but these look less masculine and more inviting with throws and pillows woven with bright blues and greens. The furniture faces another wall of windows that look out over the city. But what grabs my attention is the telescope set beside the glass practically begging for use.

"I was just telling Tyler this is where you'll be while we're here." Nessie grins as my attention shifts to her. Then her eyes slowly move to Coop still at my side, his arm draped over my shoulders. Her lips fall with a gentle frown, her shoulders bowing.

I hate to see my sister upset, even more so when I'm a contributing reason. But this is Cooper, my best friend, the person who knows me nearly as well as Nessie. It draws my realization and fears back to how much is going to change this year.

I look across the room at Tyler, feeling his stare as well. His blue eyes are calculating again, and for a second, I wonder what he's thinking. How he's reading this current situation. Is he regretting us being here? Does he think we're using him? *Are* we taking advantage of him? Before the rest of the questions or a single answer can be considered, he moves to the nearest door. "This is the first bedroom."

We follow him into the room themed in dark stone colors with a king-size bed that sits against the far wall. Two chairs, a full dresser, and an expansive fireplace with a giant TV over the top complete the room. I'm fairly confident the room is bigger than the apartment we're renting in Seattle this year.

"This is the master?" Nessie asks.

Tyler shakes his head.

"We can totally take this," she tells him.

"You might change your mind when you see the other rooms," he says, nodding in the direction of the doorway.

Manners can be such a strange set of rules, I realize, when Tyler again waits for us to exit the room first. We step out and move to the side so Tyler can lead us to the next bedroom. The second room is both bigger and lighter. It's decorated in muted grays and beiges with patterned wallpaper that makes the focal wall appear to almost move like grains of sand after a wave crashes. There's a large picture window with a built-in bench seat filled with cushions and a couch with a chaise. The king-size bed has a tufted headboard that makes me want to run my fingers across the surface and forget about the giant TV on the wall.

"Sorry, Coop. We get this room," Nessie tells him, moving to the couch where she sets her purse down and moves to look out the window. She's itching to go out and see the city. She turns to face us. "This is amazing, Tyler. Thank you so much for everything." It's sincere and kind and completely appropriate, and I'm beyond relieved she included me in the sentiment because I'm not sure I could thank him.

"Are you sure you don't want to see the master?" he asks.

"This is beyond perfect," she tells him.

Tyler nods. "I have to make a couple of calls before dinner," he says, excusing himself.

We collectively watch him leave the room before turning to each other, eyes wide with the shock. "Is this the kind of room we'll be staying in the entire time?" Nessie asks, looking at Cooper.

He shakes his head. "I have no idea. I mean, I knew he was loaded, but I didn't know he was *this loaded*. I've only seen his place in Seattle."

"This is crazy," I echo, staring across the room and at the ornate details that are so subtle and yet each scream of wealth.

"I'm going to gain twenty pounds on this trip if the restaurants are as fancy as the room," Nessie says.

I shake my head. "Fancy restaurants always serve tiny portions."

She laughs. "Just remember to use the silverware on the outside and work your way in."

5

TYLER

I need a drink, a gym, and some really loud music.

Instead, I'm leading the Robinson twins and Cooper into Taste, our renowned two-Michelin-star restaurant within the hotel.

"Good evening, Mr. Banks, Mr. Sutton, Ms. Robinson, and Ms. Robinson," Gregory greets us. He's the reason this restaurant has become what it has and also why the restaurant hasn't managed to earn a third Michelin Star. He's talented, driven, and so stuck in his ways he refuses to go in new directions.

Chloe takes a subtle step sideways as we begin to move, allowing Cooper to walk beside Vanessa. Cooper told me he's never admitted to Chloe how he feels about Vanessa—their one secret—yet, I can't help but wonder if she has an inclination considering how long Cooper's liked Vanessa.

Gregory stops at a table that overlooks a wide window. It's a seat my dad would request, one that is prominent and will make those waiting on us more apparent to garner attention and intrigue from fellow guests.

Chloe's gaze skates across the room as she grips the back of a chair, ready to pull it out. I place a hand on her lower back, my thumb following the curve of her hip. She startles, her shoulders snapping straight as her attention jumps to me. I grab the chair, and she releases it, mumbling an apology as her cheeks flush. She takes a seat and grips the bottom of the chair to pull herself closer to the table, and we do an awkward shuffle as I try to help scoot her closer. Across from us, Cooper's brows are lowered, watching me and wondering what in the hell I'm doing as he takes his seat. Arse.

"Chef Babineaux will be right out to tell you about today's specials," Gregory says as the other two members of the wait staff spread napkins across our laps.

"We're really underdressed," Vanessa says, fidgeting in her seat across from Chloe.

"No one cares what we're wearing," Chloe tells her. "They're all wondering if one of is famous because we have an entire entourage."

I glance out at the other patrons, noticing many are indeed looking our way.

"Is this normal?" Vanessa asks, looking at me.

I shake my head and then stop, shrugging because while it's not necessarily normal, it's not far from it. "It's worse in London. Here, few have any idea who I am."

"All of Brighton knows who you are," Chloe says, turning to look at me. Her green eyes make a quick descent when I meet her gaze. She reaches for her filled water glass and takes a long drink before fixing her attention on Vanessa. I swear the two have an entire conversation without a single word being shared, and at the end of it, Vanessa grins widely.

"Good evening. Welcome to Taste," Chef Babineaux appears, drawing more attention from the other guests. She begins explaining the menu and her suggestions for us based upon our preferences and tells us where everything has been harvested and raised.

In her seat beside me, Chloe leans as far from me as possible while Vanessa straightens her silverware and tells Cooper about classes for this upcoming year. The girls are exactly the type that most guys dream of bringing home to their mother: accomplished, sweet, polite, well mannered, and the win-win for both the guy and their mother is how blatantly innocent they both are. Not in the virginal sense necessarily, though I could easily be convinced to bet my left bollock that at least one of them is a virgin. No, it's in the way the hotel left their jaws hanging and how they are unsuspecting of the uglier sides life often presents.

I'm definitely not most guys, though.

I prefer a girl with a past who wants to work her aggression out between the sheets and leave me like a bad habit.

Attachments make me uneasy, which is why I had no problem choosing dare every time while playing the game on our drive here. I don't want anyone in my life. The only reason Cooper is as close to me as he is, is because he doesn't want or expect anything—at least, not yet. That's the sad part of our relationship. Our brotherhood, while strong, sometimes leaves me leery and waiting for the other shoe to drop because what I've learned in life is that money is power and power is absolute. Everyone wants to wield it, and few are capable.

And I have no desire to entertain even a fling with Chloe, knowing that it would be like putting myself between a bullet and a target—guaranteed to end badly. She knows it as well, which is likely why she pretends she never kissed me and has been avoiding me like the plague since.

"Okay, so, what do you guys think about going to Bourbon Street after dinner?" Cooper asks.

"Um, yes!" Vanessa nods enthusiastically. "Definitely."

Chloe traces a pattern in the condensation on her glass of water, a resigned smile on her face as she watches them.

"We need to go out and get drunk tonight," Vanessa continues. "Celebrate that Chloe is staying at Brighton."

"Staying?" my thought slips out as a question.

She takes a fleeting glance in my direction then quickly resumes staring at her glass. "I applied to a program that would have had me moving to Virginia for much of the year," she says, her attention still on her glass that she's wiping the condensation clean from for a second time. "But I wasn't chosen." She glances up at me and takes a deep breath that hollows her cheeks and much of her exposed collarbone. I notice her eyes are several shades lighter than Vanessa's.

"Forget them. We and Brighton know how amazingly awesome you are. And tonight, we're going to celebrate you," Vanessa says.

Chloe's fingers slide down the glass, leaving three lines before she moves her hand to the apex where her shoulder and neck meet and digs her fingers into the flesh there.

Sympathy, or maybe it's compassion, has me staring at Chloe for longer than I should. Unlike her, I'm working to change my future and the many signs telling me I can't, whereas she's resigned to let one of her dreams slip away.

I raise a hand when one of the servers looks our way. She hustles to our table. "Yes, sir?"

"Could we get a round of drinks, please?"

She hesitates for a second, likely wondering if she should be asking for our IDs or if that would be insubordination.

"Four Sazeracs," I tell her.

She nods and disappears into the kitchen.

"What in the hell's a Sazerac?" Cooper asks.

"You'll like it," I tell him. "New Orleans is famous for them."

"I thought they were known for hurricanes?" Vanessa asks.

I nod. "Those too."

"We should make a boozy bingo card," she says.

Chloe shakes her head. "We only have a couple of days, and I don't want to spend one of them in bed with a hangover."

"I didn't say we had to complete the card tonight," Vanessa replies.

Before Chloe can respond, the waitress returns with a tray of drinks, curled pieces of lemon peel around the top of each glass, and passes them out. "Is there anything else I can get for y'all?"

"Could we get two sweet teas?" Cooper asks.

She nods and looks at Chloe and then me. "What about for you guys?"

"Um, actually, one of the sweet teas is for me," Chloe says.

The waitress raises her eyebrows but does a quick job of hiding her confusion and looks at Vanessa. "Would you like anything?"

Vanessa smiles, shaking her head. "This is perfect, thanks."

When the waitress turns her attention back to me, I simply point at my Sazerac.

Cooper's the first to raise his glass. "Tonight, we celebrate friendship and our final weeks of summer."

"Cheers," we echo, clinking our glasses.

Chloe takes a small whiff of her drink and blinks quickly. "That smells strong."

Vanessa laughs. "Whenever it comes out in such a small pour, it's pretty much guaranteed to be straight alcohol."

Chloe turns her attention to me, pushing her hair back and exposing her collarbone again. "We sip it?"

I nod. "It's not a straight shot. Made well, a Sazerac deserves a little time."

She raises the glass to her mouth and rolls her tongue over her lips.

I take a sip of my drink in an attempt to swallow the desire her lips evoke. I lean back in my seat, watching the long wave of her lashes fall against her cheek as she tips the glass back to get a taste.

She turns to face me again, surprise evident in her wide eyes. "That's so different. It's sweet and spicy and almost herbal."

"All I taste is whiskey," Vanessa says as she tosses her drink back like it's a shot.

Chloe chuckles, shaking her head. "You're going to make me play tourist alone tomorrow, aren't you?"

"Cooper will go with you," Vanessa tells her.

Cooper gives a sideways look. "I don't know. D.C. kind of scarred me for life. I saw one too many hats and shoes from people in history at the Smithsonian Museum."

"That was three years ago," Chloe protests.

"And I'm still recovering," he says.

Vanessa laughs as she nods.

"You guys are going to miss out. I've heard the beignets are out of this world. Supposedly, powdered sugar trails for blocks because that many people order them every day."

Before we can discuss it further, our food arrives. Platters with neatly arranged *hors d'oeuvres* fill the table, and we dig into the unique flavors of New Orleans that express so much history and culture.

"Should we change?" Vanessa asks as we pass the elevators. "Do we need to dress up?"

"Only if you want to see Coop and me get into a fight," I tell her, already wondering if I should be asking for someone with security to go with us because the Robinson twins attract attention even in jeans and sweatshirts, much less the short shorts and form-fitting tops they're in tonight.

"Is it rowdy?" she asks.

"It's packed. People are going to be wasted and stupid. Just stick with us, and you'll be fine." I make a silent oath for this to be my first and only night of babysitting.

Cooper exchanges a questioning glance with me. Uncertainty is clear in his gaze.

"It'll be fine," I assure him.

"Mr. Banks." A man at the valet desk raises his hand to catch my attention. "The car is ready, sir."

"We're driving?" Chloe asks, sounding disappointed.

I nod. "It would take us an hour to walk it."

Before she can respond, Vanessa takes her hand, tugging her in the direction of the black Mercedes used to drive VIP guests around the city. The three of them squish into the back, and I sit in the passenger seat, next to our driver.

"Chloe, truth or dare?" Vanessa asks.

Chloe laughs. "I'm going to regret this, aren't I?" Vanessa doesn't reply. "Dare."

"I dare you to collect five strands of beads tonight."

Cooper groans.

The girls laugh.

"Be careful. They'll arrest you for indecent exposure," our driver warns them.

"She knows I won't flash anyone. She's trying to make me fail," Chloe explains.

"And you can't buy them," Vanessa tacks on.

"So many rules," Chloe objects.

Vanessa laughs. "You love rules."

The driver pulls over a few minutes later, and I tip him as the others climb out of the back seat.

Music flows through the air along with the chatter of voices. Buildings line both sides of the narrow street, decorated with neon lights.

Vanessa coughs. "It stinks," she says.

I nod. "The only time this place doesn't smell is in the morning after they've hosed it all down."

Chloe's nose crinkles, but only slightly, her curiosity stronger than the putrid scents of urine, alcohol, and sweat. Her gaze crosses the street and roves over the crowds before she looks back at us, her lips tipped with a smile. "It's loud."

I struggle not to laugh, knowing that Chloe Robinson is one of the most observant people and certainly took in far more than the most obvious fact she just shared.

"Let's go." Vanessa leads the way, her grip on Chloe tight, pulling her toward the traffic light that allows us to cross onto Bourbon Street.

And without thought, I'm traipsing after them, crossing the busy street as cars honk and men yell their awareness of the sisters.

"I'm going to hate this city, aren't I?" Cooper grumbles.

Ahead of us, Chloe bestows a smile on an unsuspecting bloke who looks like he walked around with binoculars and a wide-brimmed hat all day. He's startled by her, caught off guard by her quick approach and even more so by her beauty. She's too far away for us to hear what she says, but we watch as he takes a strand of beads from around his neck and gives them to her.

She turns back toward Vanessa, victory shining in her bright eyes as she hurries back over to her.

"Yup," I answer Cooper.

"Let's get something to drink," Vanessa says. "I read that there are bars down here that have specialty drinks. I want to try a hurricane."

Chloe shakes her head. "I think I still feel a buzz from that drink at dinner."

Vanessa laughs. "It was *one* drink."

Chloe shrugs, her attention bouncing between the buildings and balconies and the busy street. "Although, a bar might be a good spot to get..."

I lean closer, missing the last of her words as we pass open doors where the music pours onto the street, competing with the music from other nearby bars and restaurants and the buzz of conversation

Vanessa turns to me, wearing a smile I recognize because while I haven't seen it on her, it's the same look a girl gets when she's about to ask me for something. "Which bar should we go to?"

I shrug. "Depends on what you're wanting."

"Fun," she says. "I want to have fun." She glances at Chloe, and I understand her intention—she wants her sister to have a good time. I think of our brief conversation at dinner about Chloe being declined admittance to the program she'd applied for and their plans to get drunk, and though there's a warning in my head saying this could go very badly, I jerk my chin forward.

"There's a place up here with live jazz music and the best hurricane you'll find on Bourbon Street."

Her smile radiates with appreciation.

Then some fucker with too much liquid courage stops in front of Chloe, his gaze lewd and purposefully slow as he takes her in. His glassy stare settles on her face. "You're so hot, my zipper's falling for you."

I wait for her to ask us for help or to make a retort to him—anything except for what she does—which is asking him for some of the beads around his neck.

I slap a hand to Cooper's shoulder. "You're going to have your hands full."

He pulls his chin back. "What are you going to be doing?"

I grin. "The question is *who* will I be doing? And we're going to find out soon."

The bar is crowded when we step inside, and it takes approximately three seconds before news of twins starts circulating through the bar and another two for guys to start flocking their way toward them.

The band is loud, the bass pulsing through my body. The energy in here is enough to give anyone a strong hit of dopamine, leading me to gaze across the sea of people, waiting for the high to take me over and lead me to the nearest hot girl. But my thoughts are tangled with my meetings tomorrow as I consider what the management team is going to tell me and if I'll be able to offer any suggestions or even ask the right questions to find the root of the issues.

The bombardment of thoughts ruins my mood and leads me to the bar, where I take a seat and nurse a drink. I try to plan for my first meeting and avoid the pull to watch the three of them having fun and dancing.

6

CHLOE

Normally, I would have said no to last night.

But in an effort to be more *fun*—whatever that means—I went out and matched Nessie drink for drink, dance for dance, until we hit our third round. Then I accepted her whining about how we are only twenty-one once, how our time in NOLA is going to pass in the blink of an eye, and every other attempt to get me to continue partying with her. I switched to water, gathered the last of my beads from guys who undressed me with their eyes, and started to make a list of all the places I wanted to go today.

With Bourbon Street checked off the list, I planned to spend most of the day back in the French District:

- Jackson Square
- St. Louis Cathedral
- Frenchmen Street
- Shrimp po'boys and jambalaya
- Find some beignets on the way back to the hotel

WE TRAVELED all thirteen blocks of Bourbon Street last night and learned why it smells so awful after witnessing several people vomit and even more relieving themselves in a shallow corner, not to mention the vast amount of trash strewn across the narrow street.

"Ness," I say, shaking her. My patience wears thin as I catch sight of the alarm clock, which tells me it's nearly noon. "Vanessa." I shake her again.

She groans incoherently.

"Wake up," I tell her. "We have places to go. Things to eat."

She grumbles something that sounds like a threat before burying her head under her pillow.

"I'm going without you," I warn her.

Nessie raises a hand and blindly waves.

I want to tell her she's going to regret spending the entire day sleep-ing.—that the pictures of mine she's going to see later are going to make her wish she'd gotten up and walked around and saw everything New Orleans has to offer—but I know doing so would make me sound like our dad, and after how much she drank last night, a dark and comfort-able room is likely exactly where she wants to be today.

I grab my purse, checking to ensure I have my portable charger, wallet, and phone before escaping out to the smaller living room upstairs.

The room has been untouched, which is kind of a shame. It feels like either option is a loss at this point: spend time in this beautiful city I've never seen and have dreamed of visiting for years or spend the day in a hotel room that is fancier than anything I could have ever imagined. It's not an easy decision.

I run my fingers gently over the telescope as I pass the window. The sky's a bright shade of blue with fluffy white clouds that seem so perfect, they almost look fictional.

Downstairs, the kitchen has a tray of Danishes, muffins, and bagels that make me regret not having come down sooner, but after finding Cooper in a similar state as Vanessa, I spent my morning finalizing my plans for the day and taking a long shower in our en suite that had been designed by gods. The shower has five showerheads and expensive products, all in elegant French script, that smelled better than any hair salon I've ever visited.

I take a croissant and practically moan when my first bite exposes rich dark chocolate in the center.

I wipe my crumbs from the counter, grab one of the key cards lying beside the tray of food, and head toward the elevator that will bring me to the lobby.

When the doors open, the perfumed air greets me along with the brightly polished floor. The atrium taunts me, calling for me to discover all that a luxury hotel offers its guests—how the other half lives, as Cooper put it. But, I opt to explore it later tonight when I don't have the distraction of a full and untouched list on my mind.

"Good afternoon, Ms. Robinson." Natasha, my inspiration to attempt appearing elegant and put together this morning while I got ready, greets me with a smile. My khaki green shorts with the cute belt now seem simple, and my white tank top with patterned buttons down the front scream their discounted price as she wipes a piece of imaginary lint from her fitted purple blouse with an elegant and sexy neckline that she paired with a killer black pencil skirt. "How was your evening? Did you have a nice time at Taste?"

"It was amazing," I tell her. "That was the best shrimp I've ever tasted."

She smiles, but it lacks friendliness and sincerity. "Wonderful. I'm so glad to hear that. Can I help you with something? Do you need a car? A reservation? Would you like to visit the spa?" I swear she looks from my hair to my bare nails.

"Thank you, but I'm just going to head out and do some sightseeing."

She nods. "Perfect." Maybe it's a coincidence that she walks me all the way to the front door, but it almost feels like she's escorting me, like she doesn't trust me to be in here unattended.

I smile at her before moving through the revolving doors at the front, determined not to let a stranger spoil my day. After all, this is pretty high on describing a perfect day for me: sun, summer, a new city, and a plan.

The air is thick with humidity and feels warmer after the coolness of the hotel, but I welcome it, knowing I'm about to endure ten months in the Pacific Northwest where I'll be homesick for the humidity and warm summer days.

I pull up the map app on my phone that's already programmed with my destinations, and follow narrow streets lined with a canopy of oak trees with thickly wavering branches covered in broad, green leaves that shield me from the sun. When I cross the street, large plots are marked with mansions that are set back from the road. Pristine yards with crepe myrtles and their two-toned trunks and millions of blooms, brightly colored bougainvillea, angel trumpets, and hibiscuses are artfully planted among massive magnolia trees with giant waxy leaves that are almost as beautiful as the homes tucked behind them.

It feels like I'm on a movie set, each block an image of perfection and money that turns into a new wave of history. I come to a stop in front of giant cement structures that are equally eerie and beautiful and surrounded by a black wrought iron fence that I follow to where the doors are propped open. The fence winds its way up into an arch that reads: "Lafayette Cemetery No. 1."

I've never seen an above-ground cemetery, and like everything else in this city, it screams of intrigue and history, forcing me to add another item to my to-do-later list so I can remain focused on my current sight-seeing list.

I walk by row houses that lead me into a more industrial district, where the heat isn't as charming, and when a driver slows down to yell something from their window, I wish I'd made Nessie or Cooper come with me.

It takes me a full hour to reach my first destination: Jackson Square. I'm so glad I read the suggestion to approach from Decatur Street to see the park with St. Louis Cathedral in the background and the statue of President Andrew Jackson at the forefront. It's picturesque; something from a postcard that has me standing in place for several long minutes, taking in the view before I snap a picture and send it along with a quick text to Mom and Dad.

I SPEND the afternoon checking each item off my list until my phone rings, and Nessie's face appears on the screen, her tongue out.

"Hey."

"How's sightseeing?" she asks.

"I'm moving here," I tell her.

She laughs. "Me too. I'm pretty sure that bed is a cloud."

It's my turn to laugh. "Don't tell me you're still in it."

She sighs happily. "Actually, Cooper and I went and tried bubble tea and walked around the Garden District."

"Bubble tea?"

"Add it to your list. You'll love it. Also, the Garden District is fab. It's so beautiful."

"The French District is pretty amazing as well. You won't believe some of these pictures I've taken. Did you know the city was under French rule, then Spanish, and then French again before America purchased it?"

"Did you know the hotel makes a jambalaya with shrimp and has an outdoor pool with a full bar where they come to your beach chair and take your order?"

"So, you're telling me you stood me up to hang out with your crush and then sunbathed like a celebrity?"

"Pretty much."

"I'm eating the beignets I bought you as we speak."

She laughs. "When are you on your way back? Tyler and Cooper made plans for tonight."

"What kind of plans?"

"A masquerade club. I looked it up, and it says it's super hard to get into, and we have VIP passes."

"We aren't going to do the bar and club scene every night, are we?"

"I'm going to pretend I didn't hear that question. Where are you? How far away are you?"

"I'm back at Jackson Square. I basically made a giant circle today and came back to get more beignets and coffee at Café Du Monde."

She repeats my location to Cooper.

"Tyler's going to send a car to get you."

"I can take an Uber or a Lyft or something," I protest.

"Too late. He's already calling someone."

"How will I know which car it is?"

She repeats my question.

"He said it's the same car that dropped us off last night."

"Did you tell him I can't remember what car dropped us off last night?"

"Nice. Black sedan."

"I feel like it's necessary to tell you I see six nice, black sedans right this very second."

"Don't get into the wrong one. You may not get to sleep on our cloud bed again."

I chuckle. "I'll see you soon."

"I was kidding. Stay on the phone with me."

I do, but it turns out to be unnecessary because the same driver from the night before finds me sitting on my park bench, fingers still sticky with powdered sugar, and calls me by name.

"I'll see you in fifteen," I tell Nessie and dust off my hands. I grab the paper bag filled with beignets and my purse, and follow him to the car.

"Thank you," I tell him as he opens the door for me.

He nods. "Ms. Robinson."

"You can call me Chloe."

"You can call me Miles." He smiles before closing my door.

"How was your afternoon?" he asks, and unlike this morning when Natasha asked me about last night, Miles makes eye contact with me in the rearview mirror, like he's genuinely interested to hear my answer.

"It was amazing. This city is filled with so much history and beauty and food. I think I could spend two weeks here and still not see everything."

He chuckles, navigating us carefully through traffic. "I'm glad you were able to come visit. Maybe on your next stay at the Banks Hotel you can stay longer."

"Oh, I..." I stumble over my thoughts, trying not to sound rude or like the freeloader I kind of am. "My best friend is also best friends with Tyler. I don't really know him. This is kind of a weird set of events that has us staying here, but we're very grateful for the experience," I tack on. "The hotel is amazing." We drive past the same path of oak trees, the sky darkening to a deep shade of violet behind them.

"Thank you so much for coming to get me. I really appreciate it," I tell him.

"It was my pleasure. You're here for one more full day?"

I nod.

"If you want to see something kind of fun, there are quite a few haunted tours. I recommend heading back into the French District, but there's one on the edge of town that starts at a mansion and will bring you to the cemetery you were admiring. I've heard it's a lot of fun." He pulls up to the hotel where someone immediately comes to open my door. The trek that took me over an hour earlier this afternoon takes us only fifteen minutes, all of it in air-conditioning.

"Thanks again, Miles."

He grins. "Have a good night, Ms. Robinson."

The hotel lobby is busy tonight, which makes a pang of regret slip to the front of my thoughts. I wish I'd taken the extra hour to explore the hotel when it was still quiet and mostly empty this afternoon.

When the doors to the suite open, that regret lessens with the reminder we still have two nights and a full day here.

"Chloe!" Nessie calls my name from where she's perched on the couch. "Are you hungry? Tyler made reservations for the steakhouse downstairs."

I clutch the white bag of beignets that are bleeding grease and promising the same delicious sweetness I experienced earlier. Inside the living room, Nessie is wearing a bright yellow sundress, but her hair is done for a night of going out. Cooper is on the couch, scrolling through his phone, dressed in a Brighton tee and shorts. "Not really. I feel like I ate my way through the city like The Very Hungry Caterpillar," I tell her.

She laughs. "You have to make room for something. Tyler says he wants our feedback on the environment and any food we eat."

"He's not coming?" My voice goes too high, my relief audible.

Cooper gives me the side-eye. "It wouldn't kill you to be nice to him."

"It might," I answer instead of trying to argue the fact that I have been trying to be nice.

He tries to hide his smile and look annoyed, but I see through him.

"I am nice to him," I say.

"You're civil," Coop argues.

"Civil *is* nice."

Again with the side-eye.

"He means you act a little bitchy when you're around him. Sterile, if you will," Nessie says.

"Civil and bitchy are on opposite ends of the field," I point out.

She scrunches her nose. "Not always with you."

I look at Cooper for him to disagree, but instead, he shrugs.

"How do I come across as bitchy?" I ask.

"It's not that you're bitchy, it's just you aren't friendly—warm," Nessie says. "You like your rules and your schedules, and you sometimes get a little ... uptight. Rigid."

"I went out last night. Drank. Danced. Collected beads."

"For a while..." Nessie says.

The weight of Ricky's words replay in the forefront of my thoughts: *uptight, cautious, serious.* Those were some of his favorites to describe me, even from the beginning when he said them with a smile like he thought they were cute and endearing rather than points of contention like near the end of our brief span of dating.

I drop my head back, but before I can arrange my thoughts, the elevator doors open, and Tyler steps into the hotel room, dressed in a white dress shirt and a blazer that highlights the broadness of his shoulders. His dress slacks fit so well I have no doubt they were tailor-made, and his shoes are as stylish as they are expensive. The only thing that's not perfect is his slightly disheveled hair that looks like he rode up on the elevator doing a scene from a hot romance novel—effectively making the imperfect feature only more perfect. His angular jaw is tight, his blue eyes emotionless. In his hand is a large brown bag with handles.

"Everything okay in the lobby?" Coop asks him.

Tyler steps forward but pauses before he gets too close.

Why am I considered uptight and bitchy, but no one mentions how he comes across as a complete asshole most of the time?

"It was nothing. A misunderstanding with management." He extends his arm, revealing a shiny, silver watch. "Our reservation's in an hour. We can go from the restaurant to the club."

Questions pop into my thoughts about the masquerade club—where it is and what we should wear—but all of them seem to follow the narrative of the old me. The uptight me.

Tyler's gaze flashes to the bag in my hand. "You made it to Café Du Monde."

I glance down at the crinkled bag and nod. "Yeah. Thanks for sending a car."

He nods dismissively. "You should have taken one when you left. Tomorrow, just let them know where you want to go. Someone will take you."

Would it be rude to say no?

"It was a nice walk," I say instead.

He nods, and that short spark of interest that I saw when he noticed my bag dies as he excuses himself and heads toward the stairs.

"Double standard much?" I grumble to Nessie as she stands so we can get ready as well.

7

TYLER

Cooper's story about a sports headline becomes jumbled as the girls step into the living room. At first sight, they're harder to tell apart tonight. Chloe, who usually stands an inch taller, is the same height as Vanessa, but her hair is down. Vanessa's is still tied back as it was before they went to get dressed, and she's wearing a black mini skirt and a black top that nearly causes me to owe an apology to Cooper for checking out her cleavage. Beside her, Chloe's wearing a dress that looks like sin. It's made of black lace and keeps tearing my attention to different areas of her body to see if I'm seeing an illusion or skin. Her red lips flash as a warning sign to stop staring.

Cooper lets out a low whistle. "Look at you two clean up."

Vanessa smiles. Chloe ... well, she tries to smile, but it looks more like a grimace. I want to laugh, assuming this is because of Cooper's reaction or an annoyance due to something that happened before they came downstairs, but then Chloe pulls in a breath as her eyes track down the front of herself. When she looks back at us, I spot the vulnerability that has her gaze wavering between Cooper and me. She's uncomfortable. Nervous.

I can't imagine why or how because she looks like perfection wrapped in lust and tied up with every sexual fantasy.

"We need a picture," Vanessa says, waving us over. We move in closer to fit on Vanessa's screen, Chloe doing her best to inch away from me.

Vanessa takes a series of photos before we retreat for the elevator, where the sweet and citrusy scent that follows Chloe hits me like a tidal wave.

I think back to freshman year and Cooper telling me his best friend was a girl. He was dating Claire Mayfair at the time, so I'd chalked up his immunity to Chloe as respect for Claire, not realizing for months that it was actually because he'd fallen for the other sister.

Dinner is a repeat of last night—the manager and head chef greeting us and telling us about the menu, massive amounts of food, and fellow patrons staring—only tonight, rather than questioning glances about why we're receiving preferential treatment, the sisters are drawing all the attention.

The manager brings a bottle of a dry merlot that is supposed to enhance the flavors of the aged steaks and fills our glasses.

"Could we also get four Vieux Carré?"

"How do you know all these drinks?" Vanessa asks when the manager leaves.

I grin. "In England, alcohol isn't so taboo."

"Why'd you choose to come to college in America?" she asks, lifting her wine glass.

"Because I'm American."

This seems to draw Chloe's attention from looking around the restaurant and over the menu to me. "You are?"

I nod. "I have dual citizenship, but I've spent half my life in America."

"You guys spent time over here because of the hotels?" Chloe asks.

I shake my head, smiling because I know they're about to balk with surprise. "My mum's American. She's from Ohio."

"Ohio?" Vanessa says, a bit too loudly.

Our drinks arrive, orange peels and ice dancing in each of the glasses.

"What shall we toast to tonight?" I ask, lifting my glass.

Vanessa shakes her head. "I have a thousand more questions."

I grin. "I'll give you two."

"So, you're British and American, and your mom is from Ohio, but you live in Miami. But why do you have a British accent?"

"I lived in England, growing up. Trips to America were for business and vacation."

"I'm reserving my right for my last question," she says.

"To friendship," Cooper says, lifting his glass.

"And Ohio," Vanessa adds on.

We look at Chloe, who releases a breath and raises her glass a little higher. "And the French for settling this city ... twice, and bringing really good food."

"To whiskey," I say, and we clink our glasses.

"HEY, MILES," Chloe greets our driver as we pile into the car, piquing my curiosity.

"Nice to see you again, Ms. Robinson."

"Nice to see you, too," she says in response.

"You guys know each other?" I ask, turning in time to catch the smile she sends him.

"He picked me up and brought me back to the hotel this afternoon," she explains.

From his seat beside me, Miles looks at me. "Ready, Mr. Banks?"

I nod, and the engine hums as we move forward and drive the short distance to the notorious and inconspicuous club.

"This is it?" Vanessa asks, looking around where industrialized buildings sprawl in every direction.

Chloe waves goodbye to Miles and turns her attention to us, the shadows casting a glow that makes the planes of her cheekbones appear sharper and her eyes darker.

I open the bag Anika had delivered to the hotel, and withdraw the four masks inside. "I was told these are required."

"Oh! They're beautiful." Vanessa reaches for a black mask with rhinestones and glitter dusted around the eyes, cut into an intricate pattern, while Cooper takes the single white plain mask, leaving me the black one and Chloe with a mask constructed of black lace that matches her dress nearly perfectly. She glances at it and then me as Cooper and Vanessa help each other with their masks.

Slipping my mask back into the bag so I can put hers on, I motion for Chloe to turn around. She does so slowly. I take a measured step forward as she places the mask against her face, the silk ties resting against her hair. I deftly tie it in place.

She turns, her green eyes brighter as they flash at me like a second warning of the night. I put my mask on and turn so she can tie it for me, and then the four of us cross the street, approaching the line of people that winds into the alley.

Chloe moves toward the end of the line, and I set my hand on her back, guiding her toward the door.

"Right here," I say. She glances at the people who are watching us with the same level of curiosity we received last night at the restaurant.

I flash my ID at the doorman who's wearing a purple mask, and he signals to someone and wraps lime-green bracelets around our wrists.

"Welcome to Façade, Mr. Banks," a woman with sleek dark hair and a matching purple mask greets us. "Please, follow me."

Behind me, Cooper moves to walk beside Vanessa. I place a hand on Chloe's waist, guiding her into the club. We're met with green and purple lights offset by strobes of white across the room, pulsing music, and masked faces creating a maze that assures me this would be the place to come if you didn't want to be found.

The woman leads us to a set of black wrought iron stairs where she briefly pauses to say something to the bouncer who's monitoring the space. He nods, releasing the red rope that blocks off the VIP area.

We climb the stairs that open to couches, tables and chairs, and music a few decibels quieter.

"If you want drinks or any food, your bracelets will ensure our servers help you right away. You're also welcome to place your orders here. This entire section has been closed and reserved for you tonight. We have a round of Patrón on its way up. Is there anything else we can get you? Champagne, perhaps?"

I glance at the others who look nearly as shocked as they do confused.

"Maybe in a bit. For now, we're fine," I tell her.

She nods. "There's a phone in the corner. If you need anything, just pick it up."

"This is straight crazy," Cooper says, laughing as he approaches the railing. The floor turns to glass at the edge so he can see the dance floor beneath him and out across through the waist-high glass banister.

Chloe follows him, the heels she's wearing flexing her calves as she looks out across the club. She says something too quiet for me to hear over the music, but Cooper laughs, and then so does she.

A waiter arrives with another telltale purple mask and sets four drinks on the table. I pass him a few bills. It's as much to ensure they'll be fast to bring new drinks as it is because it's expected with my name.

Cooper has one arm around Chloe's shoulders as they step away from the edge and reach for a shot glass.

"Hey, Coop," Chloe says, holding her shot glass. "Truth or dare."

He groans. "Dare."

"At the bar downstairs, you have to order a slippery nipple."

Vanessa straight cackles. Chloe works to keep a straight face, but as Cooper slowly shakes his head, she breaks, her lips curving into a wide smile that her lipstick accentuates.

"Let's go!" Vanessa says, tipping her head back and pouring down the shot in one quick drink.

We follow Cooper to the bar, and like promised, a bartender moves over to us instantly. "What can I get you?"

Cooper glances at Chloe and shakes his head. "Two slippery nipples."

The bartender pauses, but then Chloe giggles, and his attention shifts to her. The obscure drink order is all but forgotten, as he's clearly distracted for a full minute as he takes her in. He finally turns behind him, constructing the two drinks that he sets on the bar.

Cooper slides one of them to Chloe. "Drink up."

"But it's your nipple," she says, shaking her head. The guy off to her side hears the particular word, his gaze dropping to her chest. "His nipple, not mine," she tells the stranger, who looks at Coop.

Vanessa giggles. "Drink, and let's go!" she says.

Cooper shakes his head, pushing one of the drinks toward her again. She accepts it this time, and the two toast. Her smile is impossibly bigger as she chews the maraschino cherry at the bottom of her glass.

"How are you feeling?" Vanessa asks the pair of lightweights.

"Warm," Chloe admits, fanning herself.

"Well, let's get you hot." Vanessa grabs her hand, and the two lead us out toward the dance floor where steam billows into the air and the lights flash, adding to the anonymity. The DJ spins a new song, and the girls stop, arms raised as they dance together, attracting the attention of a group of guys who begin to move closer but stop when Cooper moves into a possessive stance between the girls and the interested party. Vanessa moves toward him, dancing against him.

Chloe grins and begins dancing with another guy who approaches her. She closes her eyes as the music seems to take over her body. It's hypnotic and addictive in a way that makes something dark and aggressive bloom in my chest.

A waitress weaves through the crowds. I catch her attention by raising my hand, her gaze landing on my bracelet.

It only takes her a few minutes to return with the shots I ordered. I down two of them and carry the third to Chloe.

She looks at me, a thin cloud of confusion in her eyes before she accepts, placing those red lips to the glass and swallowing it down.

I wrap my fingers around her waist, pulling her against me, and lower my mouth to her ear. "Tonight, we call a truce."

She pulls back, tipping her chin to one side as her eyes narrow with question. "Do we need a truce?"

"You don't like me much," I point out.

She says something, but I can't hear her over the noise. I grip her hip a little tighter, dropping my ear closer to her mouth. "I don't know you," she repeats.

"I'm an arse."

She laughs. "That part, I know."

"Don't forget it."

"How do you propose a truce with that caveat?"

I flash her a smile that promises promiscuity, but instead of leaning into me, she backs away, shaking her head as she looks at me.

She stops a few feet away, dancing with a guy who moves in beat with her, her hips rolling with his like she's just offered me the next round of truth or dare.

I should turn around and spend the night surrounded in booze and hot skin that would be guaranteed to end with meaningless pleasure.

I should be going up to the VIP section and focusing on the meeting from this morning and what was relayed to me—and more importantly, what wasn't.

I should be erasing these thoughts and the image of Chloe *fucking* Robinson, and the way I want to decipher the silent glances she tucks away when she looks at me.

Tomorrow, I tell myself. Tomorrow, I'll care about the fucking rules.

I close the distance between us, my intention clear as I make eye contact with the guy she's dancing with, who reads my thin veil of patience and takes the hint to move.

I slide my hand over her waist and down her hip, trailing across the lace fabric. She watches me, a dozen questions and objections clear in her gaze as I move closer. The tempo is fast, but the beat is slow, carrying her body to move against mine.

It's then I realize the orange scent is from her hair, and the floral scent is her skin as I slide against her.

We move like we know each other, know each other in intimate ways that dictate how our bodies move together with hunger. And when she turns, pressing her arse and back against me, I run my hand over her body and up through her breasts, across her sweat-dampened skin and along her neck, holding her there, feeling her breaths and the race of her heart.

It's fucking intoxicating.

She turns again, eyes dilated, hands balanced on my waist, and my thoughts are lost in a deep ravine between yesterday morning and tonight. I consider what it would feel like to kiss her properly. What she would taste like and if it would make it easier or harder to finish the rest of this trip.

Chloe raises her hand, instantly catching the waiter's attention, and though I was ready to drag her upstairs to the VIP lounge and make the absolute best use of the privacy, my thoughts cool as she steps away to place her order.

"Hey," Cooper says, wrapping a hand around my shoulder. "This place is fucking lit."

I nod. "Good. Enjoy it. I have a meeting in the morning and need to prepare for it."

Cooper raises his eyebrows. "You can't leave now."

I grin. "I've got like ten spreadsheets I haven't even started on yet. Have whatever you guys want. They'll send the bill to the hotel."

"Dude, we're not here so you can pay for everything. That's not why I invited you on this trip." There's a scratch of annoyance and an even deeper one of offense on Cooper's face.

"I know. I want you to have a good time. Vanessa's having fun. Dance with her. Drink. Do whatever. The lounge is yours all night."

"Are you going to the hotel or upstairs?"

"Upstairs for now. I need to make some calls and go over some shit they sent over."

"Okay. Well, if you need anything…"

I shake my head. "Have fun."

I disappear through the crowds of people, making my way back to the VIP lounge where I pace across the floor, my body restless and tightly wound.

"Hey." Chloe's voice pierces the space, making me feel vulnerable and messing with my headspace. "Is everything okay?" She holds two shot glasses filled with a blue liquid. She raises them. "Sometimes I get stuck in my head. I'm trying to do less of that… I think." Her pointed heels accentuate her long legs that are swallowing the space between us. She hands me one of the glasses.

I accept it, throwing the fruity chick drink back.

"Is everything okay?" she asks for a second time.

I shake my head. "Don't look at me like that,"

She blinks too fast, her glass untouched. "Like what?"

"Like you want me to take you up against that wall and let everyone watch me claim you."

Her face pales, but her eyes dilate. "I came up here because you went AWOL."

"That may be what you're telling yourself, but your body says differently."

Her eyes widen with alarm and offense. "That was *dancing*."

"We basically fucked with our clothes on."

She pulls her chin back, repulsion puckering her lips. "You're a disgusting drunk."

I laugh mirthlessly, closing the space between us and slipping my hand through her hair, brushing it from her face, the floral and citrus scents of her hitting me like a drug. Her breath hitches, and her eyes shift to me, but she doesn't move. "I'd do it," I tell her. "I'd fuck you until you couldn't remember another guy's touch or name. Fuck you until you screamed and let them all watch you as you came. But that would be it. That's where it would end."

The contents of her drink splash across my face. "It never started. Get over yourself."

8

CHLOE

My thoughts are still buzzing, too loud to let me sleep.

I roll over and reach for my phone to check the time.
Four-thirty.

I've been awake for the past two hours. The first thirty minutes were spent listening to Vanessa give me the detailed play-by-play of her night with Cooper, including details of what she felt while dancing with him —details I'd rather not know or think about my best friend—until she happily passed out with a smile on her face.

I, on the other hand, am already dreading the rest of this day. How in the hell am I supposed to face Tyler after how things ended?

And how had I felt guilty for thinking he was a jerk, and then right when my defenses lowered, he proved just how big of an asshole he is.

I flip off the covers, too agitated to sleep or remain still.

My toes sink in the plush carpet as I tiptoe across the room, silently open the door, and slip out into the air-conditioned living room upstairs where the telescope sits.

My gaze settles on the telescope, my breath leaving me with a sigh as my shoulders relax.

I move closer, the lights of the city making it easily bright enough to see as I graze my fingers over the expensive tool and the sleek lines. I can't fathom having something this expensive just sitting out for anyone to touch.

I find the brightest spot in the sky—guaranteed to be Venus—and release the clutches to align the telescope with the glowing object and look through the eyepiece, slowly twisting the focus knob until the image becomes sharp and clear.

"What are you doing?"

I jump, nearly knocking the telescope over.

Cooper grabs the telescope, chuckling as he rights it. "Sorry. I thought you'd jump, but I wasn't trying to send you out the window."

"Liar."

His smile broadens, and then he points at the telescope. "Tell me something nerdy."

I take a deep breath, moving to be in line with the telescope again. "Did you know it's silent in space?"

He raises his eyebrows. "*Silent* silent?"

I nod. "Sound waves require a medium to travel through, and since space is a vacuum with no atmosphere, the realm between stars is silent."

"What about on other planets?"

"They have noise, like Earth, but depending on the air pressure, it would sound different."

Cooper raises both hands to his head and makes an explosion sound. "That's awesome."

"Glad I could blow your mind." I pretend to shine my fingernails on my pajama shorts. "Why are you awake?"

"Why are *you* awake?" he counters.

I shake my head. "We don't answer questions with questions. It violates every friend rule."

He backs up, sitting on the couch and crossing one ankle over the other. "Are you doing okay?"

"Me? Yeah. Of course. Why?" I wonder if Tyler told him what he'd said to me?

Coop rolls his shoulders. "You've been kind of absent lately."

"I have?"

He shrugs again. "I don't know, maybe I'm in my own head, but it just seems like something is bothering you. I thought it was because of Ricky..."

I shake my head. "Definitely not. I'm done wasting brain power or another second on Ricky. We'll file that one under mistakes and embarrassing stories we don't bring up."

He nods. "Good. He's a fucking dick."

We went to high school together. Our short fling this summer was mostly because we worked together, and I think a little because he had never given me a second of attention in high school and then seemed infatuated with me this summer.

I abandon the telescope and reach for a soft throw, joining Cooper on the couch. "I wonder if there's a drink I can make you order with the word dick in it?"

His eyes slide to me, narrowed and lacking humor.

"Your face was priceless."

He shakes his head. "Just wait, Robinson."

"Oh, don't worry about me. I'll be sleeping with one eye open." I close a single eye as an example.

"Did you have fun tonight?" he asks, ignoring my attempts at making him laugh.

I nod. "Yeah. It was fun," I lie.

Coop shakes his head. "I had no idea Tyler was this loaded. No. Idea. I mean, I knew he was rich, but it seems like a third of the student body at Brighton is rich. But this is like next-level rich."

"Too bad he can't use all this money to buy himself a nice personality."

Coop stifles a laugh.

"I'm serious. I don't understand how you're friends. I keep my thoughts to myself most of the time, but he's a jerk."

"He's the first person to offer help in any situation," Cooper objects. "And he covers for anyone, no questions asked. Last season, when Arlo got hurt and Ty took his starting position, guess what the first thing Tyler did was? He sat down with Arlo and told him he wasn't going to compete for the spot—that it was his as soon as he was strong again. Every time Coach complimented Tyler, he attributed it to Arlo. Every. Single. Time. And when Paxton, our quarterback, had to change up his schedule for a couple of weeks because of a class, Tyler fucking moved everything and got everyone on board with changing it up so it wouldn't negatively impact Paxton.

"He likes women and can be sarcastic as shit, but he's not an asshole."

The words to object and expose just how big of an asshole he is and was to me last night are hanging on the tip of my tongue, but I remain silent, unable to tell him because while Tyler Banks has shown me his ugliest sides, there's also little question to how much he cares for Cooper. He helped him through his breakup with Claire, offered him a place to stay when his roommate ghosted and ended up moving out of state, and as much as I hate admitting it—picking up the slack of being a best friend when I've gotten busy with school and work.

"He's kind of an asshole," I say.

Cooper shoots out an arm, surprisingly fast, making me jump again before pulling me against him and running his hand over my hair to mess it up as much as he can before I pull free.

"I hate you," I tell him, trying to pat my hair down.

"You love me."

I sigh. "Why are you really up?"

"Are things going to be okay with us?"

"Are we talking about Nessie?"

He blanches, and for a second, he reminds me of my friend from middle school when books and good movies stopped being enough to fuel our friendship and we started talking about things that mattered— feelings and emotions about others and situations. How much it bothered me to watch our forty-fourth president stand behind bullet-proof glass when giving his victory speech, though we were supposedly more human and accepting than ever in history. How more prisons are becoming privatized, turning over seven-billion dollars a year. How Cooper's father is in one of those prisons, sentenced to twenty-five-years for his possession of marijuana with an intent to sell while watching a minor—a.k.a., Coop. "I didn't mean to... I don't want you to..."

I hold up my hand to stop him. "Nothing will change between us. But you know Ness. She has a shorter attention span than Tyler, and I just don't want you to get hurt."

He sighs. "Trust me. I've thought about that a million times."

"I know," I admit because as much as I've dreaded having this conversation, I've always known Cooper watched Nessie—paid attention to the way she moved and what she said in a way that I could tell that it mattered to him.

"And while I agree to help with birthday and holiday shopping, I refuse to ever partake in disagreements or arguments. And your first child has to be named after me."

Cooper throws his head back, laughing quietly into the darkened space. "Any more rules?"

"Oh, please. You know me. I need time to construct my full list." I pull in a breath. "This went fast. I thought I would have at least a solid week or two until we had this conversation."

"Tonight kind of accelerated the situation. She told me she liked me."

I nod, not surprised. Nessie's never been known for her patience, and with alcohol and all their dancing, I can see how it likely felt appropriate.

Cooper shoves me. "I kind of thought something was happening between you and Ty. I saw you guys on the dance floor. Hell, we *all* saw you."

"No," I say instantly. "*No. No. No.* What you saw was alcohol and a good beat."

"But better than avoiding each other, right?"

I shake my head. Not even a little. "You should go to bed. Tomorrow we're going on a ghost tour. Miles recommended it and said it's fun."

Cooper grins. "You don't like ghosts or scary stuff."

"Didn't," I correct him. "Remember, I'm trying to loosen up and be all go with the flow and shit."

He laughs at my impression that wasn't intended to sound quite so stoner-like and more cool and fun.

"We have to check out the pool tomorrow."

"Deal. Ghost tour, then pool." I offer my hand that he accepts, shaking on our deal. "Also, shrimp jambalaya. I *needs* it," I joke, adding the 's' to the verb like we have since we were young, since before inside jokes mattered and we cared to remember their roots.

"Done."

"You should go to bed," I tell him.

He nods. "I'm going. I just wanted to make sure things were good between us before..."

Before everything in our roles changes.

Before the rules change.

Before it goes from Cooper and Chloe to Cooper and Vanessa.

"I just want you to be happy." He stands, pulling me up and into him, hugging me. "I love you, Chloe."

"I know," I tell him.

I feel his abs constrict as he laughs. "Nice Han Solo."

"Thank you. Thank you very much."

His arms fall, and he turns to retreat to his room. "Love you, Coop."

He looks back, flashing a smile. I watch his door close, and though he's no farther away than he was before this conversation, it feels like he's just traveled to another state.

"CHLOE," Nessie sings my name, inches from my face.

"Why are you so mean?" I mumble.

"What time did you go to bed?" she asks.

"Late. Early. What time is it?"

"Almost three."

I sit up, glancing in the direction of the window where the shades are pulled shut, making it appear like it's still the middle of the night, though I know it's not because I didn't come back in here until the sun was starting to glow on the horizon.

"You missed breakfast and lunch, but I love you and saved you some breakfast. It's in the fridge."

"What was it?"

"Sweet potato pecan waffles. They're amazing. Life-changing."

I slide my legs out from the weight of the blankets and yawn. "Is there coffee?"

"There's a Keurig in the kitchen, a regular coffee pot, and a coffee shop in the lobby that will deliver."

"I might need all the options."

Nessie laughs. "So does your hair," she teases.

I raise a hand, feeling the fine hairs that are sticking up, and try in earnest to relax them. She laughs. "It's the only part of you that's up."

"Hilarious," I tell her.

She bends at the waist, her laughter growing.

I face the mirror and cringe before reaching for some product in an attempt to tame my hair. I get dressed, and apply some light makeup to conceal my short night.

My thoughts wander to the conversation with Cooper, wondering how things will change as I descend the stairs. I come to an abrupt stop when I round the kitchen and nearly run into Tyler.

"Sorry," I mumble, taking a step back, remembering he's the actual reason I couldn't sleep and trying to create more space between us.

"Chloe, what's the name of the tour you want to go on?" Cooper asks from where he's leaning against the sink, a can of soda in his hand.

"I don't know? He mentioned it was in the French District at a mansion that comes back here to the cemetery."

Cooper looks at Tyler for clarification.

"There are several tours in the French District," Tyler says.

"Do you have a preference?" Coop asks.

I shake my head.

"This one sounds like it might be the one," Cooper says. "We can check it out and then come back here and get in the pool."

I can't register his words because the word *we* is stuck in my throat like a gumball.

What we?

I need coffee. Stat.

Nessie points at the coffee machine, the blue light reading that it's on and hot. "You're my favorite sister," I tell her, reaching for a nearby cupboard and finding a coffee mug.

"As your only sister, that's touching," she says, handing me a small basket of sugars and creamers.

"Let's do that one," Cooper says, pointing at something on his phone. "I'll call them and see if they have availability."

Tyler shakes his head. "Natasha will have contacts. I'll call her." He pulls out his phone, moving toward the living room as he calls her.

"See?" Cooper says.

I take a drink of the coffee, not caring that it's still too hot. I need caffeine to process the situation. "I thought he had meetings?"

"He did. He just got back."

I glance in his direction as his phone call ends. He turns around, catching me staring. Rather than be embarrassed, I glower, hoping it might make him change his mind and find something else to do besides hang out with us.

"Okay. We have to get going now," he says.

"Now?" I ask, still not accepting that he's coming with us.

He nods.

I take another sip of my coffee before regretfully setting it in the sink, and opening the fridge. I grab one of the waffles stacked on a plate, surrounded by small dishes of whipped butter and syrup that I have no doubt would taste like perfection.

Nessie chuckles. "Let's go so we can grab you some coffee to go. We'll meet you guys in the lobby."

While Tyler and Coop go to grab their shoes and sunglasses, Nessie and I head down in the elevator, and even though the waffle is cold and plain, it's delicious and still pillowy soft.

"Feeling better?" Cooper asks as I take a long sip of my iced coffee once they meet us in the lobby.

"Give me ten minutes."

He chuckles, waiting to keep stride with Nessie. It's sweet and thoughtful and only marginally painful to watch.

My dress is white and ends at my knees, shifting with the warm breeze as we step outside.

A car is parked at the curb, waiting for us. Miles is not.

The ride is mere minutes. We've barely gotten ourselves situated before our driver is pulling over for us to get out again at a large mansion with a crooked sign, the paint cracking and rippled from sun exposure.

"Welcome. Welcome," a woman greets us with a thick Southern accent. A half dozen others are standing outside that we join. "Twins! Now, this should make for a very interesting tour. Did you know twins used to be considered bad luck and only recently have been known as good luck?" I swear she leers at us.

Nessie grips my hand, and we exchange a look as we join the rest. *This lady's nuts, and I'll kick her in the vajayjay if she tries anything.*

"We're so glad you're here—and by we, I mean myself and the ghosts who live here—because this building, in addition to many others in New Orleans, is occupied with ghosts, and they love visitors." The tour guide rubs her hands together. "Has anyone been to New Orleans before?"

A few raise their hands.

Tyler does not.

I know he's been here, but apparently participation is low on his list, along with being decent.

"I hope you've all had some good food and drinks, and are enjoying the music and sights. This afternoon, I'll be giving you a little bit of history while also introducing you to some of my friends. If I go over anything too quickly or if you have any questions, please feel free to ask me. Also, please make sure you stay with the group. The ghosts are friendly when we're in large numbers, but that can change quickly if you wander off by yourself."

Several laugh and make jokes about this possibility, while I cast a look at the mansion, realizing this might be one of my worst ideas because though her warning is cheesy, the hairs on my arms are already standing on end, regardless of the heat and humidity that has most of the crowd fanning themselves.

"As some of you may know, Louisiana was named after King Louis the Fourteenth after France took control over the territory for a second time. And New Orleans is considered the most haunted city in all of America. Why, you might ask? New Orleans has faced numerous grisly tales, ranging from pirates to yellow fever, which lasted for over a hundred years and was responsible for over forty thousand souls, the heartless murders of slaves, fire, and many more tragedies. Some say those who die here can't rest because there's no solid ground. Others attribute it to the many who practice mystical arts, from voodoo to vampires and witches. You will quickly realize that New Orleans is home to a diverse population, and many refuse to leave it even after death.

"This part of the tour is my absolute favorite. We're going to go inside of this mansion that was at one time a gorgeous and highly coveted hotel, but no one has been able to occupy it for the past seventy-five years because the ghosts refuse to allow anyone to live here." She waves a hand forward. "Let's go inside."

We follow the others who are pointing to a group of crows, trying to add their presence as a factor for this place being haunted.

"Was this rated on a creepy scale?" Nessie asks. "Like, I need to know now if I'm going to be able to pee alone for the foreseeable future."

Cooper chuckles. "It's all for tourism."

"Okay," the tour guide says. "Please be sure to silence your cell phones, and make sure if you're taking any pictures, you have the flash turned off. We're going to be calling our ghosts, and they prefer the lights to be off."

"I'm going to hate myself for this," I whisper to Nessie, taking a step back so that our arms brush.

"Now don't worry. We'll still be able to see. We're just going to dim the lights, but be careful and watch your step. Also, if you feel a cool breeze followed by a blast of heat, that's a ghost."

"And I'm done," I say as the lights dim, and she proceeds to explain all the tools they're using to detect said ghosts.

Something falls, and half the group screams. I reach for Nessie, but she's pretzeled herself around Cooper. I pull in a deep breath through my nose, reminding myself this is likely staged. *It's fake. It's fake. It's fake*, I tell myself.

The guide starts telling us about the house's previous occupants, and my attention floats across the antique furniture and all the dolls that are staring at us—creepy, like they're watching me—when she stops talking. "Oh, do you feel that? We have a change in temperature. The ghosts are coming."

"Oh, hell no," I whisper.

A woman screams, and something else falls, and before sense can stop me, I'm clutching Tyler's arm, burying my face into his bicep.

"We're going to take you upstairs to the bedrooms. A ghost who we believe was a nurse still lives up there, so if you feel someone stroking your arm, you'll know it's her. And there's also a couple of children who like to play tricks and laugh."

I still hate Tyler.

I'm still not about to let go of his freaking arm.

As the tour continues, the space between us lessens until I'm plastered to his side, jumping each time someone screams or claims to feel something.

My muscles are tight, and my shoulders ache as we finally leave the house, and I'm not proud of the thoughts that have me wanting to cut in front of everyone so I can get back to the safety of the street. Still, I remain anchored to Tyler's side.

"Okay, we're going to continue down this way to an above-ground cemetery," the guide says.

"We aren't going to talk about this," I warn Tyler. "Ever. I'm using you, and that is all this is." I refuse to look at him as we continue the few blocks, listening to the guide talk about the traps some would place on their houses so men couldn't get in to steal their daughter's innocence, and thank goodness Tyler is either amused enough or has grown enough of a conscience not to make any jokes about using me in turn.

"Are we really going into a cemetery?" Nessie asks. "This seems like a terrible idea. Like, I knew that wasn't real, and I was still scared out of my mind. This is going to be so scary, I might cry."

"I kind of want to see it, though. What if we go and bail out before they start the actual tour?" Cooper asks.

Before we can answer, the tour guide starts talking again. "Now, in addition to ghosts, we have a large number of vampires in New Orleans, so once again, staying together is the safest way to travel, especially when we're going into a cemetery."

"Fuck me," Nessie says, shaking her head. "Sparkly ones. Please be sparkly ones."

Cooper chuckles because like always, he's practical and has already chalked this all up to old tales and has discounted any potential threat. While my major of astrophysics consists of laws, rules, and theories, right now my thoughts have abandoned all reason and sense and are currently theorizing all the ways we're going to be killed as we cross past the gates of the cemetery.

9

TYLER

I made a vow last night to avoid Chloe Robinson.

That vow died a quick death this morning when I went to work out with Cooper, and he told me about how much he'd appreciated me making an effort with Chloe and how she had given her blessing for him and Vanessa to pursue things.

I'd told him that it wasn't her choice, and in turn, Cooper tore out a page from his childhood, back from when he was first sent to live with his grandma after his dad's arrest. He shared how most of the kids avoided him and called him names for his father's crimes and how it had been Chloe who stood up for him and even went as far as punching a kid in the nose when he called Coop a drug dealer.

The problem is, as much as I admire her for standing up for Cooper, there's something about her that makes every bad decision seem good. I know that if I turned on the tap, everything would overflow and drown us both because she's not the kind of girl you can forget—which is why when I'm around her, everything turns into chaos, making all of my emotions feel like lies.

This tour—her breasts pressed against me, perfume staining me, fingers marking me—is not helping a single damn thing.

"I'm done," Vanessa announces as someone in our tour group starts sharing a picture of a blur she believes is a ghost.

A cat darts out from behind one of the tombs. A cacophony of screams echo through the cemetery as it sprints away. Chloe wraps her arms around my waist, moving even closer. "Done. Done. Done," she chants.

I read the reluctance on Cooper's face, the perverse way he's enjoying this moment having Vanessa so close, but he glances around, trying to retrace our steps. "All right, let's get out of here."

Chloe's grip loosens, and she moves so she's walking beside me, relieved by just the realization this is about to be over.

"What do they mean, vampires live here?" Vanessa asks. "Like people here drink each other's blood?" That's all it takes before Chloe slips her arm back through mine.

I pull out my phone to text Natasha to send a car.

"I'm sure it's just to scare people and add to the experience," Cooper says.

"What did you think, Ty?" Vanessa asks.

"You never want to go to the Czech Republic," I warn her. "It's supposed to be the most haunted country in the world."

"Noted," Chloe says.

"Hey, Chloe, truth or dare?" Cooper asks.

"No. No. No." She shakes her head.

Cooper laughs so hard he nearly trips. "I wasn't going to. I mean, you did this to yourself. You knew you were going to hate it and still did it. That's either really brave or really stupid."

"Being fun is so overrated," Chloe says.

As we get back to the hotel suite, my phone rings.

Dad.

Shit.

It's late there—or very early—which means there's a problem.

"You ready?" Coop asks from where we're gathered in the living room, plans of the pool on a brief hiatus as the girls exchange their experiences with the ghosts. Chloe's sitting in a single chair—the farthest seat from where I'd sat down—the past few hours forgotten.

"Yeah, I've got to take this really fast. It's my dad. I'll meet you down at the pool."

Coop gives a tight nod of understanding. We've exchanged enough stories about our fathers and their shared drive to always to be the best that sometimes left us forgotten.

I step out onto the balcony, closing the door behind me. "Hello?"

"What's going on in New Orleans?" Dad asks, cutting out pleasantries. That's okay, most will say I'm not pleasant, either.

I work to recall some of the data and figures I'd requested this morning after sitting in a conference room for over fourteen hours yesterday to understand how the New Orleans site has lost money in the past nine months when it was once one of our most profitable hotels. "We're spending too much," I begin to explain my thoughts, and then stop. I haven't shared anything with him thus far. This is my project, and we're supposed to discuss my findings and recommendations next month when he and Lewis return from Europe. "Are you checking in on me?"

"Natasha called and said you checked in with three guests. I thought you were taking this seriously? Tell me they're not prostitutes. And why were you late for your meeting yesterday? And why didn't you invite Avery to fly over?"

I laugh. "That's rich, Dad, especially coming from you. This is the first hotel, and you're already having your minions spy on me? And no, I didn't invite Avery. I don't want the management company's opinions."

"They're not spying. They work for me."

"Three people are traveling with me. All of them attend Brighton. All of them have been professional, and none of them are prostitutes. One is Cooper, and the other two are sisters." It's better to give him facts, so he stops spying.

"They reflect on you, Tyler. Every decision you make, every person you call a friend—it all reflects on you, Son."

"I'm perfectly aware of that."

"Don't embarrass our family name." He hangs up.

I clench the phone in my fist, and for a second, I consider how it would feel to chuck it off the balcony and break my contact with the outside world for just a single day.

Anger prickles at my skin as I recount what the girls wore last night when we went out and the night before when we arrived. Did they say or do something that made them come across as opportunistic or inappropriate? It shouldn't matter—it doesn't matter.

With anger still thrumming through my veins, I go back inside. The girls are gone, only Cooper is here. I head straight for the mini bar, grab a filled bottle, and bring it to the kitchen where I use a steak knife to break the seal.

"Didn't go well?" Coop asks, leaning against the fridge in his bathing suit with one shoulder, arms crossed over his chest.

"I need to fire someone."

Coop's eyebrows jump. "Post drink?"

I swallow two fingers and set the glass and bottle on the counter. "Yeah, it's a phone call."

"He asked you to do it?"

I shake my head.

"Who is it?" he asks.

"The GM here."

"Natasha? The hot one?"

I nod.

"No wonder you're drinking. Perk: once she isn't your employee..."

He's trying to make me laugh, not encourage me to add another poor decision to my already long list of bad decisions, but the exhaustion of this moment and the betrayal it's packed with prevent the idea from being even remotely funny.

"You guys go down to the pool. I'm going to make this call, and I'll be down shortly." I start to turn toward the staircase and stop. Chloe is making her way down the stairs in a one-piece bathing suit that is sexier than any bikini I've ever seen. It's green, and the top dips between her breasts to nearly her navel, the two pieces laced together with a matching piece of fabric below her breasts.

She stops, her eyes lifting to mine, greener and brighter with the bathing suit. A shy smile teases her lips. "Sorry," she says quietly, before continuing down the steps with her bare feet that reveal multiple tan lines from summer.

I consider moving so she can't pass me and forcing a conversation. Try to draw out some apology for last night and remind her that I'm an arse, and that's the one part about me she can always count on.

She slips past me without even a glance, and I hear Cooper talking about what truth or dare question he's going to ask Vanessa, and Chloe laughing in return.

FIRING NATASHA WASN'T HALF as rewarding as I'd hoped. She's damn good at her job, but it was a necessary decision. I knew she'd keep my father apprised of everything—expected it in fact—but her lies crossed too many lines. I would never be able to trust her, and if she was willing to cross me so quickly just to earn the praise of my father, who else would she willingly stab in the back? She wasn't upset in the least, which I quickly realized meant she'd be calling my father in the morning to appeal the decision, and I'm not fully sure he'd support my choice, which means I'll need to reach out to him first. The idea of asking him to stand by me on this—of having to defend myself when he should have been the one who fired her when she contacted him—ratchets up my anger. My thoughts splinter into the realm of *what-if?* when I think about the possibility of my father choosing Lewis as the incoming CEO, and I pour myself another drink.

I consider what would happen if I invested in Cooper and his business ventures—living on the island the three of them have painted numerous times while discussing their future. The four of us with our feet in the sand and not caring about budgets or bottom lines or trends. The idea leads me to my wardrobe, where I rifle through my clothes that the hotel's staff hung and laid out for me, finding a pair of swim shorts that I quickly change into and tossing my phone on the bed on my way out.

I take the elevator down to the outdoor patio, finding the others gathered around the table as thunder rumbles in the distance.

"We're debating if it's worth getting in. The girls think they've already pushed their luck with the ghost tour and that if they get in, the storm will start." Another roll of thunder cracks as he finishes telling me this.

The pool is small but deep, not made for much aside from to impress. Still, the privacy is welcomed.

"Hey, Ty," Coop says as I look across the brightly lit city.

"Yeah?" I say, instantly hating the jarring smile he flashes.

"Truth or dare."

"Bloody hell."

Chloe and Vanessa laugh, waiting to hear what I choose.

"Dare."

Cooper rubs his finger against his chin like he does whenever he deserves a kick to the gonads. "I dare you to lose your shorts and jump in."

"No way," Chloe says. "There have to be some boundaries. I made you order a drink. These dares are starting to—"

Her words come to an abrupt stop as I throw my shorts at her and jump into the pool.

Laughter greets me when I surface, and then there's a squeal and a splash as Cooper tosses Chloe into the pool after me.

"Cooper Ronald Sutton, we're no longer friends," she warns him, brushing the water from her face.

"Ronald? Your middle name's Ronald?" I ask.

Coop flips me off. "You said you wanted to go swimming. You needed a little push."

Vanessa howls with laughter.

"The water's nice, yeah?" I ask Chloe when she looks at me.

She glances away, her cheeks tinted with embarrassment.

"Are you embarrassed?" I ask her, knowing full well that she is.

Vanessa throws my swim shorts into the pool. They fall a couple of feet away and float along the surface.

"That's okay. It actually feels pretty nice," I say, stretching to my back and kicking my feet up to glide backward.

"Oh, God," Cooper grumbles.

"If you've got it, flaunt it, right?" I say.

Chloe has her back turned to me. I'd bet this hotel that her eyes are closed.

"I thought we were swimming?" I yell to the others.

"Put your fucking shorts on," Cooper says.

"You dared me to take them off."

"I need a drink," Coop grumbles.

"Ditto," Vanessa pops up from her chair.

"Get dressed by the time we come back, or I'm posting this all over your social media," Cooper warns.

The two disappear into the elevator, leaving Chloe and me alone in the pool.

"Will you put your shorts on?" she asks, chancing a look at me.

"Does my being naked make you uncomfortable?"

"It makes *everyone* uncomfortable, hence the alcohol."

"You're talking to me again," I point out.

She sighs, turning to face me as she treads water.

"See?" I say. "You can't even see anything."

"You're still naked."

"Can you see my cock?"

"There's a principle here."

"And what's that?"

"There are laws about decency."

"I'm on private property," I counter.

She shakes her head. "Do you always argue this much?"

"You'd know if you didn't avoid me all the time."

"I don't avoid you."

"No?"

"I pretend you don't exist."

I don't mean to laugh, but she has a pirate smile, working to either goad me or ensure my ego is completely shattered. "Why do you pretend I don't exist?"

Her smile slips, but then her eyebrows rise as she continues to tread water. "Does it matter?"

"It depends."

Her smile resumes. "On?"

"If it's true or not."

"It is."

"You don't know me."

"I know enough."

I swim closer, catching the uneasy glint in her eyes that only fuels my confidence like a textbook sadist. "What's that?"

"Why are you trying to make me nervous?"

"Do I make you nervous?"

She remains still, only turning to watch me as I circle her. "In the same way swimming beside an alligator would."

I move closer, knowing the water is clear and lit well enough that she could see every part of me if she looked. "You don't trust me."

"You have a reputation."

I flash a shark smile—predatory and intentional. "The rumors are all true."

"They're nothing to be proud of."

I shrug. "Debatable." I move closer, noting the way the tip of her nose and cheeks are red from getting too much sun yesterday, and that the faint indent above her lip can be traced to her chin with a shallow dimple there. "Just ask," I tell her. "Ask me to kiss you."

She rolls her eyes. "Was I not clear enough last night?"

I lean closer still as a particularly loud crack of thunder followed by a burst of lightning highlights the sky. Her foot brushes my leg as she continues to tread water, and I run my tongue over a drop of water along her jaw.

Chloe raises her hands, pushing away from me. "I don't know why you're doing this, but you need to stop. I'm not playing some game with you." Anger and hurt flash in her eyes before she turns and swims to the edge of the pool and gets out.

"Are you guys crazy? Did you see the lightning?" Cooper asks as the elevator doors open. "Let's go upstairs and celebrate our last night in New Orleans."

Chloe grabs a towel, wrapping it around herself. "I'm tired. I think I'm going to bed."

Cooper turns his attention to me. "Tell me you put some shorts on."

"You might want to close your eyes if you don't want feelings of inadequacy to haunt you."

The last thing I hear before the elevator doors close is Cooper chuckling.

10

CHLOE

"I don't think I'll ever find a bed this comfortable again," Nessie says, spreading her arms over it like she's making a snow angel.

"They probably have the same beds at all the locations," I tell her. "But I'm bummed to leave as well. I never had jambalaya, and I really want more beignets."

"I bet Tyler could arrange it so you could get both before we leave."

I shove the last of my makeup into my overnight bag and move to pack it in my suitcase. I didn't tell her about the club or the pool. I can't even figure out why. Maybe it's because I think she'll tell me he was teasing or joking? Or because it might create a point of contention that would make the next fifteen days painful and awkward? "That's okay. Austin is supposed to have good food, right?"

She laughs. "That's something I'd be asking you. You looked this stuff up. I barely looked anything up for Austin because I knew we were staying just one night."

We turn as Cooper knocks on the door. "They're here to grab the bags. You guys ready?"

I look across our bags and empty room. "Yeah."

He nods. "We can meet Tyler in the lobby. He said he'd be ready by ten so we could head for Texas."

Nessie woke me up and dragged me out of bed at six this morning to go for a jog with her, saying I owed her after the ghost tour. I would have complained more if it hadn't allowed me to get a longer look at the Garden District.

"He's not back yet?" Nessie asks.

Cooper shakes his head. "Maybe he had a meeting or something?"

I shrug, giving a final glance at the room. "I want to see the atrium down in the lobby. Let's go see if we feel any cool breezes followed by a warm gust."

Nessie shudders. "Still not funny."

I grab my purse, and we move slowly through the hotel suite, parting ways with the beautiful space.

"Should we try calling him?" Vanessa asks, tossing her empty coffee cup in the recycle bin.

Cooper glances at his cell phone that confirms we've been down in the lobby for three hours. We've seen the entire thing, twice. We saw the shops where I bought a T-shirt and a postcard to send to Mom and Dad, the full atrium filled with exotic plants and a small waterfall, and even the crocodiles. When it hit noon, Cooper texted him, but when he didn't hear back, we crossed the street and had lunch at a small restaurant. Lunch ended up being a silver lining because I finally got my shrimp jambalaya, and it was definitely worth the wait. We ate in a hurry so that we'd be back to the hotel, not wanting to delay the seven hours and change we have to drive to reach Austin.

"I'll send him another text. He said ten, right?" He looks at Nessie because I held to my word last night, though they both teased me about being a party pooper, and went to bed where I read until I fell asleep.

My ego still feels bruised, certain Tyler's playing some kind of head game with me. And I hate the fact I can still smell him and recall the warmth and strangely erotic feeling of his tongue against my skin. I brush my fingers across the same expanse of skin in an attempt to rid the memory.

"There he is," Vanessa says, pointing back toward the steakhouse we ate at the night before last. He's wearing a pair of jeans and black tee that reveals some of the ink I'd seen last night when he came down to go swimming—before everything got ruined by that stupid dare. His dark blond hair is finger-combed to one side, but these details quickly fade as he raises a hand and places it on the waist of a short brunette who is all hair, boobs, and ass, wearing a skin-tight red dress and black heels that scream s-e-x.

He waves at us, and for a second, I think he's going to bring her over here and make this moment even more awkward, but instead, he faces her and says something that makes her laugh. Then he bends, kissing her mouth and burying his hands in her hair.

"He seriously ghosted us to hook up with some chick?" Nessie asks.

"They were in the restaurant. I doubt they hooked up," Cooper says.

"It doesn't open until five," I point out, my attention still on Tyler, watching his hand slide down her back to cup her ass.

"He had to fire someone. Maybe she's the replacement," Cooper says.

"He kisses all his employees?" Nessie asks.

"Is it our place to judge?" Cooper asks. "We got a couple more hours to hang out and have some good food. It hardly seems fair we're going to be pissed off about this when we got to stay here." Leave it to Cooper to not only be reasonable and logical but also stick up for the manwhore.

I scrub at the same spot on my jaw again, hating the fact the memory is stained there and burns more prominently, as she reaches for him before waving goodbye and blowing him kisses.

"Hey," Tyler says, crossing the rest of the distance to us. "You guys ready to go?"

"We've been ready to go," I say.

Tyler's blue gaze travels to me, humor shining like he knows I'm irked, which only annoys me more. "Sorry about that. I got a little carried away after meeting Opal." He turns, waving at the woman again.

She waves back, and I have to bite the inside of my cheek to keep from saying something that will make me sound either jealous or snarky —neither of which I am.

"Well, let's get going, shall we?" He spreads his arms, walking toward the front doors of the hotel.

Nessie rolls her eyes and shrugs, following after him.

"Would you mind switching seats?" Cooper asks in a hushed tone.

"No way."

"Come on. Please? I'll owe you so big."

I shake my head. "Hard pass."

"Chloe," he whines. "Come on. Do this, and I will try and get you a day at the Redwoods."

"Sit by Satan for a maybe? Terrible negotiating skills, Sutton."

He gives me an exhausted stare that plays on my emotions—a similar expression to the one Ricky bestowed on me so many times when he thought I was being difficult and uptight. "Fine. Fine. But you have to orchestrate it. I don't want him thinking this was my idea."

Cooper's brow knits, and he laughs. "Why would Tyler care?"

It's not intentional, but it twists that knife that got lodged in my back last night when they left me in the pool with him alone.

I shake my head. "Never mind."

He wraps his arm around my shoulders and gives me a brief squeeze before hurrying to catch up with the other two.

Our bags are already loaded into the back of the Tesla, and I don't miss the look one of the valets shoots Tyler, likely because he was also expecting us three hours ago, and it's led to confusion for them as well.

Cooper walks around the car and gets into the seat behind Tyler, laughing at something Nessie said. I pull in a breath, reminding myself this leg is just shy of eight hours. I'll finish my book, take a nap, start another book, and we'll be there. Thank God for e-books.

The valet opens the passenger door for me, and I square my shoulders as I slide onto the soft leather of the front seat, working to ignore Tyler, who turns to look at me. "Asked Coop for a favor?" he teases.

"Are you ever humble?"

"What's that?"

I fasten my seat belt, ignoring him as I open my book and hug myself as close to the door as possible.

THREE HOURS INTO THE DRIVE, and I'm considering potential rules for the rest of this trip, starting with I get to sit in the back seat because right now, as Cooper and Nessie sleep in the back and I reread the same page for the fourth time because Tyler keeps looking at me, I'm debating walking to Austin.

"Why are you looking at me?" I ask, turning to face him.

"Are you ever humble?" he returns my earlier question.

I roll my eyes and take a deep breath through my nose to keep myself from yelling because although I'm known for having a lot of patience, Tyler manages to defy that fact and pushes me right to the brink of my sanity.

"I'm tired," he says. "I need you to talk to me. Keep me awake."

"Wake Cooper up."

"He's tired."

I rub my fingers along my forehead. "What do you want to talk about?"

"Football?"

I frown. "Seriously?"

"Do you have something you'd rather talk about?"

There are a thousand things I'd rather talk about, and considering he was naked and licking my face last night and accusing me of wanting him the night before and then kissed another girl's lipstick off, it seems there's a much larger issue we should be talking about—or possibly several—but I scoff and shake my head. "No. By all means, let's discuss football."

"Brilliant. Do you like the game?"

"How do you even play football? You're British. Aren't you supposed to play soccer or cricket or something?"

"I'm American."

"And British, and you grew up there."

"Did you Google me?"

I sigh deeply, my attention moving to the window in an attempt to find my patience that he just successfully destroyed. "You told us. Remember?"

He grins. "I was kidding." He passes a slow-moving vehicle and then glances at me. "My uncle, on my mum's side, lived with us for a while. He's a big football fan. Taught me most of what I know."

I glance across the space at him, the same tattoo I'd seen when he was kissing the woman winking at me from the inside of his bicep. It's only the edge of the tattoo, tickling my memories of last night as I work to recall what is tattood on his skin.

"We moved to Miami when I was thirteen, and football was the quickest way to make friends. I joined a team, and I went from being the kid with the weird accent to the kid who could run really fast."

"Yeah, right. Even our dad swooned at your accent."

He looks at me briefly, and I'm pretty sure it's the first time I've seen him surprised, his lips slowly fighting a smile that he quickly loses to. He moves, rubbing his hand over his bicep and sliding the sleeve up, revealing the hard planes of muscles. "Swooned, did he? You think thirteen-year-olds swoon when they hear someone they can't understand?"

It's difficult for me to imagine anyone not swooning.

I don't tell him this, though, no need to add more wind to his sails.

"So, my American side won out with football, but I prefer tea in the morning."

"I only watch football because Cooper plays."

"Not a fan?"

I shrug. "I don't know. It just seems dangerous and slow and aggressive."

He laughs, tipping his head back slightly as he rights his sleeve and moves his hand back to the steering wheel. "You sound like my mum. She hates it. She'd prefer I played chess or water polo."

"Water polo is shockingly difficult. It might be the most underrated sport for difficulty."

He laughs.

"I'm serious. We had to play once for PE, and it was intense. There are no fouls, and you can't reach the bottom, and you're supposed to swim while throwing a ball." I shake my head. "Grossly underrated."

"Besides your brief water polo career, did you play sports?"

"Very brief," I point out. "I played soccer."

He nods. "I can see that. But not in college?"

I shake my head. "Nope."

"More time to study?"

I glance at him again. "Kids aren't much nicer when someone passes out in the middle of a game."

His blue eyes meet mine, his brow furled. "What happened?"

"It's a long story."

"Good thing we have five hours, and I need you to keep talking."

"I was born with a hole in my heart, and we didn't know about it. Atrial septal defect."

"Fucking hell," he says, sympathy cutting his mouth into a frown that I itch to erase.

"It's fine. *Totally* fine," I tell him. "They fixed it. I just stopped playing because it was hard for others to forget that moment. I was no longer Chloe. I was Chloe, the girl who passed out and had to have emergency heart surgery. Everyone looked at me like I was about to keel over again and wouldn't pass me the ball, and the coach wouldn't make me run—"

"Sounds totally fine," he says, his gaze dropping to my neckline, likely looking for a scar.

"I had a cardiac catheterization, so they were able to go in through a small incision on my leg." I trace the tiny scar through my shorts. "But, seriously, it's all better. They fixed it, and now I see a cardiologist every couple of years, and they tell me everything's normal." I rush to add the words, regretting having told him because though I'm technically better, the memory still makes me feel weak.

He looks at me again but doesn't say anything.

"My vagina is also pierced."

His eyes open wide with shock, and the car weaves.

"Kidding. Kidding. Completely kidding," I say, shaking with laughter. "You were just way too serious, and I could tell you were starting to regret acting like a total asshat for the wrong reasons, so I needed to get your attention for a second."

Tyler shakes his head. "But it's a big deal. Does Vanessa have it also?"

"What, a clit ring?" I burst out laughing again, proud of myself for letting go and living in the moment.

Tyler still isn't amused.

I shake my head. "Thankfully, no, her heart is hole-free. And it could have been a big deal, but I was lucky. I didn't have a very large hole, and they were able to repair it easily. I spent one night in the hospital and two weeks at home and was given a clean bill of health. Not many can say that about a heart condition, so I prefer not to tell people about it so they don't react the way you are."

"It doesn't still impact your life?"

I shake my head. "Not even a little. I can exercise, run, jump, go on haunted ghost tours..."

He smiles. "You did that as an excuse to touch me, didn't you?"

I roll my eyes. "You have me all figured out."

"So, you're saying you thought last night was hot?"

"Not even a little." I subconsciously wipe that same spot on my jaw again, my thoughts traveling to what Cooper had said. "Coop mentioned you had to fire someone last night."

His lips toy with a smirk. "It wasn't nearly as satisfying as I'd hoped."

"It wasn't Miles, was it?"

I count the second time I've seen Tyler Banks surprised as he looks at me. "Miles? Miles the chauffeur?"

"Pretty sure he's more than a chauffeur, but yes."

"You're more observant than I realized."

"What does that mean?"

"You realized I didn't like that you knew his name, didn't you?"

This time, it's my turn to be surprised. "Why would you care?"

He stares at me a moment too long, considering he's driving. "I didn't fire Miles. I gave him a raise and an extra week of vacation."

My surprise quickly becomes shock. "You did?"

"He took the time to know your name and remember it. Went and got you within seconds of my calling and delivered you safely. Then took the time to listen to you and offer suggestions for a ghost tour. He deserved it."

Certainly, it's not meant to be personal, but it just sounds and feels incredibly personal when he keeps putting it in reference to me and staring at me like he is—like he wants to lean across the center console and demand I ask him to kiss me again.

I don't want that, I remind myself, adding the memory of him kissing that woman just hours before to finalize that realization and recalling dozens of other memories of him kissing girls that has my upper body shifting back closer to the door and farther from a very bad idea.

11

TYLER

I sit in the swivel chair at the end of the conference table, a mess of spreadsheets in front of me as well as three laptops, nothing on them reflecting anything that makes sense.

I scrub a hand over my face and stand, my muscles constricted and restless. Our next hotel isn't until Santa Fe which, when we started to plot this trip, didn't seem like that big of a feat, but after all of yesterday being spent in the car and still fighting to get the information I'd requested, that eleven hours to New Mexico is feeling like a life sentence.

"Mr. Banks," Anika answers on the second ring.

"Anika, I need a hotel reservation for somewhere between Austin and Santa Fe. Four rooms, please."

"For tonight, I presume?"

"That's correct."

"Your options are limited."

Tell me about it. "We'll make it work."

"There's a small city called Odessa, Texas. It's going to be about five and a half hours from where you are."

I rub my eyes with my thumb and forefinger, wondering how the others will take this news. "Okay. Yeah. That works."

"I'll email you a reservation. Anything else?"

"N... Yes. Atrial septal defects. It's a heart condition, a hole in the atrial septum. I want to speak with a specialist to ask some questions." I read about the condition in detail last night, yet, I still want some assurance from a specialist.

"When would you like me to set it up?"

"As soon as possible."

"I'll make an appointment for after you meet with Santa Fe."

"Thank you."

She hangs up, and I roll my shoulders before heading for the door, looking for Sid, the general manager here who has the attention span of a toddler.

"Sid, where are the expenditures for the past three years?"

"Aren't those in there?"

I shake my head. "No."

"Let me go find them."

He starts to turn. "I also need the variable expenses to calculate the contribution margin as well," I tell him.

As I open the conference room door, my phone rings. "Your ears burning?" I ask my Uncle Kip.

He laughs. "What are you doing, kid?"

"Currently, just trying not to gouge my eyes out from boredom."

He clicks his tongue with disapproval. "I taught you better than that. You know what I'll tell you: find a hottie or a football."

I lean back in my chair, laughing at the sentiment he's instilled in me for as long as I can remember. "Been there, done that."

"Rinse and repeat, kid. Rinse and repeat."

"I'm on a business trip."

"How in the hell did you get roped into that? Was it your mom? Need me to put in a good word for you? I can call her and remind her about that time she ran off to Colorado after graduation before she met your dad."

I cringe, not wanting to think about the implications of that story. "No. My choice."

"Your choice?"

"I'm trying to show initiative."

"I'm sorry, I think I dialed the wrong number. I'm looking for my nephew. He's a good-looking fucker, who's been all over college sports news because of his new role with Brighton as a starting running back. They're talking about how he's going to change things up with his speed. They're calling him The Flash."

"That was spring league," I tell him. "It hardly counts."

"Oh, trust me. It counts. I've seen your mug on the TV a dozen times this week. Go put this on in whatever fucking hotel you're in. Plaster it all over the lobby and in every guest room. You'll have chicks lining up to suck you like a goddamn lollipop."

"Choke on me, you mean."

He cackles. "Better yet, tell me where you are. I'll send the party to you."

"Can't. I'm about to leave. We're doing a road trip across the country."

"We?"

"One of my teammates and a couple of friends."

"Ah, so you brought a mobile party."

Sid returns, opening the conference room door, holding a file and another laptop.

"Sorry, Uncle Kip, but I've got to cut it short. I'll give you a call when I hit Seattle."

"All right, kid. I'll smell you later."

I hang up and turn my attention to Sid and the mess he's trying to hand off to me, wrestling with facts and stats that all seem tangled in a web that appears to be growing larger and larger with every question.

"Sid, let's be frank here. Your budget isn't adding up. You have dozens of expenses that don't make sense. A pool renovation, new company cars, a fucking water feature that isn't here. And apparently, the laptop to employee ratio is three to one. You're bleeding money."

He blanches. "People don't want luxury anymore."

I stare at him, waiting for him to continue. Several moments pass, and he drops my stare, a red stain creeping up his neck and reaching his face. At least he has some sense.

"Explain."

"People want more privacy. They don't want the traditional turndown service because they don't want people in their space. And they don't need the best concierge in town telling them where to find the best drink or steak in Austin because now they have Google."

"It's not just turndown service and a good concierge," I argue.

"It's not?" He raises his eyebrows. "Our cheapest room is three hundred and fifty dollars a night before tax, and people are starting to care less about the exclusivity perks and are choosing someplace more affordable with free breakfast and a warm cookie when you check in."

"Bullshit. People don't care about a free breakfast or cookies. They care about image, which is why you see people stopping to post pictures to their social media account every damn second, and why every teenager has a thousand-dollar cell phone."

"But people want luxury on a budget."

"Three hundred and fifty dollars a night is a budget," I tell him.

He shakes his head. "Not anymore."

I stand, ready to flip the table. Not because this location means anything—we could easily close it, cauterize the bleed and be no worse for wear. No, this irritation stems from his complete lack of desire for this place to remain open. If he, as the general manager, has so little regard for the hotel, then I can't expect his staff to, either.

"I need a break. Let's meet back in an hour to finalize things, and then I've got to go."

Sid pops out of his chair like I've just said the magic word to free him of a lifelong servitude, dashing out the door before I'm out of my seat.

I call Cooper as I make my way down the hallway to the elevator.

"Hey, man."

"Where are you guys?"

"In the lobby."

"You could've stayed up in the room. I told them we'd have a late checkout today."

"The girls were restless. Since we have a long drive, they wanted to walk around for a while. What's going on with you?"

"I'm on my way down. Where are you guys?"

"Near the koi pond."

"I'll see you in a minute." I hang up as the doors shut and descend the multiple floors to the lobby, where I find them laughing over something. We arrived late last night after having to stop to charge the car and electing to eat dinner at the same time. It was a small dive bar with "spicy" and "fried" describing everything on their menu.

When we checked in, we did a much faster tour of the suite, sitting out on the balcony while they brought in our luggage and discussing the plan for today. The hotel had an entire team set for the task, and because we were only staying the one night, I requested they didn't unpack our bags as had been done in New Orleans, which led to me slipping away to catch some sleep even faster.

"Thank goodness you're done. These two are delirious and need a nap." He looks between the twins and shakes his head.

"He's projecting," Vanessa says. "We're great. We're just naming all the fish."

"Naming the fish?" I ask.

"None of them are appropriate, so don't ask," Cooper says, shaking his head.

"Who doesn't love a good pun?" Chloe replies. She's wearing a pair of gray shorts with a loose-fitting sweater, a coffee in her hand.

"Hey, so, I think I left a hat in New Orleans," Cooper says. "Do you think I could contact someone and have them ship it to me?"

I suggest telling him just to buy a new one but stop, knowing Cooper has a limited income and that it might hold sentimental value. "Yeah. I can have Anika message them and have it sent to Seattle."

He smiles with relief. "Thanks, man."

I nod.

"Are you ready to go?" Vanessa asks me.

I shake my head. "Unfortunately, there's been a change in plans. I need a little more time here, so we're going to drive halfway today and stay overnight, and we'll drive to Santa Fe in the morning."

Vanessa nods—an easy sell. "I don't think I could have survived eleven hours in the car." She stretches. "Do you have some time? You want to grab something to eat? We need a tiebreaker. There's supposed to be a really good Mexican restaurant and Chinese restaurant both within two blocks."

"There are three of you. By default, you can't have a tie," I point out.

"Oh, I'm not getting in the middle of this," Cooper says, shaking his head.

I glance between the sisters, considering which restaurant each chose. "I have a little time."

"Perfect. Chinese or Mexican?" Vanessa asks.

"Mexican," I tell her. "We're in Texas."

Vanessa frowns. "Fine, but I get to pick dinner." She links arms with Cooper and starts toward the front doors.

"Everything okay?" I ask Chloe when she refuses to look at me or attempt small talk.

"Yeah, I'm fine."

"You don't seem fine. You seem annoyed."

"It's stupid." She shakes her head and pulls her shoulders back.

I stop walking and turn to face her, causing her to stop as well. Her attention shifts from me to Coop and Vanessa and the building gap as they continue walking. "You guys grab a table, we'll be right there," I tell Coop.

He nods without a sign of hesitation.

"What's stupid?" I ask her.

A narrow line forms between her brows as apprehension becomes visible. "It's just the way you come across sometimes. Changing plans and taking another day isn't a big deal, but you didn't even discuss it with us. You just made the plans and expect us to go along with them."

"This is my business trip," I remind her.

"Sure, but that doesn't mean you don't need to consider us when making decisions that affect everyone."

"I don't," I tell her. "You guys are getting a free trip, all expenses paid. Why does one more night matter? I'm not going to waste thirty minutes to check in with you guys on a decision that needs to be made and benefits all parties."

Her green eyes narrow. "*This* is why I avoid you." She starts to turn, but I reach for her hand.

"Because I made a decision without asking you?"

"Because you assume you know everything, and you don't."

"I'm right about this. Just like I'm right about the fact you wanted me in that club. You wanted me, and you didn't care who watched. I might be a bossy son of a bitch, but you're so stubborn you refuse to admit I'm right."

She shakes her head. "You're wrong. I tolerate you for Cooper. That's it. That's all this is. That's all it will ever be."

12

CHLOE

Reasons I hate Tyler Banks:

- He's a bossy asshole
- He's a REALLY bossy asshole
- He drives like a maniac when angry
- The infuriating way he smiles like he knows I want to punch him but can't because it would drag Cooper into this mess
- He's begun walking around the hotel like a nudist, refusing to put on a shirt

"Chloe, are you ready?" Vanessa enters our shared room wearing shorts and a sports bra because apparently not wearing a shirt is becoming contagious.

I set down my notebook filled with random lists. "How far is this hike?"

"Come on. It will be fun."

We're in Scottsdale, Arizona after having spent one night in a small town, in a hotel that was still fancier than most, and a single night and half day in Santa Fe, New Mexico, where I convinced Cooper and Nessie to go to a history museum with me.

This is our first stop with a full day and two nights in the same city since New Orleans, and I'm strangely relieved to have the consistency. While living out of a suitcase isn't something I necessarily mind, there's some comfort in recalling where my phone charger is plugged in and where the light switches are.

Tyler offered us—and by us, I mean Nessie because he hasn't spoken to me since our altercation in Austin—spa passes, but with all the eating we've done over the past week, Nessie insisted we spend our morning hiking.

Cooper is meeting a friend and one of their teammates, Jackson, leaving it to be just Nessie and me for the first time in a week, so despite the fact being outside in the intense heat of the Arizona desert sounds less than ideal, I agreed, even with the four thirty wakeup time she insisted we had.

"Did you put on sunscreen?"

Nessie rolls her eyes. "It's still dark out."

I toss the bottle of sunscreen into my bag and an extra T-shirt, along with several bottles of water and some granola bars I picked up in Odessa when we were across the street from a convenience store.

We silently head out to the living room, and both of us jump when Tyler flips on the lights. "Did you feel a cold rush followed by a strange warmth?"

Nessie laughs. "You startled us. What are you doing up?"

Again, he's shirtless, only wearing a pair of black mesh shorts and tennis shoes. I notice he wears ankle socks, and for some reason, I like this more than I should because it means he doesn't chase every trend.

I quickly avert my gaze when he catches me staring too long at the tattoo that wraps around his shoulder. "I'm going down to the gym. Where are you two sneaking off to?"

"We're going to hike Camelback Mountain," Nessie tells him.

He nods. "Good idea to get an early start. It's going to be hot today. Did you arrange a ride with the front desk already?"

"We were just going to call a Lyft."

He frowns. "Go to the valet desk. I'll let them know you're on your way down. They'll get you over there and leave you a card so you can call when you're ready to be picked up."

"You're the best," she says. "Thank you!" She takes my hand and pulls me toward the elevator that leads us to the lobby.

And just like he told us there would be, a driver is waiting to take us.

"ARE you sure it's safe to hike? It's not even light yet." I turn on the flashlight on my phone as more experienced hikers pass us with their bags and headlamps.

"We just have to stay on the path."

"We don't have to worry about it being steep or coyotes or anything?"

Nessie shakes her head. "There are too many people for coyotes, and everything I read said the path is well marked." She fans herself. "But it's already hot. How can it be so hot? The sun isn't even up."

We head forward on the trail where warning signs advise us it's a double black diamond. "I'm going to like you by the end of this, right?"

Nessie laughs. "Come on."

We start on built-in stairs, pointing out cacti and the rock formations that offer an entirely different beauty than what we're used to in Florida and Washington.

"How are things going with Coop?" I ask.

She beams. It's an automatic response that makes me stumble, the toe of my tennis shoe catching on the stair.

"You okay?" another hiker asks.

I nod. "Yeah, just clumsy."

He appears to be twice our age, sporting a full set of hiking gear. "You guys should be careful. This isn't an easy hike."

I want to tell him my tripping had nothing to do with the trail and everything to do with the smile my sister gave at the mere mention of Cooper's name. "Thanks," I tell him. "We'll be safe."

He looks reluctant but nods as he continues past us.

"You really like him, don't you?"

Nessie grins, almost sheepishly this time, like she's embarrassed over the fact. "I always thought Cooper was too smart for me, you know?"

I shake my head because Nessie has always done well at school, she just doesn't have much interest in computers and new technology like Coop does. "Are you kidding? He forgot his hat in New Orleans, his sunglasses in Austin, and his freaking phone charger in Odessa. It's like he's leaving a trail of breadcrumbs."

Nessie giggles. "You know what I mean. And Coop's nice and sweet and funny, but it's kind of scary because he already knows all my worst sides and habits, and he's still interested in me. It's a little unnerving." The stairs taper off, and we hike the moderate incline. "I'm trying to take things slow and make sure we do this right, but it's kind of weird because we know each other so well. It's not like we need the customary intro period to learn if the other person is a serial killer or hates Christmas or something else equally tragic, you know?"

"He likes you a lot," I tell her, and rather than saying it in a way of warning to ensure she handles his feelings with care, I say it as an assurance. "You guys should go to dinner or something together."

"You wouldn't mind?"

I shake my head. "I'll order room service and watch a movie and pretend I'm Kevin McCallister from *Home Alone.*"

Nessie laughs. "You're sure?"

"Totally."

"How are you doing with the whole Ricky thing?"

"Ricky who?" I ask.

She looks at me and right through me, just like she's always been able to do. Maybe it's because people are right, and twins do have a shared connection, or maybe it's because we've been so close our entire life, but Nessie's always been able to see through all the bullshit and nonchalance I use to disguise the ugly truth. "Are you going to tell Cooper?"

I shake my head. "Cooper never liked him, and it's over." I shrug. "Besides, it's not really like there's anything to say or do."

"Guys should come with a full report," she says. "Like a resume. Something that states their strengths and weaknesses. His would say charming but a complete toad."

"You want Cooper's full report?"

She laughs easily, already knowing most of it.

The trail inclines and steals my breath as I look up at what appears nothing like a hiking path and more like a steep, dirt hill with a long metal rail halfway up where the trail becomes steeper, which most hikers are gripping to hoist themselves forward.

"I'm so eating dessert tonight," I tell her.

Nessie grins, moving beside me as we climb what feels like a giant rock with some loose red dirt to make it slightly slick.

"Oh, we're adding whipped cream to our desserts," Nessie says when we reach the top and face another incline with another long metal handrail going down the middle, only now, the trail is covered in large, misshapen rocks.

"But look," I say, turning toward the ledge where the sun is slowly beginning to rise, skating across the city and turning the sky into several brilliant shades that the red rock beneath us compliments so beautifully.

We share a bottle of water as we appreciate the view and then tuck the empty bottle back into my bag and continue, our breaths growing labored as it gets even warmer. When we get to the top of the hill, we step to the side to allow others to continue up to the summit. We're not at the top yet, but still, we whoop, feeling accomplished and proud as we stop for a rest and visit with an older couple who are local to the area and tell us all the best places to go. The woman teaches us about the creosote bushes that she explains are native to the Southwest and smell like rain when you rub the leaves together. It's such a small and simple beauty and yet thoroughly captivating as we laugh and rub the plant again to ensure it wasn't our imaginations.

The path flattens out, less steep, and is peppered with beautiful yellow flowers, cacti, and other small bits of color, the sky blooming a brighter shade of blue that contrasts against the rock and makes the sky a more vibrant color.

"Is that a joke?" Nessie asks, coming to a stop. I look around, realizing the trail sign points toward a pile of boulders and large rocks, sans the metal rail this time. "Don't snakes and scorpions hang out on the rocks?"

"Probably, but it won't be the first snake we've kissed."

She laughs, putting both hands on her hips as she looks toward the trail.

"Come on. We'll order pasta *and* dessert."

"And garlic bread," she says, following me toward the rocks.

"*Extra* garlic bread."

With each rock, we add a new thing to our dinner menu until we've named practically every entrée, side dish, and dessert when we finally reach the summit.

We find a flat rock and circle it twice to ensure there are no snakes before we climb on top of it and take a seat, our feet dangling over the edge as we admire the city and view of the mountain. It feels amazing, and for a few minutes, I forget about school and our trip and Cooper, and I enjoy these moments with Nessie as we laugh and celebrate our feat.

"IT's STILL EARLY," Nessie says as we come down the Cholla trail on the other side of the mountain, which feels like a house cat compared to the lion we climbed on our way up to the summit. The descent takes us a mere thirty minutes in comparison to the two-hour trek up. "Cooper said he and Ty wouldn't be back until after five. There's another area we could hike. Or we could go back and cash in the spa treatments Tyler offered?"

My pride—which doesn't want to take a thing from Tyler at this point—leans heavily toward another hike, but as the sun climbs higher into the sky, the idea of a spa sounds heavenly. "I'm game for whatever," I tell her, unwilling to make the decision.

Nessie leans against a rock and pulls out her phone. "I didn't charge my phone last night, and it must have lost reception because I've got like two percent battery," she says, unlocking her phone. "I'm going to call the driver and have him bring us to the Tom's Thumb trail, and then we can head back for lunch and still sneak in a massage before they're back."

THE DRIVER ARRIVES with bagged lunches and extra water bottles, courtesy of Tyler, and though I want to refuse it all and send it back with him, I'm starving and thirsty and appreciate the care package.

"If this is carb-free, I'm going to be really sad," Nessie says, digging into one of the paper bags as we take a seat at a picnic table.

Inside each bag is a club sandwich, a banana, an orange, some energy bars, and two giant chocolate chip cookies.

"Sorry, Coop. I'm using my last one percent to text Tyler and say thank you," Vanessa narrates her action, while I dig into my sandwich, practically moaning as the smoked turkey and salted bacon mix with the juicy tomatoes and rich, creamy wedges of avocado. "Oh my gosh. Give me a bite," she says.

I shake my head. "You have your own."

"But I'm too weak to open it. I'm starving. One bite."

I laugh as I shake my head and hand her the sandwich.

"Oh my gosh," she says with a mouthful of sandwich, her eyes rolling back in her head. "So good. *So good.*"

I set my sandwich down and unwrap hers to ensure she can't pull the same excuse before returning to mine.

We pack the rest into my backpack to snack on as we go, apply a thick layer of sunscreen, and head out into the desert.

"ARE you sure we didn't come from that way?" Nessie asks, pointing away from me.

I shake my head. "I have no idea. It all looks the same." The trail itself stopped being blatant once we passed the 'thumb' rock, and since that point, it's just been rocks and sand and the occasional half-mile marker. It's been hours since we passed one of those markers or any other hikers, which has us dancing around the realization that we're lost.

"Okay. We are two smart, capable women. We just have to pay attention, and we can figure this out. Footsteps, a trail marker, something." Nessie sweeps her attention both ways, hoping to find something over the same expanse we've searched dozens of times already. "How many acres do you think this place is? I mean, do we just keep walking straight until we reach something? Or will that take us days?"

I shake my head. "It would depend on which way we go. I don't know where we are or where we started." I shake my head again as Nessie looks at me.

"But you can figure out which way we're facing?"

"An approximation, maybe? But I don't know if it will help. I don't know which direction we need to go."

Nessie scrubs her palms against her eyes. "I'm so hot."

I lower my bag, reaching for another bottle of water that I pass to her. "You need to drink."

She takes it, drinking a quarter of the bottle in one sip. "Are you sure your phone's not in your bag? You checked all the pockets?"

I check it again, though I've already emptied the contents a handful of times. "I took it out in the car to charge. It has to be in there."

Nessie drops her head back with defeat. "It's okay. It's getting darker. Cooper will get back soon, and when he realizes we're gone, he'll figure it out, right?"

I nod, feeling hopeful and doubtful all at the same time, and then stop. "Oh my goodness."

Nessie freezes. "What?" she whispers.

"Don't move."

"Chloe."

"Don't move," I tell her again.

She takes a step as she moves to look behind her. "If you're pulling a prank..."

I grab her arm. "Stop moving."

She goes still, her eyes meeting mine. "What is it? Is it a snake?"

I swallow, knowing snakes are Nessie's greatest fear. "A small one," I lie.

Her nostrils flare, and her shoulders go rigid. "What kind of a snake?"

I already know it doesn't matter. Nessie is terrified of all snakes, and I have no idea how to tell them apart. "I'm going to hand you my bag, and you're going to hold it in front of you, and we're going to move backward really slowly."

"Chloe, is it a rattlesnake?"

"It doesn't matter. Everything's going to be fine. You just have to move slowly, okay?"

She whimpers. "I hate snakes."

"I know. But I'm here." I slowly shift my bag so she can take it, the slight movement making the snake coil, and then it releases the warning as its tail shakes.

"Oh, God," Nessie says, gripping my bag with her shaking hands and slowly moving it to cover her legs.

"Okay. Okay. Good. We've got this." I place a hand on her hip and take a step back as I seek out any abnormalities that might be another snake, since this one had camouflaged itself so easily we nearly stepped on it.

"It's hissing," Nessie says, shuddering as she reaches back for me.

"I know. Just keep going."

"Chloe, he looks pissed."

"He's probably just as scared as we are."

"Doubtful." She squeals as it starts to shake its tail again.

We're about twenty feet away when I pull her a bit closer. "Okay, okay." I hold her hand so tight my fingers ache. "We need to pay attention. Everything in the freaking desert is deadly."

"Too soon," she says, her gaze still focused on the snake that's now a good thirty feet from us and still rattling its tail.

"Let's go this way," I say.

"You think it leads to the trail?"

"I have no idea, but the signs said to avoid plants because that's where most snakes hide, and this way is pretty much just sand."

"Should I mention now that there's a hunting reserve near here?" She hands me my bag and holds my hand as we comb over the ground.

"At least we're not in a cemetery near vampires and ghosts."

Nessie chuckles. "I don't know. Those ghosts don't seem so scary right now."

I cut my eyes to her. "They were, you're just forgetting. I was willing to hold Tyler's hand the whole freaking time. I'd say they were pretty damn scary."

Nessie giggles so hard she pauses to gain her breath. "Do you really hate him?"

"Sometimes," I admit.

She snickers again. "I think it's because you guys are attracted to each other."

"Oh, no." I shake my head, temporarily forgetting to look at where we're going because, like everything that revolves around Tyler, it takes too much of my attention.

"You don't have to like him to think he's hot."

I shake my head. "Still not happening."

"If he wasn't best friends with Cooper, would you like him?"

I consider her question for too long, making her laugh again. "Maybe if I could duct tape his mouth shut."

Nessie drops her head back, giggling so loud the sound becomes cathartic, and before long, I join in.

"SHIT!" Nessie yells, jumping up and down.

We've been wandering for what feels like days. The sun is beginning to set, which gives me hope that Cooper will soon start to question our whereabouts and start looking for us. But it's also concerning as I try to recall all the nocturnal desert animals we learned about while visiting the natural science museum in Austin. I have no idea how Cooper will find us even if he knows where to start looking. And if we know he's looking, do we stop and wait for him? Do we keep walking? Is it safe to walk at night in the desert?

Nessie jumps again.

"What?" I ask, looking around. "What?" I ask again, more concerned when she continues screaming and jumping.

She points at a rock where a giant tarantula sits, spanning far larger than any spider should. "Oh, God," I cry as goosebumps reign across my skin. We back up, and that's when I see it: a trail marker.

"Oh, thank goodness!" Nessie says as I point it out. She wraps her arms around me. "We did it!"

I laugh, half delirious with the realization we had a hard enough time sticking to the path in the light, and the sun has almost set, and the signs warned us there would be more snakes once it started to get dark.

"Which way do you think we should go?" she asks.

I swing my attention in both directions, hoping something will magically point us in the right direction.

"Wait, do you hear that?" I ask.

Nessie moves closer to me, and I hear it again, the faint sound of a voice yelling.

"Please be Cooper," Nessie says, gripping my hand and pulling me to the left toward the direction of the voice.

"Watch for snakes," I remind her as we hurry along what we hope is the path.

"Vanessa! Chloe!" the person yells.

"Cooper!" we yell back.

"Watch, it's going to be like a forest ranger. We're going to get ticketed for getting lost in the desert, and we're never going to hear the end of it," Nessie says. "If it's not Cooper, and we get out of here, let's never tell him."

"If Cooper isn't looking for us, he's getting coal for Christmas."

As if on cue, we hear our names being yelled again. "It's him," Nessie says, putting her hands on both sides of her mouth as she calls out his name again.

"Chloe!" Cooper hollers, coming into view.

"Cooper!" we practically scream.

A second figure joins Cooper's, and my relief is so instantaneous, I nearly cry.

Vanessa releases my hand and starts running, and like some cheesy scene out of a movie, Cooper catches her, and they kiss, and it's so perfect and romantic and ridiculous that I can't tear my eyes away for a solid minute.

"What in the hell have you guys been doing?" Tyler's words are a slap of accusation. "Where were you?"

I kind of want to punch him in the throat, but I'm so freaking glad I don't have to spend the night out here that I also kind of want to hug him. Instead, I laugh. I laugh so hard I probably sound crazy, and still, I laugh harder.

"Fucking hell," he says, shaking his head.

13

TYLER

"Six snakes," Vanessa corrects Chloe as she recounts their day in the desert. "A tarantula, a few enormous centipedes, and some black flying bug that we didn't get close enough to see if it played nice."

"Jesus," Cooper says. "We had no idea where you guys were. We found Chloe's phone in the back of the car, but your phone kept going directly to voicemail."

"Dead battery," Nessie admits.

"We didn't know if you guys were lost or hurt or if you were..." Cooper releases a deep breath, refusing to say the word abducted—the suggestion from the head of security at our hotel when we discussed the situation with him, and he voiced his concerns about human trafficking and kidnappings.

Vanessa stops speaking, sensing the seriousness in Cooper's tone. "Snake," she finally says, pointing in the distance.

"I'm so over this hike," Chloe says, taking another drink from the water bottle I handed her. I scan over her a third time.

"It's moving," Cooper says. "It's just crossing the trail."

Chloe looks at me, likely feeling my stare. The challenge is missing from her gaze. She looks exhausted, and try as I might, I can't get the idea of her heart condition out of my thoughts, even though a cardiologist assured me her prognosis would be excellent and that later complications would be incredibly rare. I didn't want to hear rare—I wanted to hear impossible. "Do you need to sit down for a few minutes?"

One side of her lips curl. "Is this one of those situations where you don't have to be faster than the bear, just faster than your friend?"

Cooper chuckles.

Knobhead.

"It's late. You guys have been out all day," I say.

"I'm okay," she says. "I might need like four showers to get all this sand out of my hair, though."

"And food. You guys should have seen our first hike. We earned pasta, dessert, and double garlic bread all before noon," Vanessa chimes in. "I don't even know how that's a trail, to be honest. Half of it was giant rocks we had to climb over, and the other half was a very steep and uneven hill with a railing."

"Now you admit it," Chloe says.

Vanessa laughs. "We should have gone to the spa."

Chloe smiles. "But we decided the ghost tour was still scarier."

Vanessa shakes her head. "No way. That snake was out for blood."

"We don't have much longer," Cooper says. "Probably another half mile or so, and then you guys can sleep in the car tomorrow on our way to Vegas."

A noise several kilometers from us has us all pausing for a second, but we continue until we finally hit the parking lot when we can't find anything with our flashlights.

"Do you have a towel or something in the trunk?" Chloe asks, stomping her feet. "We're filthy." She brushes at her legs.

"I don't give a single fuck about the car getting dirty."

Vanessa stops, wrapping her arms around me and taking me by surprise. "Thank you for coming out here and finding us." She releases me and slides into the back where Cooper gets in beside her.

Chloe watches their doors close, and I move closer to her, brushing a streak of dirt that crosses her cheek with my thumb. "This has been a really long day. I just need you to get in the car so it can finally be over."

She closes her eyes for a brief second, and when she looks at me again, I see it—recognize that confusion and muddled hope. "Thank you," she says.

I swallow before taking what feels like my first breath in several hours. "I'm still an arse."

"Oh, I know." She flashes a smile, and then turns, getting into the passenger side of my car.

"WE'RE LIKE PIGPEN," Vanessa says. "Leaving a trail of dirt behind us."

Chloe scrunches her nose. "At least the lobby was pretty empty."

"Seriously. It gave a whole new meaning to the walk of shame."

Chloe chuckles as she toes off her shoes in the entryway. "You want to shower first?"

"Use my shower," I tell her.

She cuts her eyes to me like I've just invited her into my bed.

"I'm not going to spy on you."

Vanessa laughs, but doubt has Chloe's eyebrows hitching.

"Come on," I tell her.

"I need my shower bag," she protests.

I shake my head. "It's stocked with any amenity you could need."

She bites the inside of her lip like she does when she's nervous—it's one of the many details of Chloe Robinson I've learned and memorized in the past eight days without thought or choice.

We pass her bedroom door and reach the master suite. I push the door open, the motion-sensing lights instantly illuminate the long rectangular room and wall of windows that render Chloe speechless. It's twice the size of the bedroom they're sharing, with a full sitting area and king-size bed.

"Wait until you see the bathroom," I tell her.

We step into the en suite, and her eyes dance around the space before finally landing on me.

"Truth or dare?" I ask her.

Her eyes flare with surprise, and then she blinks several times. I know it's not a fair request—she's exhausted and dehydrated and likely has heatstroke.

"Can I hear both before I decide?"

"No."

She holds her breath for several seconds before releasing it slowly. "Truth."

I was hoping for dare, but this works, too.

"Why do you avoid me?"

"I already told you why."

I shake my head. "You've avoided me since before you even knew me."

"Dare," she whispers.

"You know what I'm going to dare you to do."

Her skin is at least two shades darker than when she left this morning, streaked with dirt and sand that I imagine myself rubbing from her body.

"Who was she?"

My thoughts complete a full somersault, and I shake my head, struggling to think of anything but Chloe naked. "Who?"

"The girl in New Orleans."

I shake my head again. "Who?"

"Never mind. It doesn't matter. It's none of my business." Something snaps in her attention, the edge of vulnerability she had edged toward now far in the distance. "I avoid you because you overwhelm me. Because I like rules. Because you're Cooper's best friend and I'd never make him choose. Because I know the score with you—know I would be a blip on your radar." She stares at me, brazen, and completely closed off.

My thoughts churn between each of her points that likely reveal far more than she intended—proves she's thought of me. *Thinks* of me. She tries to barricade herself from those thoughts and me, and right now, I'm on the other side of that door, and I can tell she senses it as she works to decide if it's me or her insecurities who has her thoughts balanced on the ledge.

She starts to turn away and I lift my arm, my palm connecting with the wall, caging her in. That spark lights in her green eyes as she looks at me, panic and lust and desire burning so fucking bright I can feel the heat. "You changed and said dare."

Chloe's eyes narrow.

"I answered your question."

"With half-truths."

She raises her chin, confirming I'm right.

"Do you know what I'm going to dare you to do?"

She rolls her eyes and sighs before gritting her teeth. "Tyler, will you kiss me?" She couldn't sound more petulant if she tried.

I grin, feeding her anger. "I was just going to dare you to smile."

Her frown deepens. "I'm taking a shower. Watch if you want. I don't care. You'll do whatever you want anyways." She twists away from me, shoving at my arm. I move, allowing her space, realizing too late that she'd cracked the door with her half admission and has slammed it shut as she rips her tank top off, the red dirt from the desert, staining the gray fabric. She pulls open the shower door, staring at the multiple levers for several seconds before her shoulders sink.

I step behind her, placing a hand on the bare skin of her waist, and turn the shower on, lowering the heat from the scalding temperature I prefer. "The amenities are under the counter, and there's a robe on the back of the door," I tell her. And with a single look, she guts me, her eyes glassy and jaw clenched with pride.

"Chloe," I begin.

But she shakes her head. "It's been a really long day. Can you just give me some space?"

I remain in place, wanting to say no, wishing to apologize, needing to know if she's okay. I think of a thousand things I should have asked her and offered.

"Please?"

I close the bathroom door on my way out and drop my head against it as I pull in a long breath, willing myself not to go back in there and beg for forgiveness because I went too far this time, crossed a barrier when she was her weakest like a selfish fucking bastard.

In the hallway, I run into Vanessa, a towel wrapped around her hair as she dons a pair of pajamas that reveals her sunburn. "Vanessa, I messed up."

She stops, tilting her chin to the side as though working to process my words and the implications. "I was a dick, I..." I shake my head. "Can you go talk to her? Make sure she's okay."

Vanessa glances in the direction of my door and then at me. "Once. I'll only clean up your mess once." She disappears into my room, closing the door behind her.

Cooper's in the living room, his hands gripping both sides of his head. "Man. What a crazy-ass day. Thank you. Thank you for everything. I know you sounded the alarm and had a lot of people and groups going into motion to find them, and I can't tell you how much I appreciate it. I mean, I care about Vanessa, shit, I, well, you know ... and Chloe..." He licks his lips and diverts his gaze as the weight of his words become too much. "I don't know what I would have done if something had happened to them. Either of them."

His appreciation is like a dull knife twisting in my stomach.

"Order room service. Anything you guys want. Order it all. I've got to get a little more work done so we can get out of here before noon tomorrow."

He grins. "Vegas, baby!"

I nod, trying to hide the cynicism in my smile. "I'll be up late." I grab my gym bag as I head for the door.

I SPEND the first two hours at the gym, trying to run from my thoughts, and when that doesn't work, I aim for physical exhaustion as I hit the weights.

Finally fatigued, I shower and find an empty conference room to hide out in. The Scottsdale location is one of the few we're staying at that isn't having any issues. Everything about this location is seamless perfection, so rather than searching for holes, I'm looking for any anomalies between here and the past couple of hotels in an attempt to compare them.

SPREADSHEETS ARE BURNED to the back of my eyelids when I make it back up to the suite, finally checking my phone because I have no doubt my dad heard about my red alert and order to move all hotel security to find Chloe and Vanessa this afternoon. But the first message is from Cooper from two hours ago, sending me a heads up that Chloe's asleep on the couch.

I toe off my trainers to silence my steps, slip my phone back into my pocket, and move to the couch where Chloe is asleep, hands tucked under her cheek, bare arms exposed.

I slide my hands under her, taking her weight and carrying her toward my room.

She opens her eyes as we pass through my bedroom door, and she startles at the sound of the latch clicking in place. "What are you doing?" she asks.

I have no fucking idea. "I won't touch you. I swear."

The lights are set to dim, all on a smart timer so only the ones along the bottom of the bed and beneath the desk stream a faint glow as I lay her on the king-size bed. I send Sid, the general manager back in Austin, a mental fuck off as I thank fuck for turndown service. I leave the throw across her and lift the blankets to cover her up to her shoulders.

"My bedroom's just down the hall," she says.

"Did you eat?"

She stares at me, hair curtained around her neck, teasing my pillow. I trace my finger across her temple, gently pushing more of her hair back in an attempt to make an easy excuse to touch her.

"I can't do this," she says, rolling to her back. She lifts both hands to cover her face.

I sit on the bed, kicking my legs out over the top of the covers, still wearing my jeans and a T-shirt from my family's hotel in Athens, Greece that I'd changed into post-workout. "She was no one," I admit. "I hired her because the GM called my father, accusing me of doing things I wasn't. So I needed to know who else might rat me out and piss him right off at the same time. It was only kissing, and it meant nothing, and I've fucking regretted it every second of every fucking day since it happened because you've been looking at me like you hate me ever since."

"I don't hate you," she says. "Sometimes I want to."

A quick chuckle bursts from my lips because the feeling is mutual. "I want you to hate me."

She tips her face toward me as the lights fade and turn off. "Why?"

"It would make everything so much simpler."

I try to read her expression in the darkened room, realizing that although I've come a long way, I'm still barely adept at understanding her.

"I'm pretty sure we're breaking the rules," she says. "It's easier to hate you when you avoid me and act like a bitter asshole."

"I'm a bitter arsehole."

"Why did you bring me in here?"

"You were supposed to be back at two, three at the latest. We didn't find you until after nine. I need you to be here so I can breathe—so I can think. Because for the better part of today, I wasn't able to do either."

She stares at me, a dozen questions visible in her eyes, but they never make it to her lips. "I'm sorry. I really am."

I shake my head. "You don't need to apologize."

"We should have brought a map, and I should have made sure my phone was with me."

"I'm not looking for an apology."

"I know, but I'm still offering one."

"I don't want it."

Her brow creases. "What do you want?"

I stare at her, sick and tired of asking myself that very same question.

Several minutes pass before she looks away. "I'm not the only one who avoids contact," she says before she rolls over.

I quietly sigh, feeling the truth of her words inching into my chest. I ignore them and the thoughts they carry as the lights dim so the room is the color of pitch, and I can only see a faint outline of Chloe. "Are you sure you're okay?" I ask her.

The sheets rustle as she moves. "I'm just tired."

I nod into the darkness. "We should have taken you guys to the hospital. You probably need IVs."

"Just sleep," she mumbles. "Goodnight, Ty." The blankets shift again as she cuddles down in the bed.

The dim lights flicker back on as I stand and move to the closet to find a pair of sweatpants. After making the promise that I wouldn't touch her, they seem like a necessary barrier because sleeping naked, like I prefer, would absolutely turn me into a liar. I lose my T-shirt, brush my teeth, and silently cross to the bed again. Her eyes are closed, one hand curled into the comforter. I lie down behind her and close my eyes, taking long, deep breaths as my thoughts twist into a dozen situations that explore what I would have done had we not been able to find them. Where would we be? Who would I be paying off? Bribing?

"Your thoughts are too loud. Go to sleep," she says.

I hook a hand around her waist and haul her back against my chest. Her hair doesn't smell like oranges, and the floral scent on her skin is masked by whatever soap she used in my shower. My shower. I can't decide if I love or hate this.

"Fair warning, I kick while I sleep."

"You would." I slide my hand over her hair, pulling it to one side of her shoulder when it tickles my face. Then, I pretzel our legs and wrap my arm around her slender waist and close my eyes, finally able to fucking breathe.

14

CHLOE

I wake up to an empty bed. Tyler is gone, as are my senses, evidently.

I have no idea why I stayed. Maybe I can claim heatstroke or exhaustion or these beds that make me feel drugged, allowing me to sleep better than I've ever slept before.

I roll with the intent to get up and pause, catching the scent of his cologne on the pillow. It's spicy and sweet, mixed with the aromas of eucalyptus and mint, and because I'm alone, I bury my face in the pillow, reluctant to move again.

Nessie.

Cooper.

I sit up, searching for a clock to see how late it is. What will they think if they find out I slept in Tyler's room? Nothing good.

I flip off the covers and discover a silent living room and kitchen. Relief floods me as I make my way out to the patio. The railing is glass, and though it's another bright and sunny day, all I can see is a dark club and bright lights, bodies dancing, and Tyler's intense gaze as he accused me of wanting him in New Orleans.

I expel a deep breath and abandon the patio in search of coffee.

· · ·

"Hey, look. Another desert. You guys want to take a little hike?" Cooper teases from the back seat of the Tesla.

"Shut up," Nessie says, finishing another sports drink. "I don't look sunburned, but I feel sunburned," she says.

"Bloody hell, what do you expect?" Cooper asks, trying to impersonate Tyler, who pulls his chin back and looks at me as I laugh.

"I don't sound like that."

"Yeah, you do," Nessie says.

"Bloody hell," he says, shaking his head and making Nessie and me laugh even harder.

"Throw in a wanker or a shite," Coop says.

Tyler shakes his head again, flipping him off.

"What are we going to do tonight?" Nessie asks. "It's Saturday, and we're about to be in Vegas. We need plans."

"Are you guys sure you're up for going out?" Tyler looks in his rearview mirror at Nessie. For much of our three-hour drive, he's barely looked at me and hasn't addressed me directly once.

I hate how uncomfortable and self-conscious it makes me feel—how exposed and vulnerable and rejected I try to *avoid* feeling. I lean my head back, closing my eyes as Nessie assures him we're okay and want to go out.

I don't argue and say that I don't. Being out in public is better. I need to be around others because it allows me space from him.

"Where do you want to go?" Tyler asks her.

"A club. I've heard stories, and I want to see if they live up."

"Mr. Banks?" I open my eyes as an unfamiliar voice fills the car.

Tyler calls her Anika and asks her to get passes to a club with a foreign name and confirms a reservation and what time we expect to arrive in Vegas.

I spend the next two hours resting, sometimes in a full sleep and other times relaxed, keeping my eyes closed. I don't have the energy to join in the conversation, and everyone seems to accept that. I don't open my eyes until Nessie exclaims about the size of a hotel. We're on the Vegas Strip. I sit up to get a better view, taking in the sidewalks filled with people and the casinos that stretch on for blocks.

Cooper whistles under his breath. "This is crazy."

"I can't believe we're in Vegas!" Nessie says, gripping the back of my seat and leaning forward so her face is right behind my headrest. "Are you seeing this?"

Tyler turns into the Banks Hotel, the building so tall I can't see the top half. Everything is gold and white, a massive fountain in the front that we pause in front of when a group of pedestrians walks past us, dressed like they just walked off a fashion runway.

I glance at my sweatpants and Brighton tee. I'd chosen them based solely for comfort, knowing we'd change when we reached the hotel, and regret the decision nearly as much as not having packed more water for our hike yesterday. Pathetic. Shallow. I know.

Tyler slowly pulls forward and puts the car in park. Our doors are opened, the heat of the desert rushing to battle the air-conditioned interior.

"Welcome to Las Vegas, Ms. Robinson," the man says, offering me his hand.

"Thanks," I respond, still feeling awkward about these moments, though it occurs at each stop—except for our brief stay in Odessa, where we had to bring in our bags and check in at the front desk like everyone else. Aside from New Orleans, every other hotel we've stayed at Tyler scans something from his phone in the elevator when we arrive, and we find a stack of key cards and a welcome gift that is always in the form of food, usually fruit and desserts from their renowned restaurant that the area is known for.

Nessie is wearing a pair of blue denim shorts that are fashionably distressed and a blouse that falls off one shoulder. She meets me on the sidewalk, her hand sliding into mine as she silently checks in with me. *Are you okay?*

I nod to confirm I am, and she gives me a gentle smile. "I look like a bum," I tell her, watching more people exit the hotel who look at us with mild curiosity before looking away. Everyone staying here is loaded, unimpressed with Tyler's extravagant car.

"No one cares," Nessie assures me. "You should drink some more Gatorade."

I chuckle. "Just to see Tyler's expression when I tell him that I need to pee again."

She laughs outright because we had to ask him to pull over three times, extending our drive by over an hour.

We step into the lobby, the same sweet and rich perfume that is in the air of all Banks Hotels greets us, but unlike the others, this hotel was made for guests just as much as it was made for tourists not staying here, the lobby more opulent, with wider halls to accommodate more foot traffic. A series of fountains is in the middle of the lobby, with small seating areas arranged throughout the space.

"Let's go," Tyler says, leading us through the extravagant space. Cooper, Nessie, and I trail behind him, trying to take in each detail. The elevators are gold with a hammered finish that, like most things in the hotel, adds a sense of wealth and style. We pass them, stopping at the end where the elevator has a stone finish.

We get inside, and Tyler flashes his phone. "Welcome, Mr. Banks," a speaker in the elevator says as the doors slide shut.

"This is ridiculous," Coop says, shaking his head.

When the doors reopen at the top floor, the shock and amazement that hits me each time we walk into one of the rooms is even stronger as this room might be the most extravagant of them all, which is fitting, considering this is the city of lights, known for glamour and everything being over the top. I try to count the chandeliers, each dripping with beveled glass and opulence. As in New Orleans, there are multiple seating areas, each tied together with matching furniture and massive area rugs.

We pass all of them, then follow the wall of windows into the kitchen. It's small and gourmet—made for looks rather than use, I've realized. I'm sure most who can afford to stay in this room have little to no use for the kitchen unless they have a personal chef who travels with them, which strangely seems like a reality as we tread into our ninth day of living in this extravagant lifestyle.

"Champagne," Nessie says, stopping at the counter where the bottle sits in an ice bucket, surrounded by a small mountain of chocolate-dipped strawberries, a full charcuterie board, and a small bottle of whiskey.

"Damn, this looks good," Coop says, inspecting the charcuterie board that has started to become a staple with our last few stops.

"We should make a toast," Nessie says, reaching for the champagne. "Ty, do you have to work much, or do you have the weekend off?"

Tyler picks up the bottle of whiskey and twists it around in his hands. "I have to get some work in. This location has been under new management for six months, and during that time, half the staff has turned over."

I stare at him—it's difficult not to stare at Tyler—because the moody and bossy and confounding man is easily the hottest guy I've ever seen. All angular lines and chiseled features, perfectly mussed hair, and lips that are so distracting you can't help but stare when he talks and imagine what it would feel like to kiss him. Mix that with the devious glint in his eyes and the rewarding feeling of catching one of his rare smiles, and it makes it nearly impossible not to stare. I wonder if he's regretting last night—if that's why his gaze seems almost glacial today. Is it because he told me that girl meant nothing? Because he revealed a thin sliver about caring what I thought?

The thoughts compound and overwhelm me, making me feel suddenly exhausted all over again. I wish I had allotted some of our time yesterday in the desert to talk about this with Nessie. Maybe she would have some insight, or at the very least, an unbiased opinion.

Nessie screams as the top of the champagne pops as Cooper opens it. She follows it with laughter that Coop joins in, and for a second, I feel a sense of melancholy as my attention turns to them. I don't know how I didn't see that they were perfect for each other years ago. I'm envious of how determined they were to be together and how completely smitten they are. How quick they are to laugh and how both of them seem on a constant quest to bring the other one happiness.

Cooper fills four glasses with the bubbly liquid. "To Vanessa and her wild sense of adventure that thankfully led her back to me."

I grin, shifting my gaze to Nessie. "To Tyler, for hooking us up on the most epic adventure ever."

They turn to Ty, who's standing beside Nessie. "To being halfway done with this exhausting trip," he says, his expression once again impassive.

"Cheers to that," I mutter, tipping my glass back before it's my turn to say anything because at this point, I have nothing more to say.

. . .

NESSIE and I spend well over an hour getting ready in our mini spa of a bathroom decorated in teal and gold and looks so gaudy and yet extravagant enough that it somehow works. And when Nessie suggests I wear a black dress she bought for Vegas that is shorter and tighter and more revealing than anything I'd normally wear, I don't object. Tonight, I want to draw attention to myself and go back to ignoring and avoiding Tyler and not caring about why he's being hot or cold and worrying that I'm the cause.

Nessie is in a silver dress with a deep cowl neck that she rocks like it was made for her. Nerves dance through my belly at the prospect of seeing Tyler, but when we step into the living room, Cooper is sitting on the couch and watching the news. His eyes shift to us, and then he blinks and does a double take, a goofy grin curling his mouth.

"Wow. You look ... amazing." He stands, walking over to Nessie and pressing a kiss to her cheek. I remember when he used to look at new gaming and computer stuff with that same envious stare, and it makes my lips twitch with a smile as I redirect my attention to the mostly empty bottle of champagne, choosing to finish it straight from the bottle instead of pouring it into a glass.

"Are you guys ready?" he asks.

"Where's Ty?" Nessie looks around.

"He had to go do something for work. He said he'd meet us there."

"Poor guy. It's Saturday night," Vanessa says.

I reserve my right to roll my eyes as I set the empty bottle down and lead the way to the elevator.

We could take a car, but since this is our first time in Vegas, we opt to walk. Each casino is different, the architecture, the colors, the plants all competing to be the most extravagant. The Banks Hotel is non-gaming and vastly smaller than the ones we pass through, which all have row upon row of brightly colored slot machines and posters with half-naked men, contrasted with class and luxury displayed in the architecture and elaborate décor.

Nessie's hair is straight as pins while mine is in waves, but hair and dress differences aside, I still hear whispers of twins nearly always followed up with a crude remark that has me regretting the tiny dress and craving the comfort of my sweatpants again.

"They're gross. Ignore them," Nessie says, linking her arm with mine. "Don't let it get in your head. You're gorgeous and sexy, and you should own it tonight. Forget stupid boys, forget all your rules, and just have fun."

She's right, of course. My thoughts are still stuck on details, wondering what others think of me rather than on the here and now and having a good time. I square my shoulders, and when a guy turns to leer at us, I stare at him with a challenge that has him ducking his head.

I expel a deep breath, confidence radiating from me as we make the long walk to the hotel the club is in, and I don't waste another second thinking or caring about anyone else as we explore the casinos, talking about which ones we want to come back and explore more of tomorrow.

"Are we really going to cut the line again?" I ask.

Cooper grins. "Party like a rockstar."

Nessie laughs. "It's crazy to think in a couple of weeks we're going to be going back to work and school and eating Top Ramen again."

Before we can reply, the bouncer at the door looks at us. He's well over six feet and solid, likely intended to look like a threat, or at least make people question doing something stupid. His bald head shines with sweat as he greets us with a straight face. Cooper shows him his ID, and the bouncer looks over a shortlist on a clipboard and then nods, beckoning us forward. He places bright pink bracelets around our wrists. "My friend Angel is going to show you guys around. Please let us know if you need anything."

It's obvious that Tyler called ahead because there are three shots on the table when we reach the private VIP room: slippery nipples.

Cooper laughs, damning him before he takes the shot and downs it. "Let's go have fun."

I lose the rest of my thoughts to the music, the lick of alcohol still hot in my throat. The dance floor accepts us, swallowing us into the beats and writhing bodies. We're so close together, and the lights are constantly changing and flashing, making it nearly impossible to tell who I'm dancing with and whose hands run over my body. I hardly care as I try to erase my thoughts of this week, the memory of Tyler's cologne, and weight of his arm, the flash in his blue eyes whenever he smiles. I work to forget each detail—every new memory that I try to pry from my thoughts where they're working to burrow far deeper.

Nessie grips my arm, a smile splitting her face. She leans in, yelling over the noise of the club, "I need to pee."

Cooper stays on the floor as we use the buddy system to head to the restroom. The door is in sight when I see him: charcoal gray suit with a black dress shirt and attentive blue eyes. His intensity stops me in my tracks.

Nessie notes my hesitation and glances around, spotting him. I hate that I noticed him so quickly when she had to work to spot him. It's becoming a trend that I've been trying to ignore and avoid because it's becoming increasingly obvious.

"There's an attendant at the door," Nessie says. "I'll be right back." She waves to Tyler as he moves closer, and I'm torn between wishing she would stay and being grateful for her momentary absence as he finally looks at me.

He stops in front of me, dropping his dilated eyes to my mouth, and for a second, I'm so sure he's going to step forward and kiss me that I'd bet my private invitation to the planetarium next week on the fact. I've been on the receiving end of this look before, with the same guy. I've seen this exact brand of need and desire darkening his gaze when he invades my space and pushes every limit. I'm so confident he will kiss me that I tilt my chin up to receive him, regretting the instant that I do, because it's not a thought or a need that dictates the movement —it's him.

He releases a quiet noise that sounds so much like a scoff. I instantly pull back, humiliation already tinting my cheeks.

"Maybe next time you'll get your wish."

"I don't know what you're talking about," I tell him.

His eyes are sharp as they come down on me, a wolf smile. "You're a terrible liar." He turns on a heel and heads toward the stairs that lead to the VIP section, taking them two and three at a time.

Anger quickly follows embarrassment like a shot of liquor, contorting the memory and making everything sting as I wait for Nessie to return.

15

CHLOE

"I'm too sober, and it's too early," Nessie says when she comes into the kitchen where I'm nursing my second cup of coffee and talking to Cooper. "We're in Vegas. Where's our tiger? Why isn't anyone missing?"

Cooper laughs. "Morning, babe."

I try not to respond to the pet names they're beginning to use with each other, reminding myself this is my new normal.

She pouts. "I'm kind of serious."

"We have two days to make bad decisions. Don't get disappointed yet," I tell her as Tyler comes down the stairs, another hiatus on shirts as he scrubs a hand across his bare chest.

She points at me. "This is why you're my favorite sister."

I smile at her, but the joke falls flat as my confidence wanes, the memories of dancing and having an amazing night with Vanessa and Cooper forgotten as my brief interaction with Tyler comes to the forefront of my mind.

"We should get going so I can win my millions at the slot machines," Nessie says.

Cooper looks horrified, his brow knit and mouth parted. "You realize slots have your worst odds, right?"

She grins. "Of course, but they're fun."

Tyler shakes his head. "I'm going to a poker game this afternoon, but if you guys want to head out, we can go check out the Strip."

"You should take Chloe to play," Nessie says. "She's a poker shark."

Tyler looks at me, a teasing look that has me shaking my head. "That's only when my competitors include Dad and Coop," I tell her. "While you guys get ready, I'm going to head on down. There's a doughnut shop that's supposed to have a really long line, so they said to get there early." I grab my purse.

"Give me a minute. I'll go with you," Tyler says.

"It's okay. You don't have to rush."

"I just have to grab a shirt," he objects, already standing.

"That's a good idea. It's probably best to stay in pairs while we're here. There were some crazy people last night," Nessie says.

I want to remind her we've seen some shocking things in each city, but that doesn't really seem like it's going to help my argument, so instead, I finish the rest of my coffee and encourage her to hurry up and get ready.

Tyler returns within moments, a clean V-neck tee that fits him too well, acting like his smile—fully distracting. "Frozen hot chocolate and doughnuts," I remind Cooper and Nessie, realizing as I look between the two that they're likely going to be up here for far longer than I'd prefer doing things I don't want to think about.

In the elevator, Tyler stands too close, forcing me to move forward to gain some space and breathe air that doesn't smell of his cologne. Thankfully, his phone rings before he can make a joke about last night. This elevator is fancy but doesn't have a couch like the one in New Orleans. Instead, the space is open, filled with mirrors that create a strange optical illusion that makes me dizzy when I focus on any one spot for too long.

"I'm on my way down." He sighs as he hangs up. "We have a quick pit stop."

Relief tickles my nerves. "That's okay. You can go take care of whatever, and I'll just meet you later." I leave the when and where vague, hoping I don't have to see him again until much later.

The doors open, my relief spreading, and then his hand settles on my back like a flame, burning me. "It will only take a moment."

"Okay, well, then I'll see you in a few."

He pivots, standing in front of me and coming to a stop. "I'm not the possessive type, so don't confuse this with those arseholes who think they can tell a woman what to wear or do or where they can go, but if you think you're going to wander the Strip alone, you've clearly misunderstood my intentions. Half the people you're going to encounter will still be drunk from last night, and the other half will be nursing a loss of money and or pride. And as fucked up as it is that someone might look at you as a consolation prize, they will, and then I'd burn this fucking city to the ground to find the scumbag."

I'm caught off balance by his words, trying to understand what he's just told me and feeling fully dumbfounded.

"Good morning, Mr. Banks," a man wearing a navy blue suit greets us before I can contemplate a response. "Sorry for the interruption." He exudes confidence, his voice loud and clear, his stare unwavering. He reminds me of my mom's brother, Ryan, who's worked in sales his entire career.

Tyler shakes his head, a tight smile pulling at his lips and my attention. I've never seen this expression. It exudes the same level of contradiction and lies that my heart currently is. He shifts so he's beside me again, placing a hand on my lower back. "Chloe, this is Ken Avery. He works with the management company that oversees the hotels in the Southwestern and Eastern regions. Avery, this is my friend Chloe Robinson."

Appreciation dances in his gaze as he takes my hand, his handshake weak and cold. "Pleasure to meet you, Ms. Robinson."

"You as well." I discreetly rub my hand across the denim of my shorts.

"Perhaps we could sit and get some coffee?" Mr. Avery suggests, confusing me when his gaze remains on me as he poses the question.

Tyler's gaze quickly flashes to me, a sign of hesitation and annoyance. I can hear his thoughts, confirming I need to wait before heading to find doughnuts.

I plaster a fake smile on my face, hating that I'm giving in so easily. "I'll go back upstairs. Vanessa and Cooper should be ready soon."

"No. We'll make it fast." Tyler's hand at my waist strokes up my side several inches, then travels down the same span, making my heart beat erratically as we follow Mr. Avery across the lobby and past the front desk, where a woman in a cream suit smiles kindly at us and then grows brighter as she recognizes Tyler.

We stop at a door where Mr. Avery signals for someone to open it. Inside is a small room with a single round table and a row of windows along the top, too high to see out of.

"I heard you have concerns regarding some of the hotels we oversee," Mr. Avery says, smiling as he gestures to the table for Tyler and me to have a seat.

Tyler remains still, his hand stilling at my waist. Then he takes a breath, and his hand slips from my side, reaching for the chair in front of me. He pulls it out for me and takes the seat to my left.

Mr. Avery grins, revealing this is a posturing game—one for which I don't understand the rules or purpose. "I wish you had called and let me know you were going to be here. We could have gone golfing or out to dinner." Mr. Avery finally sits. "I'd like to discuss some of these questions you've been asking because you seem to be upsetting some people."

Tyler leans back in his chair and raises one hand to his jaw, where he runs his thumb along the underside of his chin, drawing my attention to the shadow from not having shaved this morning. It's deliciously distracting. "Upsetting people? If my questions are upsetting people, it just confirms I'm on the right path, wouldn't you agree?" He grins—all teeth.

Mr. Avery glances at me as my attention volleys to him. His smile is equally threatening but a much better lie. "Our company has a long-standing relationship with your father. He allows us autonomy to conduct business as we see fit, and we both benefit."

I wish I could see Tyler's expression because he's silent for too long, leaving me to guess what's going on. "Yet he was completely unaware that four of your locations were hemorrhaging money."

"Hemorrhaging?" Mr. Avery laughs. "This is a business. It has its ups and downs. The markets change, the needs change."

"Fantastic. Then get the information I've requested, and I'll gladly leave you to continue managing." Tyler pushes his chair back and stands, extending a hand to me.

I take it and follow him around the table, glancing at Mr. Avery as he remains in his seat, fingers steepled as he feigns a smile.

Tyler opens the door for me and only makes it a few steps before another man in a suit approaches him, asking for his signature on some documents he seems to be expecting. Tyler gives me an apologetic look. "It will take two minutes."

"It's okay," I assure him.

He follows the man behind the counter, their heads bowed as they go over the documents.

"Are you local, Ms. Robinson?" Mr. Avery asks, surprising me as my thoughts linger on Tyler.

I shake my head, confused by his question. "No."

His eyes deliberately scan the front of me, his gaze predatory as it returns to mine. "Here's my card. I'd love to hire you." He offers me the business card he'd been holding, clearly anticipating this conversation.

"Hire me?"

"Do you charge by the hour or day?"

My gaze narrows with realization, my shock so great I can't respond.

He reaches forward, tucking the card into my purse and turns, whistling as his dress shoes tap across the tiled lobby.

It's personal—toward Tyler, not me—I have no doubt. Still, my stomach sours, and for a moment I want to march over and show the evidence to Tyler before Mr. Avery leaves, but then doubt settles in my thoughts. Does Tyler hire prostitutes? I recall that woman he admitted to hiring in New Orleans. My blood drains from my face and goosebumps dance across my skin, making the chilled lobby feel arctic. I was mistaken for a prostitute!

Do I look like a prostitute?

I glance at my Chucks, denim shorts, and hot pink tee and feel myself spiraling with more doubt as Ricky's words continue to haunt me: *tease, uptight, prude.*

"Chloe?" I blink several times, pushing the thoughts to the back of my mind as Tyler stares at me, brows lowered with concern. "Are you okay?"

"Yeah," I answer too quickly.

"The doughnut shop is this way. Come on."

I follow him, my appetite nonexistent as we step out into the morning heat. Tyler swears, glancing skyward as his hand returns to my waist again.

Do I care if he's hired prostitutes?

Caring would insinuate it matters to me on a personal level.

His fingers gently stroke my back, and he points at one of the hotels across the street. "We need to be sure to stop in there. You'll love it, and they have a chocolate fountain that you guys will lose it over."

I glance at him, painfully aware of the pounding in my chest that happens whenever he's near is becoming louder and stronger when he reminds me that despite how long we've both worked to avoid each other—he's getting to know and understand me. I want to claim it's new, but that would just be another lie sewn into our history because it's been there since the first time I met him in downtown Seattle when Cooper and I thought he was late. Cooper apologized for his friend's tardiness as Tyler showed up ten minutes late, but when we left an hour later, a homeless person thanked him again for buying him groceries. That was my first encounter with the sour and sweet balance that is Tyler Banks, that I strive so hard to understand and evade because everything about him is as confounding as it is intriguing and terrifying, and I knew with the scores of girls who have been chasing him since the first day of school, anything between us would only ever lead to heartache.

"What's wrong?" he asks when I don't respond to his comment about the fountain from heaven.

I shake my head, busying myself with staring at the expansive lobby of another hotel. "Nothing."

"Are you sure?"

I nod again, plastering on a smile as his blue gaze flickers to mine. "Is everything okay with the hotels?" I ask in an attempt to divert, run, and hide from these thoughts and the fact he's sensing them.

His fingers at my waist constrict, and he tips his chin, indicating we need to turn the opposite direction. "They're fine, or rather, they will be. Something just isn't adding up."

"What's not adding up?"

We round the corner and find a line fifty people deep that makes Tyler frown. "I could call the concierge. They can get you every doughnut you want, and we wouldn't have to wait in line."

I scoff, moving to join the hungry patrons. "This is part of the experience. It will add to the satisfaction because you had to wait for them."

His eyes darken, and he licks his lips, and I feel that pounding in my chest that dares me to lean forward.

I clear my throat. "You don't trust the management company?"

Tyler breathes in deeply through his nose. "I don't know. Something's amiss. Take the New Orleans hotel, for instance. It's always been one of our busiest locations. It was sold out all three nights we were there, and yet the profit and loss statement doesn't reflect that."

"What could create that kind of discrepancy?"

He shakes his head. "That's what I'm trying to figure out. They're telling me it's upkeep costs and taxes, which," his eyes round, "are admittedly high—too high—but it still doesn't add up."

"You could talk to Nessie about it. She might have some ideas. She's an accounting major."

"I'm sure it's just something I'm overlooking." He stretches his shoulders, pulling them both back. "I've been around the hotels my entire life, learning the industry, but accounting was never something I spent time on. I preferred focusing on how our hotels interacted with the community and how we could give back while also remaining a sought-after experience."

"I didn't realize the hotels have been open since nineteen-thirty."

His chin tilts with surprise, and my cheeks flush with embarrassment. It sounds like I Googled him again.

"I read about the Banks Resort and Luxury Hotels while we were in New Orleans. There was a book in the living room."

He smiles, the usual glint of aversion missing. "My great grandad founded the company. He had no money, but he had a small farm, and so he paid men by giving their families food so they could build the first hotel, which was made exclusively for women and children as a shelter for the first decade. People could stay if they helped each other—watched the children, taught them to read, write, and cook."

"That's amazing."

He nods. "It was important to him to give back because he'd grown up as an orphan, and he wanted somewhere for them to stay that was safe. That site is still an orphanage, but my great granddad was so impressed with his crew that he hired them to build a second location and turned it into a hotel. He'd planned on selling it, and splitting the profits with his men and letting someone else run the hotel because he hadn't the first clue, but then people started staying there, and he began turning a profit. One of the guys who'd helped build the two locations suggested he keep it to employ more people, and he did, writing the dozen men and their families into the ownership with him."

"Do they still own it?"

Tyler shakes his head. "No, by the time he opened a second hotel, he was drowning in debt, and the others all jumped ship, assuming he'd sink."

"Wow."

He nods. "He gambled everything and nearly lost it all, but he made it."

"That's quite the history."

"It's a part of our family—a big part. I grew up in the hotels, and for a while, I thought maybe I wanted to do my own thing—be my own person—but in reality, the legacy of these hotels is what I want to continue. I want to be able to continue giving back and finding new ways our foundation can help families and children all around the world."

And just like that, Tyler Banks confirms what I've known all along and have worked to avoid: that aside from his broody and rough exterior, he's good in a way few are—all the way down to his soul.

16

TYLER

We've walked the full length of the Strip on one side, stopping in each casino along the way. We've played slots, watched the little free shows, and have posed in front of far too many landmarks by the time my patience thins beyond the point of ignoring it.

Chloe has been mostly quiet, making a point to walk ahead or behind me like she has for the past two years, but today something is different. There's a change in her, a lack of enthusiasm and humor and vibrancy that has me feeling restless.

"You guys want to go explore, and we'll meet up with you?" I extend the offer to Cooper, uncertain what his reaction will be.

"Are you sure? You won't ditch Chloe, right? I mean, don't tell her this, but I don't want her wandering around alone." He eyes another guy who openly checks her out.

"Yeah, no. I figured you and Vanessa might want some time to hang out. I can take Chloe to play poker with me."

"You're sure?" He doesn't voice it, but I can see the hesitancy in his gaze, questioning if this is a good idea because before this trip, Chloe and I have never spent time together without him.

"Positive."

He grins, turning back to the girls. "Hey, Vanessa. You want to go for a gondola ride?"

Her smile is enough of an answer, but she looks at Chloe, a silent question to ensure she's okay with it.

Chloe grins, a subtle nod of her head. "Go. Have fun."

Vanessa spins around, her smile impossibly wide as she and Coop head in the opposite direction.

"Come on," I say to Chloe.

"What?"

"I've got a poker game, and you're playing."

Shock has her lips parting. "I wasn't kidding. I'm not a poker player."

I shrug. "It's just for fun. It doesn't matter if you win or lose."

Her green eyes pinch with uncertainty. "I don't think we're going to play at the same tables."

Understanding dawns on me: money. "The game's on me. I already bought your seat."

She looks like my classmates when a professor announces there's going to be a pop quiz.

"Chloe, you went out into New Orleans alone, did a ghost hunt, and then got lost in the fucking desert. This is going to be a walk in the park. Hell, I'll throw in cake."

She scoffs. "I feel like I should apologize now for losing your money."

"That's all right because I plan on winning it back."

She rolls her eyes, making me smile. This is the side of her that's been missing all day. "Which casino are we going to?"

"We'll drive."

"Is it downtown? My dad said they have a cool light show."

I shake my head. "It's a private event."

Her green eyes narrow. "A private event? Do I want to know?"

"Probably not, but it's too late now."

WHEN WE PULL up to the industrial building once used to make and process sand, Chloe's looking at the place like the graveyard we toured on the ghost tour. "This is it?"

I nod.

"Is this a joke?" Reluctance tugs her lips into a frown.

Another car pulls up beside us; an Aston Martin.

"People get paranoid hosting high stakes games at their houses," I explain. "This place has been operating for several years, though. They're legit, and you're safe. I wouldn't bring you here if I didn't know that."

Two women get out of the Aston Martin and head toward the building.

Chloe reaches for the door handle. "Why does this feel like a really bad idea?"

We cross the parking lot, our shoes crunching against the gravel lot to a service lift that the women enter without hesitation. Chloe follows them, her gaze meeting mine when she turns around. There's that same gleam of excitement and nerves I'm starting to feel an addiction to in her eyes.

The lift sways as it hits the top floor, and Chloe remains back to allow the other two off first. I move toward her, my hand at her waist. "Stay next to me. If anyone asks, we're together. These guys think their money entitles them to everything and everyone."

Her steps falter, and her gaze becomes accusatory. "Like human trafficking level or whore level?"

I shake my head. "People are impressed by money. They don't have to buy women. Women fall for them because of what they can get. Everyone can be bought."

Her brow furrows. "That's not me. I'm not—"

"I know," I tell her, my grip at her waist tightening. "But you're an anomaly."

She shakes her head as I lead her out to the hallway. "Cooper isn't your friend because you have money."

I stop, turning to face her. "Why haven't you told him?"

She shifts her attention from looking around the building to me, her brows pinched. "Told him what?"

"What an arsehole I've been to you?"

Chloe's confidence wanes as she looks away, her lips rolling together.

"He'd hate me if he knew," I tell her.

Her green stare hits me like a brick, fast and hard. "I know. But it would hurt him. Coop's had enough loss in his life, and you not liking me shouldn't be a price he has to pay. Aside from me and Ness, he's never had many friends—people hold onto expectations even tighter than they hold on to memories. They think Cooper will be just like his dad, and he's had to live in that shadow forever. Brighton gave him a way out—*you* gave him a way out."

"You think I don't like you?"

A dozen emotions flash in her green eyes. "Sometimes." Her answer sounds like a question. "I never know what you're thinking."

"Tyler," Jericho greets me with a smile, interrupting our conversation. "Good to see you. It's been too long." He offers his hand.

I steal a look at Chloe, who takes a breath, a cross between relief and annoyance in her slightly crooked smile. My grip tightens at her waist before I release her to shake Jericho's hand. "Thanks for the invite."

He nods. "You're always welcome." His attention shifts to Chloe. "This is your plus one?" He extends his hand to her, and without waiting for a beat, she takes it.

"Chloe," she says, earning his full attention with the simple gesture. He hates demure women.

"Welcome, Chloe. Please, follow me."

We pass by a couple of men who are here as muscle in case someone tries to steal or cause problems. I tell Chloe this, making sure Jericho hears me because the reminder serves as much as an assurance as a threat. Jericho's games are private—invite only—and would come to a hard stop if rumors were to start about him or one of his guests strong-arming in any way.

Jericho nods. "My friends say I'm paranoid. I prefer the term careful." He smiles, walking us past Avery, his surprise visible as he does a second and third look in our direction. "If you'd like anything to drink, we have a full bar. Please, just let us know your preferences." He taps his wrist where a large gold watch sits. "We'll get started in five minutes."

We stop at the cashier, and I pull the envelope from my wallet. The woman opens it, counting through the stack of Benjamins. "Thank you, sir, ma'am." She nods. "We'll be drawing for seats in just a moment."

"I can't play," Chloe hisses as I place my hand on her back again and direct her toward the table where ten cards lie face down.

"Why?"

"You just gave her enough money to buy a car."

"It wouldn't be a very nice car."

Her eyes narrow. "I can't lose that much money."

"Yes, you can."

She shakes her head. "Ty, I literally can't. Go refund this. When you said poker, this is not what I had in mind."

Behind her, Avery starts to move toward us. "If you're scared, you're going to lose. It's when you play like it doesn't matter that you win."

Her brow knits. "That type of reverse psychology has never made any sense, for the record."

"It's five grand. We blew more than that at the club last night."

Her eyes grow round with alarm. "Are you serious?"

"Fear is crippling. If you're not afraid, you'll have fun, and hell, you might show us all up and end up being the shark."

She closes her eyes, a subtle shake of her head as she works to process my words.

"Ladies and gentlemen, please come select your seat," Jericho says.

"What does that mean?" Chloe asks.

"You're going to draw a card, and it's going to say where you sit. This way, it makes it fair. Hopefully, you're on my right."

"Are you ever not confident?"

I grin. "See, you knew being on my left would mean you'd lose. You understand more about poker than you're letting on."

"Fractionally."

My smile grows. "Draw your seat."

"Mr. Banks, Ms. Robinson, what a surprise," Avery says as he approaches us, drawing the card at the far end.

Chloe's back goes straight, her muscles tensing, drawing my attention to her face, which is set with a defensive edge, her lips flattened, eyes narrowed.

"Small world," I lie. I knew he would be here—it's the only reason I'm here because as much as I love to play poker, Texas hold 'em bores me, and it's the only game Jericho ever runs.

"Welcome, again," Jericho says. "If you'll all please take your seats, we'll get started. I want to introduce you all to Joseph, our dealer for tonight." A man with tire tracks tattooed down half his face nods, his hands folded in front of him.

I glance at our drawn cards and frown when I notice she's right beside Avery. "You okay sitting next to him?"

She looks at her seat at the table that's between Avery and a man wearing a cowboy hat and a tan suit. "Yeah." She slowly releases her breath as she moves toward the chair. I follow her, my intentions clear— I'm letting them all know she's here with me, which will hopefully prevent attempts to intimidate her if she's as novice of a player as she's claiming.

"Welcome, ladies and gentlemen," Joseph says as trays filled with chips are delivered to each of us. "Please feel welcome to place your drink orders at any point. If you need a waitress, please be sure to hold a finger up, and they'll get to you right away. Also, as a reminder, the blinds are twenty-five, fifty."

Chloe presses her lips together, but aside from that, she hides her shock far better than she did when she walked into the first Banks Resort.

The first deal begins, and rather than look at my cards, I briefly study everyone at the table, working to memorize their expressions because while everyone claims to have a poker face, few do. Minor details often reveal their relief or concern, and at least half of this crowd is here simply because they don't want to deal with being recognized at a casino, believing their money makes them a celebrity. The other half is here knowing these guys are easy money.

CHLOE FOLDS CONSISTENTLY for the first ninety minutes. I can tell she's nervous, see it in the way she's chewing on the inside of her cheek, and declines getting anything to drink. It's her turn to be on the button, giving her the best position because she's the last to act.

I fold pre-flop, and when a waitress walks by, I raise my hand to catch her attention. "Two Sazeracs." I point to Chloe to let the waitress know one goes to her.

Chloe's green eyes slide to me, and I nod.

"Call," she says.

"Was wonderin' if you were gonna play or just sit there and tease me." The guy in the tan suit laughs, taking a drink before he looks at me. "Don't worry, I know she's hands-off."

"She's fucking eyes and thoughts off, too," I tell him.

He chuckles. "Can't blame you." He leans back in his chair. "Call."

The driver from the Aston Martin with black painted eyelids chuckles as she calls.

Joseph flips over an ace of spades, eight of spades, and a ten of hearts.

"Check," Cowboy says.

"Check," the woman beside him echoes.

"Bet," the woman beside me with crazy long fingernails says, sliding a short stack of chips forward. If I had to place a bet on it, I'd say she's the best player here.

A man beside her, wearing a tired expression and more diamonds than sense, folds.

I take a drink as I watch Avery smile—all confidence and bullshit. He pushes a tall stack of chips forward.

Chloe takes a drink. "Call." She matches the bet.

Cowboy folds. Beside him, the woman with dark eyeshadow folds as well. Crazy-ass fingernail lady stares at Avery, running her nails silently over the felt table. "Call."

I turn to watch Joseph flip over an ace of diamonds on the turn.

The pair of aces on the table has everyone excited as we turn to crazy fingernails to hear her play. "Check," she says.

Avery grins, a sadistic glint in his eyes as he watches the unease in Chloe's expression and posture that has every one of my muscles growing strained with a restless tension. "Bet. Eight hundred." He counts out the chips and slides them forward.

Chloe blinks, staring at her cards for a long moment before setting them face down. "Call." She takes a drink.

The lady beside me shakes her head and folds.

I glance at the pot that's nearly three grand, hoping that if Chloe loses, she doesn't take it hard. The river comes as a seven of spades.

Chloe takes another drink, ignoring Avery as he attempts to make eye contact with her.

I clear my throat, ready to give him a similar warning that I gave to

Cowboy, but Chloe looks at me and shakes her head once, smiling as she does.

"Bet. Twelve hundred," Avery says.

Chloe licks her lips and finishes her drink with one pull. "All in."

Avery chuckles. "Call."

I drain my glass.

Chloe's eyes flare, and regret slides through my gut. The money is nothing, but convincing her of that fact is going to take effort if she doesn't win this hand.

Cowboy whistles. "This is gonna be good."

Avery drops his cards to the table: pocket eights, giving him a full house. Cowboy shouts out a cheer, and then Chloe flips her cards over, revealing pocket aces, giving her four of a fucking kind. My chest swells with excitement and pride and something that sits too fucking close to my damn heart as I look at her, noting the gentle smile her lips are curved into as Joseph announces her the winner.

WE PLAY FOR SIX HOURS, and though Chloe loses a few hands, she wins far more.

"So glad you came," Jericho says as we leave with our winnings. "Make sure you bring her again next time."

I give a polite nod, leading Chloe to the lift.

"How are you feeling?" I ask her.

Her green eyes meet mine, bright with the adrenaline from winning. "I think I'm shaking," she admits.

I laugh. "Now we have to go celebrate."

A smile spreads across her face. "That was crazy."

"You fucking wiped the floor."

"I got lucky," she says.

I scoff.

The lift doors part to a darkened parking lot. Two more security guys meet us, one of them following us to where we're parked.

"There's something slightly unsettling about needing someone to walk us to the car," she says as we fasten our seat belts.

"It's more to make Jericho look good rather than because there are any potential threats."

"Is it weird that Mr. Avery was here?" she asks. "I mean, what are the odds?"

I glance at her seconds before the dimmers fall and the interior of the Tesla goes dark. "I knew he'd be here."

She's silent.

"I have some suspicions, and I knew he liked to play because his ex-wife is now married to the GM of the San Francisco site. He hates Avery and is happy to tell me all about it, so, I asked Jericho to invite him."

"But you didn't even talk to him."

"I wanted to see how he played."

"Because knowing he sucked at poker told you something?"

I chuckle. "Watching him buy back in four times did."

"I'm not following."

"He lost twenty grand tonight and drank his way through a bottle of gin. He's either up to his eyeballs in debt or he's embezzling money."

17
———

CHLOE

"**E**mbezzling?" the word squeaks out of me.

"I can't prove anything yet, but remember what I said about the numbers not adding up for the New Orleans hotel?" His gaze shifts to mine as he stops at a red light. "I thought maybe I was missing something, but then when we got to Austin, I assumed that the hotel was doing shitty because the GM is a clown. But then I learned that they'd paid to do a bunch of remodeling and nothing had been done or was even scheduled. When I asked Sid about it, he didn't even know what I was talking about. So I contacted Vivian, our accountant at the San Francisco location because she's worked for the hotels forever, and my dad's always complained about her being paranoid and rigid—which means she's good—and I talked to her about the examples and hired her to start looking over the other sites.

"Before we got here, she sent me a whole list of concerns. Half of them are likely erroneous and loose bookkeeping, but there are too many inconsistencies and not enough answers from Avery. He keeps telling Vivian that he'll look into things and follow up, but he never does, or when he does, it's some bullshit answer that doesn't address the issue."

"So, you wanted to see how aggressively he'd gamble?"

"It wasn't guaranteed to tell me anything—it still doesn't. He might live far below his means and piss all his money away gambling. However, if he's doing this every week like the San Francisco GM claims, then something's amiss."

"What are you going to do?"

He glances at me. "Keep digging."

All of this is so far over my head that I can't quite wrap my mind around the implications of what this might mean as the lights of the city welcome us back to the Strip.

Tyler's phone rings through the speakers, silencing the music as Cooper's name is announced.

"Hey, Coop," Ty says.

"Where are you guys? You aren't still playing poker, are you?"

"We're on our way back to the hotel now. Where are you guys?"

"Ready to go party. Vanessa's words, not mine."

Ty chuckles. "Where do you want to go?"

I consider Tyler telling me we'd spent more than the five thousand last night at the club, likely due to the VIP lounge we didn't need.

"Vanessa says you guys can choose. She wants to do either a show or another club," Cooper tells him.

Ty glances at me. "What do you want to do?"

I shake my head, unable to make a choice when each might be associated with a matching price tag.

"We'll be there in ten, and we can figure it out," Ty says.

"Sounds good." Coop hangs up, and the music slowly grows louder again.

"You're wrong," Tyler says as we pull up to the hotel.

"About what?" I ask.

His blue eyes scan over my face, his features perfectly impassive. "About me not liking you. You've always treated me like I was a normal person, and I kept waiting, expecting you to do what everyone else does: treat me like I'm different, ask me for favors, laugh when I'm an arse—and you don't. You're probably the most real person I've ever met."

My door opens, and I ignore it and the person who's holding it open. I stare at Tyler, waiting for him to say something else, something more, because hope and reality have just gone to war in my head, and neither is willing to wave the white flag as they armor themselves with that warmth in my chest and his shiny words that wield sharp weapons.

He nods. "I know." He leans back and slides out of the car.

He knows?

He doesn't have a clue.

The war rages on, making my heart feel unsteady and my thoughts unstable as I accept the valet's hand. "Good evening, Ms. Robinson," the valet attendant says.

I smile out of obligation.

"Hey!" Nessie calls from inside the lobby, her smile radiating with energy and lust and the constant high that is palpable in this city. "How was it?"

"She was a shark," Tyler says. "Wiped the floor with everyone there."

"I didn't lose money," I clarify.

"She more than doubled it," Tyler says.

"Whoop!" Nessie high fives me. "I told you she was good." She looks back at Ty. "Did you decide what you want to do?"

"Let's hit a club tonight, and tomorrow we'll go see a show."

"I'm so on board for that," Nessie says.

"We don't have to do anything," I counter. "We could just walk through more casinos or hang out up in the room?"

Nessie shakes her head. "We're in Vegas. We're going out."

Tyler smirks. "Indeed. Hey, we'll meet you guys upstairs. I need to stop at the front desk and show Chloe something."

Nessie grins before spinning around and looping her arm with Cooper's, their steps too quick as they cross the lobby.

"I didn't tell you that shit to make you feel guilty for going out. I get deals, and it gives the hotel benefits when we spend money. Don't worry about it," Tyler says.

"I don't want you to think we're only here because you can get us into all these clubs and shows."

"If I did, I'd say so. Don't mistake my compliment for a warning or to mean something it doesn't."

Reality cries out a victory as his eyes meet mine, another expression that reveals so little that hope relinquishes its weapons.

. . .

NESSIE WHISTLES as I step out of our shared bathroom wearing one of the few dresses I packed. It's a gold cocktail dress that is simple in its design, but the way it glitters and hugs my curves has the more modest dress making me feel even sexier than last night's revealing number. "You're going to have to beat the guys away tonight."

"It's already past eleven," I tell her.

She shrugs. "In a month, we'll be at study groups at this time. Let's live it up."

I hold on to this reminder as we head out to the living room. Her sentiment feels like a truth I desperately needed to hear. This entire trip is a once-in-a-lifetime experience. We've spent most of our lives in Florida, so seeing these states and cities for the first time and experiencing as much as we can is something I pledged to do back when it was our plan with Meredith.

Tyler and Cooper are at the small bar in our suite, watching football clips on one of their phones. Tyler's blue gaze lifts to me as he's mid-sentence, his words trailing off as his eyes climb my legs to my chest and finally meet my stare. He blinks and then looks over me twice more before sliding his phone into his pocket.

Nessie nudges me with her elbow. "Told you."

"You guys look amazing," Cooper says.

My cheeks heat as I turn my attention to the safety of Nessie. She links her arm with mine like she knows I need her strength.

Cooper snaps his fingers, dancing in place to his created beat, breaking the tension that seems to swallow me as Tyler continues to stare at me.

Coop drapes an arm over my shoulders and Nessie's. "Let's go!" he says.

Regardless of it being a Sunday, the club is packed as we follow our hostess, yellow bands around our wrists, marking our VIP status. She leads us up a set of stairs where the suite looks out across the darkened club, a white couch stretching from one wall to the next, several tables spaced out along the stretch as smaller square tables line the railing, looking out onto the club with hardback chairs. Waiting on one of the tables are four shot glasses.

After my day with Tyler, I'm so desperate to silence my thoughts that

I barely hear the welcome the hostess offers as I eye the drinks and the club, making quick plans for the easiest way to get out of my head and off this battlefield: drink, find a hot guy, dance. And when the thoughts start to creep back in, take another drink, and by then, the others will likely be ready to go back to the hotel where I can climb into bed and gain a safe distance from these lingering stares and the lack of sarcasm that has kept Tyler and I separated and all the lines between us safely defined.

The hostess leaves, and the others converge around the drinks. I quickly follow suit, grabbing one of the shot glasses and not caring what it is as we lift our glasses with a silent toast and swallow the heat of the alcohol. It burns the back of my throat and my belly, promising to help the music speak louder and quiet my thoughts. Nessie flashes me a smile, her fingers tangling with mine. "Let's go. This place is amazing. The DJ is ridiculous."

"Have fun!" Cooper yells after us.

I glance back at him and catch as he gives me a subtle nod. It's his way of giving me time with Nessie after spending the afternoon with her. I smile, appreciating the time before I turn and follow her back down into the club.

The alcohol chases my inhibitions and straggling hopes that returned to the battlefield after Tyler's reaction. Nessie might be right. Maybe he's attracted to me, but that means little to nothing, and tonight I need it to mean less. Those thoughts take a backseat as we find a space on the dance floor, dancing and laughing as the world disappears into a familiar territory of Nessie and I having fun together.

Cooper finds us several songs later, and Nessie's face lights up. I wait to see Tyler behind him, but the crowd closes around Cooper, and when a guy in a deep blue shirt and New York accent asks me to dance, I don't look back.

"I need something to drink," New York yells after several more songs have played. "You want to get something?"

I glance toward Nessie and Cooper making out and back to New York. He's a good dancer, and his broad chest and quick smile have made it easy for me to forget what I was running from when we arrived. I nod. "Yeah."

He flashes another quick smile. "I'm Reggie," he says.

"Chloe," I respond.

He repeats my name. "It's nice to meet you, Chloe."

I smile, trying to remember how to flirt as his hand floats down my back, resting right above my ass. We weave through the crowd, heading to the bar, which is still overflowing with people.

"What would you like?" Reggie asks, his gaze skipping from me to the bartender as he tries to get his attention.

I shake my head because the only drink I can think about is Sazerac and slippery nipples.

Then Tyler appears, his blue eyes accusatory as he looks at Reggie's hand on my back and then me.

"I've got her," Tyler says, beckoning the same bartender Reggie's been working to catch for the past several minutes.

Reggie raises his eyebrows, his hand slipping from my back. I glance from him to Tyler, feeling irrationally angry by him interfering when I needed this—needed the attention of someone else who wanted to buy me a drink and spend time with me and chase the rest of these ghosts from my thoughts.

I sigh, moving past Tyler in the direction of the restrooms.

When I reach the hallway, a hand at my waist stops me. I turn, catching Tyler's eyes shining intensely back at me. "Are you trying to make me jealous?"

I laugh in spite of myself, fully aware he's about to lay open a new wound with the lashing of words, assuring me he doesn't get jealous, much less by me. The idea of making him jealous hadn't even crossed my mind because I knew it was impossible. My intention was purely selfish—an attempt to seek sanity, to forget him. I shake my head, not wanting to hear the verbal blows that will remind me I'm his favorite new head game.

His palms fall flush against the wall on either side of me, his mouth so close I smell that he was drinking a Sazerac. "What are you doing to me?" His gaze drops to my mouth, and the column of his throat moves slowly as he swallows. He leisurely lifts his gaze to meet mine, and there's a crease between his brows with the weight of a thought he doesn't like. "Why do you look at me like that?"

"Like what?"

"Like I'm redeemable."

I pull my chin back, surprise hitting me like a cold drink to the face as the hope in my chest slowly rises to its feet again. Of all the things I thought—*expected*—for him to say, this was not even within the same galaxy of possibilities.

"Dammit, Chloe." He leans closer to me, his forearm connecting with the wall. I trace the lines of his face with my eyes, catching a subtle scar across his jaw, the roundness of his lips, the way his stare cuts through me in a way that leaves me feeling exposed, which is both terrifying and liberating. He raises his left hand, brushing the back of his fingers from my temple to my jaw. "Tell me you want me. Tell me you're drowning in thoughts of me because I constantly feel like I'm one breath from drowning. Tell me you feel this."

Never have I questioned my cardiologist's assurances about my heart being fine, but right now, my doubts feel like a fact as my heart beats like the dryer when we put too many clothes inside—off balance and clunky. His stare pleads with mine, searching for what I fear most to expose: how much I want him. I tear my gaze from his, but he's everywhere, his lips, his scent, his warmth.

I pull in a fraction of a breath. "I don't want to be a mistake that you avoid for the next ten days."

He closes his eyes and shakes his head. "You want to know the first time I wanted to kiss you?" His eyes dip to my mouth again, and he licks his lips. "We were outside, and you were telling me how the moon was nearly the same distance across as Australia."

"I kissed you that night," I admit the moment I avidly work to forget and pretend never happened.

His eyebrows hitch. "I know, and then you started avoiding me."

"Because that guy said I was your third hookup of the night."

He pulls his chin back. "What?"

I nod. "That guy who was smoking weed," I tell him, recalling the memory like it happened last night. "He started laughing and said Tyler Banks is already on his third hookup of the night. God, he must think Americans are so easy. And your reaction was to smile."

He shakes his head. "I remember the guys, but..." He shakes his head again. "I most certainly didn't hear him because otherwise, I would have knocked out his fucking teeth. Chloe, you were the first girl at Brighton I kissed."

My heart feels dizzy as hope breaks past sense and claims an early victory.

"You're the only girl at Brighton—the only girl, period—who I want to kiss."

He ruins me with his admission.

He also raises me.

My feelings are in a constant state of contradiction and imbalance that has me fully addicted and entranced to everything about him.

His bright blue eyes dance between my mouth and my eyes, then he starts to shake his head, but leans closer with another giant contradiction. "This will change things. If you ask me to kiss you, nothing will be the same. Not this time."

"What changes?"

His eyes slowly shift between mine. "Everything. Everything will change because I want you in ways I can't even describe. I want to own you, possess you, and claim you—I want to fucking free you, Chloe."

He buries his fingers into my hair, his palm resting hot against my jaw. "People will come at you—want to be your friend, want to ask you for favors, talk about you behind your back, start rumors—it won't be easy."

I'm so entangled in his words about wanting to claim me that I can't ask logic to take a seat and join in the conversation because desire cleared that space and is lighting the candles and turning on some sexy music. "I don't care," I tell him.

Regret flashes in his eyes. "Chloe..." His gaze starts to slip, and I can feel the distance as he works to pull himself away, though he hasn't moved a single inch.

"Truth or dare?" I ask him.

He blinks, his blue gaze making a roundtrip pass over my lips again, making it increasingly difficult for me to breathe or think straight. A week ago, talking to him was difficult, now I challenge him to hold my stare and finally admit this is more than a game—more than we both want to admit.

"Dare."

It's the same choice he's made throughout the entirety of our brief game, ensuring me he'd choose it again. "Kiss me."

The air feels heavier as my dare echoes in my ears, my stomach pitched with nerves and fear of rejection.

His eyes sweep back to mine, and that desire and hunger I feel in the pit of my stomach is reflected in his blue eyes. My heart throbs, and my knees feel weak as I reach for him to balance me—anchor me—and bring him closer because I need to feel him everywhere.

He leans closer, and my breath catches.

Everything changes...

Claim you...

Only one...

I lean into him. His chest heaves against mine as his breaths drag against my cheek, the scent of whiskey hypnotizing me along with the beat of his heart against my chest. Then his hands close around my waist, and his lips come down on mine, and it feels like I'm floating as he takes my bottom lip between his teeth and tugs, his fingers grinding into my waist, pulling me closer. Or maybe I'm tugging him closer as my nails scrape against his black dress shirt, desperate to feel him and taste him.

He slants his lips over mine, his tongue sweeping across my lips, daring me to take more—to give more. I part my lips for him, and his tongue tangles with mine, and I taste the whiskey and absinthe and the sweetness from the sugar.

I groan, or maybe it's him. I can't tell anymore because as we collide in this moment, I think about cold welding: the effect in which two metals of the same type touching in space become permanently joined because of the absence of air. That is how I feel. Bonded to Tyler in a way I know will forever change who I am.

The weight of his body against mine is exhilarating and seductive, all heat and strength that disarms me as our kiss grows deeper.

"Let's go," I whisper as he kisses my top lip and then my cheek, my jaw, and my bottom lip, peppering them until I can't recall what I said.

"To the hotel?"

I shake my head. "The VIP room."

His eyes darken.

I kiss him fully on the mouth. "You said it's private. No one can see anything." I kiss him again. "Please."

He growls, his teeth grazing the top of my ear. "You know what you're asking for?"

"I want you." I've never been so sure of anything in my life as I am right now, discussing having sex with Tyler. I would likely do it right here and now against this wall with everyone watching us if I wasn't terrified my sister or Cooper might see. Nothing here seems taboo or wrong.

He threads his fingers with mine and sets his other hand on my hip, his fingers lazily tracing the line of my hip bone as he guides us toward the VIP room I'd told him hours before was unnecessary.

"We don't want to be disturbed," Tyler tells the bouncer. He nods with understanding and moves to the middle of the stairs as we ascend them, my heart and breaths growing lighter as though we're gaining actual altitude with the short climb.

Tyler closes the door behind us. The room is dark, and the music and lights still throb through the space as the lounge looks out across the club. Sheer white curtains offer a veil of privacy. Apprehension steals my breath. Is everyone going to see me? Is Tyler going to go back to avoiding me tomorrow?

"We don't have to do anything," Tyler says, moving to stand behind me, his hands settling on my hips. His lips trace the side of my neck. "We can order a drink or go back down or leave. It's up to you."

"This isn't just a drunk hookup?" I ask, turning my head to catch his gaze.

His eyes flash to mine, and then he's kissing me again. He slides his hands into my hair as his tongue twists around mine for a hot second before it ends too quickly, leaving my thoughts spinning and my breaths heavy. "How much have you had to drink?" he asks, his lips resting against my ear.

"One. When we got here."

"That was two hours ago," he tells me. "I've had two." He licks his lips. "Nothing about you, nothing about this—*us*—has come easily. This is way more than a hookup."

My body heats as his eyes convey a level of honesty my heart understands. "In New Orleans," I start, my body shivering as I recall his promise to take me then. "You put that thought into my head, and I haven't been able to get it out. Every time we step into a club, it's all I can think about."

Tyler's fingers run the length of my thighs and then back up, raising the hem of my dress higher on my thigh. His breaths are cool against my skin, which feels too hot as need courses through me. "We should slow down." His fingers press into my flesh, the roughness of calluses scratching my skin tantalizingly, contradicting his words.

I shake my head. "If we stop, I'm pretty sure I'm going to explode."

His fingers travel higher, skimming my butt before following the edges of my underwear over my hips and core, making me nearly gasp with anticipation, yet he doesn't touch me at all where I want him—need him to.

I lean my head back, my breaths uneven as his fingers skim across my inner thigh again.

"God, you're gorgeous," he says before he breathes me in, another short growl before he cups my core, offering only the slightest relief before the pressure somehow increases further. He slides his fingers over me, applying more pressure with his middle finger as he strokes up my middle, making my hips buck and my breath to come out in a gust.

The reality of this situation has me tensing, feeling self-conscious as my inexperience echoes in my ears with the unwanted memory of Ricky's taunting words.

Tyler senses my hesitation, his lips and touch pausing. I realize I've shifted, my head no longer against his collarbone. He kisses my bare shoulder sweetly, then turns me to face him. "What's wrong?"

His eyes are liquid heat, desire edged in lust that has me contemplating just staying quiet and continuing. His fingers slide along my jaw, tipping my chin up. "Tell me."

"I want this," I preface the conversation. "I want you. But this is..." My words trail off, the word virgin seeming sterile and clinical as I struggle to form the word.

His brows furrow.

"My first time..." I tell him.

His eyes flare, and as I'd feared, the words seem to make him come to a full stop as he releases a deep breath. "We should go."

"Are you serious?" I take a step back, anger hitting me like a wave, covering me with regret and resentment.

"This is a big decision," he says. "I can't..." He shakes his head. "I'm not going to take your virginity in a nightclub."

"You're wrong. The first time we met was downtown Seattle. You were late because you bought that homeless person bags of groceries, and you sat with Coop and me, and you were wearing a Beatles shirt that Cooper teased you about for being cliché, and you laughed. That was our first time meeting, and I've wanted you since. I've thought about this for two years, and I don't care if my first time is in a club, I just want it to be with you."

He tips his head back as he releases a train of curses before looking around at the space, his throat moving as he swallows, then his eyes fall back on me, that hungry need burning once again, making my skin feel ablaze. "What are you doing to me?" he mumbles. He takes my hand, leading me over to the railing that separates the club from our room with twenty feet of height. It hits the middle of my back, cold and hard against my skin. He kneels in front of me, his hands sliding my dress so it's bunched around my waist, exposing my purple underwear. Holding my dress, fingers firm against my skin, he kisses my navel and then lower, trailing his mouth and tongue down to the edge of my underwear, making anticipation return with a vengeance. Then he places his nose against me, taking a deep breath. Embarrassment tickles my thoughts, but there's something so damn erotic and sexy about the gesture that has me shamelessly spreading my legs a bit wider. He runs his nose over me, and I grasp the railing even tighter with one hand to keep myself upright, moving my other hand to his hair, tangling in the blonde locks, wanting to pull him closer to make him do it again and also away because this still seems dirty to have him eye level with my vagina. Tyler opens his eyes and looks up at me as he moves his hands to my pelvic bone, pulling me open with his thumbs. He places his mouth over me, holding my gaze as I feel the heat of his tongue through the thin barrier of my panties. He traces me with his nose again, and then takes another deep breath. "God, I want you," he says. "You smell so good. I can't wait to taste you."

He slips his fingers into the waist of my underwear and pulls them down my legs, leaving my lower half completely exposed except for my heels as he shoves my underwear into his pocket before his gaze returns to mine. "If you need me to slow down, just let me know."

I nod, trying to swallow as my grip on the rail tightens. A smile lifts the corner of his mouth, and then he moves his hands to separate my lower lips, the air dancing across my bare skin. He licks me, so soft it almost tickles. My belly clenches and desire warms my body. His tempo changes as his tongue flattens, making my hips jerk, and the air fall from me in one needy gasp.

He moans, his eyes on me again, watching my reactions as he licks and sucks with his relentless mouth until my legs begin to shake, and my hips start to thrust, desperate for a release. He closes his mouth over my clit and slides a finger into me, and the sensation tears me apart as my release rips through me in waves.

Tyler slowly stands, bestowing me with a smile that makes my heart throb. Then his finger dips back into me and then out, drawing lazy circles around my entrance and up over my clit. He kisses me, and I taste myself on his tongue as he swipes it across mine, his fingers slowly increasing with both speed and pressure. "I'm going to make you come again, and then I'm going to take you over to the couch and bury myself in you so I can watch you come again."

I whimper, and if I wasn't so turned on and desperate to feel him take my body to these impossible highs again, I might be embarrassed over the fact. Instead, I move my hips to increase the pressure of his touch.

He kisses me deeply, distracting me for a moment with his mouth as his kiss becomes more demanding, and then a delicious fullness as he adds a second finger, curling them inside of me and making my mouth part as need mounts inside of my chest.

"That's your G-spot," Tyler whispers, kissing my parted lips. "Tell me you want me. Tell me you want me to make you come."

My breaths are short and fast as his fingers continue to hit the same sensitive spot, the sound of my arousal growing louder against his hand as he quickens his pace. Then his fingers slide out of me, running over my clit, making me groan with a protest as I move my hand to his, guiding it back to my entrance.

He chuckles, kissing me. "Tell me you want me," he warns.

"I want you. I want you to make me come."

"Good girl," he says, kissing me again as his fingers slide back inside, hitting that same spot that makes the world seem to stop as pleasure consumes me. He kisses me when my breaths grow unsteady, his fingers driving me to the brink of my sanity, making me so desperate to climax again, it nearly feels uncomfortable as the pressure continues to build. Then he presses his thumb against my clit, and my release is so strong, my knees sag as his lips come over mine, kissing me fiercely as he swallows my cries as his other hand and chest support me.

His kisses become sweeter and softer as the waves recede, leaving me breathless and sated. Then his fingers slide out of me, grasping my other hip and pulling me forward. I feel him, hard against my waist. Passion and fear ignite as my desire grows, working to be eclipsed by every horror story that accompanies this moment and the pain and discomfort that comes with it. But as his blue eyes hit me, I forget every single word and thought as I lean into him, claiming his mouth the way he'd claimed mine, gripping him through his pants. He groans, his tongue sliding against mine as his hips flex into my touch. I wonder if this is the power he felt over me when he touched me? My tongue wrestles with his as I stroke him, feeling his girth and length that make that pressure between my legs return.

I reach for his belt, fumbling with it as he takes control of the kiss, his fingers tipping my head back, possessing my mouth. I slip the ends of his belt free and unbutton his pants before lowering the zipper, cupping him through his boxer briefs, the heat and length of him making me moan. He seems to recognize my need as his kisses lessen, peppering my lips as he smiles with confidence radiating off his chest. He knows his effect on me, and it makes me feel more vulnerable than it did to have his face between my legs.

"Let's go to the couch," he says, kissing my jaw.

I shake my head. "I want that fantasy you painted. I want them to see you claim me."

He closes his eyes, his chest rising as I squeeze his length. "Chloe," he groans, his eyes opening to half-mast. "That was me being an arrogant arse. I wasn't serious. I don't want anyone to fucking see you, least of all exposed."

"You're lying. You get a thrill from it, the same thrill I do. You want to, you're just worried I'll regret it."

"Fucking terrified."

I stroke him again. "I dare you," I whisper against his lips, turning so my back is to him, my dress still pooled around my hips.

"You're going to kill me," he says, running his fingers over my bare skin. "You're testing my strength, I swear to God." He leans into me, his bulge at my backside.

I gasp, my hips reflexively moving forward.

Tyler chuckles, regaining the power I'd just stolen. "Hold onto the rail," he orders.

I do as he requests, and his fingers run over my butt and down my thighs, every inch of my skin that he's touched set ablaze. Then he stops, and I hear the rustle of clothing and crinkle of foil. Looking over my shoulder, I see he's thrown his shirt aside and is tearing at the wrapper of the condom with his teeth. Seeing him like this makes me weak in the knees. He sheaths his cock and fists himself, his eyes burning into mine. "You have no idea how bad I want you."

He blows out a long breath as he leans forward and kisses my shoulder, his hand finding my waist. "Tell me if you need me to slow down." He reaches forward, tilting my chin toward him before he kisses me possessively. His other hand dips between my legs, sliding against me and parting me open. It seems impossible to feel so desperate for him already. He kisses below my ear, and I hear the hitch in his breath as he gently pushes against my entrance, sliding in part way.

My eyes snap shut as pain and desire battle for dominance, and I pull in a shaky breath. He runs a hand over my back, allowing me a moment to adjust to his size while he moves the hand from my waist down to where we're joined, applying pressure to my clit. The sensation pushes me over the edge, a moan escaping through my parted lips.

"I'm okay," I tell him.

His hand at my waist flexes as he moves his other hand back along my clit, making me forget the pain as desire burns stronger. He moves slowly, carefully, his gaze tracking each of my breaths and every flicker of pain.

"I want you, Tyler," I remind him.

My declaration must provide him with the assurance he needs because I feel him swell even more as he slides into me entirely, planting both hands firmly on my hips.

Completely bottomed out, Tyler stills again. The fullness I feel reaches all the way to my soul, and I tremble at the rightness of the moment.

"Are you okay?" he asks.

I nod, clinging to the rail and soaking up the coolness of the metal to distract me from the sting of pain as I slowly acclimate to his size. He runs his hand over my back, kissing my shoulder as I pull in a deep breath through my nose, his intoxicating scent overwhelming my senses. Opening my eyes, I see the crowd dancing below, their bodies moving in time with the music, the beats of which accompany the melody of Tyler's labored breathing behind me. Knowing someone could look up and see us at any moment only amplifies the thrill, dialing everything up to an eleven.

He finally starts to move as I squirm below him, slowly at first, allowing our bodies time to fall in sync with his gentle tempo. When I start meeting him thrust for thrust, his pace quickens, and his hands grip me tighter, digging into my flesh. My hold on the railing tightens, soaking the coolness of the metal into my overheated skin.

And as he hits that particularly delicious spot, I peer at him from over my shoulder and smile.

"You were made for me," he rasps out, his movements increasing as his hand dips back between my legs, and we come apart together.

18

TYLER

I've never felt so exhausted and so empowered as I do at this moment. I kiss Chloe's spine through her dress, running my hand down her back as I slowly pull out of her.

She straightens, tugging her dress down, and my gratification and blissful satisfaction take a back seat as I wait for her to face me, horrified I'll find regret or anger in her green eyes. But as she turns, her smile is shy and sweet and so fucking beautiful that relief floods me as I reach for her, pulling her against me. "Are you okay?"

She nods. "Pretty sure I'm way better than you in this scenario." Her smile widens, making me laugh.

"Do you want anything to drink?" I ask.

She nods.

I kiss her hairline, breathing her in again. "There's a bathroom in here," I tell her, pointing at the door. I keep my arm around her waist as I walk her to the restroom. It's small, and the lights are cheap and too bright, buzzing when I flip them on. Chloe blinks rapidly, her makeup slightly smudged. It's fucking gorgeous. I did that. I kiss her full lips again and then make quick work of ridding the condom and washing my hands, my gaze continuing to stray to her. "I'm serious," I tell her. "This changes everything. I won't keep pushing you away, and I won't let you continue avoiding me."

Her green eyes are lined with doubt—reminding me she genuinely believed I didn't like her all this time. I grip her chin between my thumb and forefinger. "I'll work for this. I'll prove to you I am the bloke you want—the man you deserve."

Her eyes grow soft, and her shoulders slowly roll forward as I kiss her again before moving to the door.

"You have my underwear," she says.

I open the door, taking a final look at her. "I know. Don't expect to get them back."

Her cheeks heat with a blush as she stares at me, dumbfounded. I grin, closing the door behind me.

I call down to order two Long Islands and give the bouncer the green light to allow people to come back up. I hang up, slip my shirt back on, and lean back in the plush white seat, staring out toward the rail where Chloe had stood and given herself to me.

The bitterness of regret skates into my thoughts as I fear having gone too far, too fast, but then she steps out of the bathroom, her makeup once again flawless. She walks toward me with a shy smile, absent of anger or remorse. I'm flooded with relief and the realization of how long I've wanted her.

I tag her waist when she gets close enough, pulling her down on my lap. I breathe her in, smelling me on her skin. She giggles with surprise, drawing at my playful side that has my fingers scavenging for every ticklish spot on her sides.

"Tyler," she says between peals of laughter. And when I don't stop, she grabs my face and kisses me. She slides her lips over mine, deepening the kiss instantly as she licks the length of my tongue, successfully distracting me from every thought except how much I want to feel her again.

"I win."

The announcement has Chloe pulling away, her cheeks turning crimson as Cooper and Vanessa step into the suite. She starts to wriggle free, but my grip at her waist tightens, securing her to my lap.

Cooper looks from her to me, his gaze a contradiction of Vanessa's, who beams. "I told Coop you guys would get together before California. I have to admit I was getting a *little* worried." She holds up two fingers with a hairsbreadth between them.

"What?" Chloe asks.

Vanessa nods, turning to look at Cooper for verification. "You guys have had chemistry forever. I knew this trip would make you guys either face it or kill each other."

"You didn't say anything to me."

Vanessa shakes her head. "I knew if I did, you'd just fight it harder, and I had twenty bucks on the line." She smiles. "We came up to find you guys because there's a guy down there who was on one of those dancing shows. He's so good."

My hold on Chloe slips free. "You should check it out," I tell her, taking another look at the apprehension on Cooper's face.

She stands, making her way over to Vanessa and Coop, where she pauses and holds his forearm as she leans into his side and kisses his cheek. I can't tell if it's an apology or a request to be kind. Either way, it's clear she also senses his unease. She looks back at me, a gentle smile that pleads with me and has my patience expanding.

I nod once, watching her and Vanessa disappear back down to the dance floor.

When I return my gaze, Coop's looking at me, his forehead creased. "You know she's my best friend, right? I mean, I'm in no position to tell you who to like, but Chloe's not just some girl—she's *important to me.* She's..." His voice waivers before he clears his throat. "She's family, and you're like my brother, so I just need to be clear that if you're interested, you're serious because you can't hurt her without hurting me."

I blow out a deep breath, knowing this is exactly what has kept me away from Chloe Robinson for the past two years. I assumed after New Orleans she would tell Coop what a bastard I was, and he'd confront me, and I'd send them to Washington on a plane and finish this trip solo— wanted to because I needed her to avoid me because I wouldn't be strong enough to avoid her. "I know," I tell him.

"Just make sure you're positive. Don't get caught up in the fact we're on this trip and staying in a hotel together. Be with her because you *like her*. *Want her*."

I nod. "You don't have to worry," I tell him. "I won't fuck this up."

He nods, but his expression doesn't change. "Good. Don't because it would fuck up everything between us."

It's a warning bell. Loud and clear.

WE WALK TO THE LIFT. Vanessa and Chloe are laughing about the dancing they'd seen at the club, distracted as Cooper trails behind. He's still tense and brooding over the news, but I have to give him credit. He's trying to accept this change, and considering it's been less than an hour, he's doing one hell of a job.

The queue is long, which has me turning to look for stairs, but before I can, Cooper clears his throat. "Give us a cool space fact, Chloe."

She grins. "Uranus was originally named Georgian."

"They should have stuck with Georgian because everyone but space geeks pronounce it your-anus, including our third grade teacher," Vanessa says.

Chloe laughs. "When William Herschel discovered it, he named it after King George III, and the French—and the rest of the world—weren't fond of this, so Johann Elert Bode, a German astronomer renamed it Uranus after the Ancient Greek god of the sky."

"That's actually kind of a cool way to get named," Cooper says. "Named after a god."

Chloe nods. "Uranus was the deity of the Heavens, the earliest supreme god. Actually, all of the planets in our solar system were named after Greek and Roman gods and goddesses—all except Earth."

Cooper laughs. "What was Earth named after?"

Chloe shakes her head. "We don't know. The name derives from both English and German words that mean ground."

"Ground?" Coop asks. "That's not nearly as cool as deity of the heavens."

Vanessa rubs her hands together, glancing at the queue that has barely moved. "Okay. Give us something else that will help us win a game of trivia."

"Scientists have confirmed more than four thousand exoplanets and are still waiting to confirm another thousand."

Vanessa shakes her head. "When you start talking about exoplanets, it feels like a vise is squeezing my head, reminding me how little I know."

Chloe scoffs. "That's the whole point of science. We learn we know nothing."

Vanessa laughs. "Then I'm a *great* scientist."

I shake my head. "What's an exoplanet?"

Chloe licks her lips, her smile growing as her gaze dips to my pocket where her underwear are. I know it's the second drink she and Vanessa drank too fast that has her eyes coming back to my mouth. "Worlds outside of our solar system that orbit other stars," she says like she's telling me the time.

Vanessa belts out a laugh, startling the lady in front of us. "Drunk Chloe is smarter than sober Chloe," she says. "It's scary."

Chloe chuckles, shaking her head. "But think about it. It's pretty cool and mind-blowing to consider there are another four thousand plus planets out there, most of them within our galaxy."

"My grandma still insists Pluto's a planet," Coop says.

Chloe smiles affectionately. "Information is constantly changing. Plus, it's hard for people to understand that our solar system is a very tiny fraction of the Milky Way Galaxy. We're tiny in comparison to the vast expanse of our galaxy. Understanding the distance and vast implications can be really difficult for some."

Vanessa nods. "Me included."

Chloe flashes a quick smile and shakes her head.

"Are we sure tomorrow's our last day here?" Vanessa asks, turning to look around.

"I'm excited for San Diego," Cooper says. "I've only been once, and it was for our bowl game last year, and I was so hungover the next day I only saw the hotel bathroom."

I grin, recalling the sorry shape I'd found him in.

"I could be a professional traveler. How do I propose this idea to the Travel Channel?" Vanessa asks, turning to Chloe. "Maybe we can sell this to them if we come as a pair?"

"We would have been fired in Arizona," Chloe says, laughing.

"No. Because we would have had a tour guide." Vanessa takes Cooper's hand as we step into the elevator and take it to the ground floor that leads to the street.

Chloe considers this. "They probably would have known way more about snakes and spiders, too."

Vanessa nods. "Definitely."

Ahead of us, two guys are stopped, their gazes predatory as they stare too long at Chloe and Vanessa, making every muscle in my shoulders tense. Chloe seems to notice them as well, slowing to walk by my side. I wrap my arm around her waist, and my annoyance with these wankers is fully eclipsed at the reality of this moment and how easy and right everything feels.

Once back at the hotel, Chloe stops to get some water while Vanessa and Cooper head upstairs to get ready for bed.

I lean against the counter, watching her bottom lip wrap around the bottle, the movement of her throat. It's all so simple, and yet I can't stop staring because I've worked to ignore these details for so long.

"You aren't really keeping my underwear, are you?"

I push away from the counter, closing the distance between us. "I intend to save an entire collection."

"Remind me not to wear any cute ones."

I chuckle, pulling her against me, her quick gasp of surprise falling against my lips. "Stay with me." I know Vanessa's been staying in Cooper's room since Arizona.

Her green eyes shift between mine, a warmth radiating in my chest that has me rubbing small circles over her hips with my thumbs. "Let's give Coop a little time to adjust. He gave me the courtesy. I feel like it's important to return it."

She's right. I know she's right, and still, I want to fight her on it. "It's probably better. I have to be up in a few hours, so I'd wake you up."

Her eyebrows jump. "A few hours?" Her gaze drops back to my mouth. "We should have come back sooner. You're going to be exhausted tomorrow."

I bury my face in her hair and breathe her in. "We should have tried being nice to each other a long time ago. We're good at this."

She tips her head back and rolls her eyes. I have to hide my smile. "For the record, I was always nice to you."

"You wouldn't have voiced concern about me not getting enough sleep before," I tease.

"Only because you would have insisted it meant something."

My smile can't be concealed. "But it would've. Isn't that what you said? Freshman year?"

Her gaze turns fiery, her lips twisting with a challenge, but before she can respond, I kiss her. Her lips are still parted and firm, assuring me I caught her off guard, but it only takes her a second to catch up, her arms winding around the back of my neck as her body molds to mine. What begins as an intense warring of tongues and wills slows with her back against the refrigerator, our lips languid as we taste each other and memorize each other's breaths and warmth.

I kiss her again, softly, sweetly, noting the way the edges of her lips curl with a grin before she opens her eyes.

When we hit her bedroom door, I consider following her inside. I already broke the rule of sleeping with a woman in my bed with her a few nights ago, so it seems like a rudimentary concern at this point. Still, there's a conflict in my chest that is nearly impossible to silence— exchanges between my parents and advice given from my father and grandad and dozens of unsolicited requests about how you can't move too fast, give too much, or expect a lot because each will lead to disappointment and all are inevitable.

Chloe reaches for me, smoothing a crease in my forehead with her finger. Her brows are cinched, and for a second, I recognize the expression, have seen it a thousand times when she and Vanessa look at each other, only with them it's as though they can each tune in to the same wavelength and understand each other's thoughts. It can be eerie and strange as shit when the two don't say a word and suddenly burst into laughter. Still, I know she's checking in with me, recognizing the change in my demeanor and mood.

Fucking expectations.

Fucking rules.

I nod and then bend to kiss her. "Have a good night."

She smiles. "You too."

I turn, heading the rest of the way to my room. Inside, I flip on the lights, feeling restless and agitated. I consider forgoing sleep altogether and heading up to the gym to workout. This trip has sent my work outs into overdrive as regret and vulnerability tread a close line that constantly leaves me off-kilter. Instead, I sit at the table in my room and turn on my laptop, opening all the spreadsheets I need to be going over for tomorrow.

An hour later, a knock at my door has me crossing the room, my chest betraying my mind. On the other side is Chloe, her lips set in a slash. Her hair is wet, and she's wearing a pair of shorts and a red Brighton T-shirt. "This was in my purse," she says, handing me an envelope.

I stare at it but don't touch it. "It's yours."

"I don't want it." She shoves it against my chest.

"Why not?"

"Because it makes me feel like a whore."

"It's your winnings."

"That I won with *your* money."

"So?"

"I told you I didn't want it." She begins to turn around, and I tag her waist, all of the fears and advice that had rained down on me a mere hour ago gone as I stare at the anger and hurt swirling in her green eyes. I toss the money onto the nearby couch so I can place both hands on her.

"That's fair. I overstepped, and I'm sorry."

Her body relaxes under my touch, but her eyes remain hard as she glances back at the money spilling out of the envelope.

"I have a balcony and an entire wall of windows you can stargaze at."

Her eyes shift to me and then over my shoulder, looking at the room.

"I'm going to take a shower, and if you're up for it, I'd like you to stay tonight. Just be here with me."

She meets my gaze. "You'll wake me up when you get up so I can go back to my room?"

"If you want me to."

She nods.

I press a kiss to her temple. "I'll be right out."

Under the hot spray of the shower, my thoughts clear as the memory of Chloe gripping the rail and standing in front of me replays in my mind. The glint of excitement, the way she bit her bottom lip with anticipation as her eyes had darkened and desire guided her. God, she was fucking beautiful—perfect. I shudder, my cock strained and desperate for her again. I turn the water to cold.

She was a virgin.

Regardless of how big of a deal this feels to me, I know it's an even bigger deal to her.

I dry off before wrapping the plush towel around my waist, finding Chloe in a chair she moved beside the window. I grab a pair of underwear and drop my towel, pulling them on as I ask, "What made you decide to study astronomy?"

She turns, her gaze crossing over my torso and the rest of my body. She swallows. I would high five myself if she weren't here to witness it, relieved I affect her in the same fucking manner she does me each time I see her. "I've always been mesmerized by the sky—the moon, the sun, the stars, how our planet can provide so many things for us..." She shakes her head. "I've always been kind of a geek for it, and when I was thirteen, my grandparents sent me to space camp as my Christmas present, and I was hooked. I always thought I wanted to be an astronaut before that, but then I learned about the complexity of space and astronomy and how many big questions are linked to it and how many things we've learned from space that have bettered our lives, and it kind of snowballed for me."

I move to stand behind her. "Your geek side is fucking hot," I tell her.

She laughs, her cheeks tinting pink. "Speaking of sides, I didn't know which side of the bed you prefer..."

I've never had sides. "Sleep wherever you want," I tell her.

She unfolds her legs and stands. I focus on remembering the icy cold water of my shower, trying to calm myself down so I don't reach for her and slip off her shorts and tee to have her naked and at my mercy within seconds. I fight the idea of her on her back, legs spread, and bared to me as I drive her to climax again. Two years of temptation and lust have been built, and now that the dam has been broken, it seems impossible to contain.

Her thigh brushes against my fingertips as she passes me, leaving the fresh scent of citrus and floral as she moves to the bed.

I grab the remote from the nightstand and close the shades and turn off the lights, loving the sight of her in my bed. "Can I ask you a personal question?" I ask, reaching for her as I slip beneath the sheet.

"Why was I still a virgin?" she asks.

"I saw you make out with Lincoln Beckett freshman year, and I'm not shaming you, I just ... you caught me by surprise."

"I prefer to pretend that night never happened."

Thank-fucking-God. "Why?"

"Because I saw your hand up some chick's skirt, and it made me so jealous, I nearly cashed in my V-card that night."

Guilt binds around my lungs, making it difficult to think as I work to recall further details of that night, but try as I might, the only thing I remember is hating my teammate and Chloe for kissing him. "I've done a lot of things I regret."

She shakes her head. "Regret is wasted energy, and some of the most beautiful and amazing things come from mistakes."

"So you didn't sleep with anyone that night?"

"I almost did ... but it just didn't feel right." She sighs. "I don't know how to explain it. I never wanted the moment to be planned or to have it be a big production because it seemed that would make it all feel orchestrated, and the entire carnal desire and lust and everything would be a calculation—a plan—and I feel like my entire life is filled with calculations and rules and plans. This was one thing I just didn't want to make rules for. And then there was this incident where I suggested to someone I was dating that we do something in the back of his truck when we were out camping with some friends, and his reaction made me feel so dirty, like there was something wrong with me."

Her words create a puzzle that seems comprised of different pieces, all evoking distinctive emotions: jealously, relief, intrigue, confusion, and so much desire I can barely think past the haze of lust that's settled across me like a fucking fog. "What a fucking idiot." I slip my hand under her shirt and grip the soft skin of her hip. I want to taste her again, feel her against me, see her fully exposed, but I have little doubt she's sore, so instead, I pull her closer, evoking another giggle from her as she turns so her back is to my front. I nuzzle against her bare neck, trying to understand how this can feel so utterly perfect when nothing about it is anything I've ever wanted.

19

TYLER

I button my suit jacket and straighten my tie.

Most say I look like my dad, but my hair is from my mum, and my height is from her side as well. I was taller than both my dad and grandad by the time I was fifteen. As I stare at myself in the mirror, I contemplate how much of them is in me that can't be reflected.

I release a sigh, flipping off the lights before I open the door so I don't wake Chloe.

She's stretched across the mattress, arms and legs extended like da Vinci's Vitruvian Man. The sheet's tangled around her right leg, her hair a maze around her face. She's fucking gorgeous.

I contemplate leaving her and messaging Cooper with some excuse. After all, it's not like we did anything here in my room. I could leave the door open so if one of them came by, they'd see her fully dressed.

The envelope of money stares at me from the couch, reminding me how little she appreciated me not listening to her yesterday after she'd refused the winnings the first time.

Instead of waking her, I open my bedroom door and check the room she shares with Vanessa, which is currently empty, and quietly carry her back to the other bed. I lay her down, and she rolls to her side, snuggling into the pillow. I lift the blankets to cover her and silently pull the door shut behind me.

Down in the hotel's reception, I stop at the concierge desk where Cammie, one of the best in the business, is seated, preparing for her day.

"Mr. Banks," she greets me with a smile. "How can I help you? Would you like me to make any reservations for you?"

"Good morning, Cammie. I'm looking for some tickets to one of the Cirque du Soleil shows. If they have any private balconies, that would be brilliant. I'd like two. Also, could you please make arrangements for Vanessa and Chloe Robinson to receive full spa treatments this afternoon?"

Cammie scribbles a note with the details. "Anything else?"

"We'll need a dinner reservation. Can you make sure we have a table available here at Fork? Something near the back that's more private."

She nods with understanding. "Absolutely. I'll be sure the chef knows you're coming. How many will join you for the reservation?"

"Four total."

She nods again, adding to her note before flashing a smile. "Perfect. I'll have the confirmation for the show sent to your email. If you need anything else, please let me know."

I weave through the hotel reception, comparing it to the others we've seen over the past couple of days, making my way to the conference room the general manager and accountant are meeting me this morning.

"Mr. Banks," Marshall, the GM says, rising from his chair. "It's so nice to see you again, sir. How have the accommodations been?" He's quick to move forward and shake my hand, smiling like we're friends, though I've only met him a handful of times, all of them involving me staying here for bender weekends that I'd tally in the regret sector of my past.

"Good, thanks." I shake the accountant's hand as well, wishing one of them would remind me of her name because I always feel like such a twat when I can't remember someone's name in intimate settings like this.

Neither does.

"We've prepared the documents you requested," the accountant says, sliding a file to me as I sit at the round table.

"Wonderful. The hotel is in pristine condition, and I know with the weather and guests we receive, that's not always easy to maintain, so please, know my compliment is sincere. Also, our room has been wonderful. Clean, updated, classy," I tick off the things we pride our hotels on. "I would like to hear from you both in regards to any concerns you might have. Obstacles with which you're struggling? Staffing concerns?" I leave it vague because each hotel has similar obstacles, as well as unique ones, and because I've apparently been too obvious in my questions about the management company.

Marshall flashes a smile. His mostly silver hair is short, a flawless fitting black suit decorating him like a figurehead. I did my research on him last night and discovered he's been with the company for fifteen years, transferring from another hotel into a management position. I don't think I would have made the same hiring decision off paper, but in person, Marshall's quick to impress, his confidence as flashy and bright as the city.

"Well, we met with Mr. Avery a couple of months ago to cover pretty much everything, and we mutually agreed we're doing quite well. We'd like to eventually expand the pool and do something a bit more impressive with a wave pool and some slides, but for now, it does the job. And the new carpeting that was delayed should be done next year, which will really add a lot to the basic suites. Hopefully, we can consider doing something with the bathrooms in about five years, incorporating some of the design elements that were suggested."

I glance over the expenditures, searching for the carpet. "You mentioned the carpets were delayed. Was that due to the contractor? Materials?"

Marshall sits up, annoyance flashing across his features as he shakes his head. "Everything that could go wrong has. But isn't that the case with all construction projects?" He laughs.

"So it's been fully funded?"

Marshall looks at the accountant for confirmation, and she nods. "Yes, sir. You can find that on line item G-five-forty-three."

I skim to the referenced line and nod. "And it wasn't refunded?"

Marshall shakes his head. "No, sir. Avery said it would help with taxes and we'd schedule it to be done next year."

I nod, noting the similarity. "How about staffing?"

Another wide grin. "We could always use more staff, but who couldn't?"

"Your check-in and check-out times always exceed goals. Where are your pain points?"

We go over how housekeeping needs additional space and discuss the contracts we have in place with the laundry and food services, and then go over forecasts and future projections and what Marshall thinks would drive traffic and make the Banks Hotel stand out amongst competitors—a question I've asked each general manager and am always surprised with the responses because rarely are they of value. Most times, it's the concierges and front desk staff who provide the most insight on what could be improved. And the housekeeping manager and maintenance manager always have drastically different challenges than what the GM shares. It has me realizing there are many areas of disconnect, or possibly our GMs have been trained to downplay or possibly conceal potential issues.

We break before the concierge team comes to meet with me, and I check my phone, discovering a text from Chloe.

Chloe: You should have woken me up. I slept in and am now at the spa. Pretty sure you drew the short stick this morning.

I grin.

Me: You were exhausted. Are you enjoying the spa?

Chloe: Immensely. Thank you for arranging this.

Me: You're welcome. I'm going to meet Cooper for lunch, and then we all have dinner plans at 6 and a show at 8.

Chloe: You need to lower the bar. This is day one.

Me: Pretty sure this is day 2.

Chloe: Depends on how we're measuring time.

Me: I've known you three weeks shy of two years because you're wrong. The first time we met was on campus, outside at a coffee cart by the science wing. You and Vanessa were ahead of me in line. You smiled at me and randomly bought my coffee in one of those American pay it forward things.

Chloe: Are you sure? I would have remembered you.

Me: I was wearing a hat and sunglasses, nursing a hangover, and you guys were in your own world, talking about some party you didn't want to go to.

Chloe: ...that's crazy.

Me: I'll see you at 6. Also, bring a jacket.

I think about the memory I shared that was seemingly innocent and unimportant, and how a month later, I was introduced to her when Cooper invited me to hang out with him and a friend in an environment that didn't involve shots or the gym. I can remember the surprise when I recognized her. Then, two weeks later, she was in front of me again, only that time it was at a party, sans Cooper. Over the past two years, she's continued to appear in my life, sometimes at the most inopportune moments and others when it seems like fate is trying to give us another chance.

Cammie and the other two concierges enter the conference room, and I tuck my phone and memories away as I ask them to tell me about their perceptions and other realities.

I STEP into the restaurant ten minutes late. My final meeting stretched on so long, I finally had to stand up to indicate I had to leave when my casual attempts to look at my watch and push my chair back didn't seem to work.

The manager of the restaurant walks me toward the back, trying to make polite conversation as we pass through the darkened space. The sun is already beginning to set in the distance, making me regret not having gone outside for one of my breaks today. That disappointment slips away as we turn the corner, and I see her: light pink dress, nude lips, bright eyes, and a smile that stretches across her entire face as she laughs at something. It seemed impossible to cross that line with her, and now it seems impossible that it took so fucking long for it to happen.

She notices me, her laughter dimming to a radiant smile as we cross the rest of the way to the table. I stop at her chair and kiss her cheek before taking the seat next to her, across from Cooper. I set my hand on hers, watching as she turns her hand over and weaves our fingers together. "You look stunning," I tell her.

She smiles, her cheeks staining a light shade of pink.

"Hey, man," Cooper says. "We didn't choose your drink, so if it's wrong, blame it on poor management." He winks.

I grab the glass, smelling the clear liquor. "Gin and tonic," I tell them. "It's my father's drink of choice." I slide it back with my fingertips.

"Ready for this, Tyler?" Vanessa asks. "Look what Chloe bought me." She pulls a shirt from a gift bag on her lap. Across the front is a green sea monster with "Nessie" written across the bottom.

Chloe laughs again, revealing it was the source of her laughter from moments ago. "I found it in the gift shop next door. This is what happens when you guys leave me unattended."

Vanessa shakes her head, dropping it back into the bag.

"How was your day?" Chloe asks, turning her attention to me.

"Good. Long. I'm glad we have tomorrow off, even if it's to drive again. The next time we do this, we're flying."

"I don't know," Vanessa says. "I'm warming up to the car."

"That's because you sleep most of the time," I point out.

She flashes an immediate smile that looks guiltier than it does joyful. "Touché. But really, with how long it takes to get through security and things anymore, I don't know that we're losing that much time."

"Flying," I insist.

"I won't argue," Vanessa says with a dismissive shrug. "Just tell me where to sign up."

The chef comes to our table before we can consider a continuation of our travels, telling us about the specials he's prepared and wines that will pair well with each dish.

Chloe slips her hand from mine to reach for her glass, and I place my hand on her thigh. I mindlessly run my fingers over her skin, brushing random patterns across the surface.

One of my favorite parts of our trip has been our dinners—like those in England, they're longer, extended with conversation and laughter as we talk about the food and our day. This one is no different, except Chloe's gaze frequents mine, and I've spent most of the time with my hand on her thigh, reliant on the feel of her skin. It's as though the simple action allows me to breathe and relax, only interrupted when we have to leave to catch the car to take us to the show.

At the theater, an attendant escorts us to our private seats. Everything is covered in deep shades of plum, blood red, and ocean blue. There's a small table with a bottle of wine and two glasses, the bouquet of red roses, and two large upholstered chairs.

"These seats are unreal," Chloe says, looking at the stage in front of us while I take in the full image of her. The dress ends a modest distance above her knees and has a sexy yet demure cut in the back that reveals a slender patch of her spine. Her heels are thin and high, and when she turns around with her lower lip tucked between her teeth, all I can think about is hiking her dress up and slamming into her again.

The attendant offers to open the champagne, reminding me of his presence.

"Yeah. That would be lovely, thank you." I step aside to give him easier access to pass and slide Chloe's chair back. Folded over her arm is the jacket I told her to bring. I hadn't considered it would be so small.

She smiles at me as she takes a seat while our champagne glasses are filled.

The attendant pulls our curtain closed behind him, leaving Chloe and me alone in the small space. I release the buttons of my suit jacket and take a seat in the chair beside her. There's a twinge of awkwardness as we're both reminded how often we avoided spending time together like this for so long. She smiles shyly, setting her jacket down beside her. "How did things go today? Did anything seem amiss?"

I lean close to her, catching her lips in a kiss that is soft and gentle, an

I've-missed-you kiss that quickly progresses into an I-want-you kiss as my tongue dances with hers, her nails raking over the short sides of my hair, drawing me closer as my fingers curl around the back of her neck, and my other hand goes to her waist, wanting little more than to pull her into my lap, lower my zipper, and have her ride me.

The lights flash with a warning that the show will be starting soon, and Chloe's kisses grow gentler before she pulls back, her green eyes shining with a desire that has me struggling to remain in my seat.

She rubs her lips together, reaching for her champagne. "I'm glad to see you as well." Her lips curl around the glass, creating an entirely new provocative thought. "What are your plans while we're in California? Will you have to work most of the time?"

I blink through my lust, attempting to focus on the question and my upcoming calendar. "I have a meeting on Wednesday morning and then again Friday morning."

"All day again, like today?"

I gently lift my shoulder, uncertain. "I'm hoping not. This was painfully long because there was a lot to discuss, and one of the managers couldn't understand me—claimed my accent was too thick."

She belts out a laugh that makes her nose crinkle in one of my favorite expressions of hers because it's pure and unedited. "How did you guys manage?" She runs her tongue along her top lip, not even realizing the effect it has on me.

"We had to wait for someone to come and be my translator."

Her shoulders shake with a gentle laugh. "But it all went okay? No issues?"

I reach for my glass of champagne, drinking half of it with one swig. "The hotel paid to be fully re-carpeted. It was a few hundred thousand dollars, and the work hasn't been done, and it's been over eighteen months."

Chloe's eyes round before she blinks. "Is that normal?"

"It's not uncommon for charges to be made in a separate calendar year for tax purposes, but eighteen months is on the cusp of being suspicious."

"I'm sorry. I wish I could help you with this."

I don't mention that the figures are minuscule enough that it doesn't raise any alarms and wouldn't make much of a difference; it's a matter of principle and trust that has me following up on this—respect because there are few things as important to me as the hotel's running successfully and fluidly. "I just want you to enjoy your time."

"You go to work, and I play all day. Pretty sure you don't need to be worrying about me enjoying myself. But, I have done a ton of research on California, and if you're able to get off at a reasonable time on Wednesday, I'm planning a date. A Robinson style date, which—warning—will likely consist of a food truck and something outdoors."

"You aren't going to get us lost in some desert, are you?"

Her mouth falls agape. "They didn't mark the trail!" she cries out.

I bend at the waist, laughing away the rest of the stress I've felt all day in my shoulders. "It's a date," I tell her.

"And..." she continues. "I told Coop to invite you a few weeks ago, but just in case Mr. Forgetful forgot to mention it, I have tickets for all of us to go to a cocktail event in San Francisco before the meteor shower. It's going to be a total geekfest with lots of astronomy students and professors and some renowned scientists, and the food is likely going to be awful compared to what we've been having, but—"

I interrupt her with a kiss as the lights begin to dim. "I wouldn't miss it," I tell her.

She flashes a smile that steals my breath—it's adoration with a shot of appreciation that reminds me how it's always been time that she appreciates most, which is why in each city she's made an effort to get us to do things all together.

The lights fall even lower, and the orchestra begins to play. Chloe slides over in her chair, sitting as close as she can, considering the expansive chairs. I set my right hand on her thigh, and she reaches for my left hand, placing it on my right thigh and weaving our fingers together. I press a kiss to her temple before sitting back to watch the beginning of the show.

The moves on stage are artistically beautiful and sexual and have my body thrumming with energy each time Chloe's gaze shifts to mine. I run my thumb across her thigh, moving my hand fractionally higher with each pass. She moves her attention to my hand and then the surrounding area before she glances at me. "We're really exposed here," she whispers. "I think we'd get kicked out."

I grin as I lean forward and shake off my jacket and drape it across her lap. "If anyone looks, they'll think I'm just holding your hand," I tell her as I reach beneath the black cover and gather the layers of her dress. Her eyes are wide with surprise, but her thighs relax as she parts them for me. I run my middle finger along her seam, her soft gasp instantly making me hard. I trace over her again, then lightly rub her clit through her panties, feeling the muscles of her thighs constrict. She rocks her hips forward against my hand. I change the motion, using two fingers to follow across her opening. "I've been thinking about doing this all fucking day," I tell her quietly. Her eyes slide to me as I slip my finger beneath her underwear, drawing circles over her exposed clit. Her heels angle her hips upward, giving me the perfect access to slide across her entrance. Her fingers constrict around mine as I lazily move closer to her core, her teeth catching her lip as she stares at the stage. "You're so wet for me."

She gasps again, shifting her hips in a slow pattern as I draw my fingers over her again. Anyone who might glance in our direction would have a difficult time seeing anything, the space is heavily shadowed with the dim lighting, but her expression is so focused with control, I'm determined to challenge her and see if I can make her façade slip.

"Take your panties off," I whisper.

She looks at me, doubt visible in her stare.

I slip my finger across her clit, making her gasp. "Off."

She turns to look behind us, then slips her hands beneath my jacket and lifts slightly from her seat before getting her underwear to her knees. I hook my fingers into the fabric, sliding them the rest of the way and freeing them from her shoes. I press the silky fabric to my nose and breathe deeply, smelling her desire for me. I shove them into my pocket before resuming our position, weaving my left hand with hers and sliding my right hand between her thighs.

I place my thumb on her clit, rubbing circles over her as I slide my middle finger lower and slowly inside her. Chloe gasps quietly, her lips parting as she raises her hips a bit higher to meet my touch. I gently thrust my fingers into her, changing the tempo of my thumb as I continue to massage her clit. Her grip tightens, and her thighs begin to tremble. I lessen the pressure, and her gaze swings to mine with a silent protest

"It's a two-hour show," I tell her.

She blinks, trying to find a foothold in her lust-drunken state.

"Relax. I'll get you there again." I run my fingers through her folds, spreading her wider as I circle her clit with my middle finger as a sign of good faith.

"I'm beginning to think you're a sadist," she says.

I grin. "I warned you I was." I increase my speed and tempo, and with her already being so sensitive, she reacts instantly, her legs spreading even wider as her hips flex again, pressing against my hand. I stop, running my fingers lower, back to her entrance where I slide two fingers inside of her, feeling her hips rock with an invitation.

She closes her eyes, her breaths uneven for several seconds as she works to gain composure.

I lean forward, grazing her ear with my lips. I lick her there, sliding my lips down to where her two earrings are, that I lap at with my tongue. "I want you to lose control," I whisper.

She looks at me, eyes dark with need. "There are people everywhere."

"Trust me," I tell her, kissing her and following the edge of her jaw back to her ear. "Lose yourself to me, Chloe." I slip my fingers back into her, rubbing her clit with my thumb. She glances at me, a silent plea to let her come as I work her back to the edge of another orgasm.

She bites her lip, and I stop, her shoulders and thighs loosening instantly as her breath falls out in a disappointed rush. She reaches for her glass of champagne, drinking the remains in one drink.

"What do you want?" she asks, her eyes ablaze with annoyance and desire.

"I want to look at your face and know I'm fingering you. I want to see you lose composure."

She starts to shake her head. "There are so many people here."

I slide my fingers over her slick opening. "No one can see you. I wouldn't let someone watch you come."

Her eyes widen again as she stares out at the hundreds of private suites we can look out upon that can do the same to us. It takes her only a second to realize she can't see their faces or expressions, only their outlines. "They can't see you," I confirm, moving inside of her again. "Only I can see you."

She relaxes with a deep breath. Then begins to move her hips against my fingers. I reward her with a flick to her clit that has her dropping her head back against her seat. Then she reaches below the jacket with her right hand, grasping my left with her other hand, entwining our fingers as I finger fuck her, moving my thumb back to her clit as she rolls forward onto her toes, tilting her entrance higher.

"There you go, baby," I tell her, kissing along her slackened jaw as she rocks against my hand, her breaths becoming uneven and ragged. Her hand presses harder against mine, and I oblige, kissing the soft spot below her ear. She moans, and I kiss her lips, swallowing the sound as I increase the pressure of my fingers, keeping the same rhythmic pace with my thumb as her breaths come so fast and hard she can't kiss me back. Her thighs tremble, and her fingers clench around mine as she groans her release around my fingers, and I kiss her, silencing her cries as she comes undone.

20

CHLOE

Blood is still rushing through my veins as I work to recover from my orgasm one hour and a glass of champagne later.

I want to regret it—consider what we did as wrong or bad—but try as I might, I can't find even a trace of shame for allowing him to finger me. And it's not just that he touched me *there, here*, it's how erotic and leisurely and infuriatingly demanding he was all at the same time. I'm terrified to consider if I'd even hesitate if he asked me to hitch up my dress and get on the floor on my hands and knees.

And the way he continues to draw delicate patterns across my thigh is not helping me to think of anything else, even as the show continues. The music and acrobatics are beyond beautiful and shocking but pale in comparison to Tyler as he sits beside me, watching the show with a casualness that makes me almost want to scream. How is he not distracted? How is he not burning up from this inside out after that? Can I return the favor?

My thoughts are racing as the crowd roars its applause, and the lights slowly bloom. The cast moves to the front of the stage, bowing as the crowds stand from their seats.

Tyler is beside me, sending out a text as I try to recall details of the show so I can discuss them with Nessie and Coop so as not to reveal that I was distracted throughout nearly the entire production.

"They're going to meet us at the car," Ty says, putting his jacket back on and tracing the slit of my dress that goes down my back with his fingertips. I shiver. It's ridiculous and embarrassing how quickly my body reacts to him—traitorous, in fact. I try to recall that night at the hotel when he jumped in the pool naked and was inches away from me. How I'd managed to ignore him and not react because I've seen him at parties, shirtless and smiling at me with innuendos and promises that I managed to avoid and act almost entirely unfazed from. Now, I'm so damn desperate for his touch I'm considering asking him to have sex with me here and now, with the lights already on and people milling around freely.

I'm pathetic.

Tyler stares at me, his chin tilted as he stops, placing his other hand at my waist. "Was that too much? I'm sorry. I shouldn't have—"

I shake my head. "You just seem so neutral and unaffected. I can't tell if I did something or didn't do something or..."

His hand at my waist constricts. "No. God, no." He shakes his head in rapid bursts, then he moves his hand from my back and wipes it down his face. He takes my hand and places it on his crotch so I feel his erection. "I don't know what in the bloody hell happened for the past hour. I've been saying my ABC's backwards and reciting the periodic table, trying to calm down and not rationalize begging you to leave with me to go back to the hotel."

I lean forward too fast, clumsily kissing him as our chests bump. I brace myself by gripping his broad shoulders, feeling the stacks of muscles under his light blue dress shirt. His fingers delve into my hair, his palm cradling my face as he matches my need and desire, nipping at my bottom lip with his teeth and then tracing the minor wound with his tongue.

"Think Coop's adjusted to us being together yet?" he asks.

I shake my head, knowing that request is impossible, and yet hoping like hell he will accept it. "I hope so."

He chuckles at my contradiction, his lips so close to mine I can't see it, but I feel the gentle rumble against my chest as I wind my arms tighter and kiss him again.

"THAT SHOW WAS INCREDIBLE," Nessie gushes as I slide into the backseat with her and Cooper. "I have now added watching every one of their shows to my bucket list."

"What did you think, Coop?" I ask him.

"It was good."

His simple and blasé answer has me peering around Nessie to look at him because my best friend is rarely simple and never blasé unless it comes to shoes or fashion. "You didn't like it?"

Nessie starts to giggle like a schoolgirl, throwing her head back as she leans into Cooper. "We barely watched it," she admits. "I mean, we watched *parts* of it, but it was dark, and that show was so sexy, and we kind of turned our private room into the back of a movie theater and made out."

Cooper rubs his fingers over his eyes, and I can sense his embarrassment before he looks at me apologetically. I understand his contradiction that's visible in his expression so well; the happiness and sadness. The thrill and regret. The excitement and melancholy. Because as they move forward and grow, our friendship changes. Some changes are minor and others greater, and this is just the beginning. I know that like me, he's wondering how many more changes will come with me dating Tyler.

We pull up to the hotel, where the valet opens our doors. Tyler climbs out of the car, his attention moving to me. "I need to grab a couple of reports. They're going to renovate a portion of the gym, and I need to get approvals over before we leave in the morning. Coop, you want to check it out?" Ty asks.

"Hell, yes."

"We'll be up soon." He kisses me sweetly. "My room tonight," he whispers against my ear before pulling away.

I feel lightheaded at the silent promise of staying with him tonight as he and Cooper disappear toward the front desk.

"I wish we could stay longer, and at the same time, am exhausted and ready to go," Nessie says, linking her arm with mine. "Does that make sense?"

I nod, laughing at how well I understand.

"The fountains are about to start! We're going to miss them!" someone exclaims to their friend as they hurry past us.

Nessie's eyes grow round. "We haven't seen the fountains." She spins to face me. "We have to see the fountains."

I nod. "It's a must."

Nessie grins. "Come on!" We head back outside, the air feeling warm in contrast to the air-conditioned lobby as we head in the direction of the iconic Fountains of Bellagio. Nessie fishes her phone out of her purse and starts texting Coop. "If I learned nothing else from Arizona, it was that we tell people where we're going," she says.

I laugh. "Look at you, creating rules."

"I think I could live in the Southwest," Nessie says as we weave through the crowds of people.

Her words catch my attention. "Yeah?"

She nods. "I like that it's warm without the intense humidity and without storming every afternoon to hatch a million mosquitoes."

"You still have the desert and extreme heat."

Our heels clip along the sidewalk as we hurry toward the fountains, though they'll play again shortly if we miss them. "Or maybe we just stay in Seattle," she suggests. "I don't like the dreary days, but I like the four seasons, and I really love the mountains."

"But what about the beach? Disney World? Walking outside during December in a T-shirt?" I ask.

"I'll miss that stuff, but I'm good with planning visits to do all that," Nessie says with a gentle shrug like she's already made up her mind. "In Seattle, we can still live by the beach or downtown or in one of those old neighborhoods with the Victorian houses you love so much."

Sometimes, these thoughts are paralyzing—the reality that we might be separated because of jobs or preferences—the reality we might choose to live on a separate coast than our family and all that we know and love. What will Cooper choose to do? What about Tyler?

My solace is knowing we still have two years at Brighton before any of these decisions have to be made.

"Did you really think Ty and I would get together?" I ask.

Her eyes grow round with excitement. We've had so little time together to gossip and talk about things. Today, many of our spa treatments were individualized and had us separated. "Oh my gosh, Chloe, *yes*! I told you freshman year that you should date him. Remember?"

"You also suggested I date Cooper freshman year," I remind her.

She cringes. "That was before Ty came into the picture. There's something about him—about you guys together. I don't know how to explain it exactly, but you just make sense. Like he brings out the playful side of you or something. Plus, he is so attentive to you. That's how I knew you guys were going to get together. Like when you fell asleep on our first day on the way to New Orleans, he was the first to notice, and he turned down his music, and when we had to stop in Texas, he didn't want you to go out to the car alone to get things, and he sent lunch to us when we were hiking. He notices things and pays attention. I'm convinced it was sexual tension that always made you guys fight."

"Pretty sure it was just him."

She laughs, pulling me tighter as she wraps her arm around my waist. "I've missed you these past few days."

I nod, leaning my head against hers. "I've missed you, too. But I'm glad you and Coop are so happy together. I should have been more supportive from the get-go."

She shakes her head. "Honestly, I'm glad you weren't because it made me have to think about things and consider what it would be like. I had to move slower, and I think that helped ensure we were both ready and had the same intentions. And I think it makes sex better. Everything is *so* good with him."

I close my eyes and shake my head to stop the images from forming. "I don't want to hear it."

"But what he does with his hands," Nessie says.

"Nope. No. Nope." I shake my head again. "I need some more time to get used to things before I start hearing these details."

She laughs at my discomfort, but it's brief as the music for the fountains begins, and we race the rest of the way to catch the fountains dance in sync to the music.

"Hey, are you guys sisters?" a guy asks us. He's middle-aged with a grizzly beard and is wearing jeans and boots that make him stand out even more as a tourist. Beside him are three guys. One stands closer that the rest with dark hair, dark eyes, and a smirk that curls one side of his uneven mouth as he listens to our interaction, while the others peer at one of their phones.

"You aren't going to answer me?" he asks, his tone turning belliger-ent. It's a situation I loathe because I'm a firm believer that everyone should act with grace and kindness, and yet I also hold strongly to the belief that politeness and obedience are oceans apart. "I think I have your card," he says, reaching into his pocket and pulling out an entire stack of the hooker cards that are passed out on corners in Vegas.

"Let's go," I say, grabbing Nessie's hand and moving toward the walk-way, content with seeing the fountains from another viewpoint—one far away from this guy.

"Don't get shy on me now," he says, his boots loud as he trails behind us. "I just want to know if you offer a two-for-one deal because my buddy's getting married..."

I spin on my heel. "We're not prostitutes, asshole."

He leers, his gaze never meeting my eyes.

Jerk.

"She talks," he says.

"Not to you," Nessie says, grabbing my hand again.

"Good. I prefer girls who are silent." He reaches forward as though he's going to touch one of us and stops when I swat his hand away.

"You're drunk," I tell him. "You're being an asshole, and you're likely going to forget this moment tomorrow, but I'm going to warn you that girls stand up for each other. I scream for help and every woman here is going to be ready to kick you in your useless balls."

Two women standing near us step away from the fence. They look around our mom's age. "I prefer to use my knee," one of them says, her attention on the stranger.

He raises his hands and takes a step back, chuckling like the situation is funny. "I just assumed twins, Vegas..." He shrugs.

Nessie looks at me, her eyebrows lowered with anger, then looks beyond him at his group of friends who are still several feet back.

"Friends of Neanderthal, your buddy needs a leash before he gets punched in the face."

A couple stops beside us, the guy glancing between the burly bearded jackass and us. "Everything okay?"

The dark-haired friend of the jerk jogs over, grabbing his friend by the shoulders and redirecting him. "Sorry. Sorry," he says, steering him back to their group.

"You guys okay?" the guy asks again, his demeanor friendly but cautious.

Nessie nods. "Yeah, thanks for stopping." She looks at the two women. "And thanks for offering to knee him in the ballsack."

The woman who made the threat smiles. "I'm a little disappointed I didn't get to do it."

We're still laughing when Cooper and Tyler appear, dressed in their suits as they laugh about something. The sight of them together— Cooper happy, Tyler unguarded—tugs at that space in my chest that has always noticed too much about Tyler. His friendship with Cooper is how, aside from all of his negative traits, I always knew he was a good guy because Coop's acceptance and tolerance for bullshit is so low thanks to having wasted so much of it on his dad.

Cooper's smile falls as he looks at me, his gaze becoming severe as he scans the others around us. "What happened?" he asks, his focus jogging between Nessie and me.

I shake my head. "Nothing."

Ty's eyebrows are drawn as they come to a stop. "What's wrong?"

"Some guy just got mouthy with them, but they were amazing. You guys should be impressed with your girlfriends because they were strong and fearless and complete badasses," one of the women who had stopped tells them.

Ty's eyebrows jump as he pulls his hands out of his pockets, still scanning over the crowds. "What happened?"

"Which guy?" Cooper asks.

Nessie glances at me and then the others. "Thanks again, guys. Have a great night." She wraps both hands around Cooper's arm and leads him to the corner so we can cross the street.

Tyler's unease is apparent, which has me offering a quick wave to the strangers and weaving my hand in his.

"Let's go," I tell him.

His muscles are constricted, reluctant to leave. "Is that him?"

I glance up at where the bearded man is waving at us like the moron he clearly is. "While I really enjoy seeing new sights, jail is not a place I want to see," I tell him. "He was dumb and drunk, and he's going to go to bed and wake up with a killer hangover and likely a broken nose if he continues this. Meanwhile, we can go and celebrate our last night in Vegas. Alone. Not in a jail cell."

His jaw flexes with irritation, and then he pulls out his phone and hits a few buttons before slipping his arm securely around my waist.

We catch up to Nessie and Cooper, who's still growling out threats and asking for details as they wait for the crosswalk.

"It was nothing," she assures him.

"I saw your face." He looks at me. "I don't understand why you guys won't just tell me what happened?"

"Because we handled it," Nessie says, placing a hand on her chest. "You heard that woman. We were badasses." She tries to dazzle him with a smile, but Coop's got his protective growly side on, the one that he's always had toward us, even when he was the scrawny book nerd before the muscles and height kicked in to make him a legitimate threat.

Cooper swings his gaze to mine. It's a challenge, a demand that stands on ten years of friendship and not keeping (many) secrets from one another.

I sigh, glancing across the street where the guy is still standing with his friends. "The guy was being a douche. He had some liquid courage and backwoods audacity and asked if we were hookers."

Tyler stiffens, and my grip on his hand tightens reflexively. "And we handled it," I repeat Nessie's words. "Team badass." We high five each other.

Cooper's eyes are sharp as they search mine to see if I'm withholding any additional details before he releases a deep sigh. "Next time, just kick the asshole in the nuts."

I grin. "Deal."

"I sent his picture to the head of security at the hotel. He'll contact the cops and have him followed, make sure he doesn't act like a fucking tosser to others." Tyler says before taking a long breath through his nose.

"Good. Hopefully, he fucks up again and gets arrested." Cooper stabs the elevator button with his finger.

I glance at Nessie, releasing a heavy sigh. I was hoping this night would be filled with laughter and fun as we celebrated our final night in Vegas, rather than being accused of being a hooker for the second time in two days. I glance at my reflection in the doors, studying my dress and hair and makeup. At the beginning of this night, I'd been concerned I hadn't looked sexy enough, my pink dress looking more like something I'd wear to a wedding than a Vegas club. Yet, the invisible label of "hooker" makes me feel tarnished in a way that makes my regret for this evening wane as my annoyance at others making me feel less with such simple and careless words burns across my skin.

21

TYLER

"Hey, Nessie, truth or dare?" Chloe says as the lift doors close. She raises her chin and straightens her shoulders, attempting to push the bullshit out. It's something she constantly does, and one of the things that's always drawn me to her. She hates to focus on the lows, which I'm convinced is the only reason she thinks I'm redeemable.

Vanessa turns to her, a smile creeping across her features. "I was wondering whose turn it was. Oh, man ... truth?"

Chloe grins. "If you woke up as a guy tomorrow, what's the first thing you'd do?"

Cooper shouts out an unintelligible objection as Vanessa laughs. "I'd freaking find out if morning wood is a myth."

Chloe's nose crinkles with a giggle. "You're so lying. You'd be outside peeing your name on the sidewalk."

"Oh my gosh, you're right." Vanessa belts out a laugh, her hand reaching for Chloe's arm as the two start giggling, talking more with hand motions than actual words.

"What would you do?" Vanessa asks, looking at Cooper.

"Are you kidding? If I had boobs, I might never leave the house again," he admits. "Tell them, Ty."

I consider the idea of waking up as a woman and shake my head. "You're not wrong."

The tension seems to stay in the lift as we pile out into the suite. "Goodnight," Nessie says, hugging Chloe and kissing her cheek. "Love you."

"Love you, too," Chloe says before giving Coop a side hug. He kisses the top of her head, an action I've seen no less than a hundred times that only tonight registers about the significance of their connection. He read her emotions so quickly, recognizing something was amiss before he even realized it with Vanessa.

Vanessa hugs me, her head turned, watching the same interaction. "It's not..." She shakes her head. "It's innocent," she tells me.

I nod, knowing it is, and yet I still feel the pang of jealousy as I watch the two laugh.

Chloe's eyes drift to mine, and her smile changes, growing as our eyes connect.

"Let's go to bed," Vanessa says, placing an arm around Cooper and heading toward the stairs.

I grab a glass and fill it with water, knowing it's a part of Chloe's nightly routine. "What are you thinking about?"

"Are you sure you want to hear all this? Because a lot is going on up here." She motions to her head.

"I want to hear it all. All the unedited contemplations of Chloe Robinson."

Chloe looks at me, her eyes deep pools of thoughts and emotions that make me want to jump into the deepest end. She walks closer, stopping at the counter across from me where she leans back, crossing one ankle over the other. "I hate that men call women whores and hookers and cunts. I hate that it bothers me when they do because I know it's a power game and that it reflects on them and not the person they're speaking to, but I really hate that it devalues my sexuality. I went from having this incredibly hot and intimate moment with you that made me feel beautiful and desired and happy, and one stupid and callous idiot said something to me, and now I'm feeling like I should be wearing baggy sweatshirts and jeans so people can't see my body.

49

"It's like if I'm too feminine, I'm a skank, and if I'm not, I'm ugly. There's this tiny fine line, and it's so easy to breach it."

The aggression I'd felt outside when Cooper recognized there was an issue comes back with a vengeance, knitting itself into my skin, wanting retribution. Yet, I have little doubt that vengeance is what Chloe's seeking. I set the glass of water on the counter, hating that this is likely only going to get worse for her when we return to Brighton and the rumors start to fly about us dating because I've seen it happen—watched as people made something out of nothing. Someone feels inadequate or jealous, and that leads to judgment and hurtful words. I want to protect her from that ugly side. "Fuck that bloke. Tonight was perfect. You were perfect."

Her eyes fall from mine, and I move closer to her, tipping her chin up with my forefinger until her gorgeous green eyes meet mine. "Chloe, you're always perfect. Whether you're wearing sweatpants or a dress, there's never a single moment I see anything except perfection. And that chap did too, and you're absolutely right, he wanted to tear you down to make himself feel like more because he probably has a pencil dick that he's trying to make up for by being an absolute tool. And to be honest, I can talk a big game about not caring about it or what anyone says, but in reality, I'd like nothing more than to make him bleed."

She smirks. "Karma will catch up with him."

I nod. "Hopefully in the form of a broken femur."

Chloe laughs, and I feel her shoulders relax. I slide my hands to either of her hips, tugging her toward me so she's pressed against my chest, her eyes brightening as she grabs my forearms to brace herself. I skim my nose across her cheekbone. "Let's go to bed. We have another long day in the car tomorrow."

She turns her neck to look at me, but she remains silent.

"What?"

She shakes her head. "Nothing." She takes a step back, reaching for the glass of water I'd filled for her, and takes a long drink before refilling it. Frustration rattles in my chest, reminding me how I've spent the past two years working not to be able to interpret all her small habits and expressions and how much I now regret it. I want to be able to read her as easily as Cooper can—know with a single glance that something is wrong and have an educated guess on what it entails.

I take her hand as she reaches for her newly filled glass, twisting her in my arms like it's a dance move. It earns me a radiating smile. "I want to know what you're thinking. I want to give you what you want." I slip my fingers into her hair, my palms resting along her jaw. Her gaze quickly diverts from mine, making me think she's going to pull away or remind me this is my own doing.

"I just..." She pauses, licking her lips. "I wanted to continue what we started at the show, and I thought when you mentioned me staying in your room you..."

Confidence courses through my veins like adrenaline. "Chloe, if you ever ... *ever* want me or want me to pleasure you, all you have to do is ask. That is something I will do regardless of the day or time or whatever is on my fucking calendar."

She moves her gaze to meet mine. "Things were going so well tonight, and then ... if we hadn't..."

I shake my head. "Fuck that guy. Fuck what he thinks. It means absolute shit to me. The only reason I care is that it affected you. I was already planning to take you upstairs and spread you in front of the Vegas skyline, but I didn't want to suggest that after that wanker made you feel like he did. This means we both want to shag, and we both think that guy is Napoleon Bonaparte level of arsehole."

Her grin returns, as well as that flash in her eyes that I'd seen when I pulled her against me, and I quickly file the detail away as pertinent information. "Well, if you're sure you're not too tired..."

In one quick move, I hoist her over my shoulder, making her yelp, followed by a train of giggles and warnings as I move toward the stairs.

"Ty!" she exclaims when I climb the steps two at a time. "I'm not wearing underwear."

I slide my hand over the back of her exposed thighs, skimming across her impossibly soft skin until I reach her exposed backside. I knead my fingers into the globe of her arse, wishing for a moment that Cooper and Vanessa weren't here because I'd make it a personal mission to have sex on every object of this hotel suite. On the kitchen island with her legs spread, on the stairs from behind, on the chair in the study... She giggles again, but it's softer, throatier. I grip her backside fully, tracing her seam as I pull my hand back so I can open the bedroom door.

I close the door and leave the lights off, the opened shades and bright skyline illuminating my path to the bed. I set her on her feet because tonight I want to see all of her, taste every inch of skin, explore every bit of Chloe. Her smile is playful as I stand to my full height. I shuck off my jacket, tossing it to the bench at the end of the bed. I release the buttons at my wrists and loosen my tie, studying her reaction to each of my movements like film for football, noting how her eyes dilate and darken with lust.

She reaches for my shirt, tugging it loose from my dress pants and quickly working through the buttons. I toss it and my tie to join my jacket, and then her fingers impatiently peel at my white tee. I reach for the hem, ridding it with a quick pull and letting it fall to our feet. Her eyes dance over my chest as her fingers slowly glide across my skin, looking at me like I'm something to marvel. Then her green gaze lifts to mine, and something registers in her eyes—an emotion that steals my breath and wayward past and makes me feel like a giant among men, all because of a single look that my mind is racing to memorize and replace all the doubt.

I slant my lips over hers, her mouth still cold from the water she drank downstairs. Her scent fills my lungs and ushers my thoughts until I'm consumed with her. Our tongues twist and breaths mingle while our hands roam possessively. I run my thumb over her breast, and her body arches as she quietly gasps, tipping me from desire to pure need.

"In the back," Chloe says, reading my thoughts. "Three buttons at the top, zipper at my back." She turns, and I follow the directions, reigning in my weakening patience to keep myself from tearing at the fabric. The pink dress slips down her soft curves, exposing a teal bra and her bare arase that have my cock straining against the fly of my pants.

Chloe turns, slipping her heels off and letting them fall with a soft thump, and then my hands are on her again as I work to unfasten her bra and rid it as well. Her nipples are peaked, inviting me to run my thumbs across the sensitive flesh. She pushes her shoulders back, her breath coming out as a pant. It's so fucking addictive that I do it again, rolling her nipples between my thumbs and forefingers, twisting and toying as she drops her head back, allowing me access to her neck where I suck and kiss along her collarbone and neck as I continue to tease her.

Her short nails rake into my hair, and my name is on her breath as she exhales. It's so fucking sexy I groan against her skin, wanting to hear my name in the same desperate plea. Her lips dot along my jaw, meeting my mouth in a kiss that is a challenge as she places her hands on my belt, releasing the clasp and making quick work of fishing it from the loops. But I'm not finished yet, so I haul her onto the bed as my belt falls to the ground with the rest of our discarded items. I climb over her, drunk on the brazen look in her eyes. I close my lips over one erect peak, and she moans my name. I swear to God, it's even sexier than when she sighed my name, giving me another new goal as I run my fingers over her bare breast while I flick her other nipple with my tongue before licking a path to her other tit, where I draw circles with my tongue and gently scrape my teeth over the erect point. Her hands bury into my hair, holding me there as she moans with pleasure.

I lap at her nipple as I trace down the path of her body to her pubic bone, and she shivers—gasps.

Fuck me.

I trace down her seam with my fingers, feeling that she's already wet for me.

Fucking soaked.

I groan against her, my tongue flat and relentless as I try to take the upper hand and find some control again.

Chloe widens her legs, and she reaches down, placing her hand on mine, and any semblance of me trying to find my control is gone as she moans with impatience, pressing my fingers down on her core. "Please," she begs.

She fucking begs.

I run my fingers over her slit, rubbing her clit with my thumb. Her pressure on my hand loosens as she sighs a quiet, "Yes."

I return to her other breast, my tongue coming down on the peak as I slide a finger inside her, and she calls out my name. I move my fingers over and inside her in tandem until she's writhing, and then I quickly finish undressing and grab a condom that I roll onto my throbbing cock and grab her ankles, dragging her to the edge of the bed, making her laugh. She falls silent as I rub my cock along her seam. I roll my thumb across her clit again, rubbing her as I slowly bury myself into her, pausing to allow her a moment to adjust as her chest rises with heavy breaths of need and a hint of discomfort that I'm grateful passes quickly. I continue to rub over her clit, trying to ensure pleasure is stronger than her soreness.

She closes her eyes, and her muscles relax under my hands. I move slowly, gently thrusting inside of her, and her reaction is a soft moan as she nods, her hair a wave behind her. I thrust a bit harder and faster, watching her face with each move, obsessed with the soft sounds she makes and how she stares at me, unashamed as I drive into her.

When her thighs start to tremble, my movements become faster as I count the number of times she cries my name like we're at a fucking stadium, and her cheer is the only one I can hear. She fists the sheet in her hands as the pleasure of her orgasm parts her lips and furrows her brow, and I chase it with my own, losing myself in this moment until I don't care about a single damn thing except being here with her.

I pull out, kissing the inside of her calf that is still resting against my chest, before I gently rest it against the bed. Her eyes are closed, and she's still except for her breaths lifting her chest.

I lean forward, brushing my lips across hers, and she reaches for me, weakly grabbing my shoulders. Her eyes slowly drift open, and she smiles, kissing me again.

"I'll be right back," I tell her.

She nods, closing her eyes again as her hands slip down my arms. I make quick work of cleaning myself up and return to the bed, pulling her flush against me.

"I feel like Jell-O," she says, brushing her hair back and nuzzling her face against my chest.

I grin, running my hand over the bare expanse of her back.

"Do you have to wake up early tomorrow?"

I shake my head. "No."

Her arm tightens around my waist. "Good."

I kiss the top of her head. "You should rest. I'm going to be waking you up soon, spreading you out in front of that window, and fucking you senseless." I point toward the floor-to-ceiling window. It's mirrored on the outside, but there's still something borderline taboo about having sex with her while we watch people pass in front of the hotel, and I can tell she agrees when she leans up with shock and excitement shimmering in her eyes.

"You're addictive," she tells me, dropping a kiss to my chest.

I run my fingers through her hair. "I feel the same way."

She releases a long breath and a quiet hum. I wait until her breathing levels, and then I close my eyes, falling asleep to the sound of her peaceful slumber.

22

CHLOE

"For the love of Christ, will you roll up your window?" Vanessa growls from the back seat.

I smile, too tired to object. Exhaustion and pleasure have me too sated and content to argue. Tyler woke me up in the middle of the night with his head between my legs and then took me while I laid on my side with a dizzying orgasm that made me lose feeling in my toes, my body was tingling so badly. Then, he joined me in the shower where I took him in my mouth, drunk on the power I felt as he groaned my name. He didn't finish in my mouth though, insisting on carrying out his promise to bend me over in front of the window. I blush, recalling the scene and what it would have looked like to anyone if they'd been able to see—me bracing myself on the window as he spread me and entered me from behind. If they could have heard me as I begged him not to stop ... seen the rhythm as our hips moved perfectly in sync with each other until we spiraled and exploded together... "We're in California. The windows are supposed to be down," I remind her.

"I swear..." she starts.

Tyler laughs, reaching across the space and running his hand over my thigh. There's something so addictive about seeing his hands on me, so completely distracting that I forget why and if I even care about the window being open and roll it up.

I trace his fingers with mine, smiling as the desert passes us, the sky a bright and welcoming shade of blue. I lean back and close my eyes, and when his pinky locks with mine, I fall asleep.

"CHLOE," Nessie calls my name, her voice impatient again.

I open my eyes and discover a black sweatshirt spread over my lap that hadn't been there when I'd fallen asleep. Tyler's light blue eyes are muted with annoyance, his lips set in a thin line.

"Sorry," I say, sitting up, shivering as the cold air from the vent blows on me.

Ty shakes his head.

"We're trying to decide if we should stop for lunch or just eat when we get there." Vanessa's tone is factual and tight, proof that she's upset about something.

I lean forward, attempting to clear the fog from my thoughts. "Um..." I glance around. "How far are we from San Diego?"

"Three hours," she replies instantly.

I nod, hearing the request in her irritated tone. "Sure. Let's stop. Stretch our legs."

"We've gone seven straight hours in the car. It's only been two," Cooper argues.

"I could use some coffee," I tell him.

I glance at Ty again, attempting to gather the pieces from what I missed while I dozed off. Everyone seems annoyed, the air tense. Ty's knuckles are white from gripping the steering wheel so tight.

"I'll see what's nearby." I reach for my phone and quickly locate a few options that I list off, only to hear silence in response. "Why don't we try this taco place?" I suggest. "They have really good reviews, and the pictures look amazing. I am all over this," I say, flipping through to their menu. "They even have fish tacos for you, Coop."

"See!" Nessie yells.

I grip the seat and twist around to finally see them. "See what? We

don't have to stop for tacos. There's a burger joint and a fish place and…"
I reach for my phone to look at the list of restaurants again.

"It doesn't matter," Nessie says, turning to look out her window.

"What's the deal?" I ask.

"Nothing," Cooper snaps.

I glance back at Ty, who slowly shakes his head like he's equally annoyed. "They've been bickering since you fell asleep."

"We haven't been *bickering*," Nessie says, her tone coated with a heavy dose of defiance.

"Fun," I say. "I was dreaming about surfing. Which is kind of strange because I've never been surfing and I'm not sure I'd like to. It seems like a lot of work, and there's something kind of freaky to me that we know more about space than we do our oceans. Like, what's below you while you're surfing, you know?"

"Not now, Chloe," Cooper says.

"Did you forget something at the hotel again?" I ask, turning my attention to him. "It wasn't your phone this time, was it?"

"He called me Chloe," Nessie admits.

"Gross. You weren't naked, right?"

"God! No!" Nessie cries as Cooper rubs his hand over his face, shaking his head.

"Then what's the problem?"

"The problem is you guys still have this connection, and sometimes I feel like I'm an interloper on the Chloe and Cooper show."

I think about this morning, how Tyler had to take a call with his dad, and how Cooper and I had sat at breakfast, laughing about football and school and how much we were both looking forward to seeing San Francisco for the first time after our upcoming couple of nights in San Diego.

I glance at Ty again, concerned about his feelings in regard to the situation. His eyes remain on the road, making it difficult for me to understand what he's thinking.

"Ness, you know it's not like that. Cooper and I—"

"Are best friends. I know," Nessie cuts me off.

"Ness," I try again, softening my voice. I select the taco shop and make it so my phone dictates directions to the restaurant. I sit back in my seat, working on sorting through the disarray of emotions that are raining down on me, questions and doubts about if I've overstepped my boundaries as a friend when their relationship is brand new and still in that honeymoon phase where both are obsessed with each other. Everything feels so fragile about each of our relationships; concerns about getting in the way of Ty and Cooper's relationship, not meddling with Cooper and Nessie's relationship, spending less time with both so they have enough time together, while also trying not to take all of Tyler's time as he searches for a balance with work and not trying to come off as too much, too soon because our relationship feels both brand new and yet our familiarity keeps creating a false sense of ripeness. It reminds me of standing outside in July while eating an ice cream cone, and each side is starting to melt, and I'm trying to catch each drip.

The moment Tyler pulls into the taco restaurant, Nessie hops out of the car.

Cooper sighs loudly. "It wasn't..."

"You should talk to her," I say, though my hand itches to grab the door handle. "She needs your assurance," I follow up, though I want to give her mine because this is how it's always been. We're there for each other and repair the walls when they start to fall.

"She's pissed at me," he points out.

I nod. "You called her by another girl's name, Coop. Any girl would be upset and feeling self-conscious."

"But I didn't call her any girl's name. I called her *your* name, and it was because we were talking about what to do in San Diego tomorrow, and usually it's you who's talking about plans."

I twist in my seat to face him, my unease growing by the second because I can feel Nessie's duress, and not responding to it makes me physically and emotionally uncomfortable as I attempt to remain patient and allow Cooper to go, knowing this is the role he's wanted for so long and the one she wants him to fill. "Coop, you have one minute to decide. You know Nessie. You know she's sensitive and impulsive and jealous. You take the bad with the good. If you want her best, you have to accept her worst as well."

He looks at me, recognition dawning in his expression. He doesn't say anything before releasing his seat belt and quickly hopping out of the car, jogging toward the restaurant.

I lean against my seat, feeling like a part of my heart has just left my body as I watch through the large picture window of the restaurant as Coop bows his head, leaning his forehead against hers.

Tyler reaches across the space, setting his hand on my thigh again. "I might need to be present each time you give Coop advice because you're pretty good at that."

I scoff, shaking my head. "It's weird," I admit. "It feels like I'm trusting someone else to do one of my most important roles in life, and even though it's Cooper and I know this is right and needs to happen, I just feel so..." I can't fill in the blank because the list is seemingly endless. "I know it's right. I know he wants to be this person for her and that he deserves to be, and so does she." I turn my attention to Tyler, combing through my hair with my fingers. "Does my relationship with Cooper bother you?"

He blinks several times, like the question has caught him off guard. He shakes his head. "I mean, I'm sure I'll feel a little like Vanessa did at times, but sometimes I'll probably feel that way with her as well. They both know you so well. Last night, I could tell something was off when I saw you, but it was Cooper who registered that something was wrong. He saw you and," he snaps his fingers, "he instantly knew there was a problem. One look—that's all he needed. You guys share a powerful bond, and sometimes it seems like more than just friendship."

"It is," I tell him. "Cooper's family. He's like a brother to me. My biggest fear as a teenager was that Nessie and Coop would want to attend different colleges because I had no idea how I'd choose. And then he met you, and I was insanely jealous."

Tyler's eyes grow wide with surprise.

I nod. "Cooper's never had another best friend. It was always me, and then he started canceling plans with me so you guys could get in more gym time and inviting me to hang out with you guys rather than vice versa, and I was crazy jealous. I think that largely contributed to why I wanted to hate you so much at first."

He smiles, his hand at my thigh constricting. "Cooper would pull the moon out of the sky for you if you asked."

"I know he'll always be there for me, but things have changed. With you and him, and him and Nessie."

"And you and me," he adds.

I glance at him, the heaviness in my heart lightening as his blue eyes anchor me, filling me with a hope I've been fighting since he first kissed me. He moves his hand from my thigh to my jaw. "You scared the shit out of me our freshman year. You still do."

I try to accept his compliment gracefully but feel the lines of confusion creasing my forehead.

"People usually always ask for favors, try to become my new best friend or girlfriend because they look at me and see opportunities and money. You've never asked me for anything."

"You know I still don't want anything, right? I don't like you because you can buy me expensive tickets and trips to the spa. I'd be fine if we were staying in Motel 6's and eating Burger King each night. It's never been about what you can buy—it's about what you do, how you make me feel."

Tyler's eyes flash with humor and warmth as he smiles.

"I don't want you to feel jealous of Cooper or anyone."

His fingers slide higher, his thumb stroking my cheekbone, making my heart accelerate as I lean closer, wanting him to kiss me so badly it's difficult to breathe. "When we get back to Brighton, I'm worried you'll see the ugly side of being with me. Rumors and arseholes trying to play head games and bullshit. I saw it this spring with Lincoln and his girlfriend. It was like as soon as he started dating her, every girl worked harder to gain his attention and make her jealous, and she became the guy every bloke wanted to date. That's going to be you now, too."

Hope is invading nearly all of doubt's place as his words struggle to infiltrate my thoughts.

"I just need to know you're going to be okay and that at the end of every night, you know that it's you I'm going to be reaching for and wanting."

This conversation seems so big and also clunky as we omit a dozen words and what they each represent. Still, I nod. "This doesn't exclude morning sex as well, right? Because I thought you were enjoying our time in the shower this morning," I tease, desperate to infuse some humor into the conversation because I'm afraid I'll be the first to knock over this stack of carefully laid words and insinuations.

His eyes darken, and he tips his head back, emitting a low growl. "That was so fucking hot." He looks at me, a conflict in his eyes as his desire tangles into our conversation. He glances at the clock, then reaches for his crotch, adjusting himself. "We should get something to eat because when we get to San Diego, we're not leaving the hotel until morning. I plan to defile you in front of every window and mirror in the suite."

I lean closer, and so does he, our lips hard and nearly punishing as we work to express our desires with only a kiss.

We step into the small restaurant, and I'm instantly famished as the scents of fresh tortillas and spiced meats and cilantro greet us. "I want it all," I say.

Ty chuckles, his hand back on my hip, which is quickly becoming one of my favorite places for his touch. I love the way he mindlessly traces my hip bone and reminds me of him gripping me when he moves inside of me. "You liked that chimichanga in Texas. Do you want to try that again? Or the street tacos? Or both?"

"Chimichanga," I say, realizing how Nessie might be right about how much he knows about me and reveling in the fact.

I turn around, wondering if we should grab a separate table when Nessie waves an arm at me, moving her purse off the table that's meant for four.

"Go," Ty says softly. "I'll order."

Hesitation lingers in my thoughts, keeping me in place.

"I'm glad you have them, and I know how important they are to you. I knew that from the beginning. I won't interfere with that. Their connections with you only make me want to work harder to be the person you would get lost in the desert with or punch someone in the face for. I don't want to replace them—I can't replace them—I want to cut out my own place in your heart that is just us—just me."

I kiss him because words aren't sufficient or adequate for how he makes me feel.

23

TYLER

I glance at the clock and sigh, rolling my shoulders in an attempt to ease the tension as I reach for my phone to text Chloe.

Me: I'm sorry. This is taking much longer than I'd hoped.

Chloe: It's totally okay. I understand.

I start a dozen responses, wondering if Cooper or Vanessa is with her and trying not to sound like a possessive dick with the questions that linger as the time stretches.

Jim, the GM for this hotel, sits down with a filled cup of coffee, his intention to sit here for several more hours clear as he takes a seat, each of his moves unhurried.

"You know, what you've sent me is a great start. Why don't you take some time to consider the questions I've asked you and compile some quotes for those projects you mentioned and we can discuss them further." Jim would try and squeeze blood from a fucking turnip, I've realized. We've spent most of the afternoon with him asking for things he doesn't need simply to increase his budget because he's got this false sense that if he doesn't get it now when he doesn't need it, he might not when he does.

"I want to discuss some line items in the budget," I continue, opening the spreadsheet I'd marked up last night while Chloe slept, her back exposed as the sheets pooled at her waist. We'd had sex with her sitting on the bathroom counter and then with her bending over the counter, allowing me an amazing view of her breasts as I thrust inside of her. I recall the curve of her back and shoulders, the pleasure that had her moaning my name. How we'd sat on the bed in our underwear, feasting on room service while I told her about the first time my Uncle Kip got me drunk when I was fourteen and how I refused to drink again until freshman year at Brighton. I can still smell her skin as I crawled over her last night and woke her up by tracing over her nipples with my tongue until they peaked—so reactive and sensitive to every touch. We ordered room service at three in the morning, and I listened to her explain how our galaxy was the shape of a fried egg and how each galaxy has its own story, potentially formed in different ways, all of which are largely debated. She listened to my questions that seemed rudimentary in comparison to the concepts she was sharing with me, patiently explaining more information that only created more questions, and with each one I asked, her eyes seemed to burn a bit brighter with an energy and appreciation as she shared this part of her life that I've always known meant a great deal. It was fucking beautiful.

"Sure," Jim says, visibly annoyed by my change in the conversation. "Which items were you curious about?"

"The concierge lounge. I like this idea, and I'm curious where it's going and what it will offer guests?"

His brow furrows. "Lounge?"

I nod, spinning my laptop to face him. "It appears there's been a budget for food, construction, alcohol, staff..."

He looks across the details and figures and shakes his head. "You must have the wrong information. Is this for San Francisco? Hawaii? This sounds like something Hawaii would implement."

I open my file to provide the hard copy I'd printed yesterday before leaving Vegas. "Unless the accountant made a mistake, this is what I received." I slide the stack of papers to him.

He shakes his head. "I'll have to ask Mr. Avery. Maybe he was planning something?" He looks at me, his confusion falling. "Have you spoken to your father? He probably knows what this is." He's smug, the cocky son of a bitch. His large salary and power over several hundred employees provide him the false sense of bravado that has me itching to flex my power over him.

I shake my head, knowing he's not worth it. He might be an annoying little shit, but he has good numbers, and his staff likes him. His issue seems to be with me alone; likely my age or possibly the nepotism, unaware that I grew up learning the ins and outs of the Banks Hotel chain. "I'll be certain to ask him because I can't imagine his surprise at finding five million dollars unaccounted for." I start to gather the papers, but he reaches for them.

"Before you call him, let me talk to our accountant. Maybe this was filed incorrectly."

I push my seat back and close my laptop as I stand. "Thank you for your time."

"I actually have a list of things I'd like to cover with you," he says, remaining seated.

"Wonderful. I look forward to receiving them along with the details of the lounge." I grab my things and head for the door.

"Mr. Banks," he objects. "With all due respect, sir—"

I shake my head. "It took you three and a half months to accept my meeting, and you were an hour late. If you want my time, you need to respect my time. Otherwise, I'll find someone who will. You're not inimitable."

His lips close and then open several times as he struggles to find a response.

"Have a good day," I tell him, leaving for my room.

After changing into shorts and a T-shirt, I climb into the back seat of a hotel car that takes me the short distance to Balboa Park, where Chloe took a car this morning. I glance at my watch, noting it's nearly four already.

Shit.

I'd told her I'd be done by noon.

Me: You wouldn't believe how boring everything is in comparison to your explanation of exoplanets.

Chloe: That's the spreadsheets talking.

Me: Where are you?

Chloe: The Air and Space Museum at Balboa Park.

I tell the driver where to drop me off.

Me: Anything you haven't seen before?

Chloe: A little. How are your meetings going?

Me: Exhausting.

Chloe: I'm sorry. Hopefully, San Fran won't be such a headache.

I spot her, wearing a pair of jeans and a T-shirt she bought in Arizona with the sleeves rolled. Her brown hair is down in waves that reach the middle of her back, her attention on her phone as she stands in front of a giant jet.

"I incorrectly assumed I'd find you in the space section," I tell her.

She turns to face me, eyes shining with surprise, and her lips spread into a wide smile as she wraps her arms around my neck. "What are you doing?"

I grin, holding her close with my hand on the swell of her backside. "I'm sorry I'm so late for our date."

She shakes her head. "It's okay. I knew you had to work. I hope you didn't rush out for me."

I wish I had sooner.

I lean forward and kiss her, reveling in the way she melts against me, her arms winding tighter around my neck like she's as dependent on me as I am her.

"Do you like planes?" I ask her when she tucks herself under my arm.

She shrugs. "I know very little about aviation."

"We could take a helicopter tour."

She shakes her head. "This is my date. You can't hijack it."

I laugh. "You're right. All I wanted was that kiss, and now I'm ready for a Robinson date."

The museum is nearly empty, with it being the middle of the week, allowing us to be louder and goofier as we pose in the spacesuit and climb into the small early planes they permit guests to sit inside. It's a side of Chloe I've only seen in fractional pieces—her carefree side where laughter fuels her while her love for adventure guides her forward.

When the museum closes a short time later, we head outside, my reluctance at returning to the hotel on the tip of my tongue. Selfishly, I want more time with her.

"Want to explore the gardens a little? And then I was thinking we could go down to Mission Beach and see the boardwalk and visit the Pacific?" She bites the inside of her cheek like she does when she gets nervous.

"Absolutely. Yes." I set a hand on her back, allowing her to choose among the dozens of gardens that surround us.

"Have you been here before?" she asks.

I nod. "But it's been quite some time. I think I was maybe twelve? Fifteen?"

"Did you travel a lot when you were young?"

I contemplate her question, realizing my reality is vastly different than most, including hers. "I did. My father always felt it was very important to be hands-on with many aspects of the company. We only hired a management company in the past ten years."

"How was that with school?"

We turn at a sign for the Australian Garden. "I lived mostly with my grandparents until I was thirteen. I had private tutors who came to their house, and I'd travel on holidays to meet up with my parents. When I was thirteen, my grandma passed away and we moved to Miami full time where I enrolled in school for the first time."

Chloe runs her hand over my forearm. "I'm sorry about your grandma."

I nod. "Me too. She was great. You would have liked her." I close my eyes, grinning when I imagine the two of them together. "She would have liked you."

A smile brightens her face. "Do you get along well with your parents?"

I don't mean to laugh, it's just hard to keep a straight face when I consider how to answer this question. Chloe's gaze is gentle, but I can tell she notices the simple changes, allowing me a bit more space as we continue to stroll along the path. "We get along fine for the most part, but in many ways, we're strangers. Even once we were living under the same roof, it was mostly my Uncle Kip who looked after me, and putting it mildly, that wasn't always the best decision." I shake my head, recalling the number of times I walked in on him drunk or having sex or both in the pool house that he claimed as his. His response was generally to invite me to join, offering me one of the girls he'd brought back from a local bar or a drink from the bottle he was finishing. "My dad and I have a shared love for the family business, but he struggles to understand my love for football, which is what started this entire trip. He thinks football's a distraction and is certain I'm going to try and make a career out of it. But that's never been my intention. I love the game. I love playing the game, but I've always wanted to help run the hotels."

Chloe doesn't say anything, occasionally making eye contact with me to verify she's listening, and I swear there are moments where she can hear the words I'm not even saying.

"My dad's in the process of training someone else to become the new CEO, so I'm trying to prove that I'm invested and want to carry this legacy on after I graduate. I just want a break from it for a while—be normal and live in one state, in one country."

"Where will you live as the CEO?" she asks, not questioning my role as anything but the CEO.

I shrug. "It won't matter. I'll have to travel a lot."

Her eyes flash to mine, hesitance and sadness evident and something that looks too close to sympathy stirring in their depths. I don't want to see any of them, much less all of them at once.

"What about you? Are you close with your parents?"

She smiles, but it's weaker than her normal brilliant smiles. "Yeah. My parents are pretty great. My mom is a lawyer, hence, Brighton. She works at preserving wildlife, and my dad's an actuary. Nessie is basically our mom: fun, outgoing, adventurous, and I'm our dad: high-strung, stubborn, and introverted."

I pull my chin back, repeating her self-assessment. "That's how you see yourself?"

"I don't mean it in a bad way. I love my dad dearly. But sometimes I'm a little envious that Nessie got all the carefree genes."

I stop, catching her waist so she hears me. "Listen to me because I am prepared to tell you this as many times as necessary. The fact that you're motivated and don't do stupid shit doesn't make you high-strung. Your love for learning and seeing new things and being kind are some of the sexiest things about you. And your stubbornness is determination, and when I see that look flash in your eyes, I feel absolutely undone."

Her gaze starts to slip, unable, or unwilling, to accept my words. "It's okay. I can admit my faults. I like rules and structure and..."

"Chloe." I duck down, so she has to look me in the eyes. "I am happy to rise to this challenge to help you see that all these things you're listing as negative traits are what make you fucking perfection. I will play and double down every. Single. Time."

Hope settles in her eyes as she stares at me, and I reach for her, sealing my lips over hers in a kiss that feels more significant as I realize how much her happiness means to me—how reliant I am on knowing she's okay. She kisses me back, her lips a complete contradiction to her words of uncertainty, demanding and inviting in ways that make me wish we weren't out here in the middle of a public park.

She kisses me once more before she leans back, a smile on her lips. "Are you done with these gardens?"

"Hotel?"

She laughs. "We leave tomorrow. We have to go see the beach first."

"I'll bring you back so you can see the beach."

She shakes her head. "I have to put my feet in the sand and see if the water is as cold as it is in Washington."

I hoist her over my shoulder, and she belts out a laugh. "I'll give you the Cliffs Notes on our drive back to the hotel."

"One hour!" she cries between peals of laughter. "I want one hour at the beach, and then I'm yours."

I slap her backside. "You're always mine."

24

CHLOE

I wake up to the sun streaming through the gauzy curtains. We must have forgotten to close the blackout shades last night after returning from the beach, our hands and thoughts preoccupied as we sought out each other's orgasms like we were competing to be the first to claim a space expedition.

He won.

But I'm pretty sure I was the winner, considering I reached my second orgasm, chasing his first while he thrust inside of me over the back of the couch with the curtains still drawn.

We showered off the lingering sand from the beach and the fresh coat of sweat we'd gained on our race to climax and feasted on room service while watching a movie.

It felt normal. Good. Happy. Easy—*shockingly* easy.

I stare at his hand, still gripping me even in sleep, the hairs peppering his strong forearms, the curve of his fingers and squared nails. Tyler's hands are flat out erotic. His fingers are long and strong, clean but not unblemished; signs of football and weightlifting and digging in the sand with me apparent. I consider all the places he's touched me and how it's always with confidence, yet measured gentleness, and always pleasurable.

My heart races with the memory, desire coursing through my veins. I press my butt against his groin, feeling his erection through his boxer briefs. His hand at my arm tightens as he releases a low growl against my ear. I press back a little farther to ensure he's awake. His lips come down on the back of my neck, kissing and licking at a leisurely pace that makes my core throb with impatience.

I lift his hand, placing it against my breast that is thinly veiled with a tank top. His fingers graze over my hardened nipple, and he growls again. This time his hips move, thrusting against my backside so I can feel the entirety of his impressive length. He rolls my nipples, the cotton creating a new sensation, one that would be hot in the back of a crowded theater or a secluded corner on campus, but it has me quickly realizing my preference for his skin on mine. As though he can read my thoughts, Ty snakes his hand under my shirt, skating across my stomach with a flat palm like he's memorizing every inch of me. He reaches my breast, kneading his fingers into my flesh as he releases another guttural growl adjoined with another thrust of his hips. I know my panties are soaked, and I wish they were gone so I could bend forward a little more and feel his hard intrusion into my entrance that makes pleasure radiate through my entire body.

"Ty," I moan his name, sounding pitiful and needy and not caring in the slightest.

He rolls my nipple as his other hand cups my core, making me gasp as he presses his fingers against me, creating a spike of desperation that has me bucking my hips and whimpering. Last night, the scientist in me tackled the awkward elephant in the room: safe sex. We'd used condoms every time, but with oral sex, I'd been regretting not having the conversation sooner.

Awkwardness tinged the conversation initially, but he quickly normalized it with stats that my sanity needed as well as the admission that few of his "conquests" were sexual victories but rather public make-out sessions, which my ego rejoiced in far more than I thought I would. It also has me feeling more adventurous and intimate as I twist in his arms and go to my knees, scooting down and taking the blankets with me, exposing his chiseled chest and abs.

I slip my fingers into the waistband of his underwear, pulling them out and down to free his hardened length. Ty leans back, tucking his hands behind his head, exposing the tattoo on the inside of his bicep—the one I'd tried to see at the beginning of our trip. It's a map of the world but artfully distorted with stitches between England and the United States. It's painfully beautiful and likely reflective of far more than I'm aware.

I run my hands down his abs, tracing each defined line, and he hisses out a breath as I make my way to his hardened cock. I grin, tracing the same pattern over his body. "You're so fucking sexy," he says, peeking at me through the fringe of russet-colored lashes.

I feel sexy.

Empowered.

Beautiful.

I slide my palm over his shaft, and he tips his chin back, seeking strength as I flash my tongue across the tip.

I lick him from base to crown, watching his cock twitch as he grinds out a swear word, his accent thicker. I lick him again and again, changing the pace and pressure of my tongue until he's fisting the sheets, his knuckles bone white. I take him in my mouth, licking over his head when he groans. "Chloe, you're going to make me come."

I lower my mouth even more, and his thighs flex under my hands as he swears again. I move, ready to lick his shaft, drunk on this power I feel. The moment I move, he's grabbing me, hauling me up and onto my back, pinning me in place with his gaze wild and bright. His lips crash against mine in a kiss that translates his hunger and desire while devouring me. I kiss him back, meeting him thrust for thrust with my tongue, gripping his shoulders in an attempt to pull him closer, wanting to feel his skin against mine.

"I need you," I say against his lips, kissing him again as I raise my hips to feel him. "I've been on birth control since I was sixteen. We're both clean. This is safe. I want to feel you."

His blue gaze casts down my body and then lands back on my face.

"I mean..." I struggle to gain sense and words that make sense and the right order to place them in. "We don't have to. If it's a rule for you, we can use a condom."

A smile curves the corners of his lips, and then he kisses away my self-consciousness. "Are you sure?"

"I want to feel you inside of me."

He closes his eyes, his nostrils flaring with a long breath. "You have no idea what you do to me," he says, opening his eyes slowly, the lust still evident, along with something that makes the butterflies in my stomach take flight and my thoughts spin in circles. I close my eyes and lift my face to kiss him again.

Tyler braces himself over me, his breath sharp as his tip nudges against my opening. Then his eyes are on mine as he moves into me in one fluid motion, his weight on his hands as he thrusts. It feels so achingly good I forget about our nine-hour car drive ahead of us and how we're quickly nearing the end of our trip and how every day I yearn and crave being around him a little more.

"God, you feel so good," he says, brushing his lips across my jaw before his breath fans across my cheek.

I feel impossibly strong and incredibly weak. Empowered, yet vulnerable.

Tyler peppers kisses across my cheek and then goes up on his elbows and starts moving, gentle and controlled as his stare seems to infiltrate my thoughts and far deeper, seeing how significant this moment—how significant he is to me.

He kisses me, moving faster and harder, his breaths heavier. The feeling of him and everything about this moment has me spiraling, and when his chest grazes mine, my thighs begin to shake, and the pressure in my core builds. He thrusts into me faster, his breaths turning harsh, his movements uneven and jerky, and I come undone, and after a few more pumps, he chases my orgasm with his own.

He slumps across my chest, still inside of me. His face is tucked against mine, his breath warm against my neck and cheek. Our hearts race each other as they settle into a slower tempo. I slide my hands into his hair, mindlessly raking my nails across his scalp, absorbing this moment and the heat and weight of him, basking in my post-orgasm bliss that makes me wish we could stay here all day.

"What if we add another day?" Tyler asks.

"Another day?" Guilt twists in my stomach because I want the same, and yet the idea of missing my invitation seems like such a hefty price.

"We can stay another day in Portland. Do nothing. Just spend the day in the hotel. You and me. I can arrange for us to have our own suite and Coop and Vanessa to have their own as well."

I weave my fingers in his hair, nodding incessantly. "Can we add a full month?"

He chuckles, the sound rich and deep. "Autumn break. Christmas break. Spring break. Next summer." He lists the periods off like they're inevitable. "Weekends," he adds, running his nose over my skin, evoking a smile. "Hell, you can stay at my place whenever you want. I'll wake you up with an orgasm every day. Bring you coffee in the shower." He kisses me again. "Keep you supplied with chocolate filled croissants."

I groan. "They're so good."

His laughter tickles my neck, followed by a soft sigh. "They're going to be up soon to gather our bags."

I hate the reminder. I'm not ready to move, and less ready to leave. "Don't say that." I turn my face, kissing him. It's quick and playful, leaving the remnants of a smile on his face that has me doing it again and again, and then he's kissing me and tickling my sides.

His phone on the nightstand buzzes. I want to tell him to ignore it and kiss him again to ensure he'll listen. But I don't.

He reaches for it and settles back against me, the movement sliding his cock inside me farther—he's hard again.

"This is Tyler," he answers.

I close my eyes, my legs falling open as I lift my hips to feel him move inside me again. He pulls out slowly and then thrusts into me equally slowly. It feels so good I nearly moan. He does it again, his eyes on me as he discusses the number of bags and makes the request that they give us another thirty minutes.

"An hour," I whisper.

He thrusts into me again, silencing me. He hangs up, tossing his phone to the floor. "You're trouble," he says.

I lift my hips, urging him even deeper, and we both shudder. He reaches for the pillow he'd used last night and slips it under my hips, and the pressure of him is so delicious my toes curl. I stretch my hands over my head and close my eyes. Ty pulls me closer to where he's kneeling in front of me, lifting my legs so my calves rest against his chest, and then he thrusts into me, and I moan out his name, unable to believe my body can feel so amazing. Then his thumb goes to my clit, and I explode around him.

THE ROAD to San Francisco is one of our longest drives, and before we even began the trek, we ate breakfast and discussed the potential of staying somewhere else for the night and finishing the drive early to allow plenty of time for my event tomorrow night.

"Hey, Chloe," Nessie says from the back seat as I read a recent article published about a new super-Earth planet.

"No," I say, shaking my head. "Ask Cooper."

Nessie laughs. "Chloe, truth or dare."

I sigh. "Truth?"

"If you had to change your degree tomorrow, what would you choose and why?"

I blink back my surprise, expecting something about Tyler or something far more embarrassing.

"Galactic astronomy."

"That's the same thing," Cooper says.

"It's so different," I tell him. "Galactic would be studying the Milky Way, and my major is extragalactic, which studies other galaxies."

"So, you wouldn't change and do something like become a science teacher or a veterinarian or something?" Nessie asks. "Something that takes less school and physics?"

I grin. "Maybe if I could be like a professional ice cream taster or coffee reviewer. Are those possibilities?"

Nessie laughs. "Absolutely. Let your mind run wild."

"Okay, then maybe a professional coffee taster slash ice cream taster. What would you do?"

"Travel blogger, remember? You'll be doing this with me, traveling to taste all your coffees," Nessie tells me.

"I'd be a Lego designer," Cooper says.

"What about you, Ty?" Nessie asks.

He shakes his head. "The hotels are all I've ever wanted to do."

Something is comforting in his answer. Maybe it's the idea of security because he doesn't want more or different, or the fact they mean so much to him because it's a huge part of his family's history and that holds significance to him, but regardless, I find comfort in his answer.

25

TYLER

"This is it," Chloe says, looking across the line of tollbooths as traffic comes to a stop before we cross the Golden Gate Bridge.

The sun is beginning to set, making the sky appear almost purple. The vibe in the car has been easy today. It's amazing how in the short period, so much—seemingly everything—has changed, including me. I consider those first hours of our trip when I was debating staying up all night to bomb it to Washington and how all the details and stops and luggage seemed inconvenient and burdensome. And now that only a few days are remaining, I'm dreading the end.

"How many days do we have here?" Vanessa asks, making me question if her thoughts are in the same lane of melancholy and denial as mine.

"Tomorrow's our only full day," Chloe says, facing the window as we inch closer to the tollbooth.

"One day?" Disappointment is apparent in Vanessa's tone, heard louder than her words. "What time does your event start?"

"Seven. But you guys don't have to go. With us having so little time here, if you guys want to go hang out, I will totally understand."

"No, we'll definitely be there," Vanessa says.

"Just think about it. You don't have to answer now. Also, if you guys want to do your own thing in the morning since it's our last city, that's completely cool with me. I think I'm going to hike to the bridge and then try to see the pier in the afternoon."

I moved my meetings up to begin at seven in an attempt to get off early tomorrow. I'm hopeful things can get wrapped up by noon so I can spend the afternoon with Chloe, but after how things went in San Diego, I'm reluctant to even mention the possibility.

"Why are you hiking to the bridge? Aren't we about to cross it?" Cooper asks.

"Yeah, but you can walk on it," Chloe tells him. "It sounds like it's a nice hike. Most of it's along the bay."

"What about Alcatraz?" Coop suggests.

Chloe shakes her head. "You have to book reservations in advance."

"I thought you did?" Vanessa asks. "Didn't you forward the ticket info to me?" I catch sight of Vanessa reaching for her phone in my rearview mirror.

Chloe tips her chin upward, closing her eyes. "They were for the wrong date."

"Wrong date?" Vanessa asks.

"We'd planned to get here last night, originally."

The reminder packs a wallop of a punch. We'd left Austin late and stayed in Odessa overnight, causing everything to get pushed back by a day, including arriving here in San Francisco.

Our conversation in the hotel reception back in Texas plays in my mind, the way she'd tried broaching her frustrations for changing our plans, and my reaction to tell her it didn't matter.

The queue of cars we're in moves forward, and when we reach the tollbooth, I shove the money toward the man, my impatience rumbling like an afternoon storm in the South. "Why didn't you tell me?" I ask her.

She glances at me, a shade of hesitancy across her features that I haven't seen in days. I haven't missed it.

I reach to hit my call button on the dash, but Chloe shakes her head. "I don't want you to get us tickets. It's totally fine. We only have one day, and Alcatraz takes several hours, so it would be difficult to make it all fit."

My thoughts turn restless as annoyance creeps over me, guilt and regret working their best to deny culpability and refute that she should have told me. We could have canceled a day in Vegas and made it here.

"This is amazing," Chloe says, her attention focused on the bridge, ducking her head in an attempt to see the high towers and cables.

"We should go and do something tonight," Vanessa suggests. "It's not that late. Even if we just take a walk or something."

Chloe brushes her hand over mine, the bridge and bay outside her window forgotten as her eyes rove over my face. "It's not a big deal."

I blow out a breath, knowing she's right and struggling to admit the fact. Her fingers weave with mine.

"We're staying by Fisherman's Wharf," Chloe says. "Let's check-in, and we can see how everyone's feeling and maybe go down to the Pier 39."

"Yes!" Vanessa answers, ducking so she can see something that she points out to Cooper.

"I expected more hills," Cooper says.

I chuckle. "Just wait. You'll find plenty of big-ass hills here." I gently squeeze Chloe's fingers, releasing a breath and the tension that threatens to spoil our limited time.

She grins, reading me like an open book.

THE HOTEL LOOKS out over the ocean, a pristine view that I know will steal Chloe's attention during our short time here.

"It smells good up here," Vanessa says, taking a deep breath from the patio we're gathered on, picking at the charcuterie board that welcomed us to the room.

"You're smelling the Italian restaurant over there," Cooper says, leaning forward.

Vanessa rolls her eyes. "It's the sea air."

Cooper's forehead creases with disbelief. "Pretty sure it's the garlic bread."

Chloe chuckles, turning to face us from the rail she's leaning against. "Forget the garlic bread. We need to go find some sourdough."

"Yes!" Vanessa says, nodding.

Chloe shivers as she takes a step closer to me. "I need to change though. It's cold tonight." It's not that cold, but compared to Vegas and the other cities we've been in, it feels chilly tonight.

I glance toward the living room where the trail of employees is starting to leave. "Our things should be in the rooms." I open the glass door that leads into the small division between the dining room that sits eight and the living room.

"This might be my favorite hotel," Vanessa says as the others follow me inside. "The chandeliers and the beige colors with dark floors and wood... It's beautiful."

"I like this one, too," Chloe says. "But I really loved the New Orleans hotel."

"Vegas was definitely the winner," Cooper says. "There was a water fountain in our living room."

Chloe laughs. "Vegas might be my favorite, too." She glances at me. "The views there were pretty flawless." Behind her benign words, I hear the insinuation, and they paint a mental picture of her up against the glass window, bringing a wave of desire to crash over me.

"I'll be right back," she says. "I'm going to change into warmer clothes."

"I need to grab my charger," I lie, following her down the hallway where she pauses, still unfamiliar with the new space we haven't yet toured.

I place my hand on her hip and guide her to the door at the end of the hall on the right. "The rooms here are smaller, and we only have two bedrooms."

Her gaze slides to me. Though she's been staying with me since Vegas, her things have still been unpacked in a third room until now. The lights turn on as we step into the room, where a large bed sits atop a rug matching the same pattern as those in the living room. There's another wall of windows, shorter than most of the hotels we've stayed at, and on the other wall is a large glass-encased shower with a tub where Chloe's attention is paused.

"There's a bathtub in here?"

"Is that a question?" I tease, and that this wows her is incredibly endearing. "It's called a wet room," I continue, "and it's in here because of the views." I sweep my arm toward the windows.

"But anyone can see in!"

"Whatever kinky thought you're considering, I'm game," I tell her.

Her cheeks darken with a blush. "Cooper and Nessie are waiting for us."

I shrug, taking a step closer to her as her gaze darts to the opened door. "Want to time how long it takes for me to get you off?"

She laughs, taking a step back as she shakes her head. "No."

I take another step, and she takes two more backward.

I charge after her like we're on the field, and she quietly squeals when I grab her. We twist and fall back on the bed, her chest pressed against mine as my back hits the mattress. She giggles, her eyes closed, not fighting to get up.

"Why didn't you tell me about Alcatraz?"

Her smile starts to slip, so I run my hand over her back in an attempt to relax her and assure her I'm not feeling unhinged about the minor detail. "At first because it didn't seem worth arguing about, but after Vegas, it seemed hurtful and silly to mention it because if we'd have left a day earlier, it might mean that everything would have changed. You might have worked more and not have gone to the club with us, or maybe we wouldn't have gone out at all, or maybe you would have canceled the poker game..." She shakes her head. "If I had to choose between going to Alcatraz and you, I'd choose you." Her green eyes balance my racing thoughts, a shy smile curving her lips that I erase with a kiss, burying my fingers into her hair. She opens her mouth for me instantly, her tongue greeting mine. Above me, she settles, the heat of her body and the demand in her kiss make me want to forget about leaving the room, drunk on my need to feel and taste her.

"Guys! Let's Go!" Vanessa yells from the hallway.

Chloe laughs against my lips.

I tip my head back and take a deep breath through my nose, my erection pressed to her core.

"Don't make me come in there!" Vanessa calls out in warning.

"I'm just getting changed," Chloe calls back.

"You have *one* minute."

Chloe smiles, dropping a kiss to my mouth. "Her threats aren't empty. Let's go check out the boardwalk, and then we can resume."

I run a hand down her back, stopping at her ass, where I gently squeeze. "They have doughnuts on the pier and a sourdough restaurant around the corner."

Her eyes flash with a smile. "You had me at doughnuts."

I scoff, watching her retreat to the closet where she slows and looks at me over her shoulder before pulling off her shirt and dropping her shorts so they pool at her feet.

She stands in the doorway in a black thong and a matching bra.

I'm off the bed in a second, thoughts of doughnuts and the pier forgotten.

"Guys!" Vanessa stands in the doorway. "What's taking so long?"

"You have the patience of a toddler," Chloe calls from the closet.

"You never have any chill when we get to a new city." She turns her attention to me. "You've ruined her."

Chloe laughs, stepping out of the closet in a pair of jeans and a long-sleeve shirt, a hoodie over her arm. "I'm ready. Let's go."

I adjust myself and try to recall what the focus for tomorrow's first meeting is to distract myself from Chloe's too-brief strip show.

We follow the sidewalk that leads into Fisherman's Wharf, where shops crowd both sides of the busy sidewalk. We stop in front of the cafe that I'd mentioned to Chloe, with extravagantly shaped sourdough creations in their windows, before we duck inside and get seated for dinner.

I set my hand on Chloe's thigh, missing the feel of her bare skin. "Did you see Ghirardelli Square is here? They have a whole menu of ice cream."

She grins. "It's on my list for tomorrow."

"We'll have to come back. There's so much to see in San Francisco. We just purchased the neighboring property and are currently in the process of obtaining all the necessary permits and quotes to join the two buildings together. We can find all sorts of excuses to come down and check on it. We could do it over Thanksgiving since you guys don't go home for the holiday."

Chloe raises a shoulder. "That sounds amazing, but I kind of like our current tradition." She sets her hand on mine, evoking a string of memories from the past two years of celebrating the holiday in their apartment with pizzas, under-baked or overbaked pies, board games, and films, reminding me that with Chloe, it's always time that holds the highest significance.

"A long weekend then."

She grins. "I can get on board with that." She takes a drink of her water, blinking as a pronounced frown mars her face. "The water here tastes like it does in Florida."

"Point for Washington," Cooper says.

My phone vibrates and then vibrates again and again in quick succession. I reach for it, noting the multiple messages are all from Vivian. I scroll through the first and second, working to read through the data and facts she's compiled because, like always, Vivian relies solely on facts and refuses to talk in layman's terms. The final message is a screen-shot of the penal code for felony embezzlement, which for Las Vegas can be charged if there's theft of property or services exceeding five thousand dollars.

I scroll back through the other two emails, realizing they're spread-sheets showing the mess of discrepancies she's caught totaling over ten million dollars.

I breathe out slowly, knowing that I need to be fully certain of this information before I take it to my dad because if I'm wrong, this will only accomplish the opposite of what I sought out to do.

"Is everything okay?" Chloe asks.

I nod, setting my phone down as I struggle to wrap my thoughts around the situation. "Yeah, it's just the accountant I've been working with in regard to Avery. She thinks Avery's embezzled close to ten million."

Cooper whistles.

"What are you going to do?" Chloe asks, setting her hand on my thigh like she needs a constant connection between us as well.

I slide my hand beneath hers and watch her fingers seamlessly align with mine as they fall together and shake my head. "Contact one of our lawyers. We can't fire him in the same manner that we would another employee. We'll need to be a hundred percent sure of everything to draw charges." I run a hand along my jaw, considering what will happen in his future and how the decision largely rests on my shoulders. The realization makes my stomach turn for a moment, my determination to prove myself to my dad now seemingly tied with a man's future.

Our waiter arrives before my thoughts can funnel very far, and we order an assortment of sandwiches and bread bowls before the girls are out of their seats and telling us they're going to be at the gift shop.

"Ten million," Cooper repeats, shaking his head. "Who does that?"

"He could go to prison for up to five years," I tell Cooper, waiting for his reaction.

"Good. He should be going to prison for longer."

I sit back in my seat, knowing Cooper's history and dislike for the prison system. "He could potentially be charged as a felon."

Cooper shakes his head, his eyes bright as he tears his eyes from following the girls and turns his full attention to me. "You're feeling bad about possibly blowing the whistle on this guy?"

"He's divorced, has two kids."

Coop blows out a breath. "Look, this is only my two cents, you have to do whatever is going to allow you to sleep at night, but this guy is stealing a ton of money from you. If you need to, check to make sure his kid isn't sick or his mom or whatever, but remember, ten million." He shakes his head again. "Did he ask for more money? Did he come to you and ask for a favor? Tell you he needed the money for anything?"

I shake my head. "He's a contractor, not an employee."

"If he'd come to you and asked for the money and you turned him down, and he felt he had no other choice to keep someone in his family alive or safe, that would be a different conversation. If he's spending this money on a mansion and cars and bullshit he doesn't need, then I'd be pushing for a full sentence. My dad is serving twenty-five years for selling a few hundred bucks worth of weed."

"It's messed up."

Coop shrugs. "It is, and yet, he was a lousy father, and all he cared about were his plants and money and getting high. I hate the prison system. I hate that he has to serve such a ridiculous amount of time in jail. I hate that I won't know him at all by the time he's out. And I really hate how prison has turned him into someone who I don't even recognize and wouldn't trust around Vanessa. But, in that same vein, sometimes I feel lucky that they took me out of that situation and placed me with my grandma because while she was probably too tired to raise another kid, I finally had some semblance of structure. I didn't have to be a parent myself at ten to my lowlife father who nearly burnt our house down on more than one occasion and couldn't hold a job to save his life —save *my* life. It just seems unfair that his life had to be ruined for mine to be saved. But that's not the situation here. You're not doing this to him; he is. Just like my father did it to himself. This guy knows what he's doing is illegal, and you can't tell me anyone assumes they can steal that kind of money without facing serious consequences."

"That poker game I brought Chloe to, he was there. Blew twenty grand in an afternoon."

Cooper winces. "Way to rub it in your face."

From our table, I catch Chloe passing through the gift shop, laughing at something.

"Are you ready to return to reality and get to double practices and classes?" Coop asks.

I shake my head in small jerks. "Not even remotely. I feel like I blinked and we're here."

"You've been working a lot."

"We could do this again," I tell him. "Stay longer at different hotels so we could have more time to hang out in different cities. We could consider it research for how we can improve things for guests. We could spend all of next summer traveling."

"I'd be game, but you might have your work cut out for you with Chloe. Change is hard for her, which is why you see her start sweating each time Vanessa talks about where she wants to move after school. Not going home for the summer would be a big change for her."

"What if I throw in the Eiffel Tower and Rome?"

"Tell me you want us to go, and I'll start laying hints now."

I laugh, imagining the four of us abroad and then flipping to this year and spending time all together and alone with Chloe—having her in my bed, wandering through downtown Seattle to find coffee, having her in the stands with my number painted on her cheek, listening to her tell me about the laws of physics and how they apply with her major. "Vanessa's right. This is going to be a good year."

Coop nods, but before he can say anything, our food arrives at the table. I turn to look for Chloe and see her checking out, Vanessa at her side. She must feel my stare because she turns, looking at me as she waits for them to bag her purchase. She smiles, her fingers folding in a small wave.

We order a round of soft drinks to replace the water as the girls return.

"You didn't buy bread to bring back, did you?" Cooper asks, eyeing Chloe's bag.

She frowns at him as Vanessa starts to laugh. "I considered it, but I told Nessie if I did, you'd give me the hardest time, so no, I didn't buy any bread."

He laughs, turning to me. "She used to always buy food when we'd go to new places and then wouldn't want to eat it because her souvenir went away."

"Oh, watch me eat all the doughnuts tonight," Chloe says, taking her seat beside me.

I move my hand across the plane of her back, my fingers catching in her hair that I slip my fingers through as I laugh. Those mesmerizing green eyes meet my stare, and I realize how this consideration regarding Avery may not have given me much debate without her. Admitting my feelings for her has seemingly destroyed my ability to not give a fuck. She leans forward, kissing me gently on the lips before pulling back, eyes still on me, as though she hears my thoughts and is trying to settle me from how overwhelming my emotions feel around her—about her.

"You guys might as well just roll me down the pier," Vanessa says as we step out of the cafe, her hands clutching her stomach. "That was so good. So worth it."

Coop slings his arm around her shoulders, following the train of people that are headed down to Pier 39.

We pass by more shops, the homeless population drawing Chloe's attention. On the corners, street performers attract a crowd.

"This breaks my heart," Chloe says as we pass a woman asleep on a piece of broken-down cardboard. "It seems like we should be able to do something to help these people and help prevent it for others."

I kiss her temple, feeling the hopelessness that shines in her eyes and slumps her shoulders. "You're right."

"Guys! Come on!" Vanessa yells, already halfway through the crosswalk as cars inch closer. We run to catch up, seeing the ocean in the background. Music plays softly through speakers, bringing the mood up as we approach the mouth of the pier.

"This is so much bigger than I expected," Chloe tells me, her gaze traveling over the two-story buildings that lead us down the pier, everything glowing with lights as tourists file around in groups.

"I've heard you say that before," I say, squeezing her shoulder.

She slaps a hand to her forehead and laughs before wrapping her arms around my waist. "Thank you," she says. "This has seriously been the best week ever."

I slant my lips over hers, forgetting about Cooper's warning that she doesn't like change. We're all afraid of change. Sometimes we just need the right motivation. I'm well aware of this as my lips dance across hers.

26

CHLOE

My fingers and lips are still sticky from the bucket of doughnuts we demolished as we window shopped and watched a magic show where a stage and benches are permanently set up near the end of the pier.

Tyler and Cooper each throw in a few bills as they pass around a hat, and then Tyler jerks his chin toward the end of the pier. "We might not be able to see them, but let's take a look."

"See what?" I ask.

He smiles mischievously in response, two of his fingers in my back pocket as we reach a set of stairs with a giant red heart in the middle that leads to an area that looks out over the bay.

The wind off the water is chillier without the warmth of the sun, but I can't bring myself to complain because this moment is so perfect, and the clear skies above only promise better viewing for the meteor shower tomorrow that has me glancing skyward. "Look," I tell them as light streaks above us. "It's the meteor shower."

"I thought it was tomorrow?" Tyler asks, glancing at the sky.

I shiver from the breeze coming off the water and move closer to him. "No, you can actually see it for five weeks. Tomorrow's just the best day when we'll be in the thick of it, but we're currently passing through the comet's orbit, so the meteors are coming into our atmosphere."

"Coming into our atmosphere?" Ty asks, his eyebrows knit like I've just told him a line from an alien takeover movie. "Does that mean they might hit Earth?"

I shrug, trying to recall all the data about comets and meteors. "Meteors generally disintegrate before they reach Earth. Most of them are only a few millimeters in diameter—dust essentially. But, once in a while, there will be a large enough meteor that it will make it to our surface, and then it becomes a meteorite."

"Weird to think we're watching specks of rock that are on fire and admiring them, right?" Vanessa asks.

"They're on fire? Is that why they glow?" Ty stares at the sky.

I glance at him, wanting to kiss him again because each time he asks a question and invests his time and interest in this part of my life and other interests of mine, I can feel another piece of my heart get lost to him.

"Is that a stupid question? Do all kids learn this in like, third grade, and I didn't pay attention?"

Vanessa shakes her head. "I just live with her and have sat through this conversation a hundred times."

I laugh, shaking my head as I try to shuffle my thoughts back to his question. "It's kind of complicated. I don't study meteors, so I can't give you the full explanation, but basically, the rocks hit our two outer regions: the exosphere and the thermosphere where there's no air, and the meteors are rocketing to Earth—like twenty-five-thousand to one-hundred-and-sixty-thousand miles per hour—but then they hit the middle layer of our atmosphere: the mesosphere, and the gasses cause friction, which heats the meteors, so they mostly burn off in the mesosphere, and that friction and their speed create the falling star."

"Mesosphere? Is that the layer we live on?" he asks.

"No, we live in the troposphere," I tell him.

"But none of this has anything to do with what you're studying?"

"Not really. All of this involves the Milky Way Galaxy. But, it's still very complex and involves multiple areas of study. During meteor showers, astronomers measure objects in the Kuiper belt, which extends into our outer solar system, because we believe some comets, like this one, might have been created in an outer solar system and then got kicked into our solar system, so lots of planetary science is involved. That's one of the coolest things about astronomy, so often it requires teams of people from all over the globe to all have the same goals and objectives to witness and capture images and facts. Much of it is interconnected."

"How does this meteor shower happen every single year?" Cooper asks, staring up at the darkened sky.

"This one, Perseids, is caused by Earth passing through the orbit of a comet called Swift-Tuttle, which is a giant comet that is constantly losing gas and dust particles, and that's what we're seeing."

"But we don't see the comet?" Nessie asks.

"Every hundred and thirty-three years, you can see it from Earth."

Coop blows out a low whistle. "That's crazy how cool dust looks in space."

I grin. "Right?"

We watch for several minutes as meteors streak across the sky, and then I hear a sound that draws my attention to the left where a crowd is gathered at the railing. "What is that?" I ask.

A smile flashes across Tyler's face. "Want to have a look?"

I'm already five steps forward before I nod, making him laugh.

"Sea lions!" Nessie cries. The water is dark, but the many lights hung along the pier allow us to see their dark outlines, so they're difficult to see but not impossible.

"If you all come back this way tomorrow, make sure to stop here. You can see them so much better during the day, and there's usually someone here who's talking about them and sharing information. You would enjoy it," he says, looking at me with another intense gaze that feels immense and heavy. Our relationship is so new and yet feels old at the same time. I used to avoid the fact I knew so much about him, and now I wish to know it all.

"Come on. We have to ride that carousel," Nessie says, turning to retrace our steps.

I grin as Cooper follows with an objection that Nessie ignores.

"Hang on," Ty says, catching my hand. He digs in his pocket for his phone.

"What are you doing?"

His fingers release mine, and he quickly types something out in an email. "Canceling my meetings for tomorrow."

"Can you do that?"

He slides his phone back into his pocket. "I just did."

"Are you sure?" I hate that my hopes feel so inflated and that this seems so momentous.

"I want to see San Francisco with you. I want to show you the bridge and take you out for ice cream."

I feel a bit guilty for feeling so excited by this. After all, Cooper and Nessie have been troopers, willing to go to so many different museums and tourist sites with me, but the idea of seeing San Francisco with Tyler makes my heart feel like it's in my throat.

"This hotel has no problems, and half the questions and concerns are going to be addressed as construction begins, so it's mostly a moot point. We can go see the bridge and Lombard Street, and the Coit Tower, and Chinatown..."

I kiss him, silencing the plans he lists that have my chest feeling light with excitement. His lips are soft and gentle, frustrating me because I feel like every second I'm around him, I lose a little more of my composure and control, and right now, he feels like the definition of control. I don't care about the crowds or that Nessie and Cooper are nearby as I move closer to him, feeling too much air, too much space, too much composure, and far too much desire culminating like a black hole making it impossible for me to escape any of it. I close the space and kiss him deeper, my hands tightening around his neck.

Tyler growls into my mouth as I trace his tongue with mine, and dig my hands into his hair as I press my breasts against his chest. The more of him I feel, the more desperate I become.

He matches me swipe for swipe, nip for nip, one hand buried in my hair at the back of my neck, and the other pulling me closer as I feel his control begin to break. He uses the last thread of strength to pull away, his forehead pressed against mine as his chest heaves while he maintains his close hold on me.

"Carousel and then hotel," I tell him.

He kisses me and then nods.

I kiss him a final time and take a step back, wrapping my hand in his and leading him back to where Nessie and Coop are in line for the two-story carousel that is lit and playing a friendly tune.

Somehow, everything feels better. The breeze, each laugh, every breath—are all more significant as we climb onto the carousel that feels like pages out of a picture book. We spin in slow circles, looking out across the pier and the crowds of people and the bay, and with each full rotation, my gaze comes back to Tyler.

On our way back to the hotel, our steps are rushed, forcing us to stop for Nessie and Cooper so they can catch up with us on multiple occasions as our eyes continue to linger on each other, silently undressing the other one as our thoughts and desires wander, quickly becoming increasingly difficult to rein in.

The elevator ride to the suite feels like torture as I breathe him in, imagining the feel of his hands on me—in me.

"Since Ty is off tomorrow and I don't think there's a chance in hell Cooper is going to agree to see the bridge again, do we need to have anything but our IDs to get into the event tomorrow if we separate?" Vanessa asks, breaking my focus.

I blink through my lust and nod. "I have tickets. I don't know if they're required, but they sent them to me. I have them in here..." I grab the thin stack of tickets in the front pocket of my purse and pull them out as we step into the suite. As I do, a card floats to the ground. Tyler bends to grab it, his brows furrowing as he turns it over.

"Avery? Why do you have his card?"

My heart beats to a different, quicker pace at the recollection. "It's nothing."

He pulls his chin back, accusation darkening his eyes as he flips it along his fingers like a magic trick. "You just happen to have his private mobile phone number?" He flips the card around to show me the number handwritten on the back.

"You're making this sound like something when it's nothing. Believe me, it's less than nothing. He put it in there, and I meant to throw it away."

He leans back, all confidence and swagger, and as far from being the Tyler I've begun to know since this trip began. "Then why didn't you tell me?"

"I could tell you guys had some history or issue or whatever, and I didn't want to make it worse. And I knew this was his attempt to make it worse."

His eyebrows jump, his eyes rounding with disbelief. "So, it's nothing, but you decided to keep it?"

"I didn't keep it. I forgot it was there. I don't want it. Throw it away."

He rips it in half and in half again, dropping the shredded pieces to the floor. "Why'd he give you his number? What did he want you to get from me?"

Confusion furrows my brow. "From you?"

Tyler grabs an empty tumbler glass that held the whiskey he and Coop had been drinking while we'd waited on the patio for our bags to be unpacked and throws it at the wall. It shatters and rains across the dark hardwood. "He's stolen ten-fucking-million dollars from me. Tell me what the fuck he wanted."

"What the fuck, dude?" Cooper steps forward.

I raise a hand to stop him.

Cooper's eyes are wide with warning. "You need to chill," Coop warns.

Tyler doesn't even give him the courtesy of a glance. His eyes remain glued to mine.

"Mind games," I tell him. "He was trying to play a mind game."

"I swear to God, if you helped him..."

I pull my chin back like he's just slapped me because in many ways, he has. "Are you kidding me? You think he wanted my help stealing from you? You think I've been in on this for however many months—*years*— it's been that he's been doing this?" I let my questions settle for only a second before I slap him with the truth. "He accused me of being a *prostitute*. He assumed you hired me, and he wanted my *services*. And I kind of wanted to punch him in the face because my tolerance for assholes who treat me like an object is already in the negative thanks to another asshole who tried to force himself on me, but I didn't because I could tell you two were both competing to be the alpha. I assumed it was a head game for you, but considering you hired a *hooker* to make out with you, who knows? Maybe he was right to assume I was a whore."

The anger in his blue eyes magnifies and expands as he remains still, too still—scary still.

"What in the fuck are you talking about?" he asks, his voice menacing. "Forced himself? Who the fuck tried to force himself on you?"

I shake my head. "I handled it. There's nothing to talk about. It's done."

"Not a chance," Cooper says, stepping forward, his shoulders tight with anger. "What in the hell are you talking about?"

I glance at Nessie, feeling this situation spiraling faster than I can stop it.

She has both hands raised on top of her head, her eyes glassy. "You need to talk about it."

"I don't because there's nothing to talk about. This conversation is about him," I point at Tyler, "accusing me of aiding and abetting a criminal. It has nothing to do with that."

"It has to do with you never telling me anything," Tyler yells.

My eyes snap to him. "I didn't need you to save me. I don't need saving. Whether it's money or muscles or whatever, I don't need it—I don't want it. Don't you understand?"

"Did you know?" Cooper asks, drawing my attention as he looks at Nessie.

She looks like a deer caught in the headlights, her loyalty to me cutting impossibly close to her affections for him.

"Of course..." Cooper scoffs as he shakes his head, moving into the suite that now feels like a maze, surrounded by traps and unfriendly surprises as I move my attention back to Tyler, my anger is too strong to care about his.

"Tell me what happened, or I swear to God..."

"What?" I ask, challenging him though a voice in my head is tirelessly working to pull in the reins and tell me to calm down.

He sneers. "You have an hour to tell me."

"Or what?"

"I start going down the list of shitheads you've dated and fuck up all of their lives. And then I find out the name of every guy who so much as looked at you wrong and do the same."

I laugh, though I want to scream. I hate that he's trying to flex his power. I hate it even more that I don't doubt he would. "You're such an asshole." I spin toward the bedroom, hating another thing as I realize I don't have my own space in this hotel.

"You have one hour," he says. His shoes clip against the floor, and then the elevator dings as it opens.

Nessie is at my side before I even realize the tears are coating my face, chasing the previous ones in a rapid race to dampen my sweatshirt.

"What just happened?" I ask her, feeling myself deflate now that Tyler stormed away.

She wraps her arms around me, holding me so tight I can't fall apart like I desperately feel I'm about to. "It's okay. I'm here."

I pull in a ragged gasp, struggling to catch a breath as my throat tightens, and my eyes blur with endless tears. "I don't want to tell him," I admit. "I don't even know why I said that. God, *why did I say that?*"

Nessie runs one hand over my hair while the other stays tight behind my back. It's a move that reminds me of our mom—of us. "Because it's still in the back of your mind. Things like that don't just go away, Chloe."

"How do I fix this?" I ask.

She shakes her head, holding me tighter. "Sometimes you have to let all of the pieces fall before you worry about picking them up, and in this case, I'm pretty sure you need to let others help pick up this mess."

My nose burns as I sniff, trying to stop my tears. "I'd rather go back to forgetting it."

Nessie sniffs in response. "You didn't forget. That's the whole point. You don't forget when someone hurts you, that becomes a part of you. *This* is a part of you."

I shake my head. "I don't want it to be a part of me. Nothing happened."

"What would've happened if I hadn't gotten home when I did? Do you really think you'd still be able to give that same excuse?"

"But you did."

"Chloe." She takes a step back, her hands fisting in her hair again. "I have nightmares about that afternoon, and I've tried talking to you, but you won't. I can't say I'm sorry Tyler's forcing your hand. You need to talk about it."

I spin on my heel, slamming the bedroom door behind me.

27

TYLER

I pace the living room, attempting to pull my shit together and stop allowing my anger to dictate my words or reactions. The problem is, every time I think about Avery insinuating Chloe was a protitute or someone touching her—non-consensual touching—anger radiates from every fiber of my being, and I want to yell and destroy everything in my path.

It's been seventy-two minutes since I stormed out of here with a demand and chased it with a threat in the same fucking manner my father used to. I called our lead lawyer to fire Avery, not giving a shit about being able to potentially charge him for embezzlement. Maybe Chloe's right, and it was a mind game. Perhaps this was his objective all along, but I can't force myself to give a single shit. I refuse to keep him employed and continue paying him and have our company associated with him when he crossed that line with her.

I pull in a deep breath through my nose and hold it, my muscles still vibrating as I cross the suite and make it to our shared room. Chloe's in bed with the lights off. She's on the very edge with her back turned to where I'll lie.

I toe off my shoes and make quick work of brushing my teeth and changing into a pair of sweatpants because although I've been sleeping in the nude since Vegas, I'd feel like an even bigger arsehole than I already do if she woke up to my hard-on pressed into her back.

I slide into bed, respecting her space as best as I can. "Chloe," I say her name quietly, not certain if she's asleep. In all fairness, she was exhausted before all of this shit, and it's late, which I realized too late was one of the many contributing reasons I shouldn't have acted as I did.

"Can we please not have this discussion tonight?" she asks.

I roll on my side so I'm facing her back. "I want to apologize," I tell her, considering her reaction if I reach across and set my hand on her. I'm so fucking desperate to feel her, it seems my entire body is depending on it. "I'm sorry for all of it. I was so far out of line. I never should have treated you that way or yelled."

The sheets rustle as she shifts, but she doesn't move any closer or turn to face me.

"I'm shit at trusting people, and just as I accused you, I have a hell of a time letting people into my life because there always seems to be a price tag tied to it. Fuck, you should meet my parents." I sigh. "They're married and haven't lived together in years. My dad has a girlfriend— fuck, probably more than one—and my mum doesn't give a shit because she's content living the life he can provide her with."

Chloe turns at this, rolling to face me. Even in the dimmed lighting from the open curtains, I can see her eyes are swollen and her cheeks tear-stained. The sight of her like this is a direct blow to my heart as I recognize that I caused that pain—albeit not single-handedly, but I certainly didn't help lessen it.

I move closer, careful to allow some space before I reach forward and brush the hair from her face and follow the paths of tears with my fingers. "I'm sorry, Chloe. I knew you were uncomfortable sitting next to Avery. I'd seen it at the poker game, and still, the second there was doubt, I dismissed everything and accused you of turning on me, using me, and that wasn't fair. I should have known—I *did know*—it just took a few minutes for my fucking sense to catch up to my anger."

"I wasn't trying to keep it from you as a secret. I just could tell there was animosity between you, and I didn't want to make it worse. He probably knew exactly who I was. Everyone at the hotel did. He was using me to piss you off, and that just made me feel like a pawn, so I just removed myself from the board."

I shake my head. "No, when that shit happens, that's when we remove *him* from the game. *We* make the rules. Not him."

"We weren't even together at that point," she reminds me.

I slip my arms around her, pulling her closer. "You may not have caught on to this yet, but you've been mine since freshman year. Delayed gratification, foreplay, call it whatever you will, but you were mine, and he knew it."

There's a flash of warmth in her eyes as she sets a hand on my chest. It feels so fucking good to have her touching me I nearly sigh at the contact. "This summer, I dated a guy for a few weeks. We'd gone to high school together, and he'd never paid any attention to me, and then all of a sudden, this summer he noticed me. And he was..." She shakes her head, her gaze going unfocused.

I place my hand over hers on my chest, hoping she can't feel how fucking unsteady my heart is beating right now as I await her next words.

"He was a mistake, and I knew that, but Nessie and Cooper were starting to hang out, and I was feeling ridiculously desperate for someone—anyone—to pay attention to me, and I realized my mistake fast. I mean, the guy doesn't eat anything but ground beef and carrots because the only thing he cares about is working out. And one night, he brought a BB gun when he wanted to hang out and started shooting at pigeons and seagulls, and rather than being smart and ending things, I kept listening to my friends from high school telling me how lucky I was that he liked me because, in high school everyone liked him." She spreads her fingers so that mine fall between hers, and then she runs her thumb across mine. "We were the worst match. He hated every time I planned anything, and he saw everything I did as being uptight and boring, and I saw everything he did as juvenile and gross.

"He showed up one day while my parents were at work and Nessie was out, and to be honest, I wasn't concerned, which almost scares me more, because I want to think I'll know who I can trust and who I can't. I invited him inside, offered him some pop, and suggested we watch a movie." She bites the inside of her cheek as my teeth clench with a level of aggression that is foreign and unbridled as I paint a story in my head that involves my own personal brand of revenge for this fuckface.

"It didn't get very far. Nessie got home and heard me yelling for help."

My heart fucking stops, anger pulsing through me in waves.

"And then I accused you of wanting me to take you and then fucking swam up to you in the pool without a stitch of clothes on like a total wanker."

She pulls her head back and rolls to sit up, her lips tipped toward the sky. "You were a cocky jerk, but you never tried to force yourself on me. There are entire galaxies that separate you and him, and not a single bit of that space has to do with your money. It's about you wanting to help those less fortunate. It's about watching you give up hanging out with us as we play and working toward your dream. It's you knowing how I like my coffee and looking for us when we got lost in the desert. It's for sending a car for me and having breakfast ordered for us every single morning. It's for last year when my car was having trouble, and you came to get me to take me to class when Cooper couldn't, and never expected anything in return. It's for coming to Thanksgiving the past two years and never complaining about how bad our pies are." She pauses to smile. "There's nothing about you that is reflected in him, which is probably the only reason I wanted to like him because I've had a crush on you for so long, and I was trying so hard to get over it."

I sit up beside her, brushing my thumb across her cheek, and she leans into my touch. "I want to be the man you deserve."

"I feel the same way. I'm terrified that your world won't accept me."

I shake my head. "*We* make the rules," I remind her.

She twists, landing a kiss on my outstretched palm. "I would never turn my back on you and try to screw you over. Even if we weren't together, I wouldn't do that. I know how much you mean to Cooper."

"I know." I lean back into the pillow. "I know you wouldn't, that was me; my insecurities and always expecting the worst." I remain still, trying to stop the mental image of another guy touching Chloe, forcing himself on her. "Will you tell me his name?"

Silence hangs in the air for several beats as I feel her lie down, the movement drawing my eyes open. She's pensive, rubbing her lips together as she stares beyond me. "I don't want vengeance. I want to just forget about it. I don't even know why I brought it up. Nessie thinks I need to talk about it because it will help me get over it, but I don't have anything to get over. I don't want it to impact me. I want to move forward and never think about him or that day again." Her nostrils flare as she slowly moves her gaze to meet mine. "Honestly, what bothers me most is the idea he'll do it to someone else, and they might not have someone walk in to help them. That, and I really hate the idea of you thinking about it and it keeping you from wanting to touch me."

I skim my fingers over her shoulder and down her arm, settling my hand on the valley of her waist.

She props her head on one hand, her elbow resting beside my shoulder. "I love when you lose control, and your hands are touching me with this level of desperation and need that makes me feel how badly you want me. I'm addicted to that feeling. I don't want him to change that. I don't want anything to change that."

"I would pay for the entire lawsuit," I tell her. "To make you, and others, feel safe. I would find you the best lawyers and put the weight of my family's name into this."

"I already know the laws. I looked them up because I didn't want him to do it again, and Florida requires penetration for sexual assault crimes, and he didn't make it that far. Nessie yelled, and it startled him, and then I kneed him in the balls." She grins, but the bright glimmer that hits her eyes when she's truly amused is missing. "I hate that I dropped this bomb on you, especially in the way that I did." She hangs her head, and I recognize the shame that mars her features.

I reach for her, hauling her across my body, the surprise making her green eyes flash to mine. "You didn't do anything wrong, Chloe. Not then, not now. He didn't take anything from us," I tell her. "Nothing changes except it's a reminder how hard I'm willing to work to ensure you're never scared or hurt again."

She shakes her head. "It's not your debt to pay."

I smooth a strand of hair behind her ear. "It's not a debt. Even if the fucker hadn't done what he did, I'd still want that for you because you're important to me and because I literally can't seem to breathe when you're hurt or there's even a chance of you getting hurt. You carved out a space in my heart, and you did it without me even realizing." I bring her hand to my chest, allowing her to feel the erratic beat of my heart. "That's you," I tell her. "That's all you."

Her smile damn near blinds me, and then she's kissing me, sweetly, gently. I savor the feel of her, the taste of her, the scent of her, allowing each detail of her to consume me completely.

Chloe

I WAKE up to discover Tyler's still asleep.

It's only the second time I've been awake before him.

I take advantage of the moment, staring at the hard planes of his cheeks and jaw, the roundness of his lips, the straight line of his nose. His hair is sexy and mussed and perfect, and his bare shoulders are broad, stacked with muscles that I've traced my lips and fingers across, and yet, I feel starved to explore every part of him again.

The shower taunts me, having gone untouched since our arrival. I make a silent pact with myself to make sure we spend some time in there before leaving.

I slip out from the covers and make my way to the living room in hopes of finding Cooper. We need to talk and resolve this stupid Ricky situation. Throughout our years of friendship, Cooper and I have only fought a handful of times, and never have I been on the receiving end of the look he shot me last night: disappointment and rage along with a heavy dose of betrayal.

The living room is empty except for a note from Nessie that tells me they'll meet us at the meteor shower tonight.

I debate whether to text or call Cooper and if doing either would be pushing the boundaries considering he's out with Nessie, who might feel obligated to choose sides or if doing so would ruin his mood and thus their day.

"Rule one, you're not allowed to get out of bed without kissing me." Tyler saunters into the living room, dragging a hand down his still bare chest, allowing me to see every hard muscle. His sweatpants ride low on his hips, and his hair is still sexy and mussed.

"You were sleeping," I tell him as his hands hook around my waist. "I might have kissed you, and you didn't even realize it."

He shakes his head. "I'd know because I'd have felt your lips," he raises one hand to cup my chin, slowly running the pad of his thumb across my bottom lip, "and you have the sexiest, softest, most erotic lips."

I lick the tip of his thumb, then close my teeth around him, sucking him between my lips.

Ty tips his head back, pulling in a long, slow breath. It's his tell that he's turned on, and it fuels me with so much confidence and desire that I forget about all the ways I've struggled to forget about Ricky's words, realizing his assessment was never a reflection of me or my worth, but rather of himself.

Tyler's skin is still hot from being under the covers as I trace over his abs and continue sucking on his thumb. Fire burns in his blue eyes as he releases a harsh breath. "Are they still asleep?" He tilts his head in the direction of the bedrooms, keeping his focus on me.

I lick his thumb a final time before freeing it. "They're gone."

His eyes dilate, the thin veil of hesitation now ash as he claims my mouth, his tongue and lips forceful and demanding as his hands skirt beneath my shirt, gripping my waist. It takes my full attention to meet the challenge his mouth offers, but when his hands don't continue to explore my body, I nip at his bottom lip and move them to cover my breast.

"I like when you're bossy," he says with a grin, his thumb grazing over my hardened nipple. His lips come down on my throat, kissing and sucking at the sensitive skin as his hands skate along the sides of my breasts. I turn my neck, wanting to feel his lips everywhere as he rolls my nipples between his fingers, his tongue tasting my skin.

I place my hand over his erection and smile when he groans against my neck, encouraging me to trace over his length.

Tyler reaches for my sweatshirt and pulls both it and my tee clean off, his hungry gaze on my chest. Then he slides his hands gently into the waist-band of my shorts and underwear, kissing me from my collarbone down to my breasts as he slowly begins to lower my shorts. He closes his lips over my nipple, gently biting into my flesh, making arousal pool between my legs. His fingertips skim over my chest, my abdomen, the few inches of my exposed backside where my shorts are still on, just lowered. He moves to my other nipple, flicking his tongue across the surface and making me moan as I bury my hands in his hair, trying to pull him closer, but instead, he traces a path down along my stomach, sliding my shorts and underwear to my ankles where they pool on the floor. He kisses me down to my pulic bone, making me shiver with anticipation. Sitting back on his heels, Ty looks up at me, like I'm something to marvel—something to praise. "God, you're beautiful." He places both hands on my hips. "Lean back."

I do without turning to see what's behind me. My trust in him has become second nature and undeniable. The coolness of the leather couch hits the back of my thighs, sending a shiver through me before his hot mouth seals over my clit, the contrast in temperatures adding to the sensation and making my breaths turn harsh. "I want to come with you," I tell him, trying to gain control over my body and fight the sparks of pleasure he's orchestrating with his tongue and mouth and lips as he devours me.

"Ty," I whimper his name, my fingers twining in his hair as the tension in me grows. "I want you inside of me."

He runs his tongue flat against me as he emits a low growl, and then he's standing, his chin wet with my arousal. I lean up and kiss him, my breasts grazing his chest as his hands cup my backside. "Turn around," he says against my mouth. I do, my heart thrumming, my skin on fire, my body craving his touch. Tyler presses against my entrance, and I gasp, pushing my hips back as the anticipation squeezes my chest. "I need to see you," he rasps.

I peer over my shoulder to meet his scorching gaze. His fingers drag down my back, and then he thrusts into me, pleasure blazing so bright I see stars as he moves inside me. His tempo changes from slow and controlled to fast and hard, his hands gripping my waist, his eyes locked with mine, tracking my reaction to each of his moves. "You ruin me," he says, his voice a low, guttural growl. "Tell me that you need me as much as I fucking need you."

He moves a hand to my clit, making my thoughts spin as I work to focus on his words through the clouds of pleasure that are making me come apart. His fingers are relentless, and his thrusts become harder and faster.

"Tell me," he demands again.

"I need you," I rasp. "I love you." The words tumble out, raw and unguarded, making me feel a million times more vulnerable than any sexual position I could imagine.

He pauses for a moment, laying kisses to my shoulder, and then his movements pick up faster, harder, losing all sense of rhythm as his fingers pinch my clit, distracting me from my admission as I begin to shatter, and then his heavy breaths grow louder as he thrusts deeper, and we explode together with an orgasm that leaves me limp as his chest comes down on my back, his arm barring around my waist. His breaths are still coming hard and fast like his heartbeats as he kisses the back of my shoulder and then slides out of me and moves back. The air feels icy against my heated body as I turn to face him.

"Do you want some breakfast?" he asks. "We could order something or go down to the restaurant or pick something up on our way to the Golden Gate Bridge?"

With the absence of him, my words sound louder, ringing in my ears, and even more deafening is the fact he didn't return them.

I don't expect him to.

Didn't expect him to.

We've only been together for a second.

I don't even know where those words came from, much less why I said them.

Truth pierces me in the lungs, calling me on my silent lie.

"I'm game for whatever."

He smiles, but something is missing, and I swear it's not just because I'm feeling so vulnerable and self-conscious.

Or is it?

28

CHLOE

"Why don't we get ready? Then we can decide."

I nod.

Tyler links our fingers, leading me to our room, where the glass shower shines with the reflection of the sliver of sunlight peeking through the curtains. He opens the glass door and steps inside, turning the knob and standing shamelessly, gloriously naked at the side of the spray as he waits for the water to warm. His gaze is on the drain, the window, the bed—everything but me.

"It's warm," he says, his eyes flashing to me before he moves to the small bench that is set back far enough not to get wet and that houses all the same products I've grown accustomed to seeing at each of our stops.

I step into the shower, struggling to get out of my head, reasoning that I'm feeling so exposed because my filter has seemingly gone from active and dependable to nonexistent in the span of twelve hours. This is me. This is in my head. Nerves are what have me feeling unsteady. I stand under the spray, letting it hit my face and body, trying to rid the feeling that has me desperate to call Nessie so we can meet up and she can organize this mess in my head.

Strong hands run over and then through my hair, the scents of the expensive French shampoo perfuming the air. My body melts like butter as he drops another kiss to my shoulder. His fingers rake over my scalp, massaging me. It feels so good an audible sigh leaves me. He kisses me again, his tongue dancing across my skin. "Tonight, I'm going to fuck you on that bench," he says, capturing my ear with his teeth. "Then, against the glass." He runs his hand under my breast, taking the weight in his palm as he grazes his fingers along the edge and avoiding my nipple. "And when you can't remember your own name, I'm going to take you on our bed and make you come again." I drop my head back against his shoulder, feeling the embers of desire stirring low in my belly, making my breath catch when his fingers slide down my abdomen.

But he doesn't touch me where I want him to. Instead, he reaches for a washcloth that he douses with soap and then rubs it together so it's sudsy before running it across my breasts. The friction of the fabric against my nipples makes me moan, and then his lips seal over mine, silencing me with his tongue. The washcloth falls to the shower floor with a *splat*, and Tyler's hand slips down my front, over my slickened folds, and two fingers thrust inside me, making me cry out. My heart pounds as the spray hits my overstimulated nipples, and he fingers me, making me forget I just had an epic orgasm as my body turns greedy with need. From his position at my side, his erection presses into my hip. I wrap my hand around his cock, stroking up the length of him. He rewards me by adding his thumb to my clit, stroking me at the same pace I do him, and just when my walls clutch his fingers, his hands fall to my hips, and he kisses me. "Ride me." His voice is gravel, sending shivers down my spine.

He sits on the tiled floor, palming his erection, the shower hitting his legs. I straddle his waist and lower myself as he guides himself to my entrance. I sink down on his cock as his eyes close, and his head falls back with bliss. He knits our fingers to provide me support and balance, giving me all the control as I move over him, discovering every angle and pace that makes his eyes darken and others that make his control so weak, he has to close his eyes again.

"Chloe," he calls my name as I speed up, and then his control snaps, and his hips move against mine, thrusting up into me as the need in our bodies builds, reaching highs that teeter between pain and ecstasy before we explode together.

I kiss him lazily, my breaths coming out in bursts as my heart works to settle, and then I'm laughing and hugging him and letting the water from the shower warm me as the heat of our movements wane.

Tyler kisses along my collarbone and up my neck. "When we get back to Seattle, I'm having a shower like this installed in my bedroom."

"We'll never get clean."

"Exactly."

I kiss his mouth, feeling his smile. And those same three words nearly fall out again, but this time, I erase them with a kiss and then slowly stand.

We take turns washing each other's bodies, and then I shampoo his hair, and he conditions mine. And though I'm starting to feel guilty for how much water we've wasted, I'm still disappointed when he turns off the shower.

OUR WALK to the Golden Gate Bridge is filled with stories of our childhoods. I learn about how he chose Brighton to gain some space from his parents, and how he hates tomatoes but loves ketchup. I repeatedly ask him to say blueberries and basil and bananas because the roll of his tongue when he says each of them is nearly as endearing as when he says my name. We talk about some ugly things like the time he was beaten up in middle school after moving to America and how his Uncle Kip worked to change his view of women, but years of memories with his grandma kept him grounded. And I tell him about when we were nine and Nessie got separated from us while we were at the state fair and was missing for the longest five hours of my life. But throughout our walk, our fingers remain linked. And even when it gets uncomfortable to discuss something, we continue, peppering in a heavy dose of humor and stopping to kiss so many times we add well over an hour to our adventure. But it only makes it better. I can feel the memories burning into my brain with each smile and shared secret.

The sun warms my face as we follow the trail of hikers up to the bridge. The thick layer of fog that threatened to ruin our view as we began our trek has nearly vanished, leaving a picturesque view of the bay and Alcatraz Island in the background, with the blue sky and orangey-red paint of the iconic bridge. "I'm really glad you were able to take today off," I say, spinning to take another picture.

His fingers skim my side as I take a couple more pictures of the bay. "We still have two weeks before football starts," he says. "What if we just stayed for a few more days? Or we can drive up the coastline and add a few days?"

"What about things with Avery?"

He shakes his head as we walk to the middle of the bridge, the cars passing loudly to our left. But they're barely even a thought as I turn the camera on Tyler and manage to get two photos of him smiling before he grabs my waist and pulls my back against his chest. He drops his face to the crook of my neck and smiles. I snap the picture and another with him kissing me. "I fired him," he tells me.

I nearly drop my phone. I twist in his arms, a new wave of regret hitting me as I consider how this might have gone entirely differently had one of us had the sense and patience to talk it out in a more constructive manner. "Will that impact your chances of charging him?"

His hands are still on my waist as he shrugs. "Charging him would be a mild flavor of justice, but it wouldn't get the funds returned. He's spent the money, and we could try suing him, but we'd likely never see a penny of what he's stolen."

"What do you want to do?"

He raises his eyebrows a few degrees. "Bankrupt him. It would take a few calls with his other clients and a couple more to have him black-listed so no one's willing to do business with him. Then, I'd turn to the casinos, get him banned from every single one, and Jericho's games, too." He lifts just one shoulder. "It would spread, and he'd be chased out of the city. Plus, the people he's working with deserve to know. He's likely fucking them over as well."

"Are you sure he did it? No doubts?"

"Positive."

"Then do it."

He blinks back his obvious surprise.

"He stole ten million dollars from you, and like you said, chances are he's stealing from his other clients. It seems like it would be immoral for you to not tell them."

Tyler pulls me closer, his hands pressing against the small of my back. "Forget Avery. Are you excited about your event tonight?"

My smile is instant and spreads to his lips. "Stupid excited."

"Are we going to stay up all night watching it before we get a replay of the shower?"

I grin. "We can, but it's actually the most visible before the moon fully rises, so ten until midnight."

"And we'll be outside?"

I nod. "Astronomers will be inside the observatory, but we won't all be able to fit, and with a meteor shower like Perseids, the best view is outside. Plus, as much as I love this, it's far outside of my field of study, so this is just icing on the cake." I glance at the sky. "Especially if it's clear again tonight, we'll have a great view."

He brushes his lips against my temple.

"I'm hoping Cooper and Nessie still come. I hate when he's mad at me."

"He's not mad at you. Trust me. He just needs some time to breathe and cool down."

His words are meant to comfort me, but I know he's wrong. Cooper was irate, and while I might be able to share some of that blame with the situation, it's my omission that lit the match. Still, I want to believe Tyler's assurance.

"Let's get a car to take us to Ghirardelli Square," he says, glancing at his watch. "We'll grab some lunch and ice cream, and then we'll need to head back so we can get ready for your big night."

Disappointment has me looking to verify the time. I'd wanted to walk through the city and see at least a few more things on my list, but he's right. We're going to be borderline late as it is.

His lips graze my cheek and then my lips. "I'll bring you back, I swear."

"I just thought we had more time, but it's okay, this morning was..." My cheeks flush as I recall the details of our time in the living room and then again in the shower. "Amazing. If that's all I was able to take out of this city, I'd be content."

He smiles fully now. "I'm still bringing you back the first chance we get." His attention falls to his phone, and his brow furrows as his eyes cut to the sky and then back to his screen.

"Is everything okay?"

He shakes his head, reaching an arm behind his back.

"Avery?"

He doesn't respond, his focus on whatever message he's sending in reply. Several minutes pass, his attention still downcast as his thumbs dart across his screen.

"Should we return to the hotel?"

"No. It's nothing."

"Clearly, it's something."

Tyler sighs, but his shoulders don't fall. If anything, they grow bigger. "I haven't checked my phone all day. I knew shit would blow up because of firing Avery, and I just wanted one day to not worry about it or bother with trying to sort through shit. I wanted one day with you. This day. Your day."

"We had Vegas," I remind him.

He shakes his head. "I still had to work, and even that stupid fucking poker game was part of it."

"You just said we have two weeks. We can stretch the trip out. We don't have to check out tomorrow. Or we can add a couple of days and go see the Oregon coast or stay in Portland? Or just head back and hibernate at your place or my place or both?"

Slowly, he pulls in a breath, and then just as slowly, he nods. "You're right. This is just the beginning."

My stomach and chest warm at his words, my heart gallops, and I smile. "Exactly."

We walk back down to the park to catch a Lyft that takes us through the city to Ghirardelli Square, where a long line of tourists stands.

"Come on," he says, taking my hand.

"We can't cut in line here. There's no bouncer, and there are kids."

Tyler flashes a devilish grin that dares me to question if he could, and I have little doubt that he would. "There's a pub in the back that most tourists don't know about, and they serve the same ice cream."

We walk around the line and red-brick building to a second entrance, where a woman greets us with a piece of dark chocolate.

"Oh," I say, tearing open the wrapper. "You should ask them if they have any white chocolate."

His eyebrows go up with surprise.

"I know a lot about you. Two years' worth of stuff and a few Google searches." I shrug when his eyes light up with another admission. "There were a lot of rumors about who you were freshman year."

He laughs. "I'll bet."

"Most were wrong," I add, thinking about the multitude of articles that referred to him as a heartless playboy.

"I've made my fair share of mistakes," he tells me as we join a shorter line to order.

"But they led you to Brighton and Cooper."

"And you," he adds, placing his hand on my hip. It's possessive and strong and like everything about Tyler, addictive.

WHEN WE FINISH our lunch and ice cream, we wait for a car from the hotel to come and pick us up, and though I'm sad not to see more of this city that has been so amazing in the tiny fraction I've seen, I feel like a kid on Christmas Eve as we pull up to the hotel, excited for this night and to share it with Tyler.

"Mr. Banks," a man in a suit says as we enter the hotel. "Sir, your father would like to speak with you."

I glance at Tyler, wondering if his father was who he'd been responding to while we were on the bridge.

"He's right this way, sir." The man holds out a palm toward the front desk.

"Now?" Tyler asks.

The man flinches, clearly uncomfortable. "Yes, sir. He insists on meeting with you right away."

"Meeting?" I ask, the word an awkward shape as it leaves my tongue.

Tyler sighs heavily, his hand at my waist loosening. "Why don't you go get changed and take a car to the event. This might take a bit." He faces me, his blue eyes roving across my face. "I will be there as soon as I can, before the speeches and champagne."

"I can wait."

He shakes his head. "I don't want you to be late. We should have just stopped and bought some clothes and gone. I had no idea he'd come all the way here." He stretches his neck, his jaw ticking with impatience. "There should be a bag inside the room. Bring it with you."

"A bag?"

"A gift."

"A gift?"

He chuckles, his thumbs brushing along my jaw. "Be careful. If you're going to repeat everything I say, I'm going to start talking a lot dirtier. To hell with having an audience."

I feel the stain of embarrassment creep along my cheeks.

He laughs, and though it's bridled, it's genuine and calms the butterflies in my stomach. "I'll see you soon." He leans forward, kissing me.

29

TYLER

I 'm escorted into the conference room like a prisoner. Inside the small room, my father sits at the head of the table, a glass tumbler in one hand.

I take a deep breath, waiting for him to begin yelling, already knowing the points he's going to hit and ill-prepared for most. After all, my decision to fire Avery was only half logic; the rest was purely personal.

Dad nods at the employee he's treated like a lackey, waiting for the door to close before turning his attention to me. "You took a very considerable risk yesterday."

I have to cock my head to the side to ensure I heard him right. My dad isn't one for small talk. He also doesn't play mind games when it comes to anger—he saves that for revenge when someone dares to cross him.

I'm still not positive I haven't.

"I spent most of my flight going over things with Phil"—my father's right-hand man—"and we agree with your decision. It was risky and impulsive, but Ken Avery was positioned to steal more from us than what we would have gained in litigation, so I stand by your decision."

I've avoided his calls, emails, and texts for nearly twenty-four hours. I know this isn't all of what he's come to say, because if it were, he wouldn't have boarded a plane and come this far. "Where's Lewis?"

Dad's smile gives nothing away, calm and reserved as if I've just talked about the nice weather or complimented his suit. "Have a seat. Let's talk."

I glance at the clock, wondering if Chloe's still upstairs getting changed or if she's left for the event. "I have plans tonight. I'm sorry. I didn't realize you'd be coming out here."

"You wouldn't. You didn't answer your phone." Another sip. This time, his eyes cut to me, the accusation clear.

"I've had a lot on my plate."

"So I've heard." He folds his hands on the table and stares at me, his face impassive, stoic. I'm still not sure what his intentions are, but I do know he's not going to discuss them until I'm seated. Regardless of which sword my father wields, manipulation always drips from his blade.

I resign and take a seat though it feels like bowing—like lying.

Dad smiles, reaching for his glass again. "Are you really in that big of a rush?"

"I have plans," I remind him.

"Tell me about her."

He knows Chloe's name. I'm sure of the fact. Likely, there's an entire history of her on company letterhead tucked into his briefcase, complete with grades, past teachers, jobs, and more. A dark side of me hopes it will mention her ex's name. I try to shy away from that thought, but it festers, making it difficult for me to focus on his question. "What more can I tell you that you don't already know?"

He flashes a crooked smile. Takes another sip. Sets his glass down. Stares at me.

"She's bloody brilliant." I don't tell him that she doesn't care about our money or about our name, because he would take that as a slap in the face rather than assurance. It's a tough line of respect and gratification that he expects.

He grins. "That's all she has going for her? That's what's had you skipping meetings and showing up late?"

My heart pounds in my throat. He's goading me, trying to get a reaction because in my father's perverse world, you constantly have to prove something's worth, and in this case, Chloe is a possession—a liability. "I haven't been late for a single meeting, and the only meetings I canceled were from today, and that's only because I knew we'd have to be on-site continuously throughout the merger and construction. It's absolutely no reflection on her. She helped me figure out what a snake Avery was."

Dad chuckles. "I know. I was pulling your leg. She seems like a real catch. And from what I've heard, much of the staff has been impressed by you—*with you*. They say you're asking good questions and finding solutions on the spot. And now, with you finding this issue with Avery..." He shakes his head. "I couldn't be prouder."

I wait for the other shoe to drop.

"Have you spoken to your mother lately?"

I work to hide my confusion and try to recall the last time I spoke with her. "Not recently. Is everything okay?"

He nods. "Oh, yes. She's fine. She's been busy, though. She's taking a stained glass class. Can you believe it? Your mum working with stained-glass?" He shrugs. "Apparently, she likes it. Says it calms her down. I thought that was what the house in Miami was supposed to do." He laughs again as if this is some inside joke, then finishes his drink.

"Stained glass?"

"That was my reaction," he says, throwing a hand out. "But you know her. This week it's stained glass, next week it's salsa dancing." Another look of disinterest. "How was your drive? I couldn't believe you lot drove across the country. I can't imagine sitting for so long. And having to stop and find places to eat..." Disgust tugs at his lips. "How was the Tesla, though? Did it handle well? I heard you can set it to cruise control and watch a film."

I glance at the clock again. It's been over half an hour. Chloe's likely catching a car now, if she hasn't already. "I don't know if you'd want to watch a film, but I like it. Powerful, efficient, comfortable. Not much more you can ask for."

He smiles again, leaning forward this time. "You've changed," he tells me. "Maybe it's Brighton, maybe it's having this work experience, but I can tell you've changed. You're thinking like a CEO. You're seeing the bigger picture and looking out for the business."

I'm getting whiplash trying to catch up with him, and still, I'm uncertain if this is a trap, half expecting for his face to turn crimson and him to start bellowing about meddling with his company.

"I want you to be my successor." The words hang in the air like a cloud—something I'm able to see and consider. I've been waiting for years to have my father take me seriously. They reverberate, echoing in my ears again and again as we stare at one another.

"What about Lewis?"

"He'll be a great second—able to help you with whatever you see fit. This was never about me trying to choose Lewis over you. I've always dreamed of you continuing the legacy of this company, but I didn't think you really wanted to do it. I assumed it only meant money and power to you, but now, I see it means a great deal more. You were able to pick out and distinguish an underlying issue without a single person having been suspicious." His eyes shine with affection in a matching expression to the one I saw when he'd found out about my snack shop in Miami.

"Dad, I've always loved the hotels. I grew up in the hotels. Jesus, I learned mathematics by listening to grandad talk about stocks and quotas and geography by traveling to the different sites."

He grins. "It's in your blood."

I want to argue and tell him it's much deeper than just in my blood. I've lived it, experienced it, invested my past and future into the business. Still, I'm shell-shocked. Though this is exactly what I'd hoped might happen, it didn't seem realistic—still doesn't. I might have been able to recognize that Avery was embezzling, but it doesn't negate the fact my entire college career was chosen based upon my role as the CEO of the hotel. Or the fact that I spent much of the summer with my father in Australia, working to find the right location for our next site, pouring over land use laws and maps, and statistics to help formulate the best plan for all parties. Or that I've helped develop half a dozen other times. It doesn't negate that I've had to step into the laundry room and help run washers when the flu was running rampant through our Oahu location, or that I've been petitioning my grandad and father to help pay for education and better insurance for employees in America. This isn't my first involvement, and though it might come with the largest dollar amount, it doesn't even feel like that big of an achievement.

Maybe because it still feels personal?

"I appreciate the opportunity. I will continue learning from you and working to uphold our family's legacy." The words sound too formal, *feel* too formal, but it's my father, after all.

"That's why I'm here." He moves so his palms are flat against the table. "Brighton is a great school, but you can go to school anywhere. Every university wants to have you. I spoke with your grandad, and we think it would be best if you transferred to London. We can work side by side, all three of us, and get you ready so that when I retire, you're ready to take the reins. I know you love football, but it's a distraction. If I retire in five years, that would only give you three years post-graduation to prepare. You'll need more time." He starts on the defense before I've even managed to get my thoughts on the offense.

I glance at the clock again. I've been in here a full hour.

"I can't. I mean…" I try to blink through the onslaught of thoughts and scenarios that are drowning me. "I have two years left." Of freedom. I remind him. "Two years left before my life becomes living out of a suit-case and always being on the road. I want this time."

"I understand, but you need to be ready, and that involves starting now."

"Dad…" I start, not even sure where I planned for the words to end because right now it seems pointless as I see the sheath of papers he produces from his briefcase, contracts from different universities around England, universities I'd been expected to attend.

"When?" I ask.

"Now. We leave in an hour."

"Now? I have friends staying at the hotel. My car…"

He waves a hand. "I'll have Phil arrange flights for them and for someone to get your car and have it shipped back to Miami."

"Dad, I can't—"

His look silences me. "I've feared you can't for a very long time. You need to decide here and now, can you do this job or not? It's that simple."

"I have to talk to her first. I can't leave without explaining this to her."

He clenches his jaw, his frown growing pronounced. Clearly this wasn't what he'd wanted to hear.

.   .   .

Chloe

NESSIE PULLS me toward the champagne and grabs two more flutes, passing one to me. "Did you try those sweet onion bites?" she asks. "Caramelized something or other? Whatever they're called, they're delicious. I might need to brush my teeth five times so I don't have onion breath, but at this point, I'm considering it worth it." She's rambling, her pity becoming more apparent as the night wears on.

Cooper stayed at the hotel, claiming he wasn't feeling well, though we both know that was a lie. And Tyler still hasn't shown up or called.

"What's this?" Nessie asks, pointing at a large screen.

"An all-sky camera," I tell her. "It's what a telescope is seeing. That's our solar system."

Nessie pulls her chin back with surprise. "Seriously?"

I nod. "See that bright dot over here?" She nods. "It's Jupiter, and this is Saturn," I tell her, pointing to a smaller glowing ball beside it. "And over here is Mars. If it were cloudy, this would be a way to see the meteor shower, but since it's clear, we'll be able to see it outside. But this shows how far each meteor travels and the trajectory to ensure it's from Perseids because they should all have the same radiant point."

"Maybe I can get some extra credits if you just keep sharing more information on our way back to Brighton?"

I scoff. This event allows me to flex and show off what I know about space, but Nessie is incredibly bright and talented.

"I'm serious," she says. "We need to figure out how it could fit into accounting so I can make a case for this with my advisor."

"Maybe we can share tips on how to file taxes while also discussing space on our travel show?"

Nessie grins. "See? You're warming up to the idea. I knew you would."

I laugh, but it's fleeting, too many of my thoughts are still tied to Tyler's absence as I carry the gift bag he'd told me to grab. "What do I do with this thing?" I ask.

Nessie licks her lips, looking around the observatory again. It's beginning to thin as more people go outside to find a seat in the grass. We've heard the speeches, the history of the Perseids meteor, and the added and unnecessary fact of it being one of Earth's greatest threats that had us missing the next speech as I quietly worked to assure Nessie that the chances of it ever hitting Earth were so minimal that she didn't need to worry. "You should open it." She nods as though trying to convince both of us that it's the right idea.

"Let's go outside. We can open it out there and find a place to sit."

She nods, finishing her champagne as we move toward the doors, setting the empty glass on a tray.

A man enters as we attempt to step out, causing us all to stop as we nearly crash into one another. We share apologies as we each quickly assess that the other is fine, but when I meet his face, his brows are drawn. "Are you Chloe Robinson?"

I nod, working to place him.

He offers his hand. "I'm Dr. Morgan, from the University of Virginia. I thought I recognized you from your application."

Dread fills me. The door is steps away, and now I'm about to have another truth rock my world.

"I was so disappointed you couldn't join us this year. I hope that we hear more from you, though." Someone behind us calls him by name, and he looks beyond me before excusing himself.

Nessie's stare is heavy and as loud as a scream as I turn to face her and the aftermath of his words that have revealed another lie, this one not entirely by omission. "You were accepted?" she asks, her voice loud and filled with accusation.

"Yes, but—"

She shakes her head. "You lied to me." The pain in her words makes my chest ache, but it's the betrayal in her eyes that destroys me.

"I know," I tell her. "But I knew you'd try talking me into it."

Her brow knits as she stares at me. "Of course, I would. Attending this program was your dream."

"I didn't want to go," I tell her.

She shakes her head again, dismissing my words. "I can't believe you lied to me."

"Ness..."

Her lips purse as she looks at me, anger vast and endless in her green eyes.

"I'm sorry," I tell her. "I wasn't ready to leave this year. I didn't want to go."

"But you lied to me about it."

"I know, and I'm sorry. I should have told you. I just knew after talking about this for so long, you would try and convince me to go."

"You're damn right I would have. Because you *should* be going."

I stare at her for several minutes, silently pleading with her to understand or listen, but with each second that passes, her eyes become more closed off, and her anger burns brighter. "Cooper was right. I should have stayed with him tonight."

My heart aches as she delivers the final punch and then spins on a heel and moves toward the door.

She's right. I crossed a line—*the* line. Honesty has always been our shared rule. Regardless of boys or jobs or school, we have always had each other and have been able to depend on the other, to be honest.

I follow her outside, calling her name several times, but she doesn't slow down as she heads in the direction of the parking lot where I know she's already calling for a ride. The lawn is covered with individuals and groups who are preparing to watch the meteor shower, and for the first time in as long as I can recall, I don't care about seeing the meteor shower or hearing any of the data they'll be sharing.

As I turn back to move to the parking lot, I'm unsure about whether I'll stay or go, only certain that I need to try talking to Nessie again and make sure she's not standing over there alone because regardless of my proclamation to be unaffected by Ricky, I am. When a man stares too long or walks too close, Ricky is my first thought—my only thought. And I hate the idea of her standing over there alone or possibly with another Ricky.

The heavy bag in my hand bangs against my shin, making me wince, and I nearly drop it as tears of anger at myself and this moment and my regrets ambush me with the excuse of pain.

"Chloe?" My heart thrums as I take a long breath through my nose, trying to clear the signs of tears as I look up at the sound of his voice. It's useless because the relief of having him here only makes more tears build in my eyes, making my vision blurry.

"Are you okay?" Tyler asks, placing a hand on my shoulder.

I blink several more times as I shake my head. "I made a mistake, and Nessie's upset with me."

Tyler's hand runs the length of my arm, stopping at my elbow, where he grips me. "I'm sure it will all be okay." His eyes shift over me, constantly moving like he can't focus on any particular spot.

"How did things go with your dad?"

"Chloe, I need to talk to you about something," he says, licking his lips.

I wish I'd turned down that champagne or that my thoughts weren't all tangled around the fact I have so few secrets and just this one lie, and somehow everything is combusting at once, distracting me from being able to focus on this moment and this expression that is so unfamiliar and for some reason hauntingly painful. I blow out a shallow breath and nod. "Yeah. Of course."

His jaw flexes. "First." He leans forward and kisses me. It's gentle and sweet and has me leaning into him, wanting more. He brings his forehead against mine for a moment and then takes a step back. "My dad wants me to be his successor. He wants me to train with him and my grandad and prepare to take over the company, possibly as soon as five years from now." He scoffs, then proceeds to shake his head. "I know it won't be five years. It probably won't be for ten years, maybe longer."

My brows furrow with his apparent annoyance. "Ty, that's great."

His jaw flexes again, his eyes boring into mine. "He wants me to learn in London. In England."

It feels like an earthquake has just hit, and the tectonic plates below us are separating, creating a massive void as I work to understand what this means. "When?"

"Now."

Tears cloud my eyes as I roll my lips together, recalling this trip and previous conversations of Ty professing his admiration and love for the hotel and his aspirations to one day lead it.

"Wait, now as in … now?"

He nods. "Tell me not to go."

"What?"

"I will tell him no."

"You can't. This is your dream—what you've worked so hard for. What you want."

He closes his eyes, pain tugging at his lips. "I want you."

I set the gift bag down and lace my hands around his neck. "I am so proud of you, and I care so much about you, but I can't ask you to give up your future, your dreams. You have to go, Ty."

His forehead rests against mine again. "We can figure this out."

I bring my arms down around his waist, holding him so close I think about cold welding again and how, regardless of distance, I know a part of me will be wherever he is.

A car horn blares, and Tyler takes a step back. His eyes rove over my face again, and I realize that he's working on memorizing me just as I am him.

"I'll have travel arranged, and if you need anything—anything at all —call me." His eyes fill with tears, which only makes my tears multiply.

He kisses me again, and it's too fast and too hard. And then he turns around and heads to the black car idling at the curb.

Behind me, someone says something, but I can't make out their words because the sound of my heart shattering is echoing in my ears.

30

CHLOE

egardless of the knowledge that he's gone, I still step into the hotel suite, expecting to find Tyler. Instead, it isn't only him that's missing, but all of his things as well. Every stitch of his clothes, his laptop, his cologne, shoes—they're all gone, and in their place is an envelope with my name scrawled across in his handwriting.

I trace over my name, my nose and eyes burning with more tears. I don't want to be in here where I can still smell him, still remember our morning in the shower, still feel his touch. At the same point, I want to roll in the bed and soak it all up because the idea of leaving it behind makes my chest ache.

The envelope is thick, too thick to be just a note. A tear slips down my cheek as I open it, finding a stack of hundreds with a paperclip holding a note to the top bill.

> *These are your winnings. I know you don't want them, but I thought we'd take*
> *them to donate to a shelter or charity tomorrow. I'm sorry I can't be there to do*
> *it with you.*
> *-Ty*

A tear splatters across the note, and then another as I realize he made his decision before he requested me to ask him to stay.

I feel so much—*too much*. My stomach is churning, and my eyes are hot with a flood of tears that has my nose running and my chest aching.

"Chloe," Nessie says from the doorway. "Where's Tyler?"

I turn to face her, my throat so constricted I can't catch a breath to reply. Apparently, she doesn't need one because she crosses the room and wraps her arms around me, holding me so tight it feels like she's keeping me from losing everything once again. Her lips brush my cheek, and when a guttural and foreign sound climbs out of my throat, she holds me tighter.

"What happened?" she asks.

"He left."

Her grip tightens still, and my tears turn into cries, which grow into sobs.

She holds me until sleep finally shows mercy on me and pulls me under its embrace.

———

THE NEXT MORNING, breakfast is delivered on carts that are filled with an assortment of foods including an entire mountain of chocolate filled croissants. I don't touch any of them.

A man dressed in a suit stands at the door as they wheel the carts back into the elevator, and it takes me a moment to recognize him as the one who'd told Tyler his dad was here to speak with him yesterday. He struggles to make eye contact with me as he clears his throat. "Mr. Banks has a flight booked this afternoon for you all to fly to SeaTac, where a car will drive you home." He withdraws a letter from his jacket. "The details for your flight are all included here. We'll have someone up to pack for you all shortly."

I head back to the bedroom before the elevator doors can close behind him. My hope that this was a mistake and that Tyler's going to walk through the elevator is fading. I know he's already on the other side of the Atlantic—I can feel his loss everywhere.

I glance at the clock, realizing I only have a few hours left in the city. I change quickly and grab the stack of money Tyler left and head back out to the living room.

"I'll be back in an hour," I tell them.

"Where are you going?" Nessie asks.

I sniffle as I shake my head. "I don't know."

She stands from her seat beside Cooper on the couch. The piece of furniture elicits another memory that cuts me as I realize it wasn't even a full twenty-four hours ago that Tyler and I were right here in this room, and I told him I loved him.

I swallow down the rush of emotions and meet Nessie's gaze. "Tyler left all this money for me to donate to a shelter or a charity. I have no idea what to do with it. I want to buy everyone in need of a pair of shoes and socks and food and..." I shake my head. "I just want to help."

Nessie places a hand on my shoulder but doesn't hug me, and I'm so grateful because I know if she were to wrap her arms around me, I'd crumble right now. "Why don't we go talk to the concierge? Maybe they can find some contacts since we have to leave soon."

I nod, appreciating her clear and decisive thoughts that help me formulate a plan. I pull in a deep breath and work to make a list of what we need to do, items that will help the most.

Nessie and I head down to the lobby, finding the concierge who we relay our intentions to. He nods patiently and then shakes his head, telling us he has no contacts or ideas.

His response feels like a bludgeon, destroying the plan I so desperately need to carry out, not only for my sanity, but because I still see the numerous individuals we passed who were trying to sleep on the lit streets for safety, regardless of the loud noises, bright lights, and constant traffic.

"I might be able to help you," an employee says as she smiles at me. "Mr. Banks had asked me to do some research on shelters and nonprofits in the area who help the homeless community, and I was planning to send it up to you this afternoon." She smiles at the concierge behind the desk. "May I?"

He moves to the side, watching as she clicks and taps several times before returning her gaze to us. "Let me print this up, and then I'll share with you my findings." She moves to the printer and then has us follow her into the lobby, where we sit at a small table, peering over the information as she explains the different services they each provide.

"If I leave some money with you, and how I want it allocated, are you able to send it to them?"

She nods. "Absolutely, Ms. Robinson."

I take one of the hotel pens from my purse along with the stack of bills, carefully tearing off Tyler's note and securing it in my wallet. I count through the cash twice before jotting down the increments and how I'd like them divided.

It's a short plan, one that is too simple and too fast, but as we head back up to our hotel room, I feel a small sense of gratitude slip around the heartache that makes each of my breaths feel too shallow.

"What happened?" Nessie asks as we step into the suite. "Did you guys break up?"

I shake my head. I don't think so. Maybe?

No. He said we'd figure it out.

Right?

My thoughts spin, and my heart clenches. It's clear she knows Tyler's gone. He would have run into Cooper yesterday when he came up to pack. Still, I understand her confusion. "His dad came and got him. They went back to London so he can start preparing to be his father's successor."

"Why didn't you tell him to stay?"

"I couldn't make him choose me any more than I could have asked you or Cooper to choose me. He loves this company. The history and legacy of it mean so much to him. I can't take that from him."

She shakes her head. "There has to be another way."

I brush away more tears. "We need to go. It's time."

OUR SEATS on the flight bringing us back to Seattle are first class.

I'd prefer the noise and bustle from the economy seats because my thoughts are deafening as the past twenty-four hours and the past couple of weeks replay again and again. I'm desperate for something to drown them out.

The sensible side of me wants to contest my sadness, provide reason and fact for why I'm overreacting, reminding me that Tyler and I had only been together for a second in the grand scheme of things.

But each time the logical part of me tries to make this a neat and organized list, my emotions crash down, and memories rain on me like a hurricane, pulling two years of stolen glances and smirks and kind gestures that he worked so hard to camouflage behind a wall of confidence and strength.

I consider if I should try calling him as I work to figure out where he might be right now.

My thoughts run freely, all ending with the same realization—this was inevitable. He told me from the beginning that the hotel was his future and that included traveling all across the world, constant meetings and obligations to honor his role. I knew he loved the company and that eventually, this choice would have to be made. This pain would have been felt now or later.

WHEN WE LAND IN SEATTLE, the skies are as overcast as my mood, but the realization we have a ton of things we need to do before school starts in a few weeks helps distract my thoughts as we find the car that was arranged for us.

"He knew we had all our stuff in storage," Cooper says as the car pulls up to the Banks Hotel in downtown Seattle.

The reservation is for two suites, smaller than the ones we've stayed in during our trip, but equally nice. Only now, I'm alone in a room that feels too big and foreign.

I take a seat at the small dining room table and find my notebook and one of the dozens of hotel pens I've somehow collected and start making a list of everything we need to do:

1. Make arrangements to pick up the car
2. Make arrangements to pick up keys for the apartment
3. Arrange U-Haul
4. Unpack storage locker
5. Moving day—move in to apartment
6. Go grocery shopping

7. Submit job applications
8. Talk to Cooper
9. Talk to Nessie.

THERE'S a knock on my door, and hope floods my heart, making it feel like an overfilled washing machine again as I glance at the clock and then back to the door.

Would he be able to fly back from England?

Did he leave?

I stand from the table and try to reel in my thoughts, knowing disappointment hurts nearly as much as regret, and I know because I've spent nearly twenty-four hours drowning in guilt for not admitting my feelings for Tyler two years sooner.

Nessie's on the other side of the door, a pillow in her arms.

"What are you doing?" I ask her.

"I thought we could have a sleepover."

My eyes begin to mist over. "Are you sure?"

She hugs me, the pillow pressing against my side, making me feel like we're in a marshmallow. "You've been so quiet," she says.

"I feel so silly," I admit to her, taking several steps back as my chin begins to shake. "I knew this would happen eventually, and we were together for only days, so it seems like this would be the best situation because it causes the least pain—and yet it hurts so much." I place a hand across my chest from where the pain seems to be radiating. "And I know you're mad at me, and Cooper's mad at me. I don't know how everything just erupted all at once." Tears blur my vision.

Nessie's arms encircle me again, sans pillow. "I don't think anyone could tell you how long it takes to fall for someone else. The heart doesn't have a timer or a calendar or a set of rules. It wants what it wants. Loves who it loves." Her voice is soft and gentle, an allowance for my tears and sadness that grow with her words.

I pull away from her again, my lips dry and my cheeks wet. I go in search of tissues and return to the living room where Nessie is sitting on the couch. She pats the space beside her, and I fill it, wiping more stray tears. "I don't even know what to think or feel," I tell her. "I mean, he just left. It's like I haven't even been able to register the reality of the situation because I don't know what the reality is."

Nessie's eyes turn sorrowful. "I know. That has to hurt a lot."

I nod, and the tears fall faster as she confirms what my mind has known and what my heart has been fighting. And then, as she has for the past twenty-one years, Nessie picks up the pieces as I shatter.

Tyler

IT'S BEEN the longest forty-eight hours of my life.

Every time a woman walks by with long brown hair, I turn. I know it's not going to be Chloe, and yet, hope gets me every single damn time.

"Tyler, I'm going to have you sit with Phil and Lewis this morning. Let you guys cover what you both learned over this summer and see if there are any best practices you can exchange," Dad says as we pull up to the Banks hotel in London—the second building my great-grandfather helped build and the first hotel site. The top floor is a presidential suite that is larger and grander than all those that we saw over the summer. It's rumored my dad had intended to live in it at one time. Now, it's rented a few times a year or donated for fundraisers. Below it is our corporate office. Two levels of private offices and conference rooms where I learned to sit on my hands with my back straight and not touch anything. I imagine what Chloe would say and how she'd react to seeing the lavish space. When we'd first arrived in New Orleans, her obvious shock as she openly stared and admired the hotel had bordered on uncomfortable. I didn't know why it bothered me as it did, but after a few days I realized it was because her reactions were so pure. I was so used to people using me and being fake, that I assumed that's what she was doing. But Chloe is one of the most genuine people I've ever met. She appreciates what others—what I—take for granted like the luxury of a hotel, the view from a bridge.

"How was your holiday?" Phil asks, as we head down a corridor. "Your dad was jumping mad when he found out about Ken Avery. What a snake that man was. He'd been so reluctant to hire a management company for so long, and now this." He pulls his lips back in a pronounced frown and takes a sharp breath. "I don't know what he's going to do. I don't see him trying to replace the management company. This could prove to be quite the headache for you, in a few years." He opens the door to a conference room.

I step inside and pause, my gaze traveling from the wall of windows and regal desk to the couch, and then back to Phil. "What's this?"

He grins. "Your new office."

Pride inflates my chest, allowing me to memorize the feeling and realization that my dream of running our family's company is becoming a reality. "Could I have a moment?"

His grin turns into a smile, he knows how much this moment—the Banks Hotels—mean to me, after all, he's been working for my dad for nearly twenty years. "Absolutely, sir. I'll grab us some tea to celebrate." He gives a brief nod and steps out.

I reach for my phone and check the time. It's just after two a.m. in Seattle.

I unlock my cell phone to see Brighton's academic calendar still there from stufying it this morning. Labor Day is only a few weeks away, and I'm planning to hold to my promise to Chloe about San Francisco. It's going to be a gruesome weekend for me to fly that far in such a short period, but I'm determined to find creative ways to make this work. If that includes staying up late or waking up early to talk or stealing weekends or catching up on a thread of text messages we each send while the other is supposed to be sleeping.

Me: How was your job interview? I'll bet they hired you on the spot.

The dots beside her name appear, and my chest constricts. We both try to blame beign used to a different time for why we can't sleep, though we know time has nothing to do with it.

Chloe: I talked too much and too fast. But, I think it still went all right. They're supposed to follow up with me next week.

I grin, remembering our walk to the Golden Gate Bridge as she explained the theory of white holes to me, and how her passion behind the subject led her to talking faster.

Me: It's going to be great. You're going to be working at an observatory.

Chloe: MIGHT be working at an observatory. I haven't been hired.

Me: Yet.

It's difficult for me not to try and influence the situation. A donation would certainly help to ensure her the position, yet, I have absolutely no doubt she'd be livid and doubt herself and her abilities if she ever found out. Still, it feels like being sidelined during an important game.

Chloe: How are you? Are you ready for your first day of work?

I send her a picture of my new office.

Chloe: Look at you! All official! Tell me there's a nameplate on the door.

Me: No nameplate. I might need you to get me one.

Chloe: With a picture of Uranus beside it.

Me: Are you calling me a god, again? ;)

Chloe: Clearly.

I laugh, hearing the sarcasm behind her words.

Me: How's the hotel?

Chloe: It's so nice. Nessie is already dreading not having one of the hotel beds. We all appreciate you allowing us to stay here. It's been nice to not have to rush through the unpacking process.

Me: I'm glad. You can stay as long as you'd like.

Chloe: Thank you. We move into our apartment tomorrow, though.

Me: September 7th you're off for Labor Day. What would you say to meeting me in San Francisco on the 3rd? You could fly home late Monday, be back for classes on Tuesday.

Chloe: Yes!!!! I'll start looking for flights.

Me: I'll take care of the arrangements. I just wanted to check with you before I made plans.

Chloe: I have a four-day weekend for Thanksgiving. I can meet you closer to the East Coast. Or come to England so you don't have to fly.

I stare at her text for a second, rereading her words that are offering to give up one of her traditions for me. I know the significance without it being spelled out.

My office door opens and Phil returns, holding two mugs with a bottle squeezed to his side with an elbow. "I thought we should celebrate with a bit of whiskey." He walks to my new desk and sets the cups down before liberally splashing a heavy hand of alcohol into each glass. "Oh, my apologies," he says, noticing my phone is out with an unwritten reply. My response to Chloe should likely be thought out or at least something more than a thumbs up, and yet, my thoughts are firing off on all cylinders, making it seem nearly impossible to find the right words.

"It's all right," I tell him. "We can get started in just a moment."

Me: I miss you. We'll figure something out for Thanksgiving. I have a meeting to attend, but I'll chat with you later, after you wake up.

Chloe: I miss you, too. Good luck on your first day.

I pocket my phone and move around to the front of my desk. It doesn't feel that far outside of my norm to be in an office setting, focusing on spreadsheets and projections, in fact, it helps to be at work where I can focus all my thoughts and efforts on things that don't have me considering how long a flight would take to get me to Seattle.

31

CHLOE

I t's been a week since we returned from California. Four days since Nessie and I moved into our apartment downtown. It's barely bigger than the suite I was staying in, and the amenities pale in comparison, but the normalcy is comforting. We have two bedrooms and one tiny bathroom, a kitchen that won't allow more than one drawer or appliance to be open at the same time, and a living room that is so small our couch has to sit at an angle for our front door to open. I don't mind the tiny space. It feels kind of cozy, and having our things out of storage and in the same place every day has been nice.

The doorbell rings, and Nessie glances at me as she straightens her hair, checking to make sure I'm ready. I pull in a deep breath and nod.

She opens the door, and Cooper stands there, his attention bouncing between Nessie and me, discomfort and hesitation apparent as his shoulders square, and he hangs back from the door.

Nessie reaches a hand out, and he takes it, stepping into the apartment. She kisses his cheek and grabs her purse. "You guys need to talk."

His eyes round as he looks from her to me and then back to Nessie. "What?"

"You guys are best friends. You need to get past this. I'm going to take a walk and pick up some pizza. I'll be back." She kisses him again.

Cooper remains by the door, his gaze over my shoulder, over my head, at my feet.

"Why can't you look at me?" I ask him, calling him on the fact.

His eyes finally meet mine, but quickly shift away. "I am."

"Why aren't you talking to me?" I ask him.

His gaze darts back to mine. "I am."

"Yeah, like we're strangers. You talk to me all formally, and you never call or return my texts. I've tried talking to you about Ricky and Tyler, and you just tell me everything's fine."

His jaw ticks, and his attention moves to the short hall that leads to the bathroom. "Why didn't you tell me about Ricky, Chloe? Why didn't you let me help you?"

My eyes flood with tears I've managed to keep away for the past two days, and a pronounced frown forms on my wobbly mouth. "Because I was embarrassed," I tell him. "I was *really* embarrassed."

Cooper says my name so quietly it sounds like a breath as he closes the short distance between us and hugs me.

"I knew how much you hated Ricky and how dumb you thought it was that I was dating him, and I felt so embarrassed by what happened, and a part of me felt like you deserved to tell me that I should have expected it. He was such an asshole in high school. I don't know how I overlooked all of it and how stupid it was that I felt special because he finally noticed me."

Cooper shakes his head. "I'm your best friend. You've seen me at my absolute worst, during stretches where I was terrified I'd turn out like my dad and when everyone made fun of me and teased me. You saw the ugliest years of my life. And it hurt that you didn't allow me in when you were hurt, when you needed me. I want to help you, just like you've always helped me, so maybe it was my pride, but I just felt like you not only kept a secret from me, but it was a secret about a situation I was supposed to be there for—a situation I wanted to be there for."

And for the first time since July, when it all happened, I cry and tell Cooper all the details of that afternoon, including all my ugly fears and admitting to him for the first time how it impacted me—how there's an edge of doubt I have about everyone I encounter. How that man in Vegas had triggered me, and how I'd been able to recall the look in Ricky's eyes, the ugly words he used as he accused me of being a tease and used them to justify what he was trying to do.

Cooper listens to each of my confessions and replaces each of them with a validation and assurance. And I know that he's right because, through all of the ugly, I've learned so much about myself.

"Knock knock," Nessie says, carrying two pizzas. She winces as she looks across the battlefield of our faces, mine likely red and tear-streaked and Cooper's exhausted. "How are we doing?" she asks.

Cooper nods. "We're good."

Nessie's green eyes return to me for confirmation, a hopeful smile curving her lips.

I nod. "Thanks, Ness."

Her smile becomes a sigh. "I'm glad. I know you guys had a lot to talk about." She comes into the living room and sets the pizzas down on our coffee table.

"Since I'm already going to need half a bottle of medicine for my crying-induced headache, can we discuss Virginia?" I move to the far end of the couch so she can sit beside Cooper.

Her eyebrows rise with surprise as she takes a seat, keeping my gaze.

"I wanted to go, but I also didn't. Leaving Florida was hard, but I had you guys, and then after that situation with Ricky, I just really didn't want to be alone for the year."

Nessie's shoulders sink as she reaches out a hand, resting it on my knee as a fresh round of tears pool in my eyes.

I continue. "I know you want what's best for me, and you're always so good at pushing me to be the best version of myself, and I knew if I tried to tell you about it, you'd want me to go because I've talked about this for so long. I know I lied and how unfair that was of me, but it just seemed like the easiest way to stay."

"I never wanted you to go," she admits. "I only wanted you to go because you wanted to go."

I place my hand on hers. "Brighton has one of the best astrophysics programs in the entire country, and more importantly, it has you, so I didn't choose Brighton to be selfless, I chose it for me because having you guys in my life means more than everything else."

Nessie wipes away a quick trail of tears that fall across her cheek. She nods as she licks her lips. "I'm glad you chose Brighton," she tells me. "And I'm sorry I didn't listen. When you explain it, everything makes sense, I was just so caught up in the fact that you'd lied. I wish you'd just told me."

"I know, and I'm sorry about that. I should've told you."

She squeezes my fingers. "But I also understand why you didn't. I know I'm not always the best listener."

I shake my head, dismissing her words.

Cooper leans forward. "If it's any consolation, I'm really fucking glad you turned them down," he says, his dark eyes intense as he swallows hard, and I know that between this and Ricky and him still missing Tyler, this has been an equally difficult week for Coop.

"I think we just start making plans for our island retreat," Nessie says, opening one of the pizzas. "We can all work remotely. Build a giant beach house with a pool."

"As long as there's coffee," I say, reaching for a slice of pizza. "Then I'm in."

Tyler

"I RECEIVED a call about a Davenport hotel in Rome going bankrupt. He hired a contractor who fucked him over. It was a mess and cost him an absolute fortune to restore it and get things back open. I've heard it's nice, but he's drowning in debt and is going to have to sell it to cauterize," Dad tips his newspaper up as he says this.

I reach for my cup of tea so I can discreetly look at my watch. It's seven a.m. here in London, one a.m. in Seattle. I always count the difference. It's a reflex that has me imagining what Chloe is doing, where she is, what she might be thinking.

"Have you arranged for your things to be shipped over, or do you need anything?" Dad lowers his paper when I don't comment on the Davenport site.

I lift a shoulder and take a long drink of my tea.

"Everything's replaceable," he reminds me. One might mistake his comment as benign, but his words are a tumor, intended to cause harm and inflict pain as his brows hitch, and his eyes challenge me to object.

I have to set my cup down so I don't throw it, my muscles strained with objections. I don't take his bait. Not again.

Grandad comes into the dining room, wearing a brown suit as he takes a seat at the head of the table, creating a wave of memories of my childhood.

"I'd like to lead the project on the San Francisco site," I tell Dad, skirting the issue entirely.

He blinks, dropping his paper. "Why?"

"I think we should utilize part of it for a charity. We could use the tax write-off, and it would be great publicity," I add when his head begins to tilt, ensuring me he's going to say no. Money is his favorite language, but accolades and good press are a very close second.

"You should let him," Grandad says as one of the house staff pours his tea. "There's only one way to know if he's going to be able to cut it."

Dad looks between us and then releases a long sigh. "I suppose. But you'll need to clear everything by Phil."

My phone vibrates against my thigh.

It's *her.*

It has to be.

"That's fair. I'll start preparing some projections and get them to Phil by next week. Excuse me." I don't give an excuse, pushing my chair back and walking the long distance to my room.

Cooper: Football starts in 2 days.

I tip my head back and pace the length of my childhood room. My father has hired an estate agent to find me a flat, but I haven't made the time to meet with him.

It's been two weeks since I arrived in London.

Every day feels longer than the last.

I call Coop.

"I figured you'd be at work," he says, his tone dry. Bored.

"I have a business proposition," I tell him.

He's silent for a beat. "As long as it doesn't involve Chloe."

Just the sound of her name sends my thoughts to splinter and my heart to race. "What would I hire you to do with Chloe?"

"I don't know. I'm just saying I don't want to be involved. I can't be on your side in this."

"Is she okay?"

He laughs, and it's cold and sardonic. "Is she okay?" he repeats my question. "I've seen my best friend cry more during this past week than I have a decade."

I swipe a hand down my face, recalling the shock and pain that she'd tried to smile through when she assured me I should go—needed to go.

"How did Coach take the news that you're leaving the team?"

"I haven't told him," I admit.

"Why?"

"It's been busy," I lie. After ten days of being here, I'm realizing that my being here had little to do with the business and everything to do with the illusion Dad was creating. I was back home, training and preparing to take over the family business. It looked regal, professional —official. It had little to do with being here because in a matter of days, my father will be leaving back for the States, and grandad will be traveling to Dubai where he lives for half the year.

"I'll be there."

"What? Where?"

"Practice."

"What?" Cooper asks.

"I have a job proposal for you that I'm going to send you. But, I'm coming back to the states. I'm going to lead the San Francisco project, and I'll need to be closer." The idea snowballs as I tear open my closet and reach for my suitcase. "I have to go."

"What do you want me to tell her?"

"Nothing. I'll tell her myself." I hang up as I reach for a hanger, and call Anika.

"Good morning, Mr. Banks."

"Anika, I need a flight to Seattle."

"For when, sir?"

"Now."

I shove the rest of the few items I'd packed back into my suitcase, grab the second, which was never unpacked, and head to the bathroom, where I stare at the few items I have in here before ignoring them and returning to the dining room where my father and grandad have received their breakfasts.

"This hotel is in my blood, but I love it for many reasons far beyond that. I love that we care about each location and work to ensure the city and it's history is reflected in the architecture, and that we find ways to give back in each community because that was where we started—where our roots were planted. I love the company, and I've always dreamed of becoming the CEO, and that's what I want to do, but right now, I want to finish school. I want to play football. I want my last two years. And I also want to take lead on the San Francisco project. And when I'm done with it, you're going to know you didn't make a mistake by choosing me because it's going to become our flagship in the States. It's going to become the hotel that everyone wants to travel to and see with renowned restaurants and luxury. It's going to be amazing, and I'm going to do it while living in Seattle and finishing my education at Brighton."

"This was not our deal," Dad says, throwing his napkin to the table as he stands to level the playing field.

"But it should have been, and it is now."

Dad tips his chin. "Lewis has more experience. He's older, more qualified."

I shake my head. "And I'll never be able to compete with that. I can't make myself age ten years overnight. He will always have more experience than me. Always." I punctuate the word, my voice rising. "But it's not his name or his family's legacy that fails if he does. I have worked my entire life to try and be good enough, and if you can't see that, then you never are."

Grandad clears his throat, setting his spoon down. "What is this nonsense about Lewis? Lewis isn't a Banks." Though his words support my position, I want to argue that my name isn't the sole reason I deserve to be my father's successor.

"It's more than that. The hotels are my childhood—my life. I want to live up to this legacy our family has built. I want to continue to make the name Banks Hotel something that makes us proud, our employees proud, and the communities we're in proud."

"How are you going to do that with football and being distracted?"

Distracted. He still won't say her name.

"Football has taught me teamwork, brotherhood, and discipline. I was a good football player when I started, and now, I'm getting news stories. I've earned a starting position. I don't need you to be proud of me but it should make you realize how hard I've worked for this and recognize that I have that same determination and drive that I'll be applying as the CEO."

Grandad leans back in his chair, his attention moving to Dad.

"What about *her*?" Dad asks.

I scoff. "If you met Chloe, you wouldn't be asking me this question. I wouldn't be here if it weren't for her. She told me to come. I wasn't going to come with you."

He blinks too fast, revealing his shock.

"*Chloe,*" I say her name again. "Her name is Chloe. And she's bloody brilliant and motivated and has more drive in her little finger than half of our general managers. She isn't a threat to me or the business. She's the promise I'm going to continue to improve and grow and work harder every day because I want to work to be the man she deserves."

Dad stares at me, and I wonder if he has any idea what I'm saying, if mum ever inspired him in the same ways that Chloe inspires me. If it's possible he ever felt even a fraction of what I do for her. I don't think so, considering I know I will go to the grave and whatever is beyond loving Chloe. It's not the kind of love that fizzles or wanes. Instead, over the past two years, it has grown and become a force that refused to allow me to try and ignore it any longer, so great it can't be contained solely in my heart, but in my soul and my brain, and every cell of my body. It reflects in my thoughts and decisions, and I know it will continue to guide me.

"You realize what this job will do to a relationship, right? What it did to your mother and me? You're going to be living out of a suitcase for long periods of the year, missing birthdays and date nights. You won't know the names of your neighbors or be there when she has a bad day."

Grandad clears his throat, regret etched across his aging face. "I want to tell you he's wrong," he says, looking sorrowful.

"I don't have all the answers. Not yet, not now, but I do know that my love for her will make me a better leader."

"Go," Grandad says, waving a hand. "You should go. Take these years. Try and figure it out."

I cut my gaze to Dad, who appears lost in memories. "Don't tell me I didn't warn you."

Anger surges in my chest, barely holding on to the reminder that his approval doesn't matter at all when it comes to Chloe.

"I'll keep you both apprised on San Francisco and can help you choose a new management company to replace Avery."

"Focus on your education," Grandad says. "Change is scary but necessary for us to remain the leading luxury resort, and the only way for us to do that is to learn and grow."

"I'll set some appointments up with you," Dad counters.

I nod, and without another word, I take my bags to the front door where a car awaits.

32

CHLOE

"Reality kind of sucks with having to wash our own laundry," Nessie says, folding a pair of jeans from one of the two laundry baskets filled with clean clothes between us.

I chuckle. "I thought for sure you were going to say it was the beds you missed most."

"That too." She leans toward the small end table beside her and grabs the coffee we'd walked to pick up while we waited for our laundry to finish drying in the basement laundry room. Truth be told, I'm kind of glad to be downtown. After our trip that had us staying in areas where it was always so easy to access so much, it kind of feels like a continuation of that to be able to do and see so much here.

"Where's Coop this morning?"

She shakes her head. "I don't know. He said he had to go do something. I'm kind of wondering if it was to get rid of that pink bear they talked about. The one from Claire."

I try to hide my smile, knowing how badly jealousy can sting, regardless of how innocent it is. "Did you ask him why he kept it?"

"He said it didn't mean anything romantic. That he didn't hold any angry feelings toward her, and it just made him think of happy memories."

"Guys are stupid sometimes. Even Cooper, but that's not the worst reason to keep something."

She shakes her head. "I know. I probably have a dozen things from exes. I don't keep them because I'm holding a torch for any of them. Some of the stuff I just like, and others..." She shrugs. "It makes me think of happy memories."

I think of the things I collected on our trip, the dozen pens from the hotels, the shirts, a sweatshirt of Tyler's that had been in my bag that he'd carried in San Diego. I can't imagine parting with any of them, regardless of what happens between us.

"How are you doing?" Nessie asks, reaching for a shirt.

Before I can respond, there's a knock on our door. "I've got doughnuts and can't reach my key," Cooper calls from the other side.

I grin, watching the smile that consumes Nessie at the sound of his voice. She jumps to her feet, tossing the shirt back to the mound of clean laundry, and unlocks the short series of deadbolts he helped install when we moved in. She freezes, her attention shifting to me, eyes wide. "Chloe, he needs your help."

"My help?"

She nods, taking a step back, opening the door even wider. She folds her lips against her teeth and waves for me to hurry up.

"Help with what? It's not your box of things that you forgot at all the hotels, is it? Because..." My words trail off as tears fill my eyes, my heart stuttering as Tyler steps into our apartment. I can't talk because my throat is filled with emotion, and I can't see him clearly because tears are spilling down my cheeks. His strong, warm hands are on either side of my jaw, kissing my cheeks and my lips as he pulls me into his arms. I'm consumed by his scent, and the strength of his chest and shoulders feels so good as I lean into him, kissing him.

"What are you doing here?" I ask. "How?"

"Well, football starts in two days, and Coach Harris is a real asshole when it comes to players being on time."

"Damn straight, he does," Cooper says, coming inside and closing the door. He sets a box of doughnuts down in the kitchen. "We'll give you guys a little time."

Nessie flashes a smile at me, and then they disappear back to her bedroom.

I shake my head, working to understand his words without hope reading too far into the situation. "What about England? What about the hotels? Your dad?"

His fingers weave into my hair, and he smiles. I don't know if my memories and pictures didn't do him justice or if somehow in eleven days, he's gotten even sexier. "Chloe, truth or dare?"

"Are you serious right now?"

He laughs at my duress, waiting for me to answer him.

"Truth?"

"Okay, I dare you—"

I laugh. "I said truth."

I feel the rumble of his laughter against my chest. "I love you, Chloe. I don't want to live in a world where you don't exist. We have two years to figure out how we can make this happen, and since you can understand exoplanets and astrophysics, I'm pretty sure this will be a cakewalk. So, truth: I want to be with you. Truth: I want to kiss you every fucking night. Truth: I want to see you at every one of my games with my number painted on your cheek. Truth: I want to make your coffee and be your sounding board when you're trying to figure out other galaxies and hypothesizing about what forever and endless really mean. Because I feel like I understand those concepts, both of them, because that's how I feel about you. I know it in my bones, this—*us*—we're endless and forever."

There are so many questions that no one understands, some of life's biggest questions like how or why we are here, and how our universe was created. We are a minuscule dot in space, and yet, as I stand here in Tyler's arms, it doesn't matter—none of it matters. Because if I have to write the book on understanding how we got here and why, he would be my answer. I was made to love him, and he was made to love me, and together this beautiful and tragic and endlessly unknown universe was made so we could be together.

EPILOGUE

Tyler

I'M SO WINDED, my lungs burn as I come to a stop.

"I didn't hear you guys. I said, are we ready?" Coach Harris places a hand at his ear.

We bellow out, "Yes!" All of us are eager for this next season after our past undefeated one.

Coach chews a wad of gum as his gaze slowly crosses each of us. He stops on The President, and then Pax, and Arlo, and then to me. My name made a short news circuit with my leaving for London and then immediately returning to Brighton, and it made its way to Coach. Thankfully, Coach isn't big on details. He just needed my assurance I was here for the team and that he could count on me.

Dependability. Loyalty. Two more strengths football has taught me.

"I'll see you guys at six tonight." He flashes a smile that promises more conditioning.

I roll my shoulders as we head into the locker room.

"Dude, Coach is serving our asses on a platter," Bobby says, slumping to a bench.

"I thought having you date his daughter would help," Quinton says, prodding at Arlo. "You didn't piss her off or anything, right?"

Paxton laughs, patting Arlo's shoulder. "You now have an entire team of relationship counselors."

The President laughs. "Coach just wants another undefeated season. Who doesn't? Fuck, I'll run the bleachers and the lines and do the box jumps. We've got this. This season is ours." He points at me. "I saw you out there, Banks. You were a force. This is going to be your year, man."

I glance at Coop and several of my teammates. "It's *our* year."

Cheers break out like we've made a toast. The energy is high, and our resolution is even higher.

Cooper's elbow clips me as I finish getting dressed. "It's done."

I pull my chin back. "Already?"

His eyebrows furrow like I've just insulted him. "Do you want to see it or not?"

"Of course, I want to see it."

He passes me his phone. The screen is a picture of the fucker Ricky. Cooper knew his name and every detail we needed. His dating profile mentions the multiple classes he failed in high school and context about how he treats women. Cooper was able to hack into multiple systems and do whatever in the hell his genius computer mind needed to get Ricky's profile on every dating site and social media site, careful to ensure there was no mention of Chloe's or any other girl's name and set alerts to notify him if Chloe's name is ever mentioned.

"Brilliant," I say, reading his profile again. "How long did it take you?"

"You're not paying me for this shit. I wanted to do this. It's for Chloe, and every girl who doesn't know this guy is a douchebag."

I want to argue and remind him this was my idea that had him investing the past few weeks into this project. Plus, it's nearly impossible for most of the guys on the team to have a job during football season because between school, practices, games, travel, and more, there's little to no time for it, and I know Cooper could use the money. I also am beginning to understand that there are people in my life who don't come with a price tag or wish list, and Cooper is one of them.

"Well, I have another job for you. This one comes with a fixed payment."

We grab our bags and head out to the parking lot.

"What kind of job?"

"I'd like you to work with a woman I hired down in San Francisco. I've just purchased a shelter that was upside down, and I want you to create a system interface that will allow them to keep track of trends, storage, what items are low in stock, what isn't being used, easy medical record access; all the stuff we're going to be adding and integrating. It will need to work in conjunction with another system I want you to design that tracks everyone's progress so people can't fall through any gaps. Something that check to see if they need counseling, doctors, dentists, schooling..." I shake my head, trying to recall the hours of emails and conversations I've had with the new director.

Cooper grins. "I can do that."

"I know you can. You're going to be the next tech giant, and I want to invest in you."

Cooper looks as surprised as he did when I first explained who I was freshman year.

"Are we good?" I ask. Cooper was far less forgiving about my quick departure. Chloe explained it had to do with abandonment issues and trust issues, and that it wasn't personal. She's probably right, but I have no doubt she's forgetting one of the biggest reasons he was upset, which was her. He was mad at me for inflicting pain on her, and I don't blame him. Not one bit.

Coop holds a hand up for me, and I clasp his, our chests meeting as we hug. "Yeah. We're good. Just the next time your dad shows up, let's make sure it's a group meeting, okay?"

I laugh as we reach my Tesla, which had to be shipped here, and I toss my bag into the trunk. "That won't do me any favors. My dad's an arse."

Coop chuckles, unlocking his car across from mine. "Are you headed to see Chloe?"

"Yeah, but not until later. She's at work. Right now, I'm going to go eat and take a nap and then see her for a couple of hours before night practice."

"Night practice," Coop groans. "These two-a-days are brutal. I'm heading to see Vanessa. I'll see you tonight."

I slide into my car as my phone rings. "Hey, Uncle Kip."

"What's up, kid? I went and saw your mom today, and she said you were in London. Don't tell me your asshole father finally relented and gave you the keys to the castle?"

"I was in London, but I left."

Uncle Kip whoops. "Did you tell him to shove it up his ass?"

"We made a deal. I get to finish school at Brighton, and then I'll head to London."

"Two years of freedom, huh?"

"I'm pretty sure I would have had plenty of freedom there, honestly. Grandad was heading to Dubai, and Dad was heading to the States. But I have friends here, and football, and—"

"A chick," he interrupts me. "I heard you've got a girl."

I grin as he spews profanities.

"Don't turn your back on me. Think of everything I taught you."

Laughter hits my lips. "Thankfully, you taught me a lot about football."

He groans. "If you'd have taken me up on just one trip into the pool house with the girls I brought home, I'm telling you, you'd be a different man right now."

He's likely not wrong, which is sobering.

"Is she cool?"

My smile returns. "Ridiculously cool."

Uncle Kip sighs. "You deserve to be happy, kid. I'm glad you found her."

"I am too."

"Don't be like me. Don't fuck it up. You lose that person, and it's like the rest of your life you spend trying to find her again in everyone, and as you know from watching me, you can't find them again."

"You will," I tell him.

He sighs again. "I better see you on the news soon, since that's the only way I see your ugly mug."

I laugh, joining in his attempts to lift the mood. "Oh, believe me, I plan to be in every reel once we get started."

"I've got to go, kid. I just wanted to touch base and make sure I didn't need to back you up." My Uncle Kip is a lot of things, but like Coop, I've never had to question if he's got my back. "Love you, kid."

"I love you too, Uncle Kip."

I pull into my driveway and kill the engine. It's quiet out here where trees are my neighbors, and the only uninvited guests I get are deer and the occasional raccoon. I forget about eating as I make my way to the master bedroom, where I hit the mattress and fall asleep to the scent of Chloe on my pillow.

I REACH OUT, sensing her before I even see her.

Chloe's gentle laughter greets me as my hand closes around her breast. "Even in your sleep, you cop a feel," she says from where she's leaned back against the headboard, her neck craned at an unnatural angle that makes my muscles cringe.

I grin, lowering my hand because I hadn't meant to aim for her breast; it was just a happy surprise. I link my arm around her waist and tug her to lie flat beside me, curling my body around her. "I thought I was meeting you?"

"I was trying to give Nessie and Cooper some time alone. For their best interest and my sanity."

I press my nose into the back of her neck, breathing her in as I chuckle.

"Plus, Coop said you guys were worked over pretty hard."

"Coach is all about making sure we're committed." I lace my fingers with hers. "How was work?"

"I have a new love/hate relationship with the place," she says, rolling to face me. "I really like the astronomer I've been assisting at the observatory, and I keep debating if I want to remain with extragalactic astronomy or consider switching or doubling." Her green eyes dance between mine.

I lean forward, kissing her. "Take some time and consider it. There's no rush."

"It could add years to my education."

I grin. "So?"

She scoffs.

"We make the rules," I remind her. "There's no timetable. Follow your passions, and I'll be here with you every step."

Her eyes flash. The look I mistook for redemption, I've realized is affection, desire, love, and it's mine.

"Come on. I have something to show you." I jackknife off the bed, realizing my shoes are still on. I reach to take Chloe's hand.

We pass through the house and head upstairs, stopping at the end of the hall, where I open the door to a currently empty room like all of my guest rooms. Chloe follows me inside, her gaze darting across the bare walls and floors. "What's this?"

"It's going to be our new room."

Her eyebrows jump, making me laugh. "I have someone drawing up some plans, but they said they could open this wall and put in more windows, so you can put a telescope in here and see everything because it aims west, away from the city and lights. We'll put the bed on this wall and cover all the walls and ceilings with mirrors so that when I'm inside of you, I can see every side of you."

The shock on her face breaks with laughter. She shakes her head. "No way."

"Maybe just one. On the ceiling. And that wall. We can have pieces of art over them. No one will know how freaky things get."

She shakes her head again, laughter quaking her shoulders, but she doesn't say no. I can tell she's considering it.

"We just have to decide if we want our glass shower in the bedroom or the master shower."

She looks around again and then back at me. "Are you serious?"

"Dead serious. I wanted to talk to you about the idea of having you and Cooper and Vanessa all move in. I mean, this place is huge. They could have their own floor. And you won't keep forgetting your knickers or toothbrush because they'll already be here."

"You steal my underwear. I don't forget them."

I grin. "Tell me what you're thinking."

She licks her lips. "Are you sure?"

"Fucking positive. I hate not having you here. I hate when I wake up, and you're gone. I hate going to bed without you. I want you here, and our trip was fab. The four of us have a good vibe, and this place allows us to just continue that, and when you get tired of me, you can go hang out with Vanessa."

"I never get tired of you." She threads her arms around my shoulders. "I never will."

I kiss her, my tongue tracing the seam of her lips.

"Truth or dare?" she says, pulling away from me.

"Both."

Her eyes flash with that same glint of love and adoration that makes me feel bigger than a man. "What would have happened if I'd have asked you to stay?"

"I would have stayed," I tell her without a second of hesitation. "It wasn't fair of me to put that weight on your shoulders. You did what you thought was best, and I love you for your sacrifice, but there's no way I would have got onto that plane had you asked me to stay. I spent that flight to London feeling absolutely gutted because leaving was the last thing I wanted to do. It was an impossible situation with no right answer."

"But you found one."

I nod.

"Because we make the rules," she says, leaning her hips against mine.

"That's right."

"I dare you to fuck me in our new bedroom."

I grin, reaching for the hem of her shirt. "That might be the best dare ever." I move my hands up to her ribs.

She smiles outright. "I love you, Ty."

I lean my forehead against hers, brushing my fingers along her impossibly soft skin, feeling her words in every part of me as she holds my soul in her hands. "I love you. I love you more than anything. More than everything."

ALSO BY MARIAH DIETZ

The Dating Playbook Series

Bending the Rules

Breaking the Rules

Defining the Rules

His Series:

Becoming His

Losing Her

Finding Me

The Weight of Rain Duet

The Weight of Rain

The Effects of Falling

The Haven Point Series

Curveball

Exception

The Fallback

Tangled in Tinsel, A Christmas Novella

ACKNOWLEDGMENTS

First and foremost, thank you so much for reading this book. I know there are hundreds of thousands of amazing books, and I truly appreciate you choosing to read this one.

A very special thanks to Karen Cundy and Lisa Ackroyd for helping me with all of my British knowledge and answering a ridiculous number of questions. You two are rockstars and I love you dearly.

To my husband who learned how to poach eggs while I wrote this book and delivered dinner to my desk most nights, you prove romance isn't always a hot makeout scene but about dependability and teamwork.

And a HUGE thank you to my editor, Arielle Brubaker, who is so instrumental to my sanity each time I get stuck! XO!

ABOUT THE AUTHOR

Mariah Dietz is a USA Today Bestselling Author and self proclaimed nerd. She lives with her husband and sons in North Carolina.

Mariah grew up in a tiny town outside of Portland, Oregon where she spent most of her time immersed in the pages of books that she both read and created.

She has a love for all things that include her family, good coffee, books, traveling, and dark chocolate. She's also been known to laugh at her own jokes.

www.mariahdietz.com
mariah@mariahdietz.com
Subscribe to her newsletter, here

Made in the USA
Columbia, SC
06 November 2020

24070979R00186